THE TICK-

GADGETS AND GEARS

THE TICK-TOCK MAN

3

# Kersten Hamilton

with illustrations by

## James Hamilton

CLARION BOOKS
Houghton Mifflin Harcourt
Boston   New York

Clarion Books
3 Park Avenue
New York, New York 10016

Clarion Books is an imprint of
Houghton Mifflin Harcourt Publishing Company.

www.hmhco.com

The text of this book is set in Plantin.
The illustrations were executed digitally.

*Library of Congress Cataloging-in-Publication Data*
Names: Hamilton, K. R. (Kersten R.) author. | Hamilton, James, illustrator.
Title: The Tick-Tock Man / Kersten Hamilton ;
with illustrations by James Hamilton.
Description: Boston : Clarion Books/Houghton Mifflin Harcourt, [2015] |
Series: Gadgets and gears ; book 3 | Summary: Wally the boy scientist and
his sidekick Noodles the dachshund help a pickpocket named Dobbin who
works for the mysterious London criminal, the Tick-Tock Man.
Identifiers: LCCN 2015034870 |
ISBN 9780544433007 (hardback)
Subjects: | CYAC: Adventure and adventurers—Fiction. |
Dachshunds—Fiction. | Dogs—Fiction. | Scientists—Fiction. | Humorous
stories. | Science fiction. | BISAC: JUVENILE FICTION / Animals / Dogs.
| JUVENILE FICTION / Robots. | JUVENILE FICTION / Science &
Technology. | JUVENILE FICTION / Action & Adventure / General.
| JUVENILE FICTION / Boys & Men.
Classification: LCC PZ7.H1824 Ti 2015 | DDC [Fic]—dc23
LC record available at http://lccn.loc.gov/2015034870

Manufactured in the United States of America
DOC 10 9 8 7 6 5 4 3 2 1
4500597945

This book is for Stormageddon.

—K.H.

*T*ick-tock.

The sound was unsettling, and when you are with a Kennewickett, anything unsettling could spell disaster.

My name is Noodles. It is my duty to keep Walter Kennewickett, boy genius and scientist in training, as far from disasters as possible. It is my privilege as his best friend to accompany him everywhere he goes.

Which is why I found myself on a dark street corner in London, trying to track the source of the mysterious sound.

London was aglow with the process of electrification and hummed with activity even at night. Cable cars mixed with horse-drawn cabs and carts, and many of the thousand lamps that lit the streets had been converted from gas to electricity.

But Wally wasn't interested in well-lit streets. The dim gaslight above was perfect for his purposes.

*Tick-tock.*

I could sense approaching danger, but I could not tell from which direction it would arrive. The sound was bouncing off bricks, glass, and cobblestones.

"What was that, Noodles?" Wally asked, lowering the handheld camera he had been adjusting.

Walter Kennewickett is a very observant boy.

"Probably a rat," his aunt Rhodope said. "London crawls with them after dark."

Miss Rhodope Pickering is the youngest of Calypso Kennewickett's sisters. The fact that Rhodope is an eccentric allows her to fly kites in the park while other people her age attend university.

The fact that she is a sought-after photographic artist allows her to keep comfortable rooms in Charing Cross. The Pickerings are an artistic family. My current conundrum was the result of Wally's mother, Calypso, mentioning that he might have inherited an aptitude for art.

An "aptitude" is the natural ability to master a skill.

There were certainly many aptitudes Wally had inherited from his prodigious parents. His attempts at art, however, were dismal—until his father, Oliver, pointed out that the correct term for fireworks is "pyrotechnics," which means "art made from fire."

Generations of Kennewicketts have excelled at blowing things up. Wally is currently creating a line of pyrotechnics you might carry in your pocket and enjoy on any street corner.

Before we traveled to London to participate in the Electromobile Road Rally, Miss Rhodope had written to him, requesting that he use his experience with explosives to create a faster flash powder for use in photography. She'd promised to arrange a breakfast with her friend Sir Arthur Conan Doyle if he did. Walter Kennewickett is a fan of Sir Arthur's books and enjoys matching wits with his fictional detective Sherlock Holmes.

Wally had not only produced the powder for his aunt, he had devised a hat to hold the flash device, and a trigger cable to attach his hand-held camera to it. We were preparing to photograph the participants in the Electromobile Rally, which would be coming down the road at any minute, followed by a small parade of Calypso Kennewickett's fans. Calypso was the only woman among the twelve participants in the three-country rally, which was a contest of speed, design, and dependability. Since Oliver and Calypso had worked together on every aspect of their elegant electrical carriage, the Zephyr, they were taking turns driving.

The Kennewicketts had won the first leg of the rally handily, arriving at Trafalgar Square two days ago to be greeted by cheering crowds. The electromobile in last place had not arrived until just after sunset today.

The crowds had cheerfully gathered again. Drivers had signed autographs and posed for pictures for the press. Now they were proceeding to the docks at the Embankment, where ships had been chartered to carry them across the channel. The second leg of the rally was to be in France.

The Kennewicketts had requested that this small street be kept free of crowds to allow Rhodope to test her new technique for photographing in the dark. When Kennewicketts ask a small favor, people tend to cooperate. They are world-famous scientists, after all.

"Attachment test," Wally said. "In three, two, one—"

The camera clicked and fire flashed, and someone uttered a terrible cry. I whirled as a tatterdemalion tumbled out of a dark doorway. A "tatterdemalion" is a person dressed in rags and tatters.

This old man's frock coat was so faded, it appeared gray in the lamplight, in contrast with his shock of wild white hair. His angular form and antique attire gave the impression that he had just fallen out of the pages of a novel by

Mr. Charles Dickens. The poor creature held his hands before his face, as if he were afraid of more flashes. He must have been looking directly at Wally when the powerful powder ignited.

He stumbled, and Wally leaped to his assistance. As Rhodope and I followed Wally across the street, I realized that we had discovered the source of the unsettling sound. The man himself was ticking.

"I'm so sorry, sir," Wally said, helping him toward a low windowsill where he could sit. "If I had known you were near, I would have called out a warning!"

"You've blinded me!" the stranger said in a strangled voice.

"It will pass presently," Rhodope reassured him. "And I'll summon a cab to carry you home."

"No, no, just let me sit," he said, still rubbing his eyes. "I'll fumble my way. It ain't far."

"I'll lead you there myself, sir," Wally offered. "If you'd only wait until the rally has passed!"

I shook my ears, thinking my instincts must have gone awry, but no — the ticking was definitely coming from the feeble old man. At any rate, it was soon drowned out by the approaching parade.

"They're coming!" Rhodope cried. "We'll have to photograph them from this side of the street. Get ready, Walter!" Wally quickly reloaded the flash powder.

The first vehicle to appear was a topedo-shaped affair driven by Camille Jenatzy, nicknamed Le Diable Rouge, "the Red Devil," because of his unruly red beard. I felt a comparison to an annoyed Airedale might be more befitting.

*Click-flash!*

Jenatzy did not look pleased to have his photograph taken. He had set a speed record of sixty-two miles per hour in a similarly shaped electric automobile just four years ago. Last year, his record had fallen to a carriage with an internal combustion engine. Word was Jenatzy had intended to take the record back on the England leg, but the Kennewicketts captured it instead.

Rhodope poured a measured amount of

powder into the contraption on Wally's head after each photograph was taken, then stepped back and shaded her eyes from the flash.

The Kennewicketts were twelfth in line.

Rhodope raised her own camera, and Wally detached his flash. The Zephyr had no batteries or Voltage Vats. It was powered by Nikola Tesla's recent invention that drew electric power directly from the aether, a mysterious medium he believes to exist in the spaces between the solid matter of the universe. I had listened attentively

to his explanations, but I still could not quite comprehend the concept or the contraption. An unexpected consequence of this type of power was the generation of radiant matter, better known as Saint Elmo's fire.

Cold blue flames played over the Zephyr's frame. Moths drawn to the light flitted through the energy field, and their wings lit with radiant matter, which didn't harm them in the least. They spun like frenzied fairies around the fantastic machine. It completely spoiled the effect. I felt that people who viewed the photos should be admiring the Kennewicketts, not some bedazzling bugs.

The Kennewicketts had requested the last place in line to allow Rhodope time to capture the phenomenon on film. Gizmo, the family's mechanical assistant, had asked for a photograph to share with the other automatons who had stayed home with her to staff the Kennewicketts' Automated Inn. They were now all powered by the same device that caused the Zephyr to glow, and free from Voltage Vats and charging stations forever. Fortunately, the effect that lit the Zephyr seemed to apply only when very large amounts of energy were drawn from the aether. Radiant automatons would no doubt have unsettled some of the Inn's guests.

"Ascot, Walter!" Calypso called as the Zephyr rolled to a stop.

I growled as one particularly persistent moth fluttered in front of the camera.

"Yes, Mother." Wally straightened his tie as he stepped forward. Walter Kennewickett is always impeccably dressed. Calypso feels that a tidy appearance is a sign of a tidy mind.

I kept my eyes on the moths. I was quite sure Calypso would not approve of an insect obscuring Walter's face in the family photo.

Wally turned to pose by the Zephyr's door. At that moment a moth made the mistake of flitting toward the fender. I leaped, and snapped my jaws about it. I did not swallow it, of course. Well-bred dachshunds do not ingest insects.

"Nicely done, Noodles," Oliver said, sur-reptitiously checking his own tie before smiling for the camera.

"No manufacture of pyrotechnics while we are gone, son," he went on, turning to Wally. "Listen to your aunt Rhodope."

"Certainly, Father."

The wiggling inside my mouth was becom-ing unbearable. I tried to distract myself by spin-ning in place.

Finally, Rhodope lowered her camera and I heard Calypso shift the Zephyr into gear.

"Spit it out, Noodles," she said. "And take care of Walter for us."

I ejected the insect onto the pavement and attempted to regain my dignity as it crawled away.

"Get a picture of the Union with the flash, Walter!" Rhodope cried as the Zephyr rolled on. She meant the members of the International Union of Women's Suffrage Societies who were marching behind the Zephyr.

"Suffrage" is the right to vote in political elections. Calypso was a founding member of the organization. She felt that it was ridiculous that women who were doctors, journalists, artists, or inventors extraordinaire could not cast a ballot. Fire flashed, and the Sisters of Suffrage—with their shoulder sashes that read "Equal Rights for Women!" and their "Calypso Kennewickett" banners—were captured on film.

Rhodope cheered as the Sisters passed, followed by two constables who appeared to be keeping an eye on them.

A "constable" is a British police officer.

"Come on, Walter," Rhodope said. "Let's see our new friend home."

Wally turned to retrieve the tattered man, but the fellow was nowhere to be found.

"The dazzle must have worn off," Rhodope said. "He's found his own way. Let's follow the parade instead!"

2

We marched along with the constables to the brilliantly electrified Embankment. The atmosphere was festive, as if a circus had spilled into the September night. Street vendors and beggars both were taking advantage of the opportunities offered.

Onlookers cheered for each of the electro-mobiles as they drove up the ramp to the ship that was to carry them across the Channel. The cheering was loudest for the Zephyr, of course. The Sisters of Suffrage saw to that.

"You are a Kennewickett yourself, if I'm not mistaken," the younger of the two constables said to Wally as the ship slipped downriver. The man was redheaded, round-faced, and had very merry blue eyes. I could tell by the tap of his tongue each time it encountered an *r* that he was from Scotland. "Why didn't you go with your parents, laddie?"

"My aunt has arranged a breakfast with Sir Arthur Conan Doyle tomorrow, sir." Wally flushed. "I'm a tremendous fan of his fictional detective!"

"Sherlock Holmes, is it? I'm a fan myself. This is your aunt?" He tipped his hat to Rhodope. "Everyone knows Miss Rhodope Pickering. Artemis Arbuckle, at your service, ma'am. Is Sir Arthur a friend of yours, then?" he asked, squatting to scratch my ear.

"I photographed a séance for the Society for Psychical Research," Rhodope replied. "Sir Arthur is a member, and was kind enough to purchase several of my photographic prints."

I presented my other ear to the officer. I was sure that Sir Arthur's fascination with flying machines had something to do with his agreeing to meet with Rhodope, Wally, and me. I expected to be asked to demonstrate the dachshund wings that had recently allowed Wally to save the world.

"When you're dining with the gent," said Constable Arbuckle, standing again, "could you ask him to be a bit kinder to the Yard?"

He meant Scotland Yard, of course, the headquarters of the London police force. The dauntless consulting detective in Sir Arthur's books was constantly making a fool of a fictional inspector who worked there.

Before Rhodope could answer, a woman in a suffrage sash rushed up, almost stepping on me in her haste.

"Sylvia's been arrested!" she cried.

"Arrested?" Officer Arbuckle asked. "For what?"

The woman pointed at her suffrage sash.

"Ah. Causing a commotion, was she?" The officer smiled.

Rhodope's chin rose. "Don't you have rounds to make, sir?" she asked. The constable blushed, tipped his hat to the ladies, and walked away.

I was sorry to see my new acquaintance go.

A constable is not a bad thing to have around when you are responsible for the safety of a Kennewickett.

"Don't get the wrong idea, Walter," Rhodope said when he was gone. "It's just that the battle for equality can become quite exciting." She considered us thoughtfully. "I'm not sure Calypso would approve of me dragging you two to the police station, and time is of the essence. Sylvia is supposed to speak at a meeting tonight!"

"We could simply buy some fish and chips

while we wait for you here," Wally suggested. I wagged my tail in agreement. A bite of fish might erase the unpleasant memory of moth legs tickling my tongue.

"Excellent! And if I am delayed?"

"We'll find our own way home," Wally assured her. "It's just a few blocks, and Noodles never gets lost. He navigates by nose."

That was true. Neither the lingering scent of flash powder nor the scent of muck and mud now seeping up from the river Thames could confuse me; after we'd left Rhodope's flat we had passed a pastry shop, turned right at a teashop that smelled of jasmine and orchids, and made a left by a butcher's, where they were making sausages. To backtrack from the Embankment to the square, we would simply retrace the route of the parade.

"All right," Rhodope said. "Meet me by the bookseller's. If I'm not back in an hour, then go directly home."

After his aunt rushed off with the suffragette, Wally purchased a paper cone full of fish and crisp potatoes from a vendor, and we shared them as we wandered down the Embankment.

We'd gone perhaps a block when we found ourselves observing a street performance. A massive man in silk sultan's robes and a tall turban bowed to the crowd. He slowly pulled a large kerchief from his sleeve and laid it on the paving stones, then produced a plate from inside his robes. I licked a bit of chip from my chops. I have an instinctual interest in plates. They often arrive with things such as sausages or bacon on them.

The giant spun the plate in the air and twirled like a dervish beneath it, his robes flaring. When he faced us again, a little girl of perhaps six had appeared as if by magic at his feet.

The child climbed onto the plate, and the giant raised it above his head. Before I could process her perilous plight, she upended into a handstand. This time the crowd not only clapped, they tossed coins onto the kerchief.

The little girl slowly lifted one hand, balancing on the other. I thought Wally's cousin Prissy would have appreciated the feat; she planned to join the circus someday herself.

I glanced at Wally to see if he was appreciating the show, but his attention had been captured by something farther down the way. A boy was performing on a monowheel. He maneuvered magnificently, while people threw pennies into a pail.

A "monowheel" is a conveyance that consists of a single large wheel, a seat for the pilot, a drive chain, and a pair of pedals. This monowheel had been modified by the addition a motor. It was two meters tall, with the seat in the center. Most monowheels are completely dependent on the driver's sense of balance. This one, however, was further modified with a toplike gyroscope suspended over the driver's head.

The boy stopped directly in front of us and stepped off the machine. The monowheel remained upright without him. He grasped it with one hand and spun it as you might spin a coin on a tabletop, seeming to transform the circle into a sphere.

The crowd rained coins on him, but his brown eyes went from Wally to me. I was studying him as well. His costume had clearly been created from bits and bobs scavenged from trash heaps. None of his buttons matched. Calypso would not have approved of the sloppy stitching.

"You're them, ain't you?" he said. "Walter Kennewickett, boy scientist, and 'is dirigible-like dachshund wot saved the world!"

I shuddered at this description. Certain journalists simply refused to believe that Wally had invented a working pair of wings for me. I'd been depicted in multiple publications as a balloon-like creature on a string.

"I read about you in the papers," the boy went on. "I'm Dobbin. Dobbin Winckles." He held out a hand encased in a grimy glove with no fingertips. I knew from Wally's large library of crime fiction that pickpockets preferred gloves of that kind, as they kept their hands warm and their fingers nimble.

"Wally," Walter said, grasping the gloved hand firmly. I have often noted the instant camaraderie that springs up among certain scientists and inventors. I was not sure what I thought about it springing up between Wally and this fellow.

"Dirigibles are lighter than air, of course," Wally noted. "Noodles is not."

Dobbin nodded. "Of course not. 'E's respectable, 'e is."

I wagged. Grimy gloves might be forgivable under certain circumstances. This was clearly a boy of keen discernment.

Wally stepped closer to the monowheel. The stroboscopic effect of the spin gave it a ghostlike appearance, but one could clearly see the inner workings.

"Is this your own design? I read of one like it in *Scientific American,* but you appear to have made modifications!"

"The problem is balance," Dobbin said. "I've added a gyroscope to keep 'er from tipping."

"And an internal combustion engine, judging from the sound," Wally said. "My own inventions are mostly electric, and occasionally dachshund-powered. I do work some with explosives, of course."

"Such as them used for blowing safes?" Dobbin asked. His eyes darted to the rooftops and searched the crowd around us. I wondered what he was looking for.

"Such as those used in art," Wally clarified.

"Never 'eard of that sort." Dobbin leaned closer to Wally. "Run, Kennewickett," he whispered. "Leave London. Tick Tock's out to nab you."

*Tick Tock!*

Fear shot down my spine. My instincts had not gone awry after all. Walter Kennewickett was in danger.

W ho?" Wally asked.

"Dob!" the angel cried from her perch on the plate before Dobbin could reply. "Peelers!"

The word "peelers" apparently applied to the two uniformed officers of the law we had accompanied in the parade. They were making their way toward us.

Dobbin grabbed his monowheel with one gloved hand to stop the spin, then jumped aboard.

"Keep it mum," he said to Wally. "Tick Tock will kill me if 'e knows I warned you!" Then the crowd scattered as the contraption careered crazily through its midst. A quick glance confirmed that the angel and the giant had made a getaway as well.

One constable set off in pursuit of the monowheel, blowing his whistle and brandishing his billy club, but our Scottish friend stayed.

"Conversing with the riffraff, were you?" Officer Arbuckle asked.

"He *seemed* like a decent fellow," Wally said.

The constable pushed his hat back. "If you mean decent at pickpocketing and acts of light larceny, I'd agree."

"Larceny" is taking someone else's property without permission. I was disturbed to learn that Dobbin would do such a thing, but I had to admit his comment about blowing up safes had been a clue that he might not be entirely on the up-and-up.

"That lot indulges in arson and occasional kidnapping," Officer Arbuckle confided. "I've never known them to burn a building down with anyone inside, so I could say there are worse. I don't suppose they have such characters as him in Gasket Gully." He looked around. "Did your aunt just leave you here?"

"We were to meet in an hour," Wally explained. "And if she doesn't return, I'm to walk home."

"I'll walk with you a bit, if it's along my beat," Officer Arbuckle said. "I'm going to the other side of Trafalgar Square before I turn."

"It is along our way," Wally admitted.

I, for one, was glad of the constable's company.

"You've got to be careful in London Town, laddie," he said as we left the bright lights of the Embankment. "A genteel thing like Miss Rhodope might not realize it, but we've got Spring-Heeled Jack on our rooftops, thieves in the streets, and sewer swine below."

"Sewer swine?"

I was glad Wally asked. I had heard of Spring-Heeled Jack, of course. He had been in all the papers of late. The rotten rogue ran across rooftops and could leap incredible distances. This might have been considered an eccentric hobby if he hadn't taken to dropping into the street and snatching purses or pocket watches from the unsuspecting before he bounced away again. I had never, however, heard of sewer swine.

"They keep that one hush-hush. Some people don't even believe in the beasts," the constable said, stopping to tap on a grimy basement window with his billy club. "Wake up, Charlie," he called. "You've got to be at work at nine!"

"I'm awake, I'm awake," a voice grumbled inside.

"Our knocker-upper is visiting his old mum," Artemis Arbuckle explained as he stepped back to the street. "I told him I'd rouse those that work the night shift. I take care of this neighborhood, as you can see. Walk the rounds all night."

A "knocker-upper's" job is to wake people so that they get to work on time.

Rhodope has photographs of lamplighters, chimney sweeps, and knocker-uppers in her rooms. A map on her wall shows the location where each picture was taken.

"Do you believe in sewer swine?" Wally asked as we started across the square.

"I do," the officer said. "They say that years and years ago, a sow in young washed down a drain in Hampstead. She proceeded to have her piglets in the sewers, where they fed on garbage and rats. The porkers multiplied exceedingly, and *adapted,* as Mr. Darwin might say. They're all white now, with razor-sharp teeth, and as ferocious as any animal in the wild."

"But has their existence actually been documented?" Wally asked.

"Ah, you're the skeptical sort, I see. Comes of having scientific parents, I suppose. It's true that some folks don't believe in them. But I've

heard their ghastly grunting through the drains, and that is as close as I ever hope to get. I want nothing to do with dark deeds beneath the streets."

I eyed the lock on the sewer grate we just happened to be passing, and silently agreed with Officer Arbuckle. Nothing on earth could induce me to venture into such a place.

"Have you ever heard of a criminal called Tick Tock?" Wally asked.

"Murder and mahem!" Constable Arbuckle cried. "Of course I have. Feared by criminals and police alike, he is." He gave Wally a rather keen look. "What brought his name to mind just now?"

"I'd rather not say, sir," Wally admitted.

Artemis Arbuckle swung his billy club thoughtfully.

"I was curious about criminals myself as a lad," he said. "But Tick Tock is another sort entirely. Every officer dreams of apprehending him, and every officer fears meeting him in the dark."

"But who is he, sir?" Wally asked.

"A shadow, a scream, a nightmare," Officer Arbuckle said with a sigh. "And one you nowise want to meet. They say Tick Tock's father was a tosher—a person who dug amongst the muck in the sewers in those days, searching for coins and jewels and watches that had washed down. He raised two sons in the tosher trade. When that line of work was outlawed, one of them became a very fine watchmaker and the other a very foul criminal."

"Tick Tock was the watchmaker, then?"

"He was the criminal," the constable corrected. "They called him Tick Tock because he had a clockwork heart. His brother made it for him, you see, after a bullet nicked his God-given ticker during the commission of a crime."

"What does Mr. Tick Tock look like?" Wally asked, and I knew that he was thinking the same thing I was thinking—like an old man in a tattered coat, an old man who sounded like clockwork.

"Nobody's ever seen him," Officer Arbuckle said, "not and lived to tell the tale. But that's one you don't need to worry about. His brother died five years ago, and they say Tick Tock followed him away. His ticker stopped, that's what I think, with his brother not around to fix it. At any rate, he's gone and we're glad of it. My beat is this way." He pointed down a dark street.

"Auntie's rooms are the other way," Wally said.

I woofed agreement.

"Take care," the constable said. "It's a good night to be inside. We'll have fog by morning, see if we don't. Give your aunt my regards!"

"What do you think, Noodles?" Wally asked as he followed me up the street. "Have we seen the Tick-Tock Man and lived to tell? Our gentleman looked a little old to be nabbing people, though." He stopped, and his hand went to his camera. "We didn't just see him. We may have a photograph of him!"

I grabbed the cuff of Wally's pants and pulled to start him on his way again. Rhodope would never have left us alone if she had heard Dobbin's warning. It goes without saying that Oliver and Calypso would not approve of their son wandering the streets under such circumstances. It was my job to get him home as quickly as possible.

"I'm coming," Wally said.

I turned my olfactory apparatus toward the scent of sausage, glancing back every now and then to make sure Wally was still behind me.

We'd just rounded the corner toward jasmine tea and orchids when I heard it.

*Tick-tock.*

"Noodles," Wally whispered, "I believe we are being followed."

I walked a little faster. As Wally's friend, I had faced my fair share of danger. But being followed through the night by a criminal with a clockwork heart unsettled even me.

*Tick-tock.*

"Run!" Wally shouted, and I ran, making sure I did not lose him as I led the way.

4

The terrible *tick-tock* of the clock-work heart drew closer as we pelted around the corner toward the shop that sold pastries. We dodged a horse-drawn cart as we crossed the street.

Suddenly, there was the sound of a scuffle behind us, and a sharp cry. We whirled in time to see something tossed into the cart. The driver leaped aboard, a whip cracked over the poor horse's ears, and the conveyance clattered away.

The street was still.

"What on earth is going on, Noodles?" Wally wondered aloud.

I had no answers.

We reached Aunt Rhodope's address without

further incident and found her landlady, Mrs. Wiggins, waiting.

"Miss Pickering called ages ago to say she would be coming in quite late," the woman said, giving me a disapproving look. I suspected that she did not like dachshunds. "A cold supper is waiting upstairs. And just because Miss is out doesn't mean you can go jumping about in her rooms. This is a respectable house!"

"Thank you, Mrs. Wiggins," Wally said as we started up. "We wouldn't dream of jumping about."

I was certain she did not like dachshunds when I discovered she had left only one covered plate on the table, and it contained just a single ham sandwich. We had finished the fish and chips over an hour ago, and there is always room for a bit of ham.

"You eat, Noodles," Wally said as he divided the sandwich in half. Walter Kennewickett is a very thoughtful boy. "I am going to develop my film." He set the sandwich before me.

Rhodope had shown him how to use her

excellent darkroom the day we arrived, but my nose was too sensitive for the chemical baths the negatives and prints were subjected to.

I devoured my half of the ham sandwich in two bites and watched Wally's half while he worked.

"I've got him!" Wally announced after he'd developed the negatives. "We'll have to see how it prints, though."

I was sure the bread was stale by the time he hung the prints to dry, but he didn't seem to care.

"It's an excellent image," he said around a mouthful. "Aunt Rhodope will not believe who we have captured on film!"

After he finished his meal, he washed his hands and brought out the photographic prints for inspection. He held one up, and I observed an angular face, hawklike nose, and deep-set eyes. I instantly knew that the feeble old fellow we thought we had seen was just an act. Every line of this lean body bespoke power.

*Run, Kennewickett.* Dobbin's warning echoed in my ears.

I knew that I could not possibly sleep until Rhodope arrived. Wally looked longingly at the array of explosive powders he had arranged on the desk his aunt was letting him use, then sighed and picked up Sir Arthur's new novel, *The Hound of the Baskervilles,* and settled into a chair.

I may have mentioned that Walter Kennewickett is a scientist in training. He is fascinated by the similarities between scientific research and the work of a detective. Both scientific experimentation and crime solving depend on the ability to form a hypothesis.

A "hypothesis" is a guess. If you pay close

attention to the clues, it can be a very good guess. Still, it is no more than a starting point for further investigation. When Sir Arthur's detective solves a crime, he forms hypotheses and tests them until he finds the facts behind the case.

"Why would Tick Tock want to nab me?" Wally wondered, lowering the book. His mind was clearly not consumed by the mystery of the hound. "And . . . what happened to him?"

At that moment someone knocked on the door. I shuddered, suddenly sure Tick Tock had found us. But Wally ran to open it before I could stop him. We found Mrs. Wiggins in her evening cap and robe. She was holding a grease-stained envelope as one might hold a recently deceased mouse.

"A note for Mr. Kennewickett," she said.

"Thank you, ma'am," Wally said, taking it from her. She stalked away to her own room.

I expected it to be a message from Rhodope, but I was wrong.

The missive, hastily penned on a piece of butcher paper, read: "NEED HELP. Come to the courtyard behind Chopin's Pub at Bow and Kemble at midnight. It is a matter of LIFE AND DEATH. You must come alone. NO PEELERS." And it was signed "D. Winckles."

"Winckles," Wally said, and began to pace. "The boy with the monowheel. Something is amiss, Noodles." He stopped on the opposite side of the room and spun around to consult the map on Rhodope's wall.

"I estimate it will take twenty minutes to get to the courtyard," Wally said. "Ten if we run. We'll wait for Aunt Rhodope."

At eleven thirty Wally read the note again. His finger tapped twice on LIFE AND DEATH.

"What would Father suggest if he were here?" he asked, and started to pace again.

I strained my ears, hoping to hear Rhodope's tread.

At eleven forty he stopped and stood very still. "I don't know what Father would suggest in the current situation," he said. "But I know what he would do, Noodles. Someone needs help."

I was afraid he was correct. A Kennewickett never turns away from someone needing help.

Wally tore a page from his notebook and wrote a quick account of the mysterious warning about Tick Tock, along with a request that a wire be sent to his parents. He ended the message with "Gone to render assistance."

I thought it was an excellent idea to wire Oliver and Calypso. I had a hypothesis as to why D. Winckles's life might be in danger.

Wally left the page along with the note from D. Winckles on the table for his aunt Rhodope to find.

Then he took a bit of string and a candle stub from a drawer and scooped up a tin of Oliver's Delightful, Dependable, and Safe Matches and two Coruscating Cannonades. They were the last pocket pyrotechnic Wally had finished before his parents had left.

To "coruscate" is to flash and sparkle.

A "cannonade" is the continuous roar of many guns.

The Coruscating Cannonade was one of Calypso's favorite pyrotechnics.

Wally looked around one last time, and then we tiptoed past Mrs. Wiggins's bedroom and crept down the stairs. The quarter bells in the clock tower at the Palace of Westminster were chiming as we came out the door.

The well-lit streets of Charing Cross were surprisingly busy even at this time of night, but everything changed as soon as we turned from the main street. The electric lamps were gone,

replaced by gas lamps that flickered as their wicks died, making our shadows jump first behind us, then before us as we passed each post.

"We're being followed again, Noodles," Wally said.

The brilliant boy was as observant as usual. The shadows thrown by streetlights could not explain the silhouette that followed on the rooftops, black as ink against the stars.

Like our own shadows, it ran sometimes behind us. But sometimes it ran ahead, as if it knew where we were going.

The quarter bells were ringing again by the time we found the alley that opened into a small courtyard behind the pub. It was lit only by light that spilled from windows.

Something moved in the darkness, just as the voice of Big Ben, the bell that spoke the hour, broke the night. *Doom, doom, doom,* it rang, twelve times, and then the giant we'd seen at the Embankment stepped into a rectangle of light. He still wore his turban, but he was shirtless now. Light glinted off a metallic rib cage that expanded and contracted with the rhythm of a metronome.

"Where is Dobbin?" Wally asked. I was wondering that myself.

The giant took a hand bellows from his pocket, inserted it into his mouth, and pumped himself full of air.

"Kenn-eee-wickett." He sighed as the air exited past his vocal cords. My hackles lifted from nape to tail. If a corpse leaked air, I imagined it would sound something like this. "Follow meeeeeeee."

"You must breathe through mechanical gills!" Wally exclaimed, and then looked embarrassed. "Pardon me, but . . . that's fantastic! I'm here to see Dobbin. He wrote about a matter of life and death?"

The giant pumped himself full of air once more.

"Liffffe." The giant sighed. "Deattthhhhh. Yessss. Hellllp ussssss."

At that moment, the shadow dropped from above.

A young man landed with a metallic *sproing* right in front of Wally. He wore leather leggings above what appeared to be thick-soled, spring-loaded boots; a red silk shirt; and a rakish cap. A dark cape draped behind him. His eyes looked black in the darkness.

"Spring-Heeled Jack, I presume?" Wally said.

"Jack will do," the young man replied. "Stop wasting time, Cy. Knock him over the head, or I will. We have to get below. There's peelers every-where tonight. I'm surprised they didn't follow him."

I growled and inched in front of Wally as the giant stepped forward.

"Oh-ho!" Jack folded his arms. "A scary sausage."

"There is no need to knock my head," Wally said, assuming a judo stance. He had practiced the sport daily since being introduced to its effectiveness by President Theodore Roosevelt. "*If* you're friends of Dobbin, I'll come peacefully. If not, you can try your luck."

"A scary sausage *and* a feisty shrimp." Jack shook his head. "Where did Dob find you? Let's see if you have the guts for the business at hand! Open it, Cy."

The half-mechanical man squatted and grasped the sewer grate. With one mighty heave, he lifted it away, revealing a black hole beneath.

Wally pulled his candle stub from his pocket, lit it, and leaned over the hole. Metal rungs descended into the darkness.

"Hurry up." Jack dropped past him. "I told you, there's no time."

"I'd like some proof that you're taking me to Dobbin Winckles," Wally said.

"Winckles said you have a 'respectable' dog and make interesting art." Jack shrugged. "I don't like dogs, and art's for namby-pambies, so it's not like I listened."

"Namby-pamby" refers to someone weak and sentimental. I am sure he meant it as an insult, but Wally just nodded.

"You'll have to wait for me, Noodles," he said, and started to climb down.

I've said that nothing on earth could induce me to venture into the sewers. I meant nothing but the thought of Walter Kennewickett going without me. I closed my eyes and leaped . . .

. . . and felt myself snatched from thin air and swung aloft. I found myself eye-to-eye with the giant. He tucked me under his arm and started down the ladder. Wally's candle flickered below us as we descended into darkness.

The feeble flame revealed a catwalk that clung to the side of the tunnel, the depths of which were lost in darkness. When I mentioned the word "sewer," I am sure many unpleasant things came to mind. The reality was even more unpleasant than can be imagined.

The smell almost made me swoon. Wally had his hand to his nose, and Jack, who had closed the grate and followed us down, pulled a black scarf over his face.

Cy merely set me down, as if he could smell nothing at all. And then he unwound his peculiar turban to reveal an even more peculiar cranium. Cy's ribs were not the only bits of iron about him. The dome of his head was ferrous as well, and there was a bulging lens in the center of his forehead.

The giant snapped his fingers, and a flame leaped to life behind it, sending out a beam like a bull's-eye lantern. As he turned his head, I took in our surroundings.

A milky green river ran beneath us, full of unthinkable things. When the beam of Cy's lamp turned toward the torrid torrent, I saw a huge river rat on a raft of flotsam.

I believe I have mentioned that dachshunds navigate by nose. My olfactory nerves were overwhelmed by the scent, and my head was swimming. By the time we arrived at a side tunnel, I had no idea what part of London might lie above us.

We turned away from the subterranean river and stepped through an arched aperture into yet another tunnel, clearly older and thankfully drier than the first.

The air was fresher here, and clean water spouted from between the bricks as if springs had been walled up inside. The water was no more than an inch deep on the floor. Crystals had formed from minerals leaching through the ancient walls, and they sparkled in the lamp's beam. Tiny pale spiders skittered among them.

We'd traveled perhaps half a mile, past openings large and small, when Jack held up his hand.

"Listen," he hissed.

I could hear a splashing far behind us.

"It's the piggies." His voice sounded far more frightened than you might expect from a hardened criminal. "Climb for your life!" We raced to the nearest sewer access ladder. Cy scooped me up and nodded to Wally, who started to climb.

Jack reached the grate that opened onto the street, but when he pushed against it, nothing happened.

"Locked," he said, swinging hand over hand out on the grate to make more room on the ladder.

And then they arrived.

These were not *piggies*.

Piggies are small and pink. These creatures were large and pearly white. Their tiny eyes flashed red in the light of Cy's lantern. In short,

they were sewer swine. They gnashed their teeth and grunted, trying to figure out a way to get us.

"You've got to get higher, Cy," Jack said. "They're going to start stacking."

But we couldn't climb any higher. Wally was in the way.

The pigs began piling one on top of another until the jaws of the topmost, an enormous boar, were snapping just beneath the giant's heels.

Cy squeezed his eyes closed.

"Hold on." Wally looped his arm through a rung of the ladder. He pulled out the tin of Delightful, Dependable, and Safe Matches.

A match flared. Wally lit a fuse and tossed his first Coruscating Cannonade.

The boar leaped, intercepting it in the air. Swine saliva swamped the fuse. The monster swallowed it whole, licked its chops, and pranced as if asking for more.

"Feeding them treats," Jack said. "What a novel idea. That will make them leave."

Wally was already lighting his second pocket pyrotechnic.

He tossed this one farther down the tunnel. The swine scrambled after it, but just before they reached it, it burst. Spinning spots of yellow, blue, and purple fire shot upward, coruscating as they rose. They ricocheted off the walls and bounced from the ceiling. And then the cannonade began, each spark emitting a *boom* as it died. The sewer swine fled, squealing and slightly singed.

Jack dropped to the floor of the tunnel as soon as the last kinky tail disappeared, but Cy would not move until their squeals diminished in the distance.

"What was *that?*" Jack asked when Wally reached the floor at last.

"Art," Wally said, taking his notebook from his pocket. "I believe it needs more purple." He made a note of it and we continued on, past ancient arches that had been bricked over, and I could only wonder what lay on the other side. Finally, we stopped before a wooden door with massive iron bands and hinges. They must have been well oiled, for the door swung open silently.

# 6

The room we entered can only be described as a cathedral of clockwork. Brass bits and bobs glowed in the gaslight from Tiffany lamps. One side of the room resembled a giant watch that had been turned inside out. Springs, weights, and gears spilled out of the wall. They looked as if they had once kept perfect time as they performed their maker's mysterious purpose. But it was clear the clockmaker was gone and that the workshop had fallen into disuse and disarray. The opposite wall looked like something from the Middle Ages, with torches in sconces.

"We brought him as requested, Dob," Jack said.

Dobbin jumped up from a cluttered workbench that looked much as I imagined the one in

Oliver's lab would have if Calypso had never set foot in the Automated Inn.

"You rotten rat!" he cried, his fingers curling into fists. "You slimy squealer!"

A growl started to grow inside me. This was no matter of life and death. Wally had been deceived into entering a den of thieves!

"I did not squeal," Wally said. "Though I did leave a message for my parents before I left. What is this about?"

"Tick Tock said 'e was going to nab you." The little angel who had warned Dobbin of the peelers stepped out of the shadows and took Cy's hand. "And now he's missing."

Of course she was part of this gutter gang. Now that I saw Dobbin and the girl together, it was clear that they were siblings.

"You're supposed to be in bed, Briney," Dobbin said. "You said you were knackered. I 'ad to carry you 'ome!"

If Walter and I had not read so many of the Sherlock Holmes stories, I might not have known that "knackered" meant exhausted.

"I'm *always* knackered," Briney said. "Bed don't help."

Cy sat down on the floor, and Briney squatted beside me. I started to back away—and then I heard it.

*Tick-tock.*

It wasn't as loud as Tick Tock's heart, but it was loud enough that I couldn't miss it. It took me a moment to realize what it meant. It seemed that Tick Tock was not the only member of this band of bandits with a mechanical heart. I sat down.

"You twig to it, Noodles?" Dobbin asked.

"Twig" is slang for "understand," and I was terribly afraid I did.

Dobbin nodded. "Dogs could 'ear it, I suppose. Show the gent, Briney."

The little girl unbuttoned a pocket in her gown to reveal a cabinet in the center of her chest. The mechanism ticking away inside was a marvel of gleaming glass and metal. A weight swung above it like a metronome.

"Incredible!" Wally cried, stepping closer. He gasped, and I knew the keen boy had seen the keyhole and understood instantly what it meant.

"Clockwork has to be wound"—Wally's hand went to his own heart—"and Tick Tock's gone missing with the keys! What time does Mr. Tock generally wind your apparatus?"

Cy blinked as if holding back tears, but Briney just wrapped her arms around me. I held very still, listening to the whir of clockwork in her chest. This was a matter of life and death after all. They might be pickpockets and thieves, but if Tick Tock did not return with the keys, both Cy and Briney were doomed.

"He winds them in the morning at seven sharp." Jack picked up a tappet wrench from the table and twirled it like a baton. "Every single day."

I thought for an instant that the child beside me was too young to understand her predicament. And then I felt her tremble. Briney

Winckles was well aware of the peril her peculiar heart put her in, but she did not want her brother to know she was afraid. I leaned against her and licked her chin. Even a desperado needs to hug a dachshund sometimes.

"You mentioned he might kill you?" Wally queried.

"It don't matter wot 'e does to me," Dobbin said, paling perceptibly. "Wot matters is that 'e makes it back before seven."

Wally cleared his throat. "That may be beyond his ability. I'm afraid Noodles and I may have witnessed Tick Tock being abducted."

Briney went still.

"Which only means we must rescue him," Wally added quickly, "rather than await his return."

"Scotland Yard's taken 'im!" Jack exclaimed.

"I don't believe so," Wally said, and described exactly what we had seen.

"It *must* 'ave been the peelers," Dobbin said.

"Perhaps," Walter admitted. "But there is someone I would very much like to consult just in case it isn't."

"*You* know a criminal mastermind?" Jack asked.

"No," Wally admitted. "But my aunt is acquainted with a deductive genius. Sir Arthur Conan Doyle."

Jack fumbled the wrench he was spinning, then snatched it from the air. "You think 'e would give us the time of day?"

"I believe so," Wally said. "I was supposed to have breakfast with him tomorrow."

"He's at his flat in Buckingham Mansions instead of his country house, then." Jack jumped down. "Let's go!"

I found it fascinating that a criminal such as Spring-Heeled Jack would know the whereabouts of Sir Arthur's flat.

"If Tick Tock 'as been taken," Dobbin said, "I expect 'e will escape. And when 'e does, 'e will come 'ere."

"But if he does not," Jack insisted, "then we have no time to lose!"

"Jack's got it right, Dob," Briney said, standing up. "We go find him." The giant, who had been sitting silently beside me the whole time, nodded his odd head.

"All right," Dobbin decided. "We go. I'll bring you pickaback, Briney."

To bring someone "pickaback" means to carry that person on one's back. The boy bent over so his little sister could climb on.

Buckingham Mansions proved to be a fortress of flats almost a block long and six stories tall. The street level was occupied by shops and guarded by a doorman.

"Pardon me," Wally said to this worthy man when we arrived. "Would you inform Sir Arthur that Walter Kennewickett wishes to see him?"

The doorman's eyes took in Wally and our three curious companions—Cy had wisely waited in the shadows on the opposite side of the street—before they settled on me.

"Get on," he growled. "No dogs allowed. I don't like dogs, nor boys nor girls for that matter."

"How about your job?" Jack asked. "Do you

like your job? I ask because Sir Arthur is expecting us."

"Is that so?"

"Yes." Not only did Jack sound sincere, but his face showed no sign of deception. Criminals of his ilk could apparently lie without blushing.

"Then you would know that he's out chasing ghosts. Yer not gettin' in. Not in the middle of the night."

I was deciding which ankle to bite when my lunge was arrested by a cry from the street.

"Wal-ter!"

Rhodope was running toward us. The gentleman following at a more dignified pace could only be Sir Arthur Conan Doyle.

Jack made a strange, strangling sound. I could understand his emotion. Sir Arthur's form engendered awe in me as well. He was not cut from the same physical cloth as his character Sherlock Holmes. The fictional detective is described as a whip of a man. Sir Arthur resembled a walrus.

"Walter!" Rhodope cried again when she arrived. "I wired your parents as requested.

They'll be here by midmorning, I'm sure. When you failed to return, I tracked Sir Arthur down at a Society for Psychical Research meeting to enlist his help. But it seems you've captured the criminals single-handedly? Bravo!"

"He didn't capture anybody, love." Jack had jerked his scarf over his face. "We kidnapped him right and proper."

"I believe 'requested my presence' would be more accurate," Wally said. I had to concur. I would never have allowed Walter Kennewickett to be kidnapped.

"Kidnapped," Jack insisted, as if his credentials as a criminal were in question. "Carried off!"

Miss Rhodope's eyes narrowed. "Do I know you, sir?"

"Not unless you consort with vile criminals," Jack growled, his voice having grown even gruffer. "The name's Jack. I imagine you've heard of me?"

Sir Arthur studied him. "Spring-Heeled Jack steals purses, then jumps walls and bounces up buildings. You'd be that Jack, would you?"

Jack made his bow and flourish.

"But he did not kidnap me, sir," Wally insisted.

"It's just as well," Sir Arthur said. "Your aunt was about to rouse the Sisters of Suffrage to your defense. I expect there would have been rioting in the streets. And who are these young people?"

Rhodope turned to the urchins as Wally made the introductions. Dobbin scowled as if he feared Rhodope might scrub him clean on the spot, but Briney smiled shyly.

"You're the picture lady," she said.

"And you are the acrobatic angel. I've seen you perform! Aren't you a bit big for your brother to be carrying you?"

"She's knackered, miss," Dobbin said. "She'd set right down in the road if I didn't carry 'er."

"Poor child!" Sir Arthur exclaimed. "You must come inside!"

It seemed as if all would be well until Cy stepped from the shadows and crossed the street. I realized with dismay that he had neglected to replace his turban.

"Good Gad." Sir Arthur's grip on his walking stick tightened. "Who might you be, sir?"

"He's a friend," Wally said quickly.

Cy produced his bellows from his pocket and pumped his chest full of air.

"A frrriiienddd," he agreed.

Even the famous author seemed taken aback.

"On my honor as a Kennewickett, sir," Wally said, "my companions harbor no ill intent."

"At the moment," Jack interjected ominously.

"The past is the past, and the future ain't here yet, if you get my meaning."

"A philosopher as well as a villain!" Sir Arthur observed. "Well, well."

"I have more where that came from." Jack had forgotten to gruff his voice, and Sir Arthur gave him a very keen look.

"Your acquaintances astonish me, Walter," he said. "Do step inside, all of you."

The doorman glared at me, but he nodded and smiled and groveled as Sir Arthur stepped past.

He rang for tea and biscuits when we reached his comfortable study. Dobbin, who had carried his sister pickaback up the stairs, settled her on the settee. I hopped up beside her, and Wally sat beside me.

A few moments later I was pleased to learn that biscuits in England were not biscuits at all, but cookies of all sorts.

"Don't you think you should take off your gloves?" Rhodope asked as Dobbin reached grimy fingers for a jam-filled confection.

"I don't take off my gloves for nobody,"

Dobbin said, slipping a second cookie into his pocket.

Briney selected a sugar wafer and offered me half. It would have been impolite not to accept.

"Now, Walter," Rhodope said, "begin at the beginning, and tell all."

Sir Arthur's brow furrowed as Wally related our adventure.

"One moment, Walter," he said when Wally revealed that both Briney and Cy had clockwork parts. "I am a doctor as well as a writer of fiction, you know. May I examine the patients?" Cy nodded at Briney.

"All right," she said. "But don't poke us with nothing like needles."

Sir Arthur assured her that he would not. His face grew grim as he examined Cy's ribs, and grimmer still when he felt Briney's wrist with his fingertips. He took a tablet from his desk and made a couple of quick notations. Walter watched with keen interest, but Miss Rhodope was staring at Jack.

"Go on," the great man said at last, resuming his seat. "If I am going to help, I must know everything." He merely gasped when Wally reached the bit about the missing keys and tapped the tablet with his pen.

"So Walter and Noodles were the last ones to have seen Tick Tock."

"I believe so, sir," Wally agreed. As he talked, I watched Rhodope edge nearer to Jack, who edged away. This curious game of cat and mouse ended with the criminal backed into a corner.

"And he was attempting to kidnap you at the

time?" He spun toward Dobbin. "What was the motive, Mr. Winckles? Money? Was he going to demand a ransom?"

"'E didn't say," Dobbin admitted. "Tick Tock keeps 'is own counsel, 'e does."

At that moment Rhodope snatched the scarf from Jack's face.

"Leander Smyth-Hops! I *knew* it was you! He is no criminal," Rhodope accused. "He's a journalist!"

"You're the one who called my last story a crime, Rho. Said I lacked research!" He turned toward Sir Arthur, his hand to his heart.

"I was inspired by your words in 'A Case of Identity,' sir:

"'Life is infinitely stranger than anything which the mind of man could invent. We would not dare to conceive the things that are really mere commonplaces of existence. If we could fly out of that window hand in hand, hover over this great city, gently remove the roofs, and peep in at the queer things which are going on, the strange coincidences, the plannings, the cross-purposes, the wonderful chains of events, working through generations, and leading to the most outré results, it would make all fiction with its conventionalities and foreseen conclusions most stale and unprofitable.'"

He continued, "Leander Smyth-Hops can't fly over rooftops or peep into houses, but Spring-Heeled Jack most certainly can!"

"Good Gad," Sir Arthur said. "You've memorized it line for line."

"That and more, sir, much more. You are my idol! And"—he seemed to suddenly realize that Dobbin, Cy, and Briney were listening—"you've completely blown my cover, Rho!"

"We already knew," Briney said.

I was distressed to note that while I had been distracted by this discourse, every single cookie had disappeared from the tray. Not only did Dobbin's pocket look lumpy, but Cy's did as well.

"You knew?" Mr. Smyth-Hops asked, paling perceptibly. "Are you telling me Tick Tock knew?"

Cy nodded, brushing crumbs from his sleeve.

"'E don't care." Dobbin was circumnavigating the room now, examining its contents. It appeared unsettlingly as if he were "casing the joint," as criminals might say. "It's rats and abaddons Tick Tock feeds to the sewer swine," the boy went on. "Not newspapermen."

An "abaddon" is a criminal turned informer, a rascal who squeals on his fellow rogues.

"I'm glad to hear that," Mr. Smyth-Hops said. "I am no fan of perishing by pig."

"Do you mean to say that sewer swine are real?" Rhodope asked.

"Real as rats," Leander assured her. "But much bigger and much, much hungrier."

"You must help me get a photograph!" she declared.

"Not on your life," the would-be criminal replied. "You're staying out of the sewers, Rho."

She gave him an icy glare, but I had to agree. Photographing the feral herd might be beyond even Rhodope's considerable skill. I doubted that the piggies could be coaxed into posing peacefully.

"By the way, Walter"—Mr. Smyth-Hops turned to Wally—"you have quite converted me. I've become an admirer of your arts!"

"Pyrotechnics," Wally explained to his aunt. "My Coruscating Cannonades proved useful in scattering the subterranean herd."

The term "subterranean" refers to things beneath the surface of the earth—a fine place for such pigs. I hoped they stayed there.

"Useful?" Mr. Smyth-Hops cried. "They

were utterly fantastic. We must have them at our wedding, Rho!"

"We could," Rhodope agreed. "*If* we were having a wedding. Which of course we are not."

"Of course we are not *yet*," Mr. Smyth-Hops declared, undaunted. "I have to be arrested, you see," he confided to Sir Arthur. "In order to finish researching my exposé on criminals and the court system. I can't possibly propose until I've made a name for myself. But I'm finding it harder than you might suppose to end up behind bars. Really, Dob, I'm not sure why you worry about Scotland Yard at all."

"Stop shamming," Dobbin suggested. "They'll lug you off to the lockup right quick enough."

"The recent purse snatchings were shams?" Wally asked.

"Setups," Mr. Smyth-Hops admitted. "Clever crimes committed under the very nose of the constables. And *still* I have not been nabbed. It's disappointing."

"Disappointing indeed," Sir Arthur said, and sighed. "But back to the problem at hand. I believe we need to notify the Yard."

"No!" Briney started up, almost toppling me to the floor.

"Journalists is one thing, but peelers is another," Dobbin said. "No peelers. They'd take Briney from me, that's wot they'd do. It's my job to take care of 'er."

Cy nodded in silent agreement.

Mr. Smyth-Hops said, "If you ask what I think—"

"No one did," Rhodope pointed out.

"I think Tick Tock will come through," he went on. "I've met the man . . . no, not man.

More a force of nature—if nature were evil, of course. The creature is ineffable."

"Ineffable" means too powerful or extreme to be explained in words.

"You're a journalist," Sir Arthur said. "Attempt it."

Leander shuddered. "It . . . it's as if he carries with him every crime he has ever committed. When he steps into a room, you feel the force of his will. If Tick Tock is expected back, he *will be*. Everyone knows he never reneges."

To "renege" is to fail to keep one's promise, or to break a contract. Dachshunds are far too noble to renege. I was surprised to learn that we could have anything in common with such a criminal.

"If he is such a sought-after criminal, he has most likely been arrested," Miss Rhodope said. "And will not be able to keep his word."

"I asked Constable Arbuckle if he knew of him," Wally said. "He felt that Tick Tock had passed away."

Dobbin glanced at Briney. "'E ain't dead. Just quiet lately. On account of me minding the shop for 'im, if you take my meaning."

"So if he ventured out, he *could* have been captured by the constables!" Rhodope insisted.

Leander held up a finger. "'It is a capital mistake to theorize before one has data,'" he declared. "'Insensibly one begins to twist facts to suit theories, instead of theories to suit facts.' Sherlock Holmes, 'A Scandal in Bohemia.'"

"You are exactly right," Sir Arthur said. "I mean *I* was exactly right. Oh, confound it! Quit quoting me."

"We need more information," Wally admitted. "We haven't got enough to form a hypothesis." The brilliant boy took his notepad out of his pocket, and I wagged. Walter Kennewickett was on the case!

"It has been mentioned multiple times that Tick Tock never reneges," he said. "Have you made a deal with him, Dob?"

"I don't discuss Tick Tock's dealings." The

boy looked up from the lamp he was examining. "Nor my own, neither."

"We can guess," Sir Arthur said softly. "Your sister needed a heart."

"The doctor said I wouldn't grow up," Briney said sleepily. "Tick Tock said I would. He said his brother would make me a heart just like his, if Dob would—"

Dobbin hushed her with a look. "That's our own biz, Briney. They don't need to know it."

He must have felt that every eye in the room was on him.

Dobbin had made a deal with the dastardly Tick Tock, a man who did not blush at lying, stealing, and murdering. A creature who fed informants to the sewer swine. What horrible crimes had the boy committed as part of this deal?

His face flushed, but he didn't look down.

"Dobbin is my friend." Wally stepped over to stand beside him. "I only suggested coming here because we needed help. What matters at the moment is finding the Tick-Tock Man. Perhaps we could come up with a list of possible perpetrators, Dob?"

"Quite right," Sir Arthur agreed. "Who might want to take Mr. Tock?"

"Well . . . there's those that want 'im for crimes 'e's committed," Dobbin said doubtfully, "and those that want 'im to commit crimes 'e 'asn't yet. Which set do you want first?"

"A more pertinent question," Mr. Smyth-Hops proposed, "would be why would he leave retirement to kidnap Walter?"

"'E didn't say," Dobbin admitted. "Someone usually pays 'im for a nabbing."

"Could it be related to the rally?" Miss Rhodope pondered aloud. "Camille Jenatzy was positively glaring as he passed us. Oliver and Calypso are ruining his chance to recover the title."

"We must split up," Sir Arthur decided. "Gather as much information as we can about what happened to Tick Tock on the street last evening."

"We have two hypotheses to explore," Wally said. "That the road rally is involved, or that Scotland Yard has taken Mr. Tock."

"Three hypotheses," Leander corrected. "I believe he may have run into trouble with the criminal element."

Sir Arthur nodded. "Three, then. We must pursue them all, seeking out any hint, any clue, no matter how trivial, that might put us on the right track."

"I'll take to the rooftops," Leander said, resuming Jack's swagger. "I've made the acquaintance of a few cat burglars and second-story men who might be of assistance." A "second story man" is a burglar who creeps in through upper-story windows. Leander paused and put his hand to his breast. "'In solving a problem of this sort, the grand thing is to be able to reason backward.' *A Study in Scarlet*! I'm off to find a fact to reason backward from. Do you mind if I exit by way of the window, sir?"

"I'd be delighted if you did," Sir Arthur said drily. "In fact, if you quote Holmes again, I might help you to do so."

Mr. Smyth-Hops opened the window and leaned out. "Fog below," he said as he stepped out onto the sill. "White as a shroud. But the rooftops and chimneys are clear. Come with me, Rho. I can see the moon and stars!"

"No," Rhodope replied. "I'm off to gather information on the participants in the road rally. I can't do that from a rooftop."

"I doubt you'll do much," Leander said. "Not in this fog. You won't be able to find your way across the street. No carriages will be traveling tonight either."

"Then I'll feel my way," Rhodope said simply. "Neither shrouding fog nor sewer swine will stop me. This mystery must be solved before morning."

In the silence that followed, I could clearly hear the soft ticking of Briney's heart. I jumped down from the couch. Rhodope was right. We had no time to spare.

"I can take you anywhere, Miss," Dobbin said. "Even through a pea souper." This apparently was a reference to the fog. "Can you mind Briney, Cy? I don't think she's up to walking."

The little girl nodded sleepily, hardly lifting

her head from the arm of the settee as the giant sat down beside her.

"That leaves Scotland Yard to Walter and myself," Sir Arthur said.

Dobbin froze.

"We must at least ascertain whether or not your monstrous mentor has been arrested, young man. I will not mention you or your sister," the famous author assured him.

"The constable I spoke with is quite a fan of Sherlock Holmes," Wally said. "I believe he would make inquiries quietly if *you* requested it, sir."

"Good Gad," Sir Arthur muttered. "Another fan. Well, if I must, I must."

# q

We hurried down the stairs and stepped outside to discover that the world had indeed been swallowed by fog. An unnatural stillness had descended on the street. Although light spilled from the doorway, the distance of a few feet turned friends into strange, unrecognizable shapes. I stayed very close to Wally.

A surprising number of citizens were out and about. I would have thought they'd all be bundled in their beds. A carriage moved cautiously through the street before us, and boots stomped by close to my nose.

"Links!" a child's voice cried, and a torch-bearing urchin appeared before us. "Links! Light your way for sixpence, sir?" He held the blazing brand aloft.

"Dob!" he said when he spotted our companion. "I didn't recognize it was you."

"I'm escortin' this lady," Dobbin replied.

"I'll take you for free, seeing as it's you," the boy offered.

"Nonsense," Rhodope said. "I'll pay the sixpence. There's only one torch escort, though. What about you, Sir Arthur?"

"I know the area quite well," the author assured her. "I believe I can manage to bump into a constable even in the dark." He turned to Wally as we set off up the street. "Mind your pockets, Walter. Footpads like nothing better than a thick fog. Where did you last encounter your constable friend?"

"Footpads" are thieves who prey upon pedestrians. I watched for such villains as Wally described the route we had walked with Constable Arbuckle. Phantom footpads formed of fog seemed to step around corners, then dissolve into the night. Smells were mixed by the mist to such an extent that I could not even discern the scent of pastries, though at this time of the early morning, the baker should have been hard at work. I had no idea which way we should go.

"No worries, Noodles," Sir Arthur said, noticing my distress. "I'll lead the way."

When we reached the first corner, our fearless leader felt the base of the gaslight.

"Each light pole has its own mark," he explained. "They were designed to help people find their way home on just such nights as this. The same marks are also put on letters to allow a carrier to know where to deliver them. Very useful for fictional detectives attempting to trace correspondence in London."

We felt our way from lamppost to lamppost until we found Constable Arbuckle waving a torch in the middle of an intersection.

He held up his burning brand as we approached.

"Sir Arthur Conan Doyle!" the constable cried in disbelief.

"Walter said his aunt knew you, but . . . what brings you out on such a night? You must know that it's not safe, sir, not safe at all!"

"We are here on a matter of some urgency," Sir Arthur said. "But before we describe it—can I rely on your discretion?"

To "rely on someone's discretion" means to trust that that person will not reveal sensitive information.

"That all depends." Constable Arbuckle rubbed his chin thoughtfully. "Onst whether or not it regards a crime in progress?"

"Certainly not," Sir Arthur said. "All we need is information."

The constable looked from Wally to Sir Arthur, and finally to me. I stood up on my hind legs and placed my paws on his belt in an attempt to express our earnestness.

"All right," he decided, giving my ears a scratch. "I'll help you if I can."

I expected no less. Dachshunds have potent powers of persuasion.

"We need to know if Scotland Yard apprehended an individual called Tick Tock as he attempted to kidnap Walter," the author said.

"Kidnap Walter?" Constable Arbuckle cried in evident alarm. Wally recounted the events of the night once more, leaving out any information about Dobbin, Briney, and Cy.

Artemis Arbuckle whistled. "So Tick Tock's still ticking, as it were, and somebody nabbed him. If you two could hold the torch here, I'll swing over to Andrew's beat. He'll know if there was an altercation on his watch."

Sir Arthur and Wally hastily agreed, and took turns waving the burning torch. We were almost run down only once, by a carriage drawn by two horribly skittish horses. I would think animals of that size might have more sense.

"Andrew hasn't heard a thing," Constable Arbuckle reported when he returned. "Aside from that bit of trouble with the suffrage ladies, it's been uncommon quiet tonight."

Wally thanked the officer for his help, and Sir Arthur signed a slip of paper for him and shook his hand.

"That leaves your aunt's hypothesis, and that of Mr. Smyth-Hops, still to be tested," Sir Arthur said as we started home. "Either the criminal element is involved, or the abduction had something to do with the rally. We have less information than I would like. We are running out of time. I did not want to mention it earlier, but we can't even know for certain whether the tattered man was Tick Tock."

"But we can!" Wally cried.

"Of course." Sir Arthur understood instantly. "You took a photograph."

I had completely forgotten it myself!

"And produced a print," Wally added. "If the man in the alley was Tick Tock, Dobbin will be able to identify him."

We hurried toward Miss Rhodope's rooms to retrieve the evidence.

When we reached Sir Arthur's flat, we found that the others had fared far worse than we.

Cy was holding a cool compress to the side of Leander Smyth-Hops's head while Miss Rhodope and Dobbin looked on. Briney was sleeping on the settee.

"Who gave you the blinker?" Dobbin asked when Cy lowered the rag.

A "blinker" was apparently a black eye. Mr. Smyth-Hops was sporting a beauty.

"A few fellows who didn't appreciate being asked their whereabouts last night," the journalist said. "They had nothing to do with the disappearance. I was sure they had. It was a disappointment."

"Did you discern this before or after they blackened your eye?" Miss Rhodope asked. "And how many is 'a few'?"

"Somewhat after, I would say. It was quite a set-to, Rho. Oh, and there were only three of them."

"You bested three ruffians?" Sir Arthur asked in surprise.

"Certainly," Mr. Smyth-Hops said. "You can't expect that I would go amongst the criminal element unprepared. I have been studying Bartitsu with Edward William Barton-Wright himself!"

"Bartitsu?" Rhodope repeated.

"A magnificent mix of cane fighting, kick-boxing, fisticuffs, and jujitsu — in short, just the thing for the gentleman who intends to do investigative reporting on the rough streets of London. How about your hypothesis, Rho? Any bets placed?"

"None," Rhodope lamented. "Scotland Yard?"

"Claims all has been quiet," Sir Arthur admitted.

"What have you there, Walter?" Leander asked.

"Photographs," Wally said, and everyone gathered around as he spread them on the desk.

"That's Tick Tock, right enough." Dobbin picked up one of the photos of the fiend. "It flattens 'im a bit, if you take my meaning. 'E's bigger in the flesh."

"He *is* more fierce in person," Mr. Smyth-Hops agreed. "And he won't be pleased that he's been photographed, I'm sure."

"So we know he was at the parade, at least," Sir Arthur said.

"Who is this?" Wally asked suddenly, pointing at another picture. "Aunt Rhodope, do you know her?"

I hopped up onto a chair and peered past Miss Rhodope's elbow at the image in question.

It was the photograph Rhodope had asked

Wally to take of the Sisters of Suffrage as they passed. Every face was forward as they marched behind the Zephyr. Every face but one. A single sister was looking directly at us—*or at someone behind us.*

"That's Myra," Rhodope exclaimed. "Myra Maybelle Thistlethorp!"

"No, it ain't. It's Bloody Belle DunKelly," Dobbin corrected. "The Butcher of Bartle Street. Ran 'er own butcher shop until 'er mister disappeared. Then they sent 'er to jail."

"But she is completely reformed and going by her given name now!" Rhodope cried.

"Would she have known Tick Tock on sight?" Sir Arthur asked.

"Oh, she knew 'im, right enough," Dobbin said. "She sometimes gave 'im bones for the piggies."

We all paused a moment to ponder this terrible thought.

"And if she had recognized Tick Tock?" Leander Smyth-Hops asked.

"The Sisters of Suffrage are completely devoted to Calypso," Rhodope reasoned. "They would never allow her son to be kidnapped by a criminal kingpin."

"'When you have eliminated the impossible, whatever remains, *however improbable,* must be the truth,'" Leander quoted. "*The Sign of the Four,* chapter six."

"Will you stop that?" Sir Arthur thundered.

"Sorry," Leander said. "But it seems the Sisters of Suffrage *have* taken Tick Tock, haven't they?"

"Wouldn't Miss Rhodope have known?" Sir Arthur asked.

"I was at Scotland Yard seeing to Sylvia's release," Rhodope replied.

"But how did they manage it?" Sir Arthur asked. "Constables and criminal kingpins alike have tried their best—"

"Do not underestimate the Sisterhood, sir!" Rhodope said, lifting her chin.

At that moment, Briney sat up. "Dob," she said, starting toward us, "I—" And she collapsed onto the floor.

I was the first to reach her side. She was breathing. I was relieved to hear her heart still ticking.

"She's fainted," said Sir Arthur as he lifted her from the floor. "I will say this while she is insensible, Dobbin. You must prepare yourself. It is as I feared when I first felt her pulse. Your sister's clockwork is a more serious problem than you know."

"What do you mean?" asked Dobbin.

"Her heart was made for her when she was younger," Sir Arthur said. "She has grown too big for it."

"Like a fuel pump that don't push enough into the engine," Dobbin said slowly. "Even if we find the keys in time, Tick Tock's brother's dead. 'E can't make another one." The boy's face went suddenly pale.

"Electrification!" Wally exclaimed. "That was Tick Tock's motive. He was not hired to extort my parents; he was going to do it himself. He'd read about our electric automatons. He was going to force my parents to replace Briney's clockwork heart with a modernized model that runs on electricity!"

We'll find Tick Tock," Miss Rhodope assured Dobbin as he sank down beside his sister. "May I use your telephone, Sir Arthur? They will have taken him to Myra's."

"The Butcher of Bartle Street?" Mr. Smyth-Hops gasped.

"She is reformed, I assure you," Miss Rhodope repeated. It was a matter of moments before the phone connected Rhodope to an operator, who in turn connected her to the line she requested.

"Hello! Winifred? Of course it's Rhodope! Who else? Listen, Win—do you have a criminal in custody? You do?" She nodded at Dobbin. "He was? No, Myra mustn't!" Her voice grew very urgent, and she frowned as she listened.

"You put it to a vote? I see. Win, darling, was he carrying keys? Brass keys such as you might use to wind a clock? I see. I'm sending someone over. Don't let them dispose of him before my friend arrives." She set the phone on its stand. "It's already done."

"What?" cried Mr. Smyth-Hops.

"Where?" demanded Dobbin.

"Confound it all! What, why, where, *and* how?" Sir Arthur asked.

"Myra did identify Tick Tock, as Wally supposed," Rhodope said. "She intuited instantly that he was after Calypso's son. She contacted Winifred and then the quilting society. Winnie's husband is a surgeon, you see."

"I don't see," Mr. Smyth-Hops admitted.

"It means she has access to diethyl aether," Sir Arthur explained. "You can render a subject unconscious by holding a rag of it to his nose."

"That was the struggle we heard," Wally guessed, "and the most dangerous part of their operation."

"Once they had him in the coach, they

searched him for sharp objects, and then, before he could awake, they stitched him between two quilts. He was quite helpless when he regained his senses."

"Then they have the keys!" Leander cried.

"They don't," Rhodope admitted. "Which means that they must be well hidden on his person. He may have been helpless, but he was not silent. His language was so"—Miss Rhodope turned pink—"*colorful,* they voted on whether they should beat him with broomsticks or call

the constables to have him hauled away. Myra is naturally opposed to constables."

"Naturally," Sir Arthur said.

"She argued for the broomstick party, but was overruled in the popular vote. The constables are on their way to collect the Tick-Tock Man as we speak."

Walter leaped to his feet. "They can't have him!"

"Tick Tock can't fix her, anyway," Dobbin said. "His brother, Basil, was the clever one that way, and he's years gone."

"Then you and I will do it," Wally said. "We need to get back to your lab. The tools there were Basil's, weren't they? He must have had schematics for Briney's heart."

Of course I knew Walter Kennewickett would not give up! The girl stirred, and I licked her face. Dobbin knelt beside us.

"Dob," she whispered, "is Tick Tock come?"

"'E's been nabbed," Dobbin said, brushing the hair from her face. "I'm going with the writer man to get the keys, on account of I can get them to the lab the fastest once they're in 'and. Cy will carry you down below, won't you, Cy?"

The giant nodded as Dobbin helped his sister up.

We stepped onto the street once more to find that an icy wind had swept the fog completely away.

"Back down the way we came up, Cy?" Leander Smyth-Hops asked. Cy nodded.

His bull's-eye lantern sliced the darkness as I trotted to keep up with Wally. When we reached the sewer opening, Cy started down the ladder. His head was barely out of sight when Leander picked me up and followed, with Rhodope and Wally right behind.

Rhodope held a kerchief to her face when she reached the bottom, but she glanced at Leander, then put it away. We hurried single file down the catwalk.

Just as we reached the corridor of crystals, I heard what I feared the most: splashing behind us.

"Do you happen to have any additional

pyrotechnics about you, Walter?" Mr. Smyth-Hops asked hopefully.

"I'm afraid not," Wally said.

"What is it?" Rhodope asked.

"Possibly nothing," Mr. Smyth-Hops replied. "Walk a little faster, if you will."

The splashing grew nearer, and I heard the unmistakable grunting of the sewer swine.

Mr. Smyth-Hops stopped beneath a sewer grate. There was no ladder here, but an electric light on the street above us shone through the bars. A pile of detritus that had washed down the drains reached almost to the ceiling and narrowed the path.

"It's still some way to the lab, Rho," he said. "I want you to go on."

"It's sewer swine, isn't it?" Rhodope asked.

"Probably," Mr. Smyth-Hops replied. "You'll be needed to assist in the procedure, Rho. Walter will be needed to manufacture the heart, and Cy must carry Briney as well as light your way. That leaves one job for me."

"Leander!" Wally's aunt cried.

"Best hurry," he urged her, taking off his hat and hanging it on a bit of broken board. He had chosen his spot well. He could see by the dim light from above, and the swine could not get past the pile of rubble on his right. "I don't know how long I can delay them."

"Leander!" Rhodope exclaimed again.

"Save Briney, Walter." Mr. Smyth-Hops removed his coat as well. "Don't let this be in vain."

"Don't give up!" Wally said, then turned and ran into the darkness with Rhodope and Cy.

My heart ached with the desire to follow him, and my knees were shaking, but my duty was clear. I took my place beside Leander Smyth-Hops.

Dachshunds do not leave comrades to die alone.

I turned to stand by Mr. Smyth-Hops's side as the first of the sewer swine stepped into the light. The boar blinked at us, and for a moment it was still, as if it could not believe its luck at finding us there.

Then it charged.

Mr. Smyth-Hops spun his coat like a cape, covering the beast's head, and then landed a terrific blow to its nose. It jumped back and he leaped after it, delivering a spinning kick to the snout. I gave a terrific growl as I followed, and then the rest of the swine joined in and the battle became a blur of tusks and fangs.

I attacked the hocks, ears, and hindquarters; my comrade was everywhere, launching himself from the tunnel walls, rebounding from the roof, and using not only fists and feet but every brick and stick and stone at hand in the battle. I found myself flung into the air, and managed to nip a porcine ear on my way down. And then I was in the thick of the fray. I fought with fang and nail, dodging among the maddened beasts.

The one thought in my mind—the only thought now—was that the swine must not pass. Not until Wally and the others were safe behind the workshop door.

The battle went on and on, surging up and down the passage. At last I could tell we were being pushed back. The end had come. I gathered myself for one more assault, knowing it would be my last.

In that dark moment, I heard a shout. Walter Kennewickett leaped past me, a blazing brand in each hand. Rhodope, with two torches of her own, was right behind him.

The swine, no doubt remembering the burns from Wally's pyrotechnics, turned and fled.

Leander Smyth-Hops sank down beside me. His clothing was in rags, and his coat irretrievable.

"We're alive, Sausage!" he said.

I was somewhat surprised myself.

Cy was holding a very still Briney in his arms when we stepped into the workshop. There were tears on the giant's face, and I thought for a moment that time had run out—but then I heard the faint *tick-tock* of her heart.

There was still a chance.

Somewhere in the night, Dobbin and Sir Arthur Conan Doyle were doubtless rushing toward us with the keys to save Cy and Briney. Somewhere farther still, Oliver and Calypso were racing back in response to Rhodope's wire.

There are situations not even a dachshund can help with. Walter was facing one now. There was nothing I could do but watch as Wally and Rhodope tore apart the room searching for schematics and spare parts.

And then the door burst open, and Tick Tock stood before us. This was no tatterdemalion but a tiger of a man, grown old but powerful still. The rags had concealed his size, and the stumbles his energy. I backed up until I was standing on Walter Kennewickett's toes.

A chill went through me as he swept into

the room. Ineffable indeed. It *was* as if he carried every crime he had ever committed with him, crimes too horrible for this room to hold. His wild and wicked eyes took in the boxes of papers Wally and Rhodope had overturned in their search and came to rest on Briney's small form.

A crowd came through the door after him— Sir Arthur, Constable Arbuckle, several other constables, and Myra Maybelle Thistlethorp herself, still wearing a Sisters of Suffrage sash.

"You brought him!" Mr. Smyth-Hops cried.

"He brought us," Sir Arthur replied.

The officers of the law were as disheveled as Mr. Smyth-Hops.

"Sewer swine?" Rhodope inquired.

"Tick Tock," Sir Arthur corrected as Dobbin rushed to Briney's side, keys in hand. "We made the mistake of letting him out of the quilt."

"Kennewickett," Tick Tock said as Dobbin wound Briney's heart spring, "you were looking for my brother's papers?"

"Yes, sir," Wally said.

"Could they 'ave done it, then? Could your parents 'ave rigged Briney an 'eart?"

"Yes, sir," Wally said.

"Then they still could," the monster muttered.

"Yes. And there was no need to try to abduct me," Wally said. "Some people will help if you ask."

"And some people won't," Tick Tock countered. "My way, they always says yes."

I heard a sob and turned to see Dobbin still beside his sister. "Something's gone squiffy," he said.

It was clear that he meant something was very, very wrong.

"I wound Briney, but she won't wake up. Not even when I shake her. We brought the keys. She should wake up!"

"Where'd that doctor go?" Tick Tock demanded. He turned around, and the constables retreated a step or two. I did not blame them.

"I'm here," Sir Arthur said.

"I'd like a professional opinion," Tick Tock

demanded, his grimace showing blackened teeth. He cleared the workbench with one sweep of his arm. "Put 'er down, Cy. Let the sawbones have a look-see."

Cy laid Briney down gently and stepped away. Sir Arthur felt Briney's pulse.

"I'm afraid it *has* gone squiffy, Dobbin," he said, laying his hand gently on the boy's shoulder. "Your sister is deeply unconscious, and she won't be waking up. Not even one of the famous elder Kennewicketts could construct a heart fast enough. I'm sorry. There is no hope."

My legs were suddenly too weak to hold me, and I sank to the floor. *No hope.*

Dobbin staggered.

"Don't give up, Dob," Wally said, and turned to Tick Tock. "We can't give up without trying. Tell me where your brother's papers are kept, Mr. Tock," Wally said. "I will do my best to build her a bigger heart in time!"

"You could do that?" Tick Tock walked toward Wally and stepped in between him and

Dobbin. He leaned over me until his nose was almost touching Wally's. "A boy like you could replace 'er ticker?"

"I could try," Wally said without backing up an inch. "With Dobbin's help and a little more time, I believe it can be done." My pulse pounded with pride for him, for his courage and conviction, and for a moment—just for a moment—I felt there might be hope.

Then the vile man tapped his temple. "My brother didn't leave no plans. 'E kept it all in 'is 'ead. Dobbin!" Tick Tock's burning eyes turned to the boy. "You made a deal with me."

"Oi." Dobbin's voice was shaking. "But you don't play fair, Tick Tock. One job, you said, but you kept the keys, didn't you? Made me work every day or you wouldn't wind Briney!"

Tick Tock sucked air in through his teeth. "Teach you to pay attention when consorting with criminals." His hand went out, and clawlike fingers brushed Briney's cheek. It was a surprisingly tender gesture.

"Nobody ever ast me to save a life before. It was murder and theft they always wanted. It was novel, that's wot. Who was I to make a deal like that?" Suddenly, his shoulders squared, and as he whirled toward, us he seemed to grow even larger. "Tick Tock, that's who! Do you intend to 'onor your end of the deal, Dob?"

"I would 'ave," Dobbin cried. "You never told me what I 'ad to do!"

"Don't rush me," Tick Tock growled. "It 'as to be something worth my time, don't it? Something wot will give you ounce for ounce as much trouble as you both 'ave given me." His eyes went to Wally once more, and suddenly he smiled. "I know wot'll do it. *Be a good man.* From this day on, you be a good man, Dob. That's my deal."

Then he turned away from us all, and a tremendous tremor went through him—and when he turned back, his own large clockwork heart was in his hand.

"What's this?" Constable Arbuckle cried, leaping to the criminal's side.

"Time," Tick Tock whispered as he sank to his knees. "Time for Briney to grow up, as promised."

And with that, he toppled to the floor.

# EPILOGUE

**B**arely avoiding being abducted." Constable Arbuckle's hands were folded behind his back as his superior at Scotland Yard filled in Oliver and Calypso on the previous night's happenings. We had all been hauled from the sewer to the Yard for questioning, and found Wally's parents just arriving there. "Consorting with criminals," the inspector said. "Sloshing through sewers."

At this point, Leander interrupted to offer the opinion that Wally had been very clever with his pyrotechnics, and incredibly brave when he saved us from the swine a second time. Sir Arthur Conan Doyle himself described the way the wonderful boy had leaped into action, his fingers as nimble as a surgeon's as he swapped one mechanical heart for another. Rhodope mentioned that Dobbin had burst into tears when his sister opened her eyes.

I was glad no one mentioned that Cy had slipped away in the darkness as we made our way from the sewer, thus evading arrest.

The inspector silenced everyone with a glare, and then turned to the elder Kennewicketts.

"So that's what your son has been up to while you were away. What do you say?"

Oliver and Calypso exchanged a glance.

"Well done, Walter!" Oliver exclaimed. "I wish we could have been here!"

"You handled the situation with compassion, courage, and intelligence," Calypso agreed. "As expected of a Kennewickett!"

"What?" The inspector stopped pacing.

"Walter did just as we would have done," Calypso explained.

"But the danger!" the detective cried.

"The outcome of adventures is always unknown," Oliver opined. "You wouldn't expect Walter to turn his back on a friend?"

"I would expect him to find his friends in better places," the detective said. "Now we've got these young ruffians to figure out."

Sir Arthur Conan Doyle stood up. "I can't approve of children being dragged away to jail."

"An asylum for orphans would be better than the sewer," Constable Arbuckle offered, but he looked uncomfortable suggesting it. "What else can we do with them?"

"We're going to take them with us, of course," Oliver said.

"Are we, dearest?" Calypso asked.

"At once!" Oliver said. "If they are agreeable."

The detective's hand went to his head. "Well, Arbuckle? It's your case. What do you say?"

"It's a big responsibility," Constable Arbuckle said, "taking on the likes of these. I don't know what the family's like, sir, and that's a fact."

"Ahem," Leander Smyth-Hops interrupted. "I say, consider the sausage!"

"He means Noodles," Wally explained.

"I have observed that a dog always reflects the family life," Mr. Smyth-Hops went on. "I've never seen a frisky dog in a gloomy family, or a sad dog in a happy one. Snarling people have snarling dogs; dangerous people have dangerous dogs. The Kennewicketts have—"

"Noodles," Wally finished.

"The philosopher has returned!" Sir Arthur said.

"Really?" Leander Smyth-Hops grinned. "Perhaps you could put that in one of your books. Sherlock Holmes could say—"

"I repent." Sir Arthur groaned. "I repent of ever creating Holmes!"

"Nonetheless," Rhodope said, "I believe there was some wisdom in his words. If you know Noodles, you know the Kennewicketts."

I realized that every eye was on me. I stopped scratching at once and tried to appear worthy of Wally—and dashingly dangerous.

Constable Arbuckle nodded. "He's a noble beast at that. What do you think, Briney? Dob?"

Dobbin Winckles was backing away, but Briney grabbed his arm.

"Please," she said. "I want to go with Noodles."

"We can give your sister a heart that never needs winding," Calypso offered.

"Come on, Dob." Wally offered his hand. "There is room for your workshop in our lab. I have some ideas for internal combustion you could assist me with."

"How do you feel about contraptions such as"—Dobbin glanced at the inspector—"men that's, say, part mechanical?"

Briney looked most intently at Walter, and I realized they were asking about Cy. The children were unwilling to leave their friend.

"There's enough room," Wally said instantly. "More than enough!"

Rhodope cheered as Dobbin's grimy glove gripped Walter's hand.

"Well, that's all gas and gaiters, then," the detective said, sounding very pleased.

"Pardon?" Oliver asked.

"He means everything's turned out right as

rain," Leander Smyth-Hops explained. Then, lowering his voice, he added, "You're taking the members of a criminal gang off his hands."

"It's settled, then!" Calypso declared.

"And who are you again?" asked Constable Arbuckle, turning to Leander Smyth-Hops.

"Oh." Rhodope reddened. "Where are my manners? Detective, Constable Arbuckle, may I present Spring-Heeled Jack?"

"At last!" the detective cried. "Someone we can arrest!"

Leander Smyth-Hops resisted just long enough to blow Rhodope a kiss behind Constable Arbuckle's back.

"Perhaps I *should* be kinder to Scotland Yard," Sir Arthur said as his greatest fan was hauled away in handcuffs.

But everything wasn't right as rain. There was no sign of the chrome-domed giant when we ventured down to collect the children's things from their subterranean lair. This may have had something to do with the presence of the armed officers who had come to protect us from sewer swine.

Briney took one last look at her former home, and tears welled in her eyes.

Dobbin took a pencil from his pocket and wrote *There's room for friends at the Kennewicketts' Inn* on the wall before we left.

Everyone was optimistic that Cy would be found; we would be in London for a month, after all, while Oliver and Calypso signed certain papers and pulled several strings to allow Briney and Dob to accompany us out of the country.

Walter and the ex-urchins spent their time searching for Cy.

But when not even Dobbin's distasteful acquaintances knew of Cy's whereabouts, the siblings were reduced to dropping notes down sewer grates, hoping he might stumble upon one.

"If we can't find him," Wally said at last, "he'll have to find us." Then he turned to the

production of pyrotechnics, consulting Oliver often regarding chemical content and construction techniques.

The night before we sailed, it seemed that all of London had spilled into the streets to see the sky over Trafalgar Square blossom with skyrockets that boomed and then burst into flowers, flags, or stars.

The grand finale was the massive shell that Wally had worked on for weeks. The crowd went still as it climbed on a column of sparks and smoke.

Then it burst, and words blossomed in the sky.

*Come home with us, Cy!*

The letters coruscated, then faded and fell.

I leaned against Briney's legs as we waited.

"'E 'as to 'ave seen that!" Dobbin cried at last. But the crowds left, and all was still.

"He could have had some distance to travel," Wally offered. We waited some more.

Big Ben had started its ten o'clock strike and

a river mist was rising around us when at last, an enormous man in silk robes and a turban strode out of the night.

Briney flung herself into his arms.

Rhodope turned to Oliver and Calypso and made the appropriate introductions, and all was gas and gaiters at last.

Of course.

Walter Kennewickett was on the case!

# AUTHOR'S NOTE

Arthur Ignatius Conan Doyle trained and worked as a physician. As a young man, he excelled at cricket, loved playing football (soccer, in Britain) and golf, and single-handedly introduced the British to the sport of skiing. But by the time he was forty, his figure, like that of Noodles, could have been described as "respectable." When the Boer War broke out, Doyle attempted to enlist, only to be told he was too fat to fight.

Doyle loved adventures, inventions, and books. His literary career began while he was still a medical student. He was friends with Bram Stoker, who wrote *Dracula,* and J. M. Barrie, who wrote *Peter Pan*. Doyle, however, was far more productive than his literary acquaintances. He wrote historical novels, science fiction, plays, romances, poetry, nonfiction, and, to his eventual regret, detective stories about Sherlock Holmes.

After publishing a few tales of the dauntless detective, Doyle grew tired of his creation. Holmes was a skeptic. Doyle was not.

In fact, Doyle believed in fairies, hunted ghosts, and attended séances. He much preferred his historical novels about archers and knights, or his science fiction featuring the passionate Professor Challenger, to his crime fiction.

Eventually, Doyle grew to dislike writing about Holmes so much that he decided to be done with the detective. First, he attempted to raise his fees so that publishers would not buy new Sherlock Holmes stories. The publishers happily paid what he asked, and fans hounded Doyle for more.

When his first plan to rid himself of Holmes didn't work, Doyle was forced to take more drastic measures. He wrote a short story called

"The Final Problem," in which Holmes plummeted to his death at the Reichenbach Falls in Switzerland. The author hoped that with the death of Holmes, fans of his work would turn to his other books with equal passion. But they did not.

Sherlock Holmes was more than a fictional character. He was a phenomenon, the most famous fictional detective the world had ever known. When "The Final Problem" was published, fans went into mourning. Some even wore black armbands in the streets to protest the fictional detective's death.

Still, Sir Arthur Conan Doyle might never have relented and resurrected Holmes if he hadn't needed money for his growing family—but he did. Ten years after his famous fall, Sherlock Holmes returned for many more adventures.

Doyle may not have enjoyed writing about Sherlock Holmes, but the character he created changed the world. When Doyle invented his detective, police depended on eyewitness reports and confessions to convict criminals. No one analyzed crime scenes, collected fingerprints, or examined blood.

Doyle was inventing forensic science—the science of collecting evidence to be used in a court of law—as he wrote. Sir Arthur Conan Doyle may not have been a skeptic, but he was as passionate about justice as Sherlock Holmes was. Twice Doyle used the "Holmes Method" in real life to prove the innocence of two men who had been imprisoned for crimes they did not commit.

After Doyle's death, a séance was conducted at the Royal Albert Hall in an attempt to contact his spirit. Thousands of loyal Sherlock Holmes fans attended, but sadly, Sir Arthur did not appear.

# ABOUT THE AUTHOR
# AND ILLUSTRATOR

KERSTEN HAMILTON is the author of several picture books and many novels, including the critically acclaimed young adult trilogy the Goblin Wars. She has worked as a ranch hand, a wood-cutter, a lumberjack, a census taker, a wrangler for wilderness guides, and an archeological surveyor. Now, when she's not writing, she hunts dinosaurs in the deserts and badlands of New Mexico and tends to the animals on her farm in Kentucky. For more about Kersten, please visit www.kerstenhamilton.com.

JAMES HAMILTON is an artist and designer who lives in San Mateo, California. This is his second book.

BOOK BY *Joseph Fields* AND *Jerome Chodorov*

MUSIC BY *Leonard Bernstein*

LYRICS BY *Betty Comden* AND *Adolph Green*

(Based upon the play *My Sister Eileen* by Joseph Fields and
Jerome Chodorov and the stories by Ruth McKenney)

# Wonderful Town

## A NEW MUSICAL COMEDY

RANDOM HOUSE, NEW YORK

**WONDERFUL TOWN** *was presented first by Robert Fryer at the Winter Garden, New York City, on February 25, 1953, with the following cast:*

(AS THEY SPEAK)

| | |
|---|---|
| GUIDE | Warren Galjour |
| APPOPOLOUS | Henry Lascoe |
| LONIGAN | Walter Kelvin |
| HELEN | Michele Burke |
| WRECK | Jordan Bentley |
| VIOLET | Dody Goodman |
| VALENTI | Ted Beniades |
| EILEEN | Edith Adams |
| RUTH | Rosalind Russell |
| A STRANGE MAN | Nathaniel Frey |
| DRUNKS | Lee Papell, Delbert Anderson |
| ROBERT BAKER | George Gaynes |
| ASSOCIATE EDITORS | Warren Galjour, Albert Linville |
| MRS. WADE | Isabella Hoopes |
| FRANK LIPPENCOTT | Chris Alexander |
| CHEF | Nathaniel Frey |
| WAITER | Delbert Anderson |
| DELIVERY BOY | Alvin Beam |
| CHICK CLARK | Dort Clark |
| SHORE PATROLMAN | Lee Papell |
| FIRST CADET | David Lober |
| SECOND CADET | Ray Dorian |

POLICEMEN Lee Papell, Albert Linville, Delbert Anderson, Chris Robinson, Nathaniel Frey, Warren Galjour, Robert Kole

RUTH'S ESCORT Chris Robinson

GREENWICH VILLAGERS Jean Eliot, Carol Cole, Marta Becket, Maxine Berke, Helena Seroy, Geraldine Delaney, Margaret Cuddy, Dody Goodman, Ed Balin, Alvin Beam, Ray Dorian, Edward Heim, Joe Layton, David Lober, Victor Moreno, William Weslow, Pat Johnson, Evelyn Page, Libi Staiger, Patty Wilkes, Helen Rice, Delbert Anderson, Warren Galjour, Robert Kole, Ray Kirchner, Lee Papell, Chris Robinson

*Production Directed by* George Abbott
*Dances and Musical Numbers Staged by* Donald Saddler
*Sets and Costumes by* Raoul du Bois
*Musical Direction and Vocal Arrangements by* Lehman Engel
*Miss Russell's Clothes by* Main Bocher
*Lighting by* Peggy Clark
*Orchestrations by* Don Walker

## SCENE

*The play takes place in Greenwich Village in the '30s.*

# MUSICAL NUMBERS

———

## ACT ONE

| | |
|---|---|
| *Christopher Street* | Sung by Guide and The Villagers |
| *Ohio* | Ruth, Eileen |
| *Conquering New York* | Ruth, Eileen, and the Ensemble |
| *One Hundred Easy Ways* | Ruth |
| *What a Waste* | Baker and Editors |
| *Story Vignettes* by Miss Comden and Mr. Green | |
| | Rexford, Mr. Mallory, Danny, Trent, and Ruth |
| *A Little Bit in Love* | Eileen |
| *Pass the Football* | Wreck and The Villagers |
| *Conversation Piece* by Miss Comden and Mr. Green | |
| | Ruth, Eileen, Frank, Baker, Chick |
| *A Quiet Girl* | Baker |
| *Conga!* | Ruth |
| | Danced by The Cadets |

## ACT TWO

| | |
|---|---|
| *My Darlin' Eileen* | Eileen and Policemen |
| *Swing!* | Ruth and The Villagers |
| *Reprise: Ohio* | Ruth, Eileen |
| *It's Love* | Baker and The Villagers |
| *Wrong Note Rag* | Ruth, Eileen and The Villagers |

# ACT ONE

# ACT ONE

## Scene I

*(In front of the curtain, which is a semi-abstract impression of Greenwich Village, a* GUIDE *and a group of gaping* TOURISTS *enter to a musical vamp in a style highly characteristic of the 1930s.)*

GUIDE

Come along!
> *(Singing in the brisk off-hand manner of a barker and indicating points of interest in a lilting song.)*

On your left,
Washington Square,
Right in the heart of Greenwich Village.

TOURISTS

> *(Looking around ecstatically)*

My, what trees—
Smell that air—
Painters and pigeons in Washington Square.

GUIDE

On your right,
Waverly Place—
Bit of Paree in Greenwich Village.

TOURISTS

My, what charm—

My, what grace!
Poets and peasants on Waverly Place—

GUIDE
(*Reeling off his customary spiel*)
Ever since eighteen-seventy Greenwich Village has been the
Bohemian cradle of painters, writers, actors, etc., who've gone
on to fame and fortune. Today in nineteen thirty-five, who
knows what future greats live in these twisting alleys? Come
along!
(*As the* GUIDE *and group cross to the side, the curtain
opens, revealing Christopher Street. The scene looks like
a cheery post card of Greenwich Village, with Village
characters exhibiting their paintings, grouped in a tableau
under a banner which reads "Greenwich Village Art
Contest, 1935."*)

GUIDE
Here you see
Christopher Street,
Typical spot in Greenwich Village.

TOURISTS
Ain't it quaint,
Ain't it sweet,
Pleasant and peaceful on Christopher Street?
(*Suddenly the tableau comes to life and all hell breaks
loose. An angry artist smashes his painting over the head
of an art-contest judge who retires in confusion.*)

VILLAGER
Here comes another judge.

4

# WONDERFUL TOWN

*(A second judge enters, examines the paintings and awards First Prize to a bewildered janitor, whose well-filled ash can the judge mistakes for an ingenious mobile sculpture. The angry artists smash another painting over the second judge's head and all freeze into another tableau.)*

GUIDE

Here is home,
Christopher Street—
Right in the heart of Greenwich Village.

VILLAGERS

Life is calm,
Life is sweet,
Pleasant and peaceful on Christopher Street,
    *(They freeze into another tableau as a cop comes in, a friend of the street, named* LONIGAN. *He goes up to one of the artists, a dynamic, explosive character named* APPOPOLOUS.)

GUIDE

Here's a famous Village type,
Mr. Appopolous—modern painter,
Better known on this beat
As the lovable landlord of Christopher Street.
    *(Music is interrupted.)*

APPOPOLOUS

    *(Breaking out of tableau. To* LONIGAN—*violently)*
Throw that Violet woman out of my building!

LONIGAN

What's the beef now, Appopolous?

APPOPOLOUS

I'm very broadminded, but when a woman gives rumba lessons all night, she's gotta have at least a phonograph!

(*Music resumes.* LONIGAN *enters building.* WRECK *exits from building, carrying bird cage with canary. He meets a cute young girl named* HELEN *on the street. As they kiss the stage "freezes" again.*)

GUIDE

Here's a guy know as The Wreck,
Football professional out of season,
Unemployed throughout the heat,
Living on nothing on Christopher Street.

(*Music is interrupted. Freeze breaks.* WRECK *kisses* HELEN.)

HELEN

Hi! Where you goin' with Dicky Bird?

WRECK

Takin' him down to Benny's to see what I can get for him.

HELEN

Oh, no, Wreck! You can't hock Dicky!

WRECK

Take your choice—we either hock him or have him on toast.

(*Music resumes. He goes off.* VIOLET *comes out of building, followed by* LONIGAN.)

VIOLET

Let go of me, ya big phony!

(*Freeze.* VIOLET *drops valise on sidewalk, leans down,*

6

*pointing angry finger at* LONIGAN. *She carries large pink doll.*)

GUIDE

Here is yet another type.
Everyone knows the famous Violet,
Nicest gal you'd ever meet
Steadily working on Christopher Street.
(*Music is cut off.*)

VIOLET

(*To* LONIGAN)
Don't shove me, ya big phony!

LONIGAN

On your way, Violet.
(VIOLET *is pushed off by* LONIGAN.)

VIOLET

(*As she goes*)
You're a public servant—I pay your salary! So just you show
a little respect!
(*Music resumes.*)

ALL

Life is gay,
Life is sweet,
Interesting people on Christopher Street.
(*Everyone dances*)
Such interesting people live on Christopher Street!

A PHILOSOPHER

(*Enters, carrying a sign*—"MEETING ON UNION SQUARE")

7

Down with Wall Street! Down with Wall Street!
(*He freezes with the others, fist in air.*)

GUIDE

Such interesting people live on Christopher Street!

YOGI
(*Enters with sign* "PEACE")
Love thy neighbor! Love thy neighbor!
(*Another freeze.*)

TOURISTS

Such interesting people live on Christopher Street!
(*Two* MODERN DANCERS *enter.*)

MODERN DANCERS
(*Working hard*)
And one—and two—and three—and four—
And one—and two—and three—and four

TOURISTS

Such interesting people live on Christopher Street.

ALL

Look! Look!
Poets! Actors! Dancers! Writers!

Here we live,
    Here we love.
This is the place for self-expression.
    Life is mad,

8

Life is sweet,
  Interesting people living on Christopher Street!
    (THE VILLAGERS *perform a mad dance of self-expression,
    which involves everything from a wild can-can to imita-
    tions of a symphony orchestra. It works its way up to a
    furious climax which ends with a last tableau like the
    opening one, the final punctuation being the smashing
    of yet another painting over the first judge's head.*)

### GUIDE
(*Leading* TOURISTS *off, as music fades*)
Come along,
Follow me.
Now we will see MacDougal Alley,
Patchen Place,
Minetta Lane,
Bank Street and
Church Street and
John Street
And Jane.

### VALENTI
(*A strange zoot-suited character struts in*)
Skeet—skat—skattle-cc-o-do—

### APPOPOLOUS
Hey, Mister Valenti, my most desirable studio is about to
become available, and I'm going to give you first chance at it.

### VALENTI
Down there? (*Pointing to bars of a basement room below
street level*) When I go back to living in caves I'll see ya,
Cornball.

(*There is a scream off stage and a kid rushes in, carrying a typewriter.* APPOPOLOUS *twists him very expertly. The kid runs off, dropping the typewriter.*)

EILEEN
(*Runs on*)
Stop him, somebody! He grabbed it right out of my hand! Ruth!
(RUTH *enters with two valises.*)

RUTH
(*To* APPOPOLOUS)
Oh, you've got it! Thank goodness! Thank you, sir. Thank you very much.

APPOPOLOUS
(*Pulls typewriter back*)
You're welcome, young lady.

RUTH
(*Holding out for case*)
Well?

APPOPOLOUS
Only how do I know this property belongs to you? Can you identify yourself?

RUTH
Identify myself?

APPOPOLOUS
Yes, have you got a driver's license?

RUTH
To operate a typewriter?

EILEEN

Now you give that to my sister!

APPOPOLOUS

How do I know it's hers?

RUTH

The letter "W" is missing.

APPOPOLOUS

Now we're getting somewhere.
  (*Opens case.*)

RUTH

It fell off after I wrote my thesis on Walt Whitman.

APPOPOLOUS

(*Closes case*)

She's right. Here's your property. The incident is closed. Case
dismissed.

RUTH

Who are you, Felix Frankfurter?

APPOPOLOUS

(*Laughs*)

You can tell they're out-of-towners. They don't know me!

EILEEN

We don't know anybody. We just got in from Columbus
today.

RUTH

Please, Eileen, they're not interested.

**HELEN**

Columbus? That's the worst town I ever played in.

**EILEEN**

Are you an actress? (HELEN *nods*) That's what I came to New York for—to break into the theatre—

**WRECK**

Well, you certainly got the face and build for it—

**APPOPOLOUS**
(*Steps in to* RUTH)
And you, young lady, are you artistic like your sister?

**RUTH**

No. I haven't the face and build for it.

**EILEEN**

Don't listen to her. She's a very good writer—and very original.

**RUTH**

Yes. I'm the only author who never uses a "W."
(RUTH *picks up case and valise*)
Come on, Eileen. It's getting late, and we've got to find a place.

**APPOPOLOUS**
(*Laughing*)
Remarkable! You're looking for a place, and I got just the place! Step in—I'll show it to you personally!

**RUTH**

What floor is it on?

**APPOPOLOUS**

What floor? Let me show you the place before you start raising a lot of objections!

**EILEEN**

Let's look at it anyway, Ruth. What can we lose?

**APPOPOLOUS**

Of course! What can you lose?

**RUTH**

I don't know, Eileen—

**APPOPOLOUS**

What do you gotta know? (*He opens door*)
Step in. (EILEEN *steps through*. RUTH *follows*)
A Chinese opium den it isn't, and a white slaver I ain't!
    (APPOPOLOUS *steps in, closes door behind him*.)

**VILLAGERS**

There they go
Down the stairs.
Now they will live
In Greenwich Village.

Life is mad,
Life is sweet.
Interesting people living on
Christopher Street.
        (*They all dance off.*)

# ACT ONE

## Scene II

THE STUDIO: *A basement horror with two daybeds, an imitation fireplace and one barred window that looks out on the street above. It's a cross between a cell in solitary confinement and an iron lung.*

APPOPOLOUS

Isn't it just what you've been dreaming about?

RUTH

It's very nice, only—

APPOPOLOUS

Note the imitation fireplace—
    (*Steps to bed, patting it*)
the big comfortable daybeds—
    (RUTH *goes to bed, starts to pat it;* APPOPOLOUS *takes her hand away and points to window.*)
Look! Life passes up and down
in front of you like a regular parade!
    (*Some people pass by—only their legs are visible.*)

RUTH

Well, really—

APPOPOLOUS

Let me point a few salient features. In here you have a model kitchenette—complete in every detail.

(RUTH *goes to door*—APPOPOLOUS *closes it quickly. He goes to bathroom door. She follows.*)

And over here is a luxurious bathroom—

(RUTH *starts to look.* APPOPOLOUS *closes door quickly.*)

RUTH

They're awfully small.

APPOPOLOUS

In those two rooms you won't entertain. (*He indicates a hideous painting on the wall*) You see that landscape? That's from my blue-green period.

RUTH

You mean *you* painted that?

APPOPOLOUS

Yes, of course. This studio is merely a hobby—a sanctuary for struggling young artists—and since you are both in the arts, I'm gonna let you have this studio for the giveaway price of sixty-five dollars a month.

RUTH

Sixty five dollars for *this*?

EILEEN
(*Weakly*)

Couldn't we stay here tonight, and then if we like it—

(RUTH *shakes head "no."*)

APPOPOLOUS

I'll do better than that. You can have the place for a month
—on trial—at absolutely no cost to you!

RUTH

Oh, we couldn't let you do that—could we, Eileen?

APPOPOLOUS

And then, if you're not one hundred percent satisfied, I'll
give you back your first month's rent!

EILEEN
(*Pathetically*)

Please, Ruth—I've got to get to bed.
(RUTH *gives her a look, sighs and starts to count out some
bills.*)

RUTH

Twenty, forty, sixty-one, sixty-two . . .
(*There is a tremendous boom from below. The girls
freeze in terror as* APPOPOLOUS *quickly grabs the money
from* RUTH.)

APPOPOLOUS

That's enough.

EILEEN

My God!

RUTH

What—what was that?

APPOPOLOUS
(*Innocently*)

What was *what*?

RUTH

That noise—the whole room shook!

APPOPOLOUS

(*Chuckles*)

That just goes to show how you'll get used to it. I didn't even notice it.

EILEEN

Get used to it?

APPOPOLOUS

You won't even be conscious of it. A little blasting—the new subway—

(*He points to the floor.*)

RUTH

You mean they're blasting right underneath us?

APPOPOLOUS

What are you worrying about? Those engineers know how much dynamite to use.

EILEEN

You mean it goes on all the time?

APPOPOLOUS

No—no—they knock off at midnight and they don't start again until six o'clock in the morning! (*Goes to door and turns*) Good night—Sleep tight!

(*He goes out.*)

RUTH

Yes, Eileen—sleep tight, my darling—and you were in such a hell of a hurry to get to bed!

###### EILEEN

Ruth, what are we going to do?

###### RUTH

We're gonna do thirty days.

> (EILEEN *exits to bathroom with suitcase.* RUTH *follows, looks in, and steps back in horror.*)

Thank God, we took a bath before we left Columbus!

> (*She opens her suitcase and starts to take out her things. Woman with dog passes at window, dog stops and looks through bars.*)

Oh! You get away from there!

> (*The woman and her dog go off.*)

###### EILEEN

> (*Comes out of bathroom, combing her hair. She is in her pajamas*)

I wonder what Billy Honnecker thinks now?

###### RUTH

He's probably at the country club this minute with Annie Wilkinson, drinking himself to death.

###### EILEEN

He can have her.

###### RUTH

Don't you suppose he knows that?

###### EILEEN

And she can have him too—with my compliments.

RUTH

That's the advantage of not leaving any men behind—you don't have to worry what becomes of them.

EILEEN

Oh, it's different with you. Boys never meant anything in your life.

RUTH
(*Going to bathroom with pajamas*)
Not after they got a load of *you* they didn't.
(*She goes into bathroom.* EILEEN *sits on her bed and a moment later a man comes in the front door and calmly crosses to a chair and sprawls out on it.*)

FLETCHER

Hello. Hot, isn't it?
(*He offers* EILEEN *a cigarette.*)

EILEEN
(*Rising fearfully*)
I think you're making a mistake. What apartment do you want?

FLETCHER

Is Violet home?

EILEEN

No. No Violet lives here.

FLETCHER

It's all right. Marty sent me.

EILEEN

I don't know any Marty. You'll have to get out of here!

FLETCHER

Aw, don't be like that. I'm a good fella.

EILEEN

I don't care *what* you are! Will you please go!

FLETCHER

Are you sure Violet Shelton doesn't live here?

EILEEN

If you don't get out of here, I'm going to call the police! (*He laughs*) All right—you asked for it—now you're going to get it!

> (*She goes to front door.*)

FLETCHER

Ha! They won't arrest me—I'm a fireman!

EILEEN

> (*In the hall*)

Help—somebody—help!

> (RUTH *comes out of the bathroom, stops in surprise as she sees* FLETCHER *and backs away.*)

RUTH

Oh, how do you do?

FLETCHER

Hello.

EILEEN

> (*Comes in*)

Don't "how do you do" him, Ruth! He's nobody! (*She runs*

20

*behind* RUTH) He just walked in and he won't go away. Make him go 'way, Ruth!

RUTH
(*Diffidently*)
Now you go 'way. And stop bothering my sister.

FLETCHER
No.
(WRECK *dashes in, still in his shorts.*)

WRECK
What's the trouble, girls?

EILEEN
This man walked in and he won't go 'way!

WRECK
(*To* FLETCHER—*who rises*)
What's the idea of crashing in on these girls?

FLETCHER
Now don't get yourself excited. It was just a mistake.

WRECK
You bet it was a mistake! Now get movin'!

FLETCHER
(*Goes calmly to door*)
Okay (*To girls*) Good evening— (*To* WRECK) You're the hairiest Madam I ever saw! (*He runs out as* WRECK *starts after him angrily.*)

EILEEN
(*Hastily*)

Oh, thank you—Mr.—

WRECK
(*Turns*)

Loomis—but call me The Wreck.

RUTH

The Wreck?

WRECK

That's what they called me at Trenton Tech. I would have made all-American, only I turned professional. Well, girls, if anyone busts in on you again, just holler. "I'm a ramblin' Wreck from Trenton Tech—and a helluva engineer—"
(*He goes off singing.*)

EILEEN

Ruth, I'm scared!

RUTH

It's all right, darling, go to bed— (*She leads* EILEEN *to a day-bed, then goes to fireplace and bumps her hips*) Aw, the hell with it! Let it spread! (RUTH *switches off light. There's no perceptible difference*) Didn't I just put out the light?
(*She pushes button again. Then, she pushes the button a third time.*)

EILEEN

There's a lamp post right in front of the window. Pull down the shade.

RUTH

There *isn't* any shade.

EILEEN

No shade? We're practically sleeping on the street!

RUTH

Just wait till I get that Appopolous! (*Sits on bed and winces*)
Boy! What Bernarr MacFadden would give for this bed!

EILEEN

Let's go to sleep.

RUTH

Maybe we can forget.

EILEEN

Good night—

RUTH

Good night—
(*A kid runs by window, scraping a stick against the
iron bars. It sounds like a volley of machine-gun fire.
The girls sit up, terrified.*)

EILEEN

What was that?

RUTH

It sounded like a machine gun!

KID

(*Runs by again, shouts*)
Hey, Walyo—wait for me!

EILEEN
(*Wails*)
Gee, Ruth—what I got us into.

RUTH
Oh, go to sleep!
(*Girls settle back wearily. Drunks are heard singing "Come to Me My Melancholy Baby." They come up to window, their legs visible.*)

EILEEN
(*Covering herself—shouts to window*)
You go 'way from there, you drunken bums!
(*Drunks stoop down, leering in.*)

FIRST DRUNK
Ah! A dame!

RUTH
You go 'way from there or we'll call the police!

FIRST DRUNK
Another dame! Look, Pete! There's two broads—one for you too!
(*Wiggling his fingers happily at* RUTH.)

EILEEN
Ruth! Close the window!

RUTH
*Me* close the window!

24

FIRST DRUNK

No—the hell with her— (*To* EILEEN) *You* close it!

EILEEN

Ruth, please!

SECOND DRUNK

Don't you do it, Ruth!

FIRST DRUNK

Leave me in! I'll close it!
(*The cop's legs appear, nightstick swinging.*)

LONIGAN

What's goin' on here? Come on! Break it up! (*The drunks hurry away.* LONIGAN *stoops, looks in window*) Oh, I get it!

RUTH

I'm awfully glad you came, Officer.

LONIGAN
(*Heavily*)

Yeah, I'll bet you are.

RUTH

We just moved in today.

LONIGAN
(*Grimly*)

Well, if you're smart, you'll move out tomorrow. I don't go for this stuff on my beat. I'm warning you.
(*He goes off. The girls stare at each other in dismay.*)

EILEEN

Oh, *Ruth*!

RUTH

(*Goes to her dismally*)

Now, Eileen, everything's going to be all right.

EILEEN

It's awful!

RUTH

Never mind, Eileen—try and sleep.

EILEEN

I *can't* sleep.

RUTH

Try, darling—make your mind a blank.

EILEEN

I did, but I keep thinking of Ohio.

(RUTH *puts arm around* EILEEN.)

RUTH

Oh, Eileen— Me too.

(*They sing, plaintively.*)

BOTH

Why, oh why, oh why, oh—
Why did I ever leave Ohio?
Why did I wander to find what lies yonder
When life was so cozy at home?
Wond'ring while I wander,
Why did I fly,

Why did I roam,
Oh, why oh, why oh
Did I leave Ohio?
Maybe I'd better go home.
Maybe I'd better go home.
  (*Music continues.*)


RUTH
(*Rises, defiantly*)
Now listen, Eileen,
Ohio was stifling.
We just couldn't wait to get out of the place,
With Mom saying—"Ruth, what no date for this evening?"


EILEEN
And Pop with, "Eileen, do be home, dear, by ten—"


BOTH
Ugh!

RUTH
The gossipy neighbors
And everyone yapping who's going with who—


EILEEN
And dating those drips that I've known since I'm four.


RUTH
The Kiwanis Club Dance.


EILEEN
On the basketball floor.

RUTH

Cousin Maude with her lectures on sin—

BOTH

What a bore!

EILEEN

Jerry Black!

RUTH

Cousin Min!

EILEEN

Ezra Nye!

RUTH

Hannah Finn!

EILEEN

Hopeless!

RUTH

Babbity!

EILEEN

Stuffy!

RUTH

Provincial!

BOTH

Thank heavens we're free!

(*By this time each is in her own bed, reveling in new-found freedom. There is a terrific blast from the subway below and they dash terrified into each other's arms and sing hysterically.*)

BOTH

Why, oh why, oh why, oh—
Why did we ever leave Ohio?

*(They cut off as music continues and go over to* RUTH's *bed, huddling together under the covers.)*

BOTH

*(Quietly and sadly)*

Wond'ring while we wander,
Why did we fly,
Why did we roam,
Oh why, oh, why oh—
Did we leave Ohio?
Maybe we'd better go home,          (RUTH: *O-H-I-O*)
Maybe we'd better go home.

*(They sink back exhausted as the lights dim. There is a fanfare of a bugle reminiscent of "Reveille," followed by the sound of an alarm clock as the lights come up sharply. It is early morning.*
RUTH *springs up as if shot from a cannon, turns off the alarm and shakes* EILEEN. RUTH *is full of determination.)*

RUTH

Come on, Eileen. Up and at 'em! Let's get an early start. We're going to take this town. Get up, Eileen!
*(She starts briskly toward the bathroom, suddenly winces and clutches her aching back, but limps bravely on. The lights black out.)*

*(There is a dance pantomime depicting the girls' struggle to get ahead in the "Big City" beginning with determined optimism and ending in utter defeat. Everywhere* RUTH *goes with her manuscripts, publishers are either out to lunch, in conference, or just not interested. Everywhere*

EILEEN *goes, looking for theatre work, she receives many propositions, but they are never for jobs. As the number comes to a finish the two sisters join each other sadly, collapsing glumly on each other's shoulders as the hostile city crowds sing to them "Maybe you'd better go home!" There is a blackout.)*

# ACT ONE

## Scene III
The street, *same as Scene I.*

ESKIMO PIE MAN

Eskimo Pies—Eskimo Pies—Eskimo Pies—
(RUTH *enters from house with milk bottles in a sack.*)

RUTH

Hey, Eskimo Pies! Will you take five milk bottles? You can
cash them in on the corner!

ESKIMO PIE MAN

I got no time for milk bottles!
(*He goes.* RUTH *puts bottles down.*)

EILEEN

(*Enters with a large paper bag*)
Be careful, Ruth—they're valuable!

RUTH

(*Wearily*)
Oh, hello, Eileen. What have you got in the bag?

EILEEN

Food.

RUTH

(*Eagerly*)

Food? Let's see! Where'd you get it?

(*They sit on the stoop.*)


EILEEN

At the food show. I saw people coming out with big bags of samples. So I went in, and I met the nicest boy. He was the floor manager—

RUTH

(*Nods sagely*)

Oh, the floor manager—


EILEEN

He loaded me up! We've got enough junk here for a week.


RUTH

(*Taking out small boxes of cereal*)

"Pep-O," "Rough-O," "Vita-Bran," "Nature's Broom." We're going to have breakfast all day long.


EILEEN

It's good for you—it's roughage.


RUTH

I'd like to vary it with a little smoothage—like a steak!

(*Puts stuff back in bag.* VALENTI *enters and crosses, snapping his fingers in rhythm.*)


VALENTI

Skeet—skat—skattle-o-do—

32

EILEEN

Oh, hello, Mr. Valenti!

VALENTI

Hi yah, gate! I got my eye on you! *Solid.*
Skeet—skat—skattle-e-o-do—

RUTH

Who was *that*?

EILEEN

That's Speedy Valenti! He runs that advanced night club—
the Village Vortex. He's a very interesting boy. He had a cow
and he studied dairy farming at Rutgers and then got into the
night-club business.

RUTH

Naturally.

EILEEN

I auditioned for him this morning.

RUTH

You did? How'd he like it?

EILEEN

He said I should get myself a reputation and he'd give me
a trial.

(HELEN *and* WRECK *enter.*)

HELEN

Oh, girls! Can we see you a minute?

RUTH

Sure, Mrs. Loomis—what is it?

HELEN

Well, this is awfully embarrassing—I don't know how to tell you—

WRECK

It's like this. Helen got a wire that her old lady is coming on, which kind of straight-arms me into the alley.

RUTH

Haven't you room?

WRECK

You see, Helen's mother doesn't know about me.

EILEEN

You mean she doesn't know that you're married?

WRECK

Well, you might go a little deeper than that. She doesn't even know we're engaged.

(RUTH *looks at* EILEEN.)

HELEN

So, while Mother's in town we thought you wouldn't mind putting The Wreck up in your kitchen?

EILEEN

What?

34

RUTH

You mean *sleep* in our kitchen?

HELEN

You'd feel a lot safer with The Wreck around. And he's awful handy. He can clean up and he irons swell.

WRECK

But no washing—that's woman's work.

EILEEN

Well, maybe we could do it for one night, but—

RUTH

Wait a minute—

HELEN

Oh, thank you, girls. You don't know how much you're helping us out!
(*She goes.*)

RUTH

But, look—we haven't—

WRECK
(*Quickly*)

Gee, that's swell! (*Follows her*) I'll get my stuff together right away!

RUTH
(*Grimly*)

Something tells me you weren't quite ready to leave Columbus.

EILEEN

*(Smiles guiltily and goes to door)*

Coming in?

RUTH

No. I'm taking these stories down to the *Manhatter*— *(Holding up envelope with manuscript)* and I'm going to camp beside the water cooler till that editor talks to me. See you later—

EILEEN

I won't be here later. I've got a date.

RUTH

With whom?

EILEEN

Frank Lippencott.

RUTH

*Who's* Frank Lippencott?

EILEEN

Didn't I tell you about the boy who manages the Walgreen drugstore on 44th Street?

RUTH

No.

EILEEN

He hasn't let me pay a single lunch check since I've been going there. Today I had a pimento sandwich, a tomato surprise, and a giant double malt—with marble cake.

RUTH

That's right, dear—keep your strength up. You're eating for two now.

36

### EILEEN

I want you to meet him, so when *you're* in the neighborhood, you can have your lunches there too.

### RUTH

Gee, since I've been in New York, I only met one man, and he said, "Why the hell don't you look where you're going?" (*Shrugs*) Maybe it's just as well. Every time I meet one I gum it up. I'm the world's leading expert on discouraging men. I ought to write a book about it. "Girls, are you constantly bothered by the cloying attentions of the male sex? Well, here's the solution for you. Get Ruth Sherwood's new best-seller—'One Hundred Easy Ways to Lose a Man.' "

> (EILEEN *laughs and goes into house as* RUTH *sings in a spirit of rueful self-mockery.*)

Chapter one—
Now the first way to lose a man—
> (*Sings with exaggerated romanticism*)

You've met a charming fellow and you're out for a spin.
The motor fails and he just wears a helpless grin—
Don't bat your eyes and say, "What a romantic spot we're in."
> (*Spoken flatly*)

Just get out, crawl under the car, tell him it's the gasket and
  fix it in two seconds flat with a bobby pin.
That's a good way to lose a man—
> (*Sung*)

He takes you to the baseball game.
You sit knee to knee—
He says, "The next man up at bat will bunt, you'll see."

Don't say, "Oooh, what's a bunt? This game's too hard for
  little me."
  (*Spoken*)
Just say, "Bunt? Are you nuts?!! With one out and two men
  on base, and a left-handed batter coming up, you'll walk
  right into a triple play just like it happened in the fifth game
  of the World Series in 1923."
  (*Sung*)
That's a sure way to lose a man.


A sure sure sure sure way to lose a man,
A splendid way to lose a man—
Just throw your knowledge in his face
He'll never try for second base.
Ninety-eight ways to go.


The third way to lose a man—
The life-guard at the beach that all the girlies adore
Swims bravely out to save you through the ocean's roar.
Don't say, "Oh, thanks, I would have drowned in just one
  second more"—
  (*Spoken*)
Just push his head under water and yell, "Last one in is a
  rotten egg" and race him back to shore!
  (*Sung*)
That's a swell way to lose a man.


You've found your perfect mate and it's been love from the
  start.
He whispers, "You're the one to who I give my heart."

Don't say, "I love you too, my dear, let's never never part"—
   (*Spoken*)
Just say, "I'm afraid you've made a grammatical error—it's
   not 'To who I give my heart,' it's 'To *whom* I give my
   heart'—You see, with the use of the preposition 'to,' 'who'
   becomes the indirect object, making the use of 'whom'
   imperative which I can easily show you by drawing a simple
   chart"—
     (*Waving good-bye toward an imaginary retreating
     figure*)
That's a fine way to lose a man.

A fine fine fine fine way to lose a man,
A dandy way to lose a man—
Just be more well-informed than he,
You'll never hear "O Promise Me"—

Just show him where his grammar errs
Then mark your towels "hers" and "hers"—
Yes, girls, you too can lose your man
If you will use Ruth Sherwood's plan—
One hundred easy ways to lose a man!
   (*She goes off as the lights dim.*)

# ACT ONE

## Scene IV

BAKER'S OFFICE *at the "Manhatter."*

AT RISE: BAKER *is seated behind desk.* RUTH *is seated in a chair opposite, talking fast.*

RUTH

—So you see, Mr. Baker, I worked on the Columbus *Globe* a couple of years—society page, sports, everything—and did a lot of writing on the side—but I'm afraid my stuff was a little too sophisticated for Columbus—so I took the big plunge and came to New York—

BAKER

(*Breaks in*)

Yes, I know—I did it myself but this is a mighty tough town —Maybe you should have come here gradually—by way of Cleveland first—

RUTH

Yes. They're awfully short of writers in Cleveland—

BAKER

Well, at least a few people in Ohio know you—

RUTH

That's why I left—

BAKER

(*Laughs*)

Look, Miss Sherwood, I'd like to help you, but I'm so

40

swamped now—If you just leave your stories here, somebody will read them.

RUTH

(*Puts envelope down*)
Are you sure? I get them back so fast that unless I take the subway, they beat me home!

BAKER

We read them, all right— (*He takes eyeglasses from breast pocket*) I had 20-20 vision when I left Duluth.

RUTH

Duluth? Maybe *you* should've come here gradually—and stopped at St. Paul—

BAKER

(*Grimly*)
Huh?

RUTH

—95 ways to go—

BAKER

What?

RUTH

Oh, dear—Mr. Baker, please—would you mind if I went out that door and came back in and started all over again?

BAKER

Forget it!

RUTH

And I was so anxious to make a good impression!

BAKER

Well, you made a strong one.

(ASSOCIATE EDITORS *enter with pile of manuscripts. They put them on* BAKER's *desk.*)

FIRST EDITOR (LINVILLE)

Light summer reading, Bob!

BAKER

Oh, no, not any more! (*To* RUTH)
See what I mean? Every one of those authors is convinced he's an undiscovered genius!

RUTH

(*Looks at pile of manuscripts, then up to* BOB)
Well, what do you advise me to do?

BAKER

(*From desk*)

Go home!
Go west!
Go back where you came from!
Oh, why did you ever leave Ohio?

RUTH

(*Rises*)

Because I think I have talent!

BAKER

A million kids just like you
Come to town every day

With stars in their eyes;
They're going to conquer the city,
They're going to grab off the Pulitzer Prize,
But it's a terrible pity
Because they're in for a bitter surprise.
And their stories all follow one line
    (*Pointing with his arm to* FIRST EDITOR)
Like his,
    (*Pointing to* SECOND EDITOR)
Like his,
    (*To himself with both hands*)
Like mine.
    (*To* RUTH)
Born in Duluth,
Natural writer,
Published at seven—genius type—
Wrote the school play,
Wrote the school paper—
Summa cum laude—all of that tripe—
Came to New York,
Got on the staff here—
This was my chance to be heard.
Well, since then I haven't written a word.

BAKER AND EDITORS
(*Strumming guitars—imaginary*)

What a waste,
What a waste,
What a waste of money and time!
    (RUTH *turns and goes angrily as* BAKER *looks after her
sympathetically.*)

# WONDERFUL TOWN

**FIRST EDITOR**

Man from Detroit—
Wonderful Artist—
Went to Picasso—Pablo said "Wow!"
Settled in France,
Bought him a beret,
Lived in Montmartre,
Really learned how,
Came to New York—had an exhibit,
Art critics made a big fuss,
Now he paints those tooth-paste ads on the bus!

**EDITORS AND BAKER**

What a waste,
What a waste,
What a waste of money and time!

**SECOND EDITOR**

Girl from Mobile,
Versatile actress—
Tragic or comic—
Any old play.
Suffered and starved,
Met Stanislavsky.
He said the world would
Cheer her some day.
Came to New York,
Repertoire ready,
Chekhov's and Shakespeare's and Wilde's—
Now they watch her flipping flapjacks at Childs'.

### EDITORS AND BAKER

What a waste,
What a waste,
What a waste of money and time!

### BAKER

Kid from Cape Cod,
Fisherman's family,
Marvelous singer—big baritone—
Rented his boat,
Paid for his lessons
Starved for his studies
Down to the bone—
Came to New York,
Aimed at the opera—
Sing "Rigoletto" his wish—
At the Fulton Market now he yells "Fish!"

### EDITORS

What a waste,
What a waste,
What a waste of money and time!

### BAKER
(*Looking off after* RUTH)
Go home! Go west!
Go back where you came from!
(EDITORS *go.*)
Go home!
(BAKER *goes to his desk, his mind still on* RUTH, *and picks*

*up the envelope containing her manuscripts. He takes
them out and starts to read one.)*

BAKER
*(Reading)*

"For Whom the Lion Roars"—by Ruth Sherwood.

"It was a fine day for a lion hunt. Yes, it was a good clean
day for an African lion hunt—a good clean day for a fine clean
kill."

*(The lights go up on stage left as BAKER continues read-
ing. In the ensuing STORY VIGNETTES, played stage left and
musically underscored, RUTH portrays all the heroines.
These are RUTH's ideas of sophisticated writing, and are
acted in exaggerated satiric style.)*

BAKER
*(Reading)*

"Sandra Mallory stalked into the clearing with the elephant
gun."

*(SANDRA MALLORY [RUTH] enters dazzlingly attired in a
glamorous version of an African hunting outfit, a huge
gun tucked casually under her arm.)*

BAKER
*(Reading)*

"Just behind Sandra was Harry Mallory, her husband, and
Randolph Rexford, the guide."

*(They enter. REXFORD is an open-shirted, tight-lipped
Gary Cooper type and HARRY is a small, ineffectual-look-
ing man in an obvious state of terror, his gun shaking
in his hands.)*

46

BAKER

(*Reading*)

"Nearby they could hear the fine clean roar of the lion."
(*There is a loud ominous lion roar.*)

REXFORD

(*Pointing out front*)

There he is, right in front of you, Mr. Mallory! (MALLORY
*points his gun toward the oncoming roars, which become
louder and louder as* REXFORD *continues*) No, not yet—wait
until you see his eyes. That will be the fine, clean way to bag
the Simba. No—not yet— Not yet, Mr. Mallory—
(MALLORY *dashes off, screaming*)

SANDRA

(*Flatly*)

My cigarette has gone out. (*She holds her cigarette up to her
mouth. Contemptuously*) He ran—Harry, the brave hunter!
(*Her hand is trembling exaggeratedly.*)

REXFORD

(*Tensely*)

Your hand is trembling, Mrs. Mallory—
(*He grabs her hand, helping her light the cigarette.*)

SANDRA

(*Conscious of his grasp*)

It is nothing.

BAKER

(*Reading*)

"He gripped her hard. It was a clean fine grip. She remem-

bered Harry's grip. Like clean, fine oatmeal. Suddenly Sandra
Mallory felt the beat, beat, beat of Africa—"
(*Drums heard nearby.*)

SANDRA
(*Sexily to* REXFORD *as she undulates to the rhythm*)
Rexford—why do you hate me?

REXFORD
(*Tight-lipped*)
I have my job—Mrs. Mallory—and Mr. Mallory is your
husband.
(*There is a roar and terrified scream from off-stage.*)

SANDRA
(*Calmly*)
He *was* my husband. (*She drops her gun and walks toward
him passionately*) Rexford—

REXFORD
(*Moving toward her with equal passion*)
Mrs. Mallory—

SANDRA
(*Stepping nearer*)
Rexford—

REXFORD
(*Nearer—and now seething*)
Sandra—

SANDRA
(*Throwing her arms around him*)
Randolph!
(*He bends her backwards in a movie kiss.*)
48

BAKER
(*Incredulous*)

No!

(*There is a blackout on the African scene, as* BAKER *picks
up the next manuscript a little more cautiously.*)

BAKER
(*Reading*)

"Twentieth-Century Blues." "It was squalid in that one room
flat in Williamsburg without the windows, with the gray peel-
ing plaster and the sound of rats scurrying inside the walls and
the scratching phonograph across the hall screaming gee I'd
like to see you lookin' swell baby diamond—" (BAKER *finally
has to take a deep breath and plunge on*) "—bracelets Wool-
worth doesn't sell baby and Danny coming in gray and drawn
like the gray plaster coming in clutching his guts with the
gray rats inside his walls too yeah the gray rat pains of hunger
yeah the twentieth-century hunger yeah—"

(DANNY *enters, a ragged proletarian figure in his under-
shirt, in the depths of despair and hunger. He is followed
by* ESSIE [RUTH], *ludicrously ragged and obviously somewhat with child. They speak in the singsong Brooklyn-
ese used in the social-problem dramas of the '30's.*)

ESSIE
(*Dully*)

Danny—when we gonna get married?

DANNY

When—when—when—always naggin'—

49

ESSIE

They're talkin'—the neighbors are talkin'. Mamma looks at me funny like.

DANNY

It takes money, dream boat, to get married. The green stuff with the pictures of Lincoln—

ESSIE

Lincoln should see me now. Remember how swell life was gonna be— We was gonna have everything—a four-star trip to the moon—diamonds—yachts—shoes!

DANNY

Baby—

ESSIE

What's left, Danny—what's left?
(*They approach each other lumberingly with the same growing passion as in the first vignette.*)

DANNY
(*Stepping closer, arms open*)

Baby—

ESSIE

Danny—

DANNY

Baby—

ESSIE
(*Clutching him in an embrace*)

Danny!

BAKER

No!

50

(*There is a blackout on the vignette as he hurls the script down and very warily picks up the third.*)

"Exit Laughing"—"Everyone agreed that Tracy Farraday was marvelous. Everyone agreed that this was her greatest acting triumph. Everyone agreed that her breath-taking performance in 'Kiss Me, Herman' was the climax of a great career."

(*The lights go up on elegantly dressed party. Guests are discovered in a tableau.*)

"Everyone agreed that the plush opening night party at the Astor Hotel was a memorable occasion."

(*Everyone is indulging in upper-class merriment, with laughter and hysterical chitchat.* TRENT FARRADAY, *a stuffy society type, is kissing a girl as he holds her in a deep embrace.*)

#### WOMAN GUEST
(*Looking off*)

Here comes Tracy now!

#### ALL GUESTS

Tracy!

(TRACY *enters in superb evening clothes—the perfect picture of the glamorous actress. She takes a glamorous pose.*)

#### BAKER
(*Reading*)

"Everyone agreed that perhaps Tracy drank a bit too much."

(TRACY *suddenly staggers in cross-eyed, exaggerated drunkenness.*)

TRACY

(*Tallulah-ish*)

Has anyone seen that silly old husband of mine?

(TRACY *staggers to* TRENT—*taps him on shoulder. He is still deep in the embrace.*)

O, Trent—(TRENT *looks up from kiss*)—Have you got a match?

TRENT

Tracy—I'm leaving—I have found someone who needs me —appreciates me—

TRACY

You cahn't!

TRENT

(*Exiting with girl*)

You are not a woman, Tracy. You are a billboard.

TRACY

(*After him*)

No, no, Trent—I'll be different—I will— Don't go!

BAKER

(*Reading*)

"Everyone agreed that Tracy was a hypochondriac. Otherwise, why did she always carry a bottle of iodine?"

(TRACY, *throughout speech, is rummaging through her purse, pulls out red bottle of iodine and downs the contents.*)

TRACY

(*With bitter abandon, giving her greatest performance*)

Everybody! On with the party!

(*She executes a wild fandango—then suddenly clutching*

*her midriff in a paroxysm of agony, she crashes to the
floor.*)

MALE GUEST

Tracy!

WOMAN GUEST

Ah—she's just passing out!


TRACY

(*Pulling herself up on one elbow with difficulty—
gallant to the end*)

Yes! Everyone agrees—I'm just passing out—exit laughing!
Ha— Ha— Ha— Ha!

(*She laughs wildly and falls back dead, after a last con-
vulsive twitch.*)

GUESTS

(*Raising glasses in a toast to a noble lady, singing
in solemn chorale fashion*)

What a waste,
What a waste,
What a waste of money and time!

(BAKER *joins in the chorus—hurling his script down on
the desk. Blackout.*)

## ACT ONE

### Scene V

THE STREET. AT RISE: MRS. WADE *and* HELEN *come on.*

MRS. WADE

Whatever possessed you to move into a dreadful neighborhood like this, Helen? How do you ever expect to meet a nice
young man down here?

HELEN

Oh, Mother, please! Let me live my own life!

MRS. WADE

(*Climbing steps—turning from top before going into house*)
Life! You're just a child! You don't know what life is!
   (*Exits into house—*HELEN *following.* VALENTI *enters, followed by two* BOP GIRLS. FRANK LIPPENCOTT *enters. He
   carries a box of candy.*)

VALENTI

Skeet—skat—skattle-e-o-do— (*To girls*) Don't bother me,
kids! Wait until you grow up!
   (*He's off, followed by kids.* EILEEN *comes on and sees*
   FRANK *peering in their window.*)

EILEEN

Oh, hello, Frank!

54

FRANK

Hello, Eileen! I just came down during my lunch hour. I've been thinking about you all morning.

EILEEN

You have?

FRANK

I brought you some chocolate-covered cherries we're running. We're featuring them all this week during our annual one-cent sale.

EILEEN

(*Taking candy from him*)

You're sweet.

FRANK

Well, I've got to get back to the drugstore. It's pandemonium down there.

EILEEN

Don't forget—we expect you for dinner tonight. I want you to meet my sister—she's in your neighborhood a lot.

FRANK

Oh—I'll be here all right.

EILEEN

Thanks for the chocolate-covered cherries.

FRANK

'Bye, Eileen—

EILEEN

'Bye, Frank!

(*She watches him go off and, starry-eyed, starts to sing*)

Mm— Mmm—
I'm a little bit in love.
Never felt this way before—
Mm— Mmm—
Just a little bit in love
Or perhaps a little bit more.

When he
Looks at me
Everything's hazy and all out of focus.
When he
Touches me
I'm in the spell of a strange hocus-pocus.
It's so
I don't know
I'm so
I don't know
I don't know—but I know
If it's love
Then it's lovely!

Mm— Mmm—
It's so nice to be alive
When you meet someone who bewitches you.
Will he be my all
Or did I just fall
A little bit
A little bit in love?

> (BOB BAKER *enters, goes to grill window and looks in.*
> EILEEN *pulls ribbon off candy box, goes to steps. She sees*
> BAKER *and stares coldly.*)

EILEEN

*Well?*

BAKER

(*Looking up from window*)

I was just looking for the young lady who lives in there—
my name's Baker—Robert Baker—

EILEEN

Did *Marty* send you?

BAKER

I beg your pardon.

EILEEN

I hate to ruin your afternoon, Mr. Baker, but Violet doesn't
live here any more.

BAKER

Violet?

EILEEN

You might tell Marty and all the boys. It'll save them a trip.

BAKER

I'm afraid you've got me confused with somebody else.

EILEEN

I have?

BAKER

Yes. I'm looking for Ruth Sherwood. She live here, doesn't
she?

EILEEN

Who—are you, Mr. Baker?

**BAKER**

I'm an associate editor of the *Manhatter*.

**EILEEN**

Oh, oh, I'm terribly sorry! Ruth'll be furious—I'm her sister, Eileen.

**BAKER**

How do you do, Miss Sherwood?

**EILEEN**

Ruth isn't in right now, but I'm sure she'll be right back. Won't you come in and wait?

**BAKER**

No, thanks. I'll drop by later.

**EILEEN**

You're sure, now?

**BAKER**

Oh, yes—

**EILEEN**

Because I know Ruth must be terribly anxious to see you—

**BAKER**

Well?

**EILEEN**

How about a nice, cool drink?

**BAKER**

Not now—thanks, Miss Sherwood—

58

EILEEN

Oh—*Eileen!*

BAKER

Eileen—

EILEEN

Mr. Baker—I mean, Robert—I have a wonderful idea! Why don't you come back and take pot luck with us?

BAKER

Well, I don't know—

EILEEN

Oh, please! I'm making a special dish tonight!

BAKER

Okay—what time?

EILEEN

Any time after seven!

BAKER

Swell, Eileen—see you later.

EILEEN

'Bye, Bob!
(*She watches him go—and, with the same starry-eyed look as before, she sings*)
Mm— Mmm—
I'm a little bit in love
Never felt this way before
Mm— Mm—(*music continues*)
(LONIGAN *enters slowly*)
O hello, Officer!

LONIGAN
(*Suspiciously*)

Yeah.

(THE WRECK *enters and goes to house. He is carrying a rolled-up Army mattress.*)


WRECK

I borrowed a mattress, Eileen. That floor in your place is awful hard!

(WRECK *disappears into house.* LONIGAN *looks warily to* EILEEN, *who turns, startled, and puts a hand to her mouth. Blackout.*)

# ACT ONE

## Scene VI

THE BACK YARD. *This is the "garden" that* APPOPOLOUS *boasts about. It's a dismal place, sunk deep among the tenements that surround it. There are a moldy tree, a couple of chairs and a bench. Across from the girls' kitchen we see the back entrance of* NINO'S, *an Italian restaurant.* AT RISE: WRECK *is at an ironing board, pressing some of the girls' things.*

WRECK

"I'm a rambling Wreck—
From Trenton Tech—
And a helluva engineer—"
  (WAITER *comes out of* NINO'S *and is joined by Italian* CHEF.)

CHEF

E arrivato la padrone— E meglio cominciare a lavorare.

WAITER

Peccato. Si sta cosi bene qui fuore.

CHEF

Be. Cosi e la vita.
  (RUTH *comes in from kitchen.*)

RUTH

Any mail?

**WRECK**

Yeah, one of your stories came back.

**RUTH**

From the *Manhatter*?

**WRECK**

No, *Collier's*. (RUTH *picks up manuscript in envelope at window sill, changing address with a pencil.*)
Hot, ain't it?

**RUTH**

Yah. I feel as if I'm living in my own little world, mailing these to myself.

**WRECK**

Hey, which way do you want these pleats turned?

**RUTH**

(*Glances at him wearily*)
Toward Mecca.
(*The phone rings.* WRECK *goes to window sill and answers it.*)

**WRECK**

The Sherwood residence—who do you want?—Eleanor? You mean Eileen—She's not in. (*Annoyed*) This is the butler—Who the hell are *you*?

**RUTH**

(*Grabbing phone*)
Wreck! Hello? . . . Who is this, please? . . . Chick Clark?
Oh, yes, Mr. Clark. This is her sister—Ruth. . . . No, she's not in right now . . . any minute . . . I'll tell her. . . . 'Bye.
(*Hangs up. Makes note on pad at window sill.*)

WRECK

That Eileen does all right for herself. And the funny part of it is, she's a good girl.

RUTH

(*Eyeing him*)
When did you find *that* out?

WRECK

No, you sense those things. I never made a pass at you, but I could swear *you're* all right.

RUTH

That's the story of my life.
(*She goes off with manuscript as* HELEN *enters.*)

WRECK

Hy'ah, Sugar Foot!

HELEN

Hi.

WRECK

Do you miss me, honey?

HELEN

Of course I miss you. Now *I* have to do all the housework. (*Looking at laundry*) Huh! You never ironed that good for me!

WRECK

Now look, honey—!
(MRS. WADE *appears in street above them.* HELEN *ducks behind ironing board, her rear facing the audience.*)

63

MRS. WADE
(*Staring at* WRECK)

Well, I never!

WRECK

What are *you* lookin' at, you old bat?

MRS. WADE

How dare you!
(*She goes off indignantly.*)

WRECK
(*Shouts after her*)
Didn't you ever see a man in shorts before?

HELEN
(*Wails*)

Wreck! That was Mom!

WRECK

You mean that old wagon was your mother?

HELEN

You've got to get out of here!

WRECK

Where am I gonna sleep?

HELEN

If we could scrape up a few dollars you could stay at the "Y" till Mother leaves.

WRECK

We're tryin' to dig up a coupla bucks and your mother's got a mattressful!

HELEN

If only we had somethin' left to hock.

WRECK

Hey—wait a minute! (*Goes to kitchen*) If anyone comes, whistle "Dixie."
(*There is a blast from the subway.* HELEN *jumps as* WRECK *reappears with* APPOPOLOUS' "*blue-green*" *canvas.*)

HELEN

That's one of Appopolous'. They won't lend you a dime on it!

WRECK

This fancy frame might be good for a coupla bucks. Take it over to Benny's and see what you can get on it!
(HELEN *exits with picture.* DELIVERY KID *enters from street with basket of vegetables.*)

KID

(*Adoringly*)
Hey, Wreck—getting ready for the football season?

WRECK

Oh, I keep in shape!

KID

(*Centering the "ball"—a head of cabbage*)
Hey—signals!

WRECK

45—26—7—hip!
(WRECK *catches ball.*)

CHEF
(*Enters in front of* NINO's—*to* KID)
E tu che diavalo fai con quel cavalo?

KID
(*To* WRECK)
Pass.
(WRECK *passes to* KID—*who passes to* WAITER, *who catches cabbage in his stomach.*)

CHEF
Che pazzerela!
(*Waving an angry hand at* KID, *who passes him basket with vegetables.* CHEF *exits.*)

KID
Well, you certainly look in good shape for the football season.

WRECK
Yeah—for all the good it does me!
(*Goes wearily back to ironing and sings*)
Look at me now
Four years of college
Famous professors
Tutoring me
Scholarship kid

66

Everything paid for
Food and vacations
All of it free
Day that I left
Everyone gathered
Their cheering still rings in my ears—
 (*Carried away by memories, he executes some of the old
 cheers with great vigor*)
Ray Wreck rah
Rah Wreck ray
Rah Wreck
Wreck rah
Rah Wreck Wreck
W-e-c, R-e-k, R-e-q
Wreck, we love you!
 (*Singing bravura*)
'Cause I could pass a football
Like nothin' you have ever seen!
 (*A crowd has gathered on the street, watching him.
 They cheer*)
Couldn't spell a lick
Couldn't do arithmetic
One and one made three
Thought that dog was c-a-t
But I could pass a football
Like nothing you have ever seen

Couldn't write my name
Couldn't translate "je vous aime"
Never learned to read
Mother Goose or André Gide

But I could pass a football
Like nothing you have ever seen

Couldn't figure riddles
Puzzles made me pout
Where the hell was Moses when the lights went out?
I couldn't even tell red from green
Get those verbs through my bean
But I was buddies with the Dean
Like nothing you have ever seen

Passed without a fuss
English Lit and Calculus
Never had to cram
Even passed the bar exam
Because I passed that football
Like nothing you have ever seen

Then there was the week
Albert Einstein came to speak
Relativity
Guess who introduced him? Me!
'Cause I could pass a football
Like nothing you have ever seen

Had no table manners
Used ta dunk my roll
Always drunk the water from the fingerbowl
Though I would not get up for any she
The Prexy's mom—age ninety-three

Got up and gave her seat to me
Like nothing you did ever see

In our Hall of Fame
There's a statue with my name
There we stand, by heck
Lincoln, Washington and Wreck
'Cause I could pass that football
Like nothing you have ever seen!
> (WRECK *and* CROWD *of assorted* VILLAGERS *do a "football"
> dance, with* WRECK *ending up with a pile of players, hope-
> lessly outclassed. He sticks his head out from under,
> weakly.*)

'Cause I could pass that football!
Like nothing you have ever—ever seen!
> (CROWD *pulls away.* WRECK *staggers and collapses in their
> arms. At the end of number, the* CROWD *goes off.* HELEN
> enters with pawn ticket.*)

HELEN

Two bucks—here's the ticket.

EILEEN
(*Enters from studio*)
Gee, Wreck—the laundry looks swell.

HELEN
(*Coldly*)
Too bad he's leaving, isn't it?

69

EILEEN

Oh, is he?

HELEN

Yes, and it's about time, too.
(RUTH *enters from alley.*)

WRECK

Stop racin' your motor! I told her there was nothing to it!

RUTH

Nothing to *what?*

EILEEN

Ruth, do you know what she had the nerve to insinuate?

RUTH

Was it something with sex in it?

WRECK

Why, if I thought about Eileen in that way— May God strike
me dead on this spot!
(*He raises his hand solemnly and there's a tremendous
Boom! from below. He shrinks guiltily.*)

RUTH

(*Looking up*)
He's everywhere all right.

HELEN

Come on, Wreck!
(*They go off.* VIOLET *enters from house.*)

70

VIOLET

(*Cheerfully*)

Hello, girls.

RUTH

(*Stares*)

Hello.

VIOLET

I'm Violet. I used to live in this fleabag before you girls got it.

EILEEN

Oh, so *you're* Violet.

VIOLET

Say, have I had any callers the last coupla weeks—since you kids moved in?

RUTH

(*Grimly*)

One or two.

VIOLET

I thought so. A lot of my friends don't know I moved yet. In case they come around—would you mind giving out my new cards? (*She takes thick pack of calling cards from purse and hands them to* EILEEN.) Thanks loads. So long.

(*She goes.*)

RUTH

The spiritual type.

(EILEEN *carries cards to window sill.*)

EILEEN

(*Looking at note pad*)

Oh, did Chick Clark call?

RUTH

Yes. Who's he?

EILEEN

He's a newspaperman. I met him in an elevator. We got to talking and I told him about you. He seemed very interested in you.

RUTH

So interested in me, I'll bet he can't wait to get you alone.

EILEEN

What've we got for dinner, Ruth?

RUTH

What do you think? Spaghetti and meat balls.

EILEEN

Haven't we polished that off yet? We've had it all week!

RUTH
(*Flatly*)

It closes tonight.

EILEEN

Well, we simply can't give that to Bob.

RUTH

Bob? I can't keep up with you. Who's *Bob*?

EILEEN

You know, Bob Baker, from the *Manhatter*. Don't play dumb!

RUTH

Mr. Baker! No! (*Turns* EILEEN *around*) Where did you meet him?

EILEEN

He dropped by to see you, and naturally I asked him to dinner.

RUTH

Naturally! (*Grabs* EILEEN, *kisses her*) Oh, darling! You are terrific! I'd never have the nerve!

EILEEN

Well, for goodness sake, why not? He's just a *boy*—

RUTH

(*Looks around helplessly*)
How can we fix this dump up a little? (*Closing kitchen door*) Eileen, promise me you won't take him in there!

EILEEN

Of course not. We'll eat in the garden—al fresco.

RUTH

Ah—

EILEEN

Oh, dear—I just remembered. I asked Frank over tonight.

RUTH

Who?

EILEEN

You know—Walgreen's—

RUTH

Oh, no! How can you mix a soda jerk with an editor?

EILEEN

He's *not* a jerk! He's the manager!

RUTH

Okay—okay— Gee, if a man like Mr. Baker comes to see me personally, he must really be interested!

EILEEN

Of course he's interested.

RUTH

And we can't even offer him a cocktail.

EILEEN

We could tell him it's too hot to drink.

RUTH
(*Nods*)
But cold enough for spaghetti.

EILEEN

Hmmm—smell that chicken cacciatori at Nino's. Maybe I ought to have a little talk with Mr. Nino.

RUTH

Do you know him too?

EILEEN

No, but I will—he's our neighbor, isn't he?

(*She goes into* NINO'S. CHICK CLARK *enters from street above.*)

CHICK

Hello. (*Coming down stairs, consulting matchbook*) I'm lookin' for a party named Sherwood—Eleanor Sherwood.

RUTH

You mean Eileen. You must be Mr. Clark?

CHICK

Yeah. Who are you?

RUTH

I'm her sister.

CHICK

(*Doubtfully*)

Her sister? She's a blonde, *good-looking* kid, ain't she?

RUTH

(*Grimly*)

Yes, she's a blonde, good-looking kid.

CHICK

(*Loosening his collar*)

Wow, it's absolute murder down here, ain't it? (*Staring overhead*) What is this—an abandoned mine shaft?

RUTH

Are you planning to be with us long, Mr. Clark?

CHICK

Eileen asked me to take pot luck with her.

75

FRANK

(*Off stage*)

Hello? Anyone home? (FRANK *appears at window in studio*)
Oh, hello, the front door was open. Is Eileen home?

RUTH

You're Mr. Lippencott, aren't you? Come in.
(*She motions to steps. Door opens.* LIPPENCOTT *appears,
carrying bottle of red wine. Trips down stairs. Recovers
himself. Pulls out comb and combs hair.*)

FRANK

Gee, I'm sorry. I didn't know there was any—
(*Shakes hands with* RUTH.)

RUTH

Oh, that's all right. Everybody does that.

FRANK

I guess you're Eileen's sister. I can see a family resemblance,
all right.

RUTH

Why, I'm very flattered.

FRANK

Of course, you're a different type.

RUTH

Yes, I see what you mean. Eileen'll be back in a minute—
(*Glancing to café*) She's just fixing dinner. (*Looking at* CHICK)
Oh, I want you to meet Mr. Clark—

76

(FRANK *goes to* CHICK, *to shake hands.* CHICK *ignores his hand.*)

CHICK

There ain't too much oxygen down here as it is.

RUTH

Mr. Lippencott is with Walgreen's.

CHICK

Yeah? I buy all my clothes there.

FRANK

No, it's a drugstore.

CHICK

(*Groans and looks at bottle with interest*)
What's in the bottle?

FRANK

(*To* CHICK *coldly*)
A very fine California Burgundy-type wine. (*To* RUTH) I thought it would go good with the spaghetti. (*Hands her wine*) It's a special we're running this week.

RUTH

(*Looking at bottle sadly*)
So's our spaghetti.

FRANK

Huh?

RUTH

Has this heat affected your business?

FRANK

Why, we pray for heat waves.

CHICK

Oh, you *do,* eh?

FRANK

Our fountain turnover is double. I'm lucky to get away at all.

RUTH

Oh, *we're* the lucky ones.

EILEEN

(*Entering, to* FRANK)

Oh, Frank, I'm terribly sorry I wasn't here to greet you! (*To* RUTH) Ruth, what do you think?

RUTH

What?

EILEEN

Mr. Nino's in Italy. He won't be back till Labor Day. (*To* CHICK, *in dismay*) Oh, hello, Mr. Clark!

CHICK

Hy'ah, gorgeous!

EILEEN

Oh, Ruth, this is that newspaper gentleman I was telling you about who was so interested in you.

CHICK

That's right. I gave the city editor a big pitch already—

(*Lasciviously*) You won't believe this, baby, but I've been turnin' you over in my mind all afternoon.

(EILEEN *laughs uneasily as* RUTH *nods.*)

Gee, this is great. I always wanted to live in the Village in a place like this.

### RUTH

What stopped you?

### FRANK

Well, in my position in the drugstore you've got to keep up appearances.

### RUTH

I see. Where the Liggetts speak only to the Walgreens and the Walgreens speak only to God.

(CHICK *grabs* EILEEN's *hand. She pulls away.*)

### EILEEN

I'd better set the table. (*Goes to kitchen*) Where shall we dine—inside or outside?

### CHICK

Which is *this*?

(BOB BAKER *appears from street, waving envelope with manuscript.*)

### BAKER

Hello!

### EILEEN

Oh, hello, Bob!

### RUTH

Hello, Mr. Baker! Sorry I wasn't in when you called.

BAKER

That's all right—

RUTH

I'd like you to meet Mr. Clark—Mr. Lippencott— This is Mr. Baker—

FRANK

Pleased to meet you.
(*Holds out his hand, which* BAKER *shakes.*)

CHICK

What the hell is this, a block party?

RUTH

You're quite a card, aren't you, Mr. Clark? (*Puts wine on window sill*) Mr. Lippencott brought you some wine, dear.

EILEEN

Oh, how sweet! Shall we sit down?
(*She motions the others to join her and there is a general embarrassed shuffling about for chairs. She pulls* BOB *down beside her on her chair.* CHICK *brings a chair forward and* RUTH, *assuming it is for her, goes toward it, but* CHICK *sits on it himself. She gets her own and the five wind up in a tight uncomfortable group facing one another with nothing to say.* EILEEN *after a pause*)
Well—here we are—all together—
(*There is a dry discordant vamp in the orchestra expressing the atmosphere of embarrassed silence, which is repeated during every pause in the following song and conversation. It seems to grow more mocking and desperate at each repetition. After another pause they all*

*start speaking at once very animatedly and then dwindle*
*off. Pause again.* EILEEN *giggles nervously. Pause.*)


FRANK
(*Starting bravely*)
At the bottom of the vanilla—
(*He has a terrific coughing fit.* BAKER *slaps his back, and*
*he sits down—and combs his hair.*)
It's nothing.
(*Vamp.*)

EILEEN
(*Singing, over-brightly, after a pause*)
Mmmm—mmmm—it's so nice to sit around—
And chat—
Nice people, nice talk,
A balmy summer night,
A bottle of wine—
Nice talk—nice people,
Nice feeling—nice talk—
The combination's right
And everything's fine—


Nice talk—nice people
It's friendly—it's gay
To sit around this way.
What more do you need?
Just talk—and people.
For that can suffice
When both the talk and people are so nice—
(*She finishes lamely as the vamp is played again. Pause.*)

FRANK

(*Settling back in chair with a hollow, unconvincing laugh*)

Ha ha—Funny thing happened at the counter today.—Man comes in—Sort of tall like—Nice looking refined type—Red bow tie—and all. Well sir, he orders a banana split—That's our jumbo special—twenty-eight cents—Three scoops—chocolate, strawberry, vanilla—choice of cherry or caramel sauce—chopped nuts—whipped cream—Well, sir, he eats the whole thing—I look at his plate and I'll be hornswoggled if he doesn't leave the whole banana—doesn't touch it—not a bite—Don't you see?—If he doesn't like bananas, what does he order a banana split for?—He coulda had a sundae—nineteen cents—Three scoops—Chocolate—Strawberry—Vanilla—

(*He dwindles off as vamp is played again.*)

RUTH

(*Making a noble attempt to save the day*)

I was re-reading *Moby Dick* the other day and— Oh, I haven't read it since—I'm sure none of us has— It's worth picking up again— It's about this whale—

(*Her futile attempt hangs heavy on the air. Vamp again.*)

CHICK

(*Even he is driven by desperation to attempt sociability*)

Boy, it's hot! Reminds me of that time in Panama—I was down there on a story—I was in this, well, dive— And there was this broad there—What was her name?— Marquita?— Maroota? (*Warming to his subject*) Ahh, what's the difference what her name was—That dame was built like a brick—

(*A sharp drum crash cuts him off and the vamp is played with hysterical speed and violence. The four others spring*

*to their feet horrified and, as* CHICK *stands by puzzled,*
*they cover up with a sudden outburst of animated talk*
*and laughter expressed by a rapid rendition of "Nice*
*People, Nice Talk" with* EILEEN *singing an insane colo-*
*ratura obbligato as the music builds to a thunderous*
*close.*)

ALL

Nice people, nice talk,
A balmy summer night,
A bottle of wine—
Nice talk, nice people,
Nice feeling—nice talk.
The combination's right
And everything's fine.

Nice talk, nice people—
It's friendly, it's gay
To sit around this way.
What more do you need?
Just talk and people.
For that can suffice
When both the talk and people are so nice
It's nice!
(*A closing orchestra chord.*)

RUTH
(*Gets bottle*)
Let's have a drink, shall we?

EILEEN
(*To* FRANK)
Do we need ice?

FRANK

No, this wine should be served at the temperature of the room.

CHICK

Then you'd better cook it a coupla hours.

APPOPOLOUS

(*Entering from stairs*)

Congratulate me, young ladies!

Today is the big day! I'm entering my painting in the WPA Art Contest!

(*He goes into studio.*)

BAKER

Ruth, who's that?

RUTH

Our landlord—Rasputin.

APPOPOLOUS

(*Comes back, heavily*)

What kind of a funny game is going on here? Where is it? Who took it?

RUTH

What?

APPOPOLOUS

You know everybody who goes into your apartment.

RUTH

We don't know *half* of them.

84

**APPOPOLOUS**

Please, I know you girls are hard up. Tell me what you did with it and there'll be no questions asked.

**EILEEN**

You don't think we stole it?

**APPOPOLOUS**

If you didn't—who did?

**RUTH**

Maybe it was the same gang that swiped the Mona Lisa.

**APPOPOLOUS**

(*Goes angrily*)

You won't be so humorous when I come back with a cop!

**RUTH**

(*To* BAKER *anxiously*)

I hope you don't take any of that seriously, Mr. Baker.

**BAKER**

Of course not.

**FRANK**

(*Scared*)

Do you think he's really going to call the police?

**EILEEN**

The police won't pay any attention to him—he's always calling them!

CHICK

Well, let's crack that bottle before the wagon gets here!

EILEEN

I'll open it and get some glasses. Do you want to help me, Frank?

CHICK

(*Stepping in*)

I'll help ya, Eleanor—(*Turning to* FRANK) You stay out here and hand them a few laughs.

(EILEEN *starts in to house.* CHICK *follows.*)

FRANK

Oh, is that so?

(*Trips up steps into house.*)

RUTH

(*To* BAKER, *sadly*)

If you'd like to make your getaway now, Mr. Baker, I'll understand.

BAKER

No, I'm enjoying it.

RUTH

Did you get a chance to read those stories?

BAKER

I certainly did!

(WRECK *and* HELEN *appear in street.*)

RUTH

Well, what did you think?

86

WRECK
(*Coming down stairs*)
Oh, I'm sorry, Ruth—didn't know you had company.

HELEN
(*With him*)
Can we come in?

RUTH
(*Groans*)
Yes, please do. (*To kitchen*) Two more glasses, Eileen!

WRECK
I talked it over with Helen, and she wants to apologize.

RUTH
(*Quickly*)
That's not necessary—Mr. Baker—This is Mr. Loomis—and his intended. (*They shake hands.* BAKER *eyes his shorts anxiously*) Mr. Loomis is in training.

BAKER
Oh.
(FRANK *enters from studio with tray and glasses of wine.*)

FRANK
(*From top of steps*)
This wine was—(*Stepping carefully down*) made by a Frenchman in California.
(EILEEN *comes through studio door, carrying two more glasses.*)

EILEEN

Oh, hello there—(*She hands glass to* RUTH. CHICK *follows through studio door, carrying his own glass.* FRANK *passes tray to* WRECK *and* HELEN *and moves upstage with tray*) What a magnificent bouquet!

RUTH

Drink up, everyone—it's later than you think! Here's to us and Burgundy, California!
> (*They all have raised glasses in toast. There's a "boom" from below.* FRANK *jumps and spills his wine all over his new white suit.*)

FRANK

Gee, what was that?

EILEEN

> (*Stares at the wine stain miserably*)

Oh, Frank, I'm terribly sorry!

FRANK

> (*Looking down at his suit pathetically*)

What—what happened?

RUTH

The new subway—
> (*Wipes off wine.*)

FRANK

> (*Wails*)

Does red wine stain?

88

EILEEN

Not if you rub salt on it.
(*Wipes off wine.*)

CHICK

You better get a bagful!

FRANK

I just got this suit. It's brand new!

CHICK

Ah, you can't even notice it!
(*He starts to laugh. They all join in, hysterically.* FRANK *stands in the center, stricken.* HELEN *sinks to the floor in her laughter.*)

FRANK

(*Backing to stairs, he starts up them*)
Well, if you think it's so funny, I'll go!

EILEEN

(*Starts to follow*)
Frank—don't go! Wait! (*Turning to the others*) Oh, dear —he's really angry.

MRS. WADE

(*Off stage*)
Helen, are you in there?

HELEN

Yes, Mother.

RUTH

Won't you come in, Mrs. Wade?

MRS. WADE

(*Entering*)

Most certainly not. Helen, I want you to come out of there immediately!

HELEN

But, Mother.

MRS. WADE

I will not have you associating with those depraved women and their consort!

RUTH AND EILEEN

*What?*

WRECK

*Who's* a consort?

HELEN

Please, Mother—

MRS. WADE

Not another word. You come right along with me. Don't you dare talk to my Helen again. You're not fit to associate with decent people!

(*She pushes* HELEN *out.*)

WRECK

I'm gonna wait till Mother's Day—(*Making fist*) and sock her!

(*He goes.*)

EILEEN

Bob, I don't know what you must think of us, but really, it isn't so.

90

BAKER

(*Grins*)

I'm sure it isn't.

RUTH

Well, you must admit—for a place with a bad location and no neon sign, we're doing a hell of a business.

EILEEN

(*Brightly*)

Dinner, anyone?

BAKER

Fine!

EILEEN

(*Going to kitchen*)

I'd better heat the entrée.

CHICK

(*Following close behind*)

We'll warm it up together, Eleanor!
(*They go off.*)

RUTH

Funny, I'm not a bit hungry.

BAKER

I'm starving. And I smell something delicious!

RUTH

(*Looks at* NINO's)

Trade Winds.

EILEEN'S VOICE

Mr. Clark, please! Not while I'm trying to cook!

BAKER

While we have a minute, before anything else happens, I'd like to talk to you about your stories—

RUTH

Oh, do, please! You mean you actually read them yourself?

BAKER

I certainly did—You have a lot of talent, Miss Sherwood—

RUTH

Do you really think so?

BAKER

Yes, I do—(RUTH *turns away, tearfully*) What's the matter?

RUTH

Nothing—

BAKER

You're crying—

RUTH

(*Turning back to him*)

It's just an allergy I have to good news—

BAKER

You really should have more faith in yourself—

RUTH

Thanks, I'm beginning to—

BAKER

And once you get on the right track, you're going to do some good work.

RUTH

Right track?

BAKER

Look Ruth. Have you ever gone on a safari in the African veldt?

RUTH

No.

BAKER

And have you ever lived in a cold-water tenement?

RUTH

No.

BAKER

Then why do you write that stuff? Write about something you know—something you've actually experienced.

RUTH

I write the things I feel! I put myself in every one of those characters!

BAKER

Then you must be hopelessly repressed.

RUTH

That's a terrible thing to say! I'm the most normal person you'll ever meet!

BAKER

That's a sure sign. All inhibited people think they're normal.

RUTH

Oh! So now I'm inhibited!

BAKER

(*Turns to her*)

I'm afraid so—if you claim you're really those frustrated heroines.

RUTH

Repressed! Inhibited! Frustrated! What *else* am I?

BAKER

Don't take it personally—

RUTH

How else can I take it?

BAKER

I'm just trying to help you—

RUTH

What are you, an editor or a psychoanalyst?

BAKER

I should've known better—You can't take it—You'll never get anywhere till you learn humility—

RUTH

When did you learn yours?

(*Runs into studio quickly.* BAKER *watches her.*)

# WONDERFUL TOWN

*(With weary anger)*

All right! Good-bye!
You've taught me my lesson!
Get mixed up with a genius from Ohio!
It happens over and over—
I pick the sharp intellectual kind.
Why couldn't this time be different,
Why couldn't she—only be
Another kind— A different kind of girl
*(As the lights dim, he pictures the kind of relationship*
*he would like to have, but has never known.)*
I love a quiet girl,
I love a gentle girl
Warm as sunlight,
Soft, soft as snow.

Her smile, a tender smile,
Her voice, a velvet voice,
Sweet as music,
Soft, soft as snow.

When she is near me
The world's in repose.
We need no words
She sees— She knows.

But where is my quiet girl,
Where is my gentle girl,
Where is the special girl,
Who is soft, soft as snow?

Somewhere—
Somewhere—
My quiet girl.

(*As he walks slowly off,* RUTH *enters from the kitchen and watches him go, with the hopeless feeling of having lost him.*)

RUTH
(*Sings*)

I know a quiet girl,
Hoping—waiting—
But he'll never know.

(*The music continues. There is a crash of dishes from the kitchen.* RUTH *turns suddenly—looks toward kitchen —her reverie broken.*)

EILEEN
(*Off stage*)

Now look what you made me do! (*Entering from studio,* CHICK *follows*) The spaghetti—it's all over the kitchen floor! Really, Mr. Clark!

CHICK

You're so darn jumpy—! (*Goes to stairs*) Okay, I'll run down to the corner and get some sandwiches and beer! Be right back!
(*He's off.*)

EILEEN

Where's Bob?

RUTH

Gone.

EILEEN

Isn't he coming back?

96

**RUTH**

If he does, he's crazy after the way I treated him.

**EILEEN**

Gee, Ruth, what happened?

**RUTH**

I'd rather not discuss it—I'm too frustrated. (*There's a "boom" from below. She looks down wearily*) Go on! Blow us up and get it over with!

**EILEEN**

Gee, Ruth, if you start to feel that way, who's going to hold me up?

**RUTH**

Oh, I'm not worried about you—not while there's a man alive.

**EILEEN**

After all, men are only an escape.
(*The phone rings.* EILEEN *hurries to it.*)

**RUTH**

Comes another escape—

**EILEEN**

(*On phone*)
Sherwood residence—Miss *Ruth* Sherwood?

**RUTH**

For *me?*

EILEEN

Who's calling please?—What? Wait a minute— Just a second! (*To* RUTH) Ruth, it's Chick Clark's paper. Mr. Bains of the city room wants to talk to you—
(EILEEN *hands phone to* RUTH.)

RUTH

Hello?—Yes—yes, Mr. Bains. This is she—*her*—*she*. Thank you, Mr. Bains. That's wonderful! Yes, yes, of course. (*To* EILEEN) Paper and pencil quick. Take this down!
(EILEEN *reaches over for pad and pencil from window*.)

EILEEN

What is it? What happened?

RUTH

Yes, Mr. Bains—I'm ready! Sands—Street—Brooklyn—I understand—Yes, right away, Mr. Bains! Thank you—thank you very much. (*She hangs up, looks up excitedly*) I can't believe it!

EILEEN

What did he say? What did he want?

RUTH

He's giving me a chance to show what I can do—an assignment over in Brooklyn!

EILEEN

Brooklyn? What happened there?

RUTH

A Brazilian training ship just came in—like Annapolis—
only these fellows are all young coffee millionaires. I'm going
aboard to get a human-interest story.

EILEEN

Coffee millionaires! Well, you're not going over there with
a run in your stocking! Take it off!
(*They sit on bench. Both remove stockings, exchange
them. Conversation continues throughout.*)

RUTH

What a break! Isn't it wonderful! I'll show him!

EILEEN

Who?

RUTH

Never mind! Inhibited, huh?

EILEEN

What?

RUTH

I'll get a job on my own! Who does he think he is? (*Finished with stocking, she jumps up*) Have you got any money?

EILEEN

Who—*me*?

RUTH

How am I going to get over there?

The milk bottles!

(RUTH *picks up bottles near door, grabs her hat and rushes to stairs.*)

RUTH

(*Climbing stairs*)

Wish me luck!

(EILEEN *follows.*)

EILEEN

Good luck!

(RUTH *exits noisily, milk bottles clanging.* EILEEN *turns back, picks up tray with wine glasses, exits into studio.* WAITER *enters with gallon glass jug of cheap wine.* CHEF *enters with two Chianti bottles in straw and funnel.*)

CHEF

Il vino?

WAITER

Porta qui le bottiglie. Eco!

(*Pulls two straw bottles from behind back.* WAITER *pours from cheap bottle into straw one. When first bottle is full,* CHEF *takes funnel and puts it into second bottle.*)

CHICK

(*Entering from street carrying package from grocery store.* EILEEN *comes out of studio*)

Dinner for two—comin' right up!

EILEEN

(*Takes sandwiches*)

Oh, how nice!

CHICK

Let's go in the kitchen. It's stiflin' out here!
(CHEF *and* WAITER *go off with bottles.*)


EILEEN

(*Going to bench*)

Oh, this is much pleasanter! (CHICK *sits next to her and makes a pass at her shoulder which she shrugs off. She puts bag with food between them*) It was awfully sweet of you to get Ruth a chance.
(*Opening wrapper, pulling out sandwich.*)


CHICK

A pleasure! (*He pats her hand and puts arm around her. She hands him sandwich in hand which has been groping around her back. He puts sandwich on bench, his arms around her again*)—And the next thing, we're gonna get your career straightened out.

EILEEN

(*Struggling, rises*)

Please! You'll have to excuse me, Mr. Clark!


CHICK

Excuse ya! After all the trouble I went to get rid of that eagle-eyed sister of yours.


EILEEN

(*Staring*)

What? That call Ruth got was from the editor, wasn't it?

CHICK

What are you worryin' about? I'm handling it—

EILEEN

It was *you*! You sent Ruth on a wild goose chase!

CHICK

(*Shrugs*)

I'll give her a coupla bucks for her trouble.

EILEEN

She was so excited. How am I ever going to tell her? You get out of here!

CHICK

Now that's a lousy attitude to take! (*Phone rings*) Let it ring!

EILEEN

Hello? Oh, Mr. Baker—hello, Bob!

CHICK

(*Into phone*)

Call back later!

EILEEN

(*To* CHICK)

How dare you! (*Into phone*) Oh, just somebody who's leaving—(*To* CHICK) Now stop this nonsense! (EILEEN, *into phone*)—Ruth? No, she's gone to Brooklyn—(*To* CHICK—*hand over phone*) Skunk! (*Into phone, elegantly*) Oh, you don't have to apologize—we never got to dinner anyway. Me? I guess I'll wait for Ruth—I always feel silly eating alone—

CHICK

Alone! How about me and them baloney sandwiches!

EILEEN

(*Into phone*)

Why, Bob, how nice! I'd love to have dinner with you—
(*Glaring at* CHICK) Yes, I'll be waiting—
(*Hangs up. Picks sandwich from window sill.*)

CHICK

That's the worst double-cross I ever got! A fine little sneak
you turned out to be! (EILEEN *starts to eat sandwich.* CHICK
*grabs it from her hand, as she is taking a bite.* CHICK *goes to
bench, picks up empty bag, stuffs* EILEEN's *sandwich into it*)
I ain't fattenin' you up for someone else!
(*Blackout.*)

# ACT ONE

## Scene VII

The navy yard. At rise: shore patrolman *doing sentry duty*. ruth *enters, passing* shore patrolman.

SHORE PATROLMAN

Just a minute, Miss! Where's your pass?

RUTH

Oh, it's all right—Press—I'm a reporter—

SHORE PATROLMAN

You gotta have a pass.

RUTH

I just want to interview those Brazilian cadets.

SHORE PATROLMAN

Look—I'm tryin' to tell you—a pass—

RUTH

Well, where can I get one?

SHORE PATROLMAN

You can't— Commandant's office is closed. Tomorrow.

RUTH

Oh, please—my job depends on it!

**SHORE PATROLMAN**

So does mine.
> (BRAZILIAN CADET *enters.*)

**FIRST CADET**

(*Eying* RUTH *with some interest. After all, she's a woman*)
Hello.

**RUTH**

> (*To* SHORE PATROLMAN)

Is that one of them? (SHORE PATROLMAN *nods. She steps to*
CADET) Excuse me, Admiral. I'm from the press, and I'd like to
ask you a few questions—
> (CADET *shrugs his shoulders, blankly.*)

**SHORE PATROLMAN**

That means he don't understand.

**RUTH**

Thanks. I know that much Portuguese myself.
> (*Seven more* CADETS *enter, enveloping* RUTH *in their
> midst, and talking loudly.*)

Ah! Any of you Admirals speak English?

**SECOND CADET**

Si! English!

**RUTH**

What do you think of America?

**SECOND CADET**

American dance—Conga!

RUTH

No, no! Conga's a Brazilian dance!

FIRST CADET

No—Cubano!

SECOND CADET

Conga *American* dance! You show Conga!

RUTH

Then will you tell me?

ALL

Si! Si!

RUTH

It's like this. One, two, three, kick. One, two, three, kick.
(*She shuffles from side to side in Conga step. They follow clumsily. She ad libs: That's fine! You've got it! That's right! But they don't quite stop. Music:*)
What do you think of the USA—NRA—TVA,
What do you think of our Mother's Day,
What do you think of the—

ADMIRALS

Conga!
(*They dance. She attempts to get her interview, but each time the* ADMIRALS *cut in with shrieks of "Conga!" As the number becomes more violent and* RUTH *is hurled about from one* CADET *to the other, she remains grimly resolved to disregard them and get her story.*)

RUTH

What do you think of our native squaws,

Charles G. Dawes,
Warden Lawes—
What's your opinion of Santa Claus,
What do you think of the—

ADMIRALS

Conga!
 (*They dance.*)

RUTH

Good neighbors— Good neighbors,
Remember our policy—
Good neighbors—I'll help you
If you'll just help me—

ADMIRALS

Conga!
 (*They dance.* RUTH *gets more and more involved.*)

RUTH

What's your opinion of Harold Teen,
Mitzi Green,
Dizzy Dean.
Who do you love on the silver screen—
What do you think of the—

ADMIRALS

Conga!
 (*More dancing, with* RUTH *struggling to get out of it.*)

RUTH

What do you think of our rhythm bands,

107

Monkey glands,
Hot-dog stands.
What do you think of Stokowski's hands—
What do you think of the—


ADMIRALS

Conga!
(*Dance*)

RUTH

Good neighbors— Good neighbors,
Remember our policy—
Good neighbors—I'll help you
If you'll just help me—


ADMIRALS

Conga!
(*By now the dancing is abandoned and wild.*)

RUTH

What's your opinion of women's clothes,
Major Bowes,
Steinbeck's prose.
How do you feel about Broadway Rose—
What do you think of the—

ADMIRALS

Conga!

RUTH

What do you think of our rocks and rills,
Mother Sills sea-sick pills.
How do you feel about Helen Wills—
What do you think of the—

108

### ADMIRALS

Conga!

### RUTH

Good neighbors— Good neighbors,
Remember our policy—
Good neighbors—I'll help you
If you'll just help me!!
> (ADMIRALS *sing serenade, strumming on imaginary gui-*
> *tars while* RUTH *stands totally exhausted. They yell*
> *"Conga!" again, and lift her on their backs. Careening*
> *about,* RUTH *still tries to get her interview.*)

Stop!
What do you think of our double malts,
Family vaults,
Epsom Salts,
Wouldn't you guys like to learn to waltz?
I know—You just want to——Conga!
> (*She is whirled about piggy-back in Conga rhythm, her*
> *hat over her eyes—and finally lifted aloft and carried off*
> *stage—as the music builds to a frenetic finish.*)

# ACT ONE

## Scene VIII

The back yard. ruth *enters, immediately after rise, on street, followed by* admirals.

RUTH

Good night! Au revoir! Auf wiedersehn! Good-bye! (*To* eileen, *who enters from studio*) Eileen. Eileen!

EILEEN

What's going on?

RUTH

The Fleet's in!

EILEEN
(*To* admirals)

How do you do?

RUTH

Listen, Emily Post— How do you say, "Get the hell out of here" in Portuguese?

EILEEN

Why? What's the matter?

RUTH

Suppose *you* take 'em outside and walk 'em around! I'm sick of having kids whistle at me.

EILEEN

You mean they don't understand any English at all?

110

RUTH

Yes—three words—American dance—conga!


A CADET

Conga! Da-da-da-da-da-da!
(*He starts to dance. The others restrain him hastily.*)


RUTH

Listen boys—Go! Leave! Good-bye!
(*She waves.* ADMIRALS *return wave, mutter happily "Goo-bye."* RUTH *turns back to* EILEEN, *shrugs and steps back to her.*)


EILEEN

What did you bring them here for?


RUTH

Bring them! They've been on my tail ever since I left the Brooklyn Navy Yard.

EILEEN

What do they want anyway?


RUTH

What do you *think* they want?


EILEEN

Oh, my God! We've got to get them out of here! Make them go, Ruth!

RUTH

Suppose you take a crack at it.

III

EILEEN
(*Sweetly*)
Look, boys. Go back to your boat. Boat!
(*She salutes.* ADMIRALS *snap to attention, salute in return.*)


RUTH
Admiral Sherwood, I presume.
(*They drop salute.*)


EILEEN
Boys—go way—please!
(*Supplicating—her arms extended—they take it wrongly
—howl and step forward after her.* EILEEN *shrieks, runs
back to* RUTH.)

RUTH
That's fine.

EILEEN
Gee, they can't be *that* dumb.


RUTH
They're *not* that dumb.


EILEEN
What are we going to do?


RUTH
I've tried everything. I guess, Eileen, we'll just have to stand
here grinning at each other.
(*She turns to* ADMIRALS *and grins broadly.* ADMIRALS *all
grin back. She motions helplessly, steps back in to*
EILEEN.)

###### EILEEN

Look—boys—sick! Very sick! (*Sits on bench—leans all the way back—on "bed"*) Bed! Bed!

> (*The* ADMIRALS *rush in at her.* EILEEN *jumps up, shrieks, makes a dash for* RUTH, *swings behind her for protection.*)

###### RUTH

For God's sake, don't let 'em get any wrong ideas!

###### EILEEN

You brought them here! The least you can do is help me get rid of them! (*The* ADMIRALS *start to toss coins*) What are they tossing for?

###### RUTH

I don't know, but I've got a hunch it's not me!

> (*An* ADMIRAL *goes to them gravely.*)

###### FIRST ADMIRAL
> (*Bowing*)

Senorita, eu tive e grande prazer de a ganhar esta noite.

###### RUTH

Isn't it a romantic language?

###### EILEEN

No understando—no spikee Portuguese—

###### FIRST CADET

American dance—Conga!

> (*He turns* EILEEN, *takes her by the wrist and other*

ADMIRALS *join in.* RUTH *dances backwards, in front of* EILEEN.)

RUTH

Eileen, we've got to get them out of here.
(*There is a blast from below. The* ADMIRALS *stop and cross themselves in fear.*)

EILEEN

Run—Earthquake!
(EILEEN *runs to doorway, hides against it, to see if* AD-MIRALS *disperse.* ADMIRALS *make for the stairway.* WAIT-ERS *and* CHEF *enter from* NINO'S. *Passers-by stop on the street to stare down. The* ADMIRALS *stop on steps, look at one another and laugh.*)

RUTH

What a performance! Helen Hayes couldn't have done bet-ter. Listen, I've got an idea. Lead 'em out through the alley and lose them on the street!

EILEEN

Okay, but tell Bob I'll be right back.

RUTH

Bob?

EILEEN

Yes, I'm having dinner with him. (*To* ADMIRALS) Come on, boys—Conga!
(*Boys make line.* EILEEN *exits into alley,* ADMIRALS *Con-gaing after her.* RUTH *stares off unhappily. The* WAITERS *from* NINO'S *start to Conga gaily.* BAKER *enters from street*

*and looks strangely at* CHEF *and two* WAITERS *in Conga line. He goes to* RUTH.)

### BAKER

Ruth, what's going on?

### RUTH

(*Looks at him and starts to Conga by herself*)
Oh, a few friends dropped in. We're losing our inhibitions!
(*She grabs piece of celery from* WAITER, *puts it between her teeth, starts to Conga wildly. She starts her own line, with* CHEF, *and* WAITERS *following. As they go off they are met by* EILEEN *coming back, still followed by the* ADMIRALS *and a huge snake line of mixed* VILLAGERS. RUTH *backs away, in dismay.*)

### EILEEN

I couldn't lose them!
(MRS. WADE *comes on with* LONIGAN *and another cop. Whistles are blown by* LONIGAN. *Meanwhile* RUTH *has been hoisted up in the air by* ADMIRALS. COP *makes a grab for* EILEEN, *picks her up. She turns in the air, kicks* LONIGAN *in the stomach. He drags her off.* MRS. WADE *has made for the stairs and stands on the first landing, motioning wildly.* RUTH *gets down from her perch and desperately starts to run across after* EILEEN. *She is grabbed by one of the* ADMIRALS, *carried, slid back and overhead by the* ADMIRALS. BAKER *runs after* EILEEN *as* RUTH *is conga-ed aloft amidst a swirl of village figures, all caught up in the frenzy of the Conga rhythm.*)

(*Curtain*)

# ACT TWO

# ACT TWO

## SCENE I

THE CHRISTOPHER STREET STATION HOUSE. *A couple of* COPS *are talking as* WRECK *and* HELEN *enter.* WRECK *is carrying a dress of* EILEEN'S.

COP

Hey, what are you doing in here?

HELEN

Good morning.

WRECK

Can we see Miss Sherwood, please?

COP

What do you think this is, the Barbizon Plaza? Miss Who?

HELEN

Eileen Sherwood.

COP

Eileen? Why didn't you say so? (*Calls off stage*) Oh, Eileen!

EILEEN

(*Off stage*)

Yes? What is it, Dennis? (*Enters. Sees* WRECK *and* HELEN. *She is carrying a malted milk*) Oh, hello, Wreck—Helen—

WRECK

Hi, Eileen!

HELEN

The Wreck ironed this dress especially. He thought you'd want to look fresh in court.

EILEEN

(*Taking dress*)

Oh, thanks, Wreck. That's awfully sweet of you. (*To* COP) Dennis—

COP

Yeah, Eileen.

EILEEN

(*Hands dress to him*)

Dennis, would you mind hanging this up in my cell?

COP

Sure, Eileen.

(*He goes off, holding dress carefully over arm.* SECOND COP *enters.*)

SECOND COP

Oh, Eileen.

EILEEN

Yes, Dan—

SECOND COP

There's a man on the phone—wants to talk to you—says it's important.

EILEEN

Who is it, Dan?

SECOND COP

Chick Clark. Says he knows you.

120

EILEEN

(*Angrily*)

You tell Mr. Clark I'm not in to him and hang up on him if he ever calls again!

SECOND COP

Leave it to me, Eileen.
(*He pats her shoulder and goes.*)

HELEN

(*To* WRECK)

And we were worried about her!

EILEEN

Oh, I'm fine. How are you two getting along?

WRECK

Pretty good. If everything works out all right we'll be leavin' on our honeymoon next week.

EILEEN

Congratulations! Are you getting married?

HELEN

We decided not to wait for the football season.

WRECK

Yeah. Ya see, Helen went to the doctor—

HELEN

(*Turns to him*)

Wreck!

**WRECK**

Anyway, the decision was taken out of our hands.

**HELEN**

Yes, we've got a plan and Appopolous is puttin' up all the dough.

**EILEEN**

Appopolous!

**HELEN**

Yes, as soon as I collect my dowry, he'll get his back rent.

**EILEEN**

Good luck. I hope you'll be very happy.

**WRECK**

Well, we've been happy so far—I don't see why marriage should change it.

(*They go off.*)

**EILEEN**

(*To* COP)

And to think I was always afraid of being arrested!

**THIRD COP**

Ah, that Lonigan's a bum sport— Just because you kicked him!

**FOURTH COP**

(*Enters*)

Eileen, there's a girl outside—claims she's your sister—

**EILEEN**

Ruth? Send her in please!

(COP *waves* RUTH *on.*)

122

RUTH

(*Embracing* EILEEN *tearfully*)

Eileen! Oh, you poor kid!

EILEEN

(*Startled*)

What happened?

RUTH

What do you mean, what happened? This!

EILEEN

Oh— Oh, yes—this!

RUTH

I've been all over New York, trying to raise your bail—
Maybe I'd better send a wire to Dad.

EILEEN

Gee, don't do that! He'll ask a lot of foolish questions—

RUTH

Well, we've got to do something.

EILEEN

I'm all right! Everybody's very sweet to me here!

FIRST COP

(*Enters*)

Phone, Eileen.

EILEEN

Who is it, Dennis?

FIRST COP

A Mr. Lippencott. He'd like to know when he can call on you.

EILEEN
(*Thoughtfully*)
Tell him—any time before five.

RUTH
(*Stares*)
Tell me, Eileen, how many do you keep in help here?

EILEEN
Huh?

RUTH
I just love the way you've done this place. Well, I've got to get to work!

EILEEN
Where?

RUTH
The Village Vortex. Your old pal Speedy Valenti gave me a job.

EILEEN
Doing what?

RUTH
(*Hesitates*)
Well, it pays—

FOURTH COP
(*Enters*)
Eileen, there's a gentleman to see you.
(*Hands* EILEEN *a business card.*)

EILEEN

(*Reading*)

Robert Baker! Why, it's *Bob*! Send him in, please.

RUTH

(*Turning unhappily*)

I'd better go.

BAKER

(*Enters*)

How are you, Eileen? (*Turns to* RUTH) Oh, hello, Ruth—

RUTH

(*Flatly*)

Hello.

BAKER

What happened to you, Ruth? I looked for you after the patrol wagon left.

RUTH

I went for a walk—had a lot of things to think over—

BAKER

You do look a little tired.

RUTH

I am. I didn't sleep all night—(*To* EILEEN)—worrying about *you*— So I sat at that typewriter and wrote the story about the Brazilian Admirals. It's a darn good story—I know it is! I took your advice—a slice of my own life—and I sent it to Chick's city editor—Mr. Bains. (*Sadly*) But they didn't print it, so I guess it wasn't so good after all—

**BAKER**

Want *me* to read it?

**RUTH**

If you feel up to it—(*To* EILEEN) Sorry to eat and run, darling—but I've got to get to work!
(*Kisses her.*)

**BAKER**
(*To* RUTH)
Did you get a job? What are you doing?

**RUTH**

Oh, it's in the advertising game. (*Looks at wrist watch*) Cocktail time, already? Well, I've got to fly! 'Bye, dear—lovely party—such fun! *Do* ask me again!
(*She hurries off.*)

**EILEEN**

Poor Ruth! I didn't have the heart to tell her. There isn't any Mr. Bains—

**BAKER**

What?

**EILEEN**

It was all a big lie! That Chick Clark's an utter snake! Oh, if I could only get out of here, I'd—

**BAKER**

Look, I'm working on this. I'm going to get you out. I just tried to pay your fine, but they haven't set it yet.

**EILEEN**

Why not?

126

BAKER

I don't know. Washington wants them to hold you here.

EILEEN

(*Gasps*)

Washington—D.C.?

BAKER

Something about Pan-American relations.

EILEEN

Oh, my God!

BAKER

But don't worry—I'm working on this.

FOURTH COP

(*Entering, making a butler's announcement*)
Frank Lippencott.

EILEEN

Send him in, Pat.

BAKER

I'm going over to see the Brazilian Consul right now.
(*He starts out.* FRANK *enters. They collide.* FRANK *carries small box.*)

FRANK

Oops! Sorry—(BAKER *exits irritatedly.* FRANK *combs his hair quickly*) Gee, this is the first time I was ever in a police station.

EILEEN

It's *my* first time, too.

LIPPENCOTT

I brought you an electric fan we're running. I thought it
would cool off your cell.

(*Holds box out to her.*)

EILEEN

Isn't that thoughtful!

LIPPENCOTT

It's given away free with every purchase over five dollars.

EILEEN

Thanks.

FRANK
(*Opening box*)

Somebody forgot it.

EILEEN

You're sweet.

FRANK
(*Removing small rubber fan from box*)

You'd be surprised at the breeze that little thing gives off—
(*He spins blade, holds it up to* EILEEN's *face*) Everybody in the
store's got a cold.

(*He hands her fan.* FOURTH COP *enters.*)

EILEEN
(*To* COP)

Pat, would you mind putting these things in my cell?

(*She gets suitcase, hands it to* ANDERSON.)

FOURTH COP

Yes, sure.

EILEEN

Thank you.
(FOURTH COP *exits.*)

FRANK

Eileen, I want to ask you something—it's the most important decision I ever made in my life—

EILEEN

Frank, you're a very sweet boy, and I'm fond of you, but I'm really not thinking of getting married.

FRANK

No, neither am I.

EILEEN

You're not?

FRANK

No.

EILEEN

Then what are you thinking of?

FRANK

Listen, Eileen—I suddenly realize I've been wasting my life—

EILEEN

What are you talking about?

FRANK

You know—*Life*—the way you girls live it—free to follow your natural bent whatever it is—

EILEEN

What's all that got to do with me?

FRANK

Don't you see? We'd have our freedom and we'd have each other. I thought we could have a sort of ideal relationship, like Helen and The Wreck—

EILEEN
(*Aghast*)

Timothy!

FRANK

Gee, Eileen, it was only an idea!

EILEEN

Show this gentleman out—and don't ever let him in here again!

(*He goes quickly. As he passes* COP, COP *stamps his foot menacingly.* FRANK *quickens speed, exits.*)

FIFTH COP
(*Enters excitedly*)

Eileen! Did you see the paper?

EILEEN

No.

FIFTH COP

Look! You're in it!

FIRST COP
(*Enters*)

Eileen's in the papers.

FIFTH COP

A big story! Your picture and everything!

EILEEN

Oh, for goodness sakes!

FOURTH COP
(*Comes in with others*)
Hey! That's me! Not bad, huh?

FIRST COP

That jerk Lonigan has his back to the camera! He'll fry!

SECOND COP

Look, Lonigan!
(LONIGAN *enters.*)

FOURTH COP

You're famous, Eileen!

EILEEN

Do you think so? I wonder if Mr. Valenti saw it? (*To* LON-
IGAN) Oh, John, it's on your beat. Would you do me a great
favor? Would you take this over to the Village Vortex and
show it to Speedy Valenti personally?

THIRD COP

He'd better!

LONIGAN

Sure, Eileen. I'll serve it on him!

131

THIRD COP

Atta boy, John! (*To* EILEEN *as music begins*) Oh, Eileen, you brought a breath of the old country into the station house.

FOURTH COP

(*In greatly exaggerated Irish brogue*)
Sure and I been feelin' twice as Irish since you came into our lives.
(*Singing à la John McCormack*)

Take it from me,
In Dublin's fair city
There's none half so pretty
As pretty Eileen.

Take it from me,
The Mayor of Shannon
Would shoot off a cannon
And crown ye the queen.

ALL

Darlin' Eileen,
Darlin' Eileen,
Fairest colleen that iver I've seen.
And it's oh I wish I were back in the land of the green
With my darlin' Eileen.

FIRST COP

I've seen them all—
There's Bridget and Sheila

# WONDERFUL TOWN

SECOND COP

There's Kate and Deli—lah
And Moll and Maureen.

THIRD COP

I've seen them all—
Not one can compete with—

FIRST COP

Or share the same street with
My darlin' Eileen.

ALL

Darlin' Eileen— Darlin' Eileen,
Fairest colleen
That iver I've seen—
And it's oh I wish I were back
In the land of the green
With my darlin' Eileen.
(*They dance a lusty jig of the Old Country, lumbering
but full of life, all vying for her attention.*)

EILEEN

(*Somewhat apprehensive, cutting them off*)
Listen, my lads,
I've something to tell you
I hope won't impel you to cry and to keen.
Mother's a Swede and Father's a Scot—
And so Irish I'm not— And I never have been—

ALL

(*They will not hear of this*)
Hush you, Eileen! Hush you, Eileen!

133

Fairest colleen that iver I've seen.
Don't you hand us none of that blarney—
You come from Killarney,
You're Irish, Eileen!

> (*The dance resumes and ends in a "hats-off" salute to the girl of their dreams,* EILEEN.)

(*Blackout*)

# ACT TWO

## SCENE II

THE STREET. AT RISE: MRS. WADE *sitting on a camp stool, posing;* APPOPOLOUS *painting her picture.*

MRS. WADE

May I look?

APPOPOLOUS

No, it's still an embryo. Let it kick and breathe first. As a model you will be immortalized like Van Gogh's herring!

(*The* WRECK *and* HELEN *enter.* HELEN *pushes him in. He wears navy-blue suit, carries hat. She motions to his head. He puts hat on, starts to step in.* HELEN *grabs him, motions to glasses. He puts bone glasses on.* HELEN *goes off as* WRECK *crosses to* APPOPOLOUS *and looks over his shoulder at canvas.*)

WRECK

Bravo! Magnificent! You've captured the inner soul of this lovely lady!

APPOPOLOUS

Thank you, Mr. Loomis. (MRS. WADE *looks at* WRECK) That's indeed a compliment coming from a great collector like you!

WRECK

Not at all!

APPOPOLOUS

May I present you? Mr. Loomis—Mrs. Wade—

MRS. WADE

Pleased to meet you.

WRECK

(*Removing his hat*)

I'm delighted. Maestro, I'd like to add this to my collection. Is it for sale?

APPOPOLOUS

Sorry! I'm presenting this to Mrs. Wade!

(HELEN *enters.*)

HELEN

Hello, Mother.

MRS. WADE

Oh, Helen. Come here a moment! I want you to meet someone! This is my daughter, Helen—Mr. Loomis.

WRECK

Daughter? You're spoofing! You look more like sisters!

HELEN

I'm very pleased to meet you, Mr. Loomis.

WRECK

Likewise, I'm sure! Well, this is delightful! May I invite you all to tea at the Purple Cow?

MRS. WADE

Oh.

**APPOPOLOUS**

Fine! You young people go along, and we'll join you in a minute.

(WRECK *smiles, offers his arm to* HELEN. *She takes it.*)

**HELEN**

Do you get down to the Village very often, Mr. Loomis?

(*They go off.*)

**MRS. WADE**

Who *is* he?

**APPOPOLOUS**

He comes from a very aristocratic family from Trenton Tech.

(APPOPOLOUS *and* MRS. WADE *go off.* RUTH *enters with* MAN *with sign. As passers-by come on, they turn on electric signs reading "*VORTEX*" across their chests.*)

**RUTH**
(*To* MAN)

I feel like a damn fool!

**MAN**
(*Shrugs*)

It's a living.

(*Another couple passes by.* RUTH *and* MAN *turn on signs.*)

**VILLAGER**

You ever been there?

**SECOND VILLAGER**

Yeah, last night.

(*They go off.*)

RUTH

I'm really a writer, you know.

MAN

I'm really an architect, but they haven't built anything since the Empire State Building.

RUTH

(*Spotting someone off stage*)

Oh, this is awful!

MAN

What's the matter?

RUTH

Here comes someone I know! Please, don't light up!

MAN

Sure! Don't worry about it.

(RUTH *turns, faces* MAN, *simulates fixing his tie.* BAKER *enters. After he has passed* RUTH, *she and* MAN *turn and stroll off.* BAKER *recognizes* RUTH, *turns.*)

BAKER

*Ruth!*

RUTH

(*Turns, brightly*)

Oh, hello there!

(*Hastily she folds her arms across the electric sign.*)

BAKER

Well, this is a surprise! Going out?

RUTH

Yes, we are—to the opera. Mr. Stevens, I'd like you to meet Mr. Baker. Mr. Stevens is in Washington with the Reconstruction Finance Corporation.

(*They shake.*)

BAKER

(*To* RUTH)

I read your piece about the Brazilian Navy. Now that's the idea! It's fine!

RUTH

Really? No repressions? No inhibitions?

BAKER

No, just good clean fun. I gave it to the boss to read. I'm sure he'll go for it.

RUTH

Oh, thank you, Bob. That's wonderful of you!

(VALENTI *enters.*)

MAN

(*To* RUTH)

Hey, Ruth, we're going to be late for the opera!

RUTH

Just a minute, please. This is important!

MAN

So is this! More important!

(*Points to* VALENTI.)

VALENTI

What's going on here? Get on the ball! (MAN *snaps light on,*

BAKER *stares in wonder.* RUTH *looks at him unhappily*.) Well? What's with you, sister—run out of juice?

### RUTH
*(Lights up and smiles feebly at* BAKER*)*
Well, it's a healthy job. Keeps me out in the air!

### BAKER
*(Pats her arm reassuringly)*
Good girl.
*(He smiles at her and goes off.)*

### VALENTI
No socializing on my time. *(Goes to* MAN*)* Here's a pitch. You take Sheridan Square. *(Hands flyer to* MAN *who exits and then hands her flyer)* Here's your spiel—come on, get a mob around you. Make with the pitch. Get hep.
*(*VALENTI *exits.)*

### RUTH
*(Tentatively)*
Yes, sir—hep. *(Reading from flyer—very tentatively to passers-by)* Step up—step up—*(Embarrassed)* Get hep—get hep—*(Suddenly, loudly)*
Step up!
*(Rhythm starts in orchestra.* RUTH *still reading from flyer, giving a very "square" rendition.)*
Step up! Step up!
Get hep! Get hep!
*(While she reads a crowd of '30's hepcats gathers around her.)*
Come on down to the Village Vortex

Home of the new jazz rage—Swing!
Rock and roll to the beat beat beat
Of Speedy Valenti and his krazy kats!
  (*Sings falteringly*)
Swing! Dig the rhythm!
Swing! Dig the message!
The jive is jumpin' and the music goes around and around—
Whoa-ho—!
Goes around and around—
Cat, make it solid!
Cat, make it groovy!
You gotta get your seafood, Mama, your favorite dish is fish,
It's your favorite dish.
Don't be square,
Rock right out of that rockin' chair;
Truck on down and let down your hair;
Breathe that barrel-house air!
The Village Vortex!
Swing! Dig the rhythm!
Swing! Dig the message!
The jive is jumpin' and the music goes around and around—
Get full of foory-a-ka-sa-ke,
Get full of the sound of swing,
The solid, jivy, groovy sound of swing!

### HEPCATS
  (*Singing and showing* RUTH *how to get hep*)
Swing! Dig the rhythm!
Swing! Dig the message!
The jive is jumpin' and the music goes around and around—
Whoa-ho—!

RUTH

*(Getting the idea)*

Oh!

VILLAGERS

Cat, make it solid!
Cat, make it groovy!
You gotta get your seafood, Mama;
Your favorite dish is fish—

RUTH

*(Catching on still more and beginning to enjoy it)*
Oh!

VILLAGERS

Don't be square,
Rock right out of that rockin' chair;
Truck on down and let down your hair;
Breathe that barrel-house air—
You gotta get with the whoa-ho-de-ho!

RUTH

*(Answering Cab Calloway fashion)*
Whoa-ho-de-ho.

VILLAGERS

The gut-gut-bucket.

RUTH

The gut-gut-bucket.

VILLAGERS

Skid-dle-ee-oh-day!

RUTH

Skid-dle-ee-oh-day!

142

VILLAGERS

Heedle heedle heedle.

RUTH

Heedle heedle heedle.

VILLAGERS

Well, all right then, cats!

RUTH

Well, all right then, cats!

VILLAGERS

Yes, yes, baby I know!

RUTH

*(By this time* RUTH *is in a glaze-eyed hypnotic trance, having got the message and as the hepcats gather around her she delivers patter in a husky dreamlike monotone)*

Well, yes yes, baby, I know!

That old man Mose

Kicked the bucket,

The old oaken bucket that hung in the well—

Well, well, well, baby, I know—

No no; was it red?

No no no! Was it green green—

Green is the color of my true love's hair—

Hair-breadth Harry with the floy floy doy

Floy doy, floy doy, floy doy, hoy!

Hoy dre(h)eamt hoy dwe(h)elt in ma(h)arble halls—

Well that ends well, well, well—

Baby I know—No, no,

Was it green?

No no no

Was it red sails in the sunset callin' me me me

You good for nothin'

Mi-mi mi-mi
Me Tarzan, you Jane,
Swingin' in the trees,
Swingin' in the trees,
Swingin' in the trees—

(*This develops into an abandoned dance in which* RUTH *not only joins but finally leads the hepcats to a "sent" finish.*)

VILLAGERS

Swing—swing—swing—swing—swing—swing
Swing—Chu-chu-chu chu-chu-chu chu-chu-chu-chu
Swing—Chu-chu-chu chu-chu-chu chu-chu-chu-chu
Swing—Chu-chu-chu chu-chu-chu chu-chu-chu-chu


RUTH

Floy-doy floy-doy floy-doy hoy!


VILLAGERS

Sh-sh-sh.

RUTH

Gesundheit.

VILLAGERS

Thanks.

RUTH

You're welcome.

VILLAGERS

Whoa!
(*Motioning to* RUTH)
Come on, Jackson, you're getting hep.

Come on, Jackson, you're getting hep.
Come on, Jackson, you're getting hep.

RUTH

I want my favorite dish.

VILLAGERS

Fish.

RUTH

Gesundheit.

VILLAGERS

Thanks.

RUTH

It's nothing!

VILLAGERS

Solid, groovy, jivy sound of swing—

FIRST MAN

Ah—do it.

SECOND MAN

Solid, Jackson.

FIRST GIRL

Seafood, Mama.

SECOND GIRL

(*A long banshee wail*)

VILLAGERS

Go go go—yah—
Swing—oh swing it,
Swing—oh swing it.

(*The dance continues, as the* VILLAGERS *back out, followed by* RUTH *in a trance.*)

RUTH

(*In a hoarse, hypnotic whisper*)

Swing— Swing
Green, no—red, no
Me Tarzan— No, no, no
That old man Mose
He kicked that bucket
Down in the well—well, well, well
My favorite dish
Ahhh—fish!

VILLAGERS

Gesundheit.

RUTH

Thank you.

VILLAGERS

You're welcome.

RUTH

(*Her hands before her, mesmerized. Walks off in a trance*)
Swing—swing—swing—swing—swing—
(*She disappears.*)

(*Blackout*)

# ACT TWO

## Scene III

THE STUDIO. AT RISE: *Stage empty. Through window,* VIOLET's *legs pass by, then man's legs.* VIOLET *stops, half turns. Man comes back and joins her. They stand, then go off together.*

(*During this scene,* APPOPOLOUS *enters carrying blue-green painting. He steps on bed, looks about for something to stand on, picks up manuscripts off typewriter next to bed, and slips one under each foot. He hangs painting, jumps down, takes valise from under* RUTH's *bed, puts it on top of bed, takes typewriter from chair next to bed, puts it on bed, gets books and candlesticks off and puts them on bed.* RUTH *enters from bathroom in her slip. She screams.*)

RUTH

Ah! What are you doing with my things?
(*She takes robe from bathroom and slips it on.*)

APPOPOLOUS

You're being dispossessed! I only hope your sister has sense enough to give the wrong address!

RUTH

Yes, imagine what bad publicity could do to this dump!

APPOPOLOUS

(*Pointing to painting*)
I found my masterpiece in Denny's. For the frame, two dol-

147

lars—for my painting, nothing! At six o'clock your current occupancy terminates! (*Knock on door*) Remember! If you're not out by the stroke of six, you'll find your belongings in the street!

> (*He goes out through kitchen. There is another knock on the door.*)

RUTH

Come in. (BAKER *enters*) Oh, Bob—

BAKER
(*Sadly*)

Oh, hello, Ruth.

RUTH

What's the matter?

BAKER
(*Angrily*)

All I can say is, he wouldn't know a good story if he read one!

RUTH

Who?

BAKER

His Highness—king of the editors—pompous ass.
(APPOPOLOUS *sticks head in from kitchen door.*)

APPOPOLOUS

Fifteen minutes!
(*Disappears again.*)

BAKER

What was *that*?

148

RUTH

Bulova Watch Time.

BAKER

I'm sorry, Ruth. He just didn't like it.

RUTH

(*Shrugs*)

Well, maybe it wasn't any good.

BAKER

It's just one man's opinion.

RUTH

That's enough.

BAKER

I still think it's a hell of a good story and I'm going to tell him so!

RUTH

Please, Bob, don't get into any trouble on my account.

BAKER

This has nothing to do with you. It's a matter of principle. Either I know my business or I don't!

RUTH

(*Nods slowly*)

I see.

(EILEEN *enters from street with* LONIGAN, *who is carrying her suitcase.*)

EILEEN

Ruth!

RUTH
(*Embracing her*)
Eileen! Darling, you're out! How did it happen?

EILEEN
Bob fixed everything. Thanks, Bob.
(CHICK CLARK *appears at window.*)

CHICK
Hello, kids.

EILEEN
Chick Clark! You get away from there, you big snake!

CHICK
Now wait a minute, Eileen! Gimme a chance.

EILEEN
You had enough chances!

RUTH
What are you talking about?

EILEEN
Ruth, when I tell you what he did—

CHICK
Wait! The city editor's read your Brazilian story and he thinks it's the absolute nuts!

RUTH
(*Going to window. Hopefully*)
He does?

150

EILEEN

Don't believe him, Ruth! He's the biggest liar!

CHICK

Go ahead—call him up! Mr. Wilson! You know the number!

RUTH

Wilson? I thought his name was Bains?

EILEEN

You see, Ruth, he's lying again! (*To* LONIGAN) John, will you do me a great favor and chase him away from there?

LONIGAN

Glad to!
(*He runs out.*)

CHICK

Now wait a minute, Eileen. You're gonna louse it up! Tell her to call Mr. Wilson—the city editor—I keep tellin' her all the time!

(CHICK *runs off as* LONIGAN *stops at window.*)

LONIGAN

(*Kneels down, offering her whistle*)
Oh, Eileen, if anything else happens, here's a police whistle.

EILEEN

(*Taking whistle*)
Thanks, John.
(LONIGAN *goes.*)

RUTH

Next week you'll have your own hook and ladder.


APPOPOLOUS

(*Sticking head through kitchen*)

Five minutes!

EILEEN

What's that about?

RUTH

We're being dispossessed.


BAKER

Where are you going?

RUTH

(*Hands* EILEEN *suitcase*)

I don't know—home, I guess.


EILEEN

We can't. What would people say?


RUTH

"Did you hear the dirt about those Sherwood girls? On account of them, we almost lost the Naval Base in Brazil."


BAKER

It's ridiculous. You can't go home now.


RUTH

But, Bob—

152

BAKER

I haven't time to argue about it. (*Looks at his watch*) I've got to get up to the office before His Highness leaves. He wants to see me—and I want to see him a damn sight more! (*Goes to door*) Now I want you to promise me you'll wait right here till I get back.

RUTH

You'd better hurry, or you may find us out in the street.

BAKER

Half an hour. Top.
(*He's off.*)

EILEEN

Isn't he nice?

RUTH

(*Sits on bed wearily*)
Um—You like him a lot, don't you, Eileen?

EILEEN

You know, Ruth, he's the first boy I've ever met who really seemed to care what happened to me—how I got along and everything.

RUTH

Yes, I know. (*Shrugs*) I guess it doesn't make any difference now anyway—

EILEEN

What?

RUTH

(*Close to tears*)
I said we're going home—so it doesn't matter about Bob.

EILEEN

(*Goes slowly to* RUTH, *putting an arm around her*)
Gee, Ruth, I never dreamed. You mean you like him too?

RUTH

Strange as it may seem—

EILEEN

Well, why didn't you say anything?

RUTH

What was there to say?

EILEEN

After all—you're my sister.

RUTH

(*Smiles at her through her tears*)
That's the side of you that makes everything else seem worthwhile.

EILEEN

Gee, Ruth—I'm sorry we ever came here.
(*Puts her head on* RUTH's *shoulder.*)

BOTH

Why, oh why, oh why—oh
Why did we ever leave Ohio?
Why did we wander to find what lies yonder
When life was so cozy at home?

Wond'ring while we wander,
Why did we fly,

154

Why did we roam—
Oh, why oh why oh
Did we leave Ohio?
Maybe we'd better go home.
    (APPOPOLOUS *enters.*)


APPOPOLOUS

Time's up! Your occupancy is officially terminated.


RUTH

We're not ready yet.
    (VALENTI *enters.*)


VALENTI

Skeet—skat—skattle-ee-o-do! (*He carries newspaper*) Where is she? I know it! I said it! I meant it! You hit me in my weak spot—(*Slaps newspaper*) Right on the front page!


EILEEN

Oh, Mr. Valenti! How did you like it?


RUTH
(*Takes newspaper, reading headline*)
Like what? "Beautiful Blonde Bombshell Sinks Brazilian Navy." Oh, my—now we *can't* go home!


VALENTI
(*To* EILEEN)
You're in the groove, babe! I'm gonna put you in my saloon for an audition tonight. If you make good, I'll sign you!

EILEEN

Oh, Mr. Valenti! Speedy! That's wonderful! (*To* RUTH)
Ruth, it's a job! My first break in the theatre.
(*They embrace.*)

APPOPOLOUS

Girls, I'm gonna extend your time until six o'clock tomorrow
morning. Make good and you can be with me for life!
(*He goes.*)

VALENTI

(*To* EILEEN)

Get over there right away!

EILEEN

Yes, yes. (*To* RUTH) Only what about Bob?

RUTH

We'll leave a note on the door.

EILEEN

What'll I wear, Mr. Valenti?

VALENTI

I'll lend you a dress. I'll lend your sister one too—(RUTH *looks
up*)—and without the lights. Now get over there. (*Goes to
door*) What are you gonna sing, Babe?

EILEEN

Ruth, remember the song we always used to do at the Kiwanis Club? The Wrong Note Rag?

156

RUTH

Oh, yes—do that one.

VALENTI

It's an oldie, but you'll never know it when I back you up with the licorice stick.

RUTH

The what?

VALENTI

My clarinet. Then for an encore— Tell me, kid—did you ever take 'em off?

EILEEN

What?

VALENTI

You know, *strip?*

RUTH

My sister doesn't strip.

VALENTI

Too bad. We're always looking for new faces!

(*Blackout*)

# ACT TWO

## Scene IV

The street *in front of the* vortex. At rise: helen *and* wreck *enter, followed by* mrs. wade *and* appopolous.

HELEN

That was a lovely dinner, Mr. Loomis!

APPOPOLOUS

(*Grimly*)

Yes, he's certainly a fine host—everything out of season!

WRECK

Why not? You only live once!

APPOPOLOUS

Only the champagne I didn't expect!

MRS. WADE

It's good, though! Hit the spot!

WRECK

There! You see, Maestro?

HELEN

Come on! Let's get a good table!

158

WRECK

Yeah.
(*They go off.* APPOPOLOUS *takes* MRS. WADE'S *arm*.)

APPOPOLOUS

One moment, Ella. They make a lovely couple, don't they?

MRS. WADE

Yes! Do you think his intentions are serious?

APPOPOLOUS

I'll vouch for it.

MRS. WADE

Did you notice he was holding Helen's hand under the table?
My, I'd love to see my Helen settled down!

APPOPOLOUS

(*Offers his arm*)
Don't worry, Ella, she'll be settled down and you'll be a
grandmother before you expect it!
(*They go off.* RUTH *and* EILEEN *hurry on*.)

EILEEN

Oh, dear, I'm so frightened!

RUTH

Now look, Eileen, you're not afraid of anything. I know you
better than that!

EILEEN

You do?
(CHICK CLARK *runs on*.)

CHICK

Hey, kids! I gotta talk to you!

EILEEN

Chick Clark, for the last time, stop annoying us!

CHICK

I tell ya! I got it all fixed!

EILEEN

All right! You asked for it—now you're going to get it!
(*She puts whistle, attached to her wrist, to her lips and
blows several times.*)

CHICK

What are you doin'? Ya crazy!
(LONIGAN *dashes on,* CHICK *runs off.* EILEEN *points in*
CHICK's *direction.* LONIGAN *follows him off.*)

RUTH

Eileen, are you sure you're doing the right thing?

EILEEN

Some day I'll tell you the truth about Mr. Chick Clark!
(*Clutches her stomach*) Oh, gee—I'm all upset again! I feel
nauseous!

RUTH

You do? Well, look—walk up and down in the air—and
breathe deeply— That's right. I'll take your case and get you
some black coffee.
(*She goes off.*)

EILEEN

Oh, thanks, Ruth.
(BAKER *enters with piece of paper*.)

BAKER

Eileen—I found your note—this is wonderful news!
(*Takes her hands*.)

EILEEN

Thanks, Bob.

BAKER

Now, no more of that nonsense about going home.

EILEEN

Oh, no. No.

BAKER

And I'll get something for Ruth—just as soon as I land a job myself.

EILEEN

Job! What happened?

BAKER

Well, I left the *Manhatter*—uh—a difference of opinion—

EILEEN

Oh, Bob—I'm awfully sorry— But I think it's wonderful that you feel that way about Ruth!

BAKER

Well, I'm very fond of her—

161

**EILEEN**

Fond? It must be more than that if you got fired on her account.

**BAKER**

I left on a matter of principle!

**EILEEN**

Principle! Don't play dumb!

**BAKER**

Dumb?

**EILEEN**

Well, you must be if you don't know what's going on in your own mind!

**BAKER**

Will you please tell me what's going on in my mind?

**EILEEN**

I suppose you don't know why you fought with your editor about Ruth's story—or why you're picking a fight with me right now! Poor Bob—you're in love with Ruth and you don't even know it!
(*Sings.*)
It's love! It's love!

**BAKER**
(*Sings*)

Come on now— Let's drop it.

**EILEEN**

It's love! It's love!
And nothing can stop it.

BAKER

You're a silly girl— It's a sign of youth.


EILEEN

(*Shakes head*)

You're a silly boy— You're in love with Ruth.
It's love! It's love!
Come on now— Just try it.


BAKER

(*Tentatively*)

It's love! It's love!

EILEEN

Don't try to deny it,
I know the signs,
I know it when I see it—
So just face it,
Just say it.


BAKER

It's love,
It's love,
    (BAKER *sings*—BIG.)
It's love!!
    (EILEEN *watches him a moment—then exits.*)
Maybe— It's love! It's love!
    (*As the realization grows.*)
Well, who would have thought it
If this is love,
Then why have I fought it?
What a way to feel—

I could touch the sky.
What a way to feel—
I'm a different guy!

It's love, at last,
I've someone to cheer for—
It's love, at last,
I've learned what we're here for—
I've heard it said,
"You'll know it when you see it."
Well, I see it—I know it—
It's Love!
    (*Exits happily*.)

# ACT TWO

## Scene V

THE VILLAGE VORTEX, *a surrealistic night club, hung with paintings from every artist who couldn't pay his tab, and dominated by a huge revolving mobile, hung from the ceiling.* VALENTI *leads the band with his clarinet as the crowd dances a slow, writhing jitterbug, packed tightly together like anchovies.*

### VALENTI
(*As dance ends and a bedlam of sound from the crowd bubbles up*)

Settle down! Settle down!

> (WRECK *has opened bottle of champagne. Rises with bottle and glass.*)

### WRECK

Folks, here's a toast to my future mother-in-law. Long may she wave!

### PATRON
(*From balcony*)

Sit down, you bum!

> (WRECK *starts to remove his coat and glasses, shakes an angry fist at patron.*)

### HELEN
(*To* WRECK)

Please, Mr. Loomis—

> (WRECK *subsides.*)

165

**VALENTI**

Cat and Gates! You've read about her, you've talked about her! Now here she is in person, fresh from a cellar in Christopher Street—Miss Eileen Sherwood!

(RUTH *and* EILEEN *enter.* RUTH *is pushing* EILEEN, *fixing her hair at the last minute.*)

Give the little girl a great big hand!

(*He leads applause.* EILEEN *climbs steps—*RUTH *sits on bottom step.*)

**CHICK**

(*Enters*)

Hey, Ruth, I gotta square myself with you.

**RUTH**

Go away—my sister's going to sing!

**EILEEN**

You get out of here, Chick Clark!

**FRANK**

(*Stepping in*)

Is he annoying you, Miss Sherwood?

**CHICK**

(*Pushing* FRANK)

Go on back to your drugstore! No! Look, Ruth! I got your press card, signed by the city editor! You start Monday!

**RUTH**

Is it true?

CHICK

It's official—I tell ya!

LONIGAN

(*To* CHICK)

All right you—come on!
(*Takes* CHICK's *arm*.)

CHICK

Ruth, tell this clown I'm okay!

RUTH

No, no, Officer—he's all right!

EILEEN

Yes, John—you can let him go now.

LONIGAN

(*Disgustedly*)

Ah!

RUTH

Oh, thanks, Chick! Eileen, I can't believe it! Look, it's a press
card! I've got a job—I can go to work!
(*They embrace*.)

EILEEN

Ruth, that's wonderful!

VALENTI

What is this—a night club or an employment agency?

VOICES

Come on! Sing it! Let's hear her sing!

VALENTI

Come on, what are you cryin' for?

EILEEN

I'm happy!

RUTH

We're both happy!

VALENTI

Well, I ain't! And the customers ain't! Sing or blow!

RUTH

She'll sing! Go on Eileen—

EILEEN

I can't—I can't just stop crying and start singing!

RUTH

Of course, you can!

EILEEN

Do it with me, Ruth, please!

RUTH

In front of all those people!

VALENTI

Come on! Come on!

EILEEN

Ruth!

RUTH

Should I, Mr. Valenti?

VALENTI

Sure! Do something—do anything!

RUTH

All right! Play the band—the "Wrong Note Rag"!
(RUTH *and* EILEEN *stand up.* RUTH *explains the routine.*
RUTH *and* EILEEN *hurriedly whisper directions to each
other during the announcement.*)

VALENTI

Folks, something new has been added. Another glorious
voice joins us. The Wrong Note Rag— Hit it, boys!
(*There is an old-fashioned blaring introduction and*
RUTH *and* EILEEN *march forward and perform the number they have known since their early childhood. They
work in a dead-pan sister-act, style circa 1913.*)

RUTH AND EILEEN

Oh there's a new sensation that is goin' aroun'—
Goin' around— Goin' around— Goin' around—
A simple little ditty that is sweepin' the town,
Sweepin' the town— Swee—eepin' the town—
Doo—Doo—Doo
Doo—Doo—Doo—Doo—Doo—Doo
They call it the wrong note rag!

It's got a little twist that really drives ya insane,
Drives ya insane, drives ya insane, drives ya insane,
Because you'll find you never get it out of your brain,
Out of your brain— Ou-Out of your brain!

Doo—Doo—Doo—
They call it the Wrong Note Rag!
(*The music and the girls' spirit and energy become infectious and the crowd joins in.*)

### ALL

Bunny Hug!
Turkey Trot!
Gimme the Wrong Note Rag!

### GIRLS

Please play that lovely wrong note
Because that wrong note
Just makes me
Doo—Doo Da—Doo, Doo—Doo—Da—Doo, Doodoo!

That note is such a strong note
It makes me

### EILEEN

Rick-ricky-tick rick-ricky-tick tacky.

### RUTH

Wick-wicky-wick wick-wick-wick wacky.

Don't play that right polite note
Because that right note
Just makes me
Blah-blah-bla-blah, blah-blah-bla-blah blah blah!

Give me that new and blue note
And sister
Watch my dust,
Watch my smoke
Doin' the Wrong Note Rag!

(*They break out into a corny ragtime dance, and the couples at the Vortex, loving it, pick up the steps and join them, building the number to a high-spirited finish. There is wild enthusiasm from the Vortex patrons as* RUTH *and* EILEEN *hug each other happily.*)

VALENTI

Well, that's what drove 'em out of Ohio. What are you gonna do for an encore?

EILEEN

Encore? Did I get one?

RUTH

Of course you did! You were terrific! Go on!

VALENTI

What's it gonna be ?

(EILEEN *whispers,* "It's Love"! *She goes upstage and all face her.* RUTH *sits on a step downstage.*)

For an encore our little premier donna is gonna get nice and mellow— Keep it low, folks.

(*The music to* "It's Love" *starts and* EILEEN *sings—all eyes on her. She is in a spotlight—and so is* RUTH, *watching her.*)

### EILEEN
(*As she sings*)

It's love! It's love!
Well who would have thought it.

> (BAKER *enters, looks about, sees* RUTH, *he goes to her and touches her shoulder. She turns, shushes him and turns back to watch* EILEEN.)

If this is love
Then why have I fought it?

> (RUTH *does a take as she realizes it is* BAKER, *but she shushes him again. This time he takes her in his arms and kisses her. Still dazed, she pushes him away, saying, "Ssh!" Then suddenly realizing what is happening, she turns back to him and rushes into his arms.*)

What a way to feel—
I could touch the sky.
What a way to feel—
I have found my guy.

### BAKER
(*Holding* RUTH, *as all turn to watch them,* EILEEN *beaming happily at them across the club*)

It's love at last,
I've someone to cheer for.

### RUTH

It's love at last—
I've learned what we're here for.

ALL
(*Singing*)

I've heard it said,
"You'll know it when you see it."
> (RUTH *and* BAKER, *holding hands, oblivious to everything but each other.*)

Well, I see it— I know it—
It's love!

(*The curtain falls*)

# WONDERFUL TOWN

·—·—·—

# FOREWORD BY SIR JULIAN HUXLEY

IT IS RIGHT and proper that T. H. Huxley should be commemorated in this centenary of the birth of the modern theory of evolution; for if Darwin was its prime creator, Huxley was its greatest protagonist. But Huxley was much more than Darwin's bulldog, and Dr Bibby has done an excellent piece of work in describing and evaluating his career as a whole.

I have always looked up to my grandfather with a blend of awe and admiration; but I had thought mainly of his scientific abilities, his sheer intellectual brilliance, and his prophetic morality. Dr Bibby has devoted most of his book to a consideration of Huxley's rôle as scientific humanist and educator. And from it I have gained a new insight into his character and his work, and am more than ever amazed by the range of his interests, his capacities and his achievements. It shows him as an outstanding figure in nineteenth-century thought, and one who left a permanent mark on the world's scientific and educational structure. He must have been endowed with a highly improbable combination of genes; and he certainly made good use of the endowment.

Within the space of one year, as an original member of the London School Board, he played a decisive rôle in implementing the Education Act of 1870, and in setting the future course of elementary education in Britain. (He was also at the time Secretary of the Royal Society, Governor of Owens College, President of the British Association, and a member of two Royal Commissions.) He helped materially to introduce more and better science teaching in the universities and Public Schools (if it had not been for his membership of the governing body of Eton, where he so strongly fostered the teaching of biology, I might never have taken up a biological

vii

career). He was a master of lucid and beautiful English prose. He was a great humanist pioneer, and always insisted that education in all fields should be broadly based and should concern itself with the arts as well as the humanities and the sciences. He was the prime begetter of what is now the Imperial College of Science and Technology, and insisted that it should be a true university and not just a technical college. He helped transform Oxford and Cambridge from homes of classical privilege to universities of the highest rank. In the evening of his days, he was instrumental in securing the emergence of the University of London as an effective federal organisation, in place of the previous chaotic welter of institutions. He was also a pioneer of adult popular education, and devoted a great deal of time and energy to his lectures to working men. Though a brilliant research zoologist, he stressed the need for better organisation of knowledge as against the mere piling up of new facts.

Dr Bibby recounts many interesting episodes in Huxley's life. How he insisted on taking his duties seriously as Rector of the University of Aberdeen. How he was able to command the respect and the co-operation of many of his theological opponents. How he slaved away to make sure that the newly instituted examination system really worked. How he took the trouble when lecturing in Tennessee to talk about the local geology. How he studied theology to such effect that he could often confute the theologians in his disputes. How he insisted on music in the general curriculum, but failed to get art included. How and why he three times refused a post at Oxford.

He tells us of Huxley's wit and humour; of his remarkable combination of stern morality with tenderness and compassion; of what one of his students called his sublime quality as a lecturer; his deep concern for the sufferings of the poor; his devotion to Darwin and his dislike of Gladstone; his early realisation that over-population was destined to be the world's gravest problem; his tireless activity and his remarkable effectiveness in promoting the causes he thought right;

his immense range of contacts in science, art, administration, politics, education and religion.

I am personally grateful to Dr Bibby for making me more than ever proud of being the grandson of T. H. Huxley, and I commend his book as a valuable study of a great human figure.

*Julian Huxley.*

# FOREWORD BY ALDOUS HUXLEY

MEMORIES ARE SHORT and our capacity for taking things for granted is almost infinite. We grumble about our educational system, but forget that less than a century ago there was no system at all, merely a squalid absence of education, with here and there an oasis of Renaissance learning, where a few privileged boys could acquire the useful arts of construing Cicero and turning Gray's *Elegy* into heroic couplets.

Dr Bibby's book reminds us that we have blessings to count as well as shortcomings to complain of, and that we owe these blessings to the labours of a few devoted and persistent enthusiasts. The most herculean of these labourers and possibly the most effective was T. H. Huxley.

Reading Dr Bibby's pages, one is constantly astonished. Astonished, first of all, by Huxley's extraordinary capacity for work and by his no less extraordinary skill in persuasion, diplomacy and the art of overcoming official inertia. And astonished even more by the extraordinary up-to-dateness of his ideas on education. Thus, we find him lecturing the classicists on the importance of science, and in the next breath lecturing the scientists on the importance of the humanities and a training in art and music. We find him anticipating John Dewey in his insistence upon the value of learning through doing and observing, in his denunciations of "mental debauchery, book guzzling and lesson bibbing"; but we find him also anticipating the critics of 'Progressive Education' in his equally emphatic insistence upon the necessity of a thorough and accurate teaching of fundamentals. We find him agreeing with the 'we-teach-children-not-subjects' school of educators to the extent of regarding "will, energy and honesty" as no less important than knowledge;

xi

but we find him sharply disagreeing with them in proclaiming that knowledge of subjects is at least as important as 'life adjustment' or a 'well-rounded personality'. In the field of university education we find him advocating the specialisation without which scientific progress is impossible; but we also find him, in the last years of his life, advocating (in vain) a complete reorganisation of the modern university with a view to prying the specialists out of their pigeon-holes and encouraging them to work with other specialists towards a synthesis of knowledge.

Education in the West still falls short of the ideals which Huxley proposed for it three generations ago. When and if these ideals come to be realised, it will certainly be better than it is today. But will it, even then, produce all the transfiguring results which the early enthusiasts anticipated—the results which, to judge by television programmes and the popular Press, by reports of mounting juvenile delinquency and spreading neurosis, it has as yet so conspicuously failed to produce? The answer is probably in the negative. As Huxley remarked long ago, there are in every school distressingly large numbers of "can't learns and won't learns and don't learns". Moreover, even among those who are able or willing to absorb the education that is given them, how few retain throughout their adult life that openness and elasticity of mind without which nobody can profit by the lessons of experience or adjust realistically to social changes, new knowledge and unfamiliar ideas! There are, throughout the world, millions of educated young men and women who develop mental arterio-sclerosis forty or fifty years before their physical blood vessels begin to harden. A system of schooling that turns out so many educated fossils, and leaves so many other fossils uneducated, can hardly be described as satisfactory. Will it ever be possible to transform the fossils into fully living organisms, the won't learns, can't learns and don't learns into wills, cans and dos? Perhaps it will—but not, I would guess, by the kind of educational methods in use today.

These methods, even the best of them, require to be supplemented by other methods as yet untried on any considerable scale.

We set out to teach our children subjects and life-adjustment; but we do nothing specifically to educate the psychophysical organisms which underlie the children's personalities and which actually do their living for them and make possible their learning. We do nothing, for example, to train the special senses, to increase the acuity of children's perceptions and to render them more prompt and more discriminating. And yet there is good reason to believe that proper training in the basic arts of seeing, hearing, tasting, smelling, touching and body-sensing could do far more to develop a child's intelligence than any of the 'mental disciplines' in use today. Again, we know that human beings can be trained to achieve a considerable measure of control over their autonomic nervous system, over their sensations of pain and fatigue, over their moods and attitudes. Technology has made it possible for us to master the external environment. It is high time that we developed (or borrowed from other cultures) psycho-physiological techniques for achieving a comparable mastery over that internal environment in which, willy-nilly, every personality must pass its life. My guess is that, if they were trained to perceive more efficiently and to be more aware of their own bodies, if they were shewn how to combine activity with absence of tension in all the affairs of life, if they were taught to use the enormous powers of auto-conditioning in a constructive way, many of the educated fossils would come to life, many of the won't learns, can't learns and don't learns would become educable.

The medal, needless to say, has a reverse to it. Like any other kind of education, psycho-physiological training may be used in an undesirable way. It is said that, in the days of Japanese militarism, officers of the imperial navy were made more ruthlessly efficient by being put through a course of Zen. And if systematic auto-conditioning can make us more in-

dependent of our surroundings and more capable of implementing our good resolutions, systematic hetero-condition-
ing, especially when undergone in childhood, can make us
more apt to implement other people's resolutions and more
dependent upon whatever environment the conditioner wants
us to be adapted to. Equally ambivalent must be our attitude
towards another mind-changing procedure, which has recently emerged from Science Fiction into the realm of fore-
seeable probability—the procedure to which one might give
such names as Pharmacological Education, Pill Morality,
Synthetic Stoicism, Chemical Christianity. Nearly harmless
tranquillisers and nearly harmless vision-inducers and cosmic
consciousness-promoters are already on the market and more
and better pills will surely follow. Recently the Russians
announced that they were half-way through a Five Year Plan
aimed at discovering a physiologically costless way of increasing psychic energy by pharmacological means. And
without the benefit of a Five Year Plan, the West is rapidly
moving in the same direction. Within a few years it may be
that we shall be treating our encysted fossils, our dull or
stubborn non-learners, not with homilies or lectures, but with
something out of a bottle. The discovery of a harmless
psychic energiser would have consequences either extremely
good or extremely bad. Administered to everybody, such a
drug might turn out to be the salvation of the democratic
system, which depends for its survival on a high level of
general intelligence and alertness. Reserved to the few, it
would tend to consolidate the rule of an *élite*, which would
then be genuinely and objectively superior to the masses.
For the educator, as for all the rest of us, the future may be
alarming; but it will most certainly not be dull.

Aldous Huxley.

# PREFACE

> Any candid observer of the phenomena of modern society will
> readily admit that bores must be classed among the enemies of
> the human race; and a little consideration will probably lead
> him to the further admission, that no species of that extensive
> genus of noxious creature is more objectionable than the
> educational bore.
>
> *Address to the Working Men's Club and Institute Union, 1877*

FOR ANY ONE proposing a study of the educational work
and significance of T. H. Huxley, his remark about enemies of
the human race stands as a dreadful warning. And, for one
whose profession is education, and who daily experiences the
awful truth of that remark, the warning has special significance. Yet one can find comfort in the fact that Huxley himself was usually scintillating and never dull, and it would be
very difficult to write a boring book about him. The risk, in
any case, must be run, for a generation seeking some synthesis
of modern science and traditional humanism cannot afford to
neglect the greatest of scientific humanists. His two grand-
sons, Julian distinguished in science and Aldous eminent in
letters, have each contributed a foreword for which I am
most grateful, and there is a peculiar appositeness about this
dual tribute to one for whom the Public Orator of Cambridge
adapted Terence to say *humani nihil a se alienum putat*.

The research on which this book is based was conducted in
the Advanced Studies Department of the University of London Institute of Education.   It involved considerable travel-
ling for the consultation of local records, and gratitude is due
and warmly expressed both to the many librarians and archiv-
ists who were so helpful and to the University of London
which made research grants towards the expenses of these

travels. I have been fortunate in the provision of facilities and the advice of friends to such an extent as to make particularised acknowledgement in this preface impossible. Inquiries have been answered by many scores of members of the academic and administrative staffs of universities, colleges, schools, scientific societies, professional associations, voluntary organisations, libraries, museums and local authorities, and to all these kind correspondents I am most grateful.

Yet the invidious task of selecting a few of these many helpers for individual mention may not be shirked. First, I must express my appreciation of illuminating conversations with Mrs Leonard Huxley and Sir Julian Huxley, who have also put me in their debt by agreeing to the publication of some hitherto unpublished material from family letters. The papers of Sir Mountstuart Elphinstone Grant Duff were made available by the Hon Mrs Ursula Grant Duff, while the Hon Mrs Maurice Lubbock allowed sight of the papers of Sir John Lubbock, first Lord Avebury. I am also most grateful to the Provost and Fellows of Eton College for permitting perusal of their Minutes and other documents, and to Sir Claude and Lady Elliott for their help and hospitality. The Linnean Society allowed access to its MacLeay correspondence, the Royal Institution to its Tyndall manuscripts, the Royal Society of Arts to its Committee Minutes, the Dulwich Reference Library to its papers relating to the South London Working Men's College, the Heston and Isleworth Reference Library to its local history files bearing on the International College in Spring Grove, the Ealing Reference Library to its material on the scenes of Huxley's early childhood, the Charing Cross Hospital Medical School to its Minutes, and the London County Council to the records of the first London School Board. To these institutions and their library staffs, and to others not individually named, I express my thanks, as I do to those who have been so helpful in the British Museum (both at Bloomsbury and at Colindale) and in the Universities of Aberdeen, Cambridge, Edinburgh, Leeds, Liverpool, London, Manchester and Oxford. I would also express gratitude for the provision of microfilm of manuscript material in the possession of the American Philosophical Society, Columbia University, Harvard University (Houghton Library), the Henry E. Huntington Library (San Marino, California) and the Johns Hopkins University (MSS. collection in the Lanier Room). Most important of all, I have had full access to the general records and to the considerable collection of Huxley's correspondence, diaries and notebooks in the Imperial College of Science and Technology, to whose Rector and Governors I am most grateful, as I am to Mr F. W. James and Mr C. K. McDowall for their continued helpfulness in the search of these documents.

Permission has been liberally granted to publish from these many sources, as detailed in the individual references, and this permission is warmly acknowledged.

It would, however, have been economically impossible to include in this book so much of the interesting material available had it not been for the generosity of the Crompton Bequest Fund of the Society of Authors, the University of London Institute of Education, the Imperial College of Science and Technology, and the Eugenics Society, whose grants in aid of publication leave me under a great obligation.

Finally, there are two friends whose aid has been so conspicuous that they must be specially thanked. Professor Joseph Lauwerys has been an invaluable counsellor over many years, and to him I have habitually turned for suggestions and for solace. Mr Frank Coles accepted the ungrateful task of criticising each chapter at each stage of its writing, and that task he discharged with a kindly ruthlessness possible only in the closest friendship. None but these two and I can know how much I owe them.

CYRIL BIBBY

*College of S. Mark and S. John,*
*University of London Institute of Education*

B

# CONTENTS

Grateful acknowledgement is made to those who have permitted and facilitated the reproduction of illustrations, as follows:

*Imperial College of Science and Technology*—'Hornet' caricature, Bassano photograph, engraving from Elliott & Fry photograph, London Stereoscopic Company photograph, self-sketch, 'Report of a Sad Case'.

*National Portrait Gallery*—Pencil sketches by Marian Huxley, pencil drawing by Wirgman, oil painting by Collier.

*Ealing Reference Library*—'Illustrated London News' woodcut, Lock & Whitfield photograph, memorial plaque by Bowcher (book jacket).

*Sir Julian Huxley*—'Vanity Fair' cartoon, 'Men of the Day'.

*Victoria and Albert Museum and Royal Society*—Oil study by Legros.

*British Museum (Natural History)*—Statue by Ford.

# LIST OF PLATES

## ILLUSTRATIONS IN TEXT

Strong natural talent for mechanism, music and art in general, but all wasted and uncultivated. Believe I am reckoned a good chairman of a meeting. I always find that I acquire influence, generally more than I want, in bodies of men and that administrative and other work gravitates to my hands. Impulsive and apt to rush into all sorts of undertakings without counting cost or responsibility. Love my friends and hate my enemies cordially. Entire confidence in those whom I trust at all and much indifference towards the rest of the world. A profound religious tendency capable of fanaticism, but tempered by no less profound theological scepticism. No love of the marvellous as such, intense desire to know facts; no very intense love of my pursuits at present, but very strong affection for philosophical and social problems; strong constructive imagination; small foresight; no particular public spirit; disinterestedness arising from an entire want of care for the rewards and honours most men seek, vanity too big to be satisfied by them.

*Huxley's own estimate of his character, given to Francis Galton in 1873*

# CHAPTER I

# A Man So Various

If there is anything I thank the Gods for (I am not sure that there is, for as the old woman said when reminded of the goodness of Providence: "Ah, but he takes it out of me in the corns") it is a wide diversity of tastes. Barred from scientific work, I should be miserable, if there were not heaps of other topics that interest me, from Gadarene pigs & Gladstonian psychology, upwards . . . the cosmos remains always beautiful and profoundly interesting in every corner—and if I had as many lives as a cat I would leave no corner unexplored.

*Letter to Sir John Simon,* 11 March 1891*

ON THE 4th May 1825, when Thomas Henry Huxley was born in the sleepy old village of Ealing, English society still had its roots deep in the eighteenth century. By the 29th June 1895, when he died at the newly developing seaside resort of Eastbourne, it was already feeling its way into the twentieth.

The Ealing of Huxley's childhood was a place of pleasant fields and farmland, where the streams and footpaths meandered across the parks and around the orchards of wealthy and aristocratic landowners. Shortly before his birth there had been a mere 228 voters in the Vestry, and the little parish church of St Mary had seating for but forty

---

* Sir John Simon (1816–1904), the famous sanitary reformer, who held a series of pioneer posts including those of Medical Officer of Health to the City of London, Medical Officer to the General Board of Health and Medical Officer to the Privy Council. His *English Sanitary Institutions* (1890) is a masterly survey of the field.

1

worshippers. There was a Poor House, no doubt badly needed even in the 'royal village', and each June a three-day fair on Ealing Green provided an occasion for jollity and racing and gambling and drinking. A fortnight before Huxley's third birthday, something of a local sensation was caused by the arrest in Ealing of William Corder, murderer of Maria Marten in the Red Barn; but this was a time when an Englishman might legally be hanged for a hundred other crimes than murder. It was when Huxley was a child of five that William IV came to the throne, and not until he was seven did the first Reform Act increase England's electorate from less than a quarter of a million to nearly three-quarters. If the inhabitants of Ealing wanted to travel, they had the choice of canal or road, and the 'Green Man' provided stabling for a hundred horses. Where Christ Church now stands there was a meadow, and young Tom Huxley must often have played about the spring and stream which Brunel covered over in 1838 with his west-bound railway.

Huxley has not provided us with more than the briefest of autobiographies, nor does his son Leonard tell us much about his childhood in the standard *Life and Letters*. It almost seems, indeed, as if Huxley deliberately drew down a screen to protect himself from memories of unhappy early years. George Huxley, the father, was mathematics master at the local school conducted by Dr Nicholas of Wadham (the original of Thackeray's 'Dr Tickle-Us'), but there seems never to have been much money to spare from his income. Their house opposite St Mary's was rated at the not inconsiderable sum of £27 per annum, but this figure takes on a different complexion when it is realised that the ground floor was a butcher's shop and the Huxley family had to make do in the rooms above. T. H. Huxley, at any rate, was always vividly aware of the conditions of life of the masses of the people, and in later years he was to declare "I am a plebeian, and I stand by my order". The Huxley boys were fortunate enough to attend the school where their father taught, but

Tom at least did not count this as good fortune. "I had two years of a Pandemonium of a school," he told Herbert Spencer, and he deliberately affirmed that, in a life which had acquainted him with the highest and the lowest of mankind, the worst society he had known was at school.

Yet there is something strange about this, for Great Ealing School was claimed to be the finest private school in England, ranking almost with Eton and Harrow. Its social standing was such that Prince Louis Philippe, the 'Citizen King' of France, taught there during his exile, and its teaching was good enough for the future Cardinal Newman to go straight to Oxford at the age of sixteen. Other pupils were Thackeray the novelist, W. S. Gilbert the librettist, Charles Knight of the *Penny Cyclopædia*, and Bishop Selwyn—and, it must be admitted to balance the picture, a lad who was later transported to Australia and by an astonishing coincidence brought Huxley his horse in a stable-yard in Sydney. The two brothers Nicholas, who conducted the school after the death of their father in 1829, were said to be fonder of riding and shooting than of teaching, yet the regular performances of classical plays were sometimes considered superior to those of Westminster School. Mathematics, however, seems to have been another story, for it was said that there was not a boy in the school who could explain the difference between an equilateral and an obtuse-angled triangle. Perhaps Huxley found life especially hard as the son of an ineffective teacher, or perhaps he was beaten and abused as a 'fag' to one of the 300-odd wealthy boys at Ealing. At any rate, he was miserably unhappy.

Leonard Huxley tells us that the school broke up about 1835, whereupon George Huxley returned to his native Coventry and became manager of a small local savings bank; but this account seems very doubtful. There is clear evidence that in 1846 the school moved to new premises on the demolition of the Old Rectory, and from 1881 to 1894 local directories list Great Ealing School on the Green in St Mary's

Road. It is just possible that the school closed down in 1835 and opened up again a few years later, but one wonders whether there might not have been some other reason for the Huxleys' departure from Ealing. Certainly the family was an unfortunate one, and letters survive which cast some light on its difficulties.

The mother, Rachel Huxley, was a slender brunette with piercing black eyes and great rapidity of thought and enormous energy, who must have passed on many dominant genes to Tom, the seventh of her eight offspring. As a child, Tom's attachment to his mother was so close (and yet, was it in some way so insecure?) that he often lay awake at night weeping for a morbid fear that she might die. Two of the children died in infancy, a common enough thing in large families of that period, and no doubt the parents were able to adjust themselves to their loss. When Tom was fourteen his sister Ellen married a Dr Cook of Coventry, and they seem to have sunk into a most lamentable state, so that by 1858 Thomas was describing his brother-in-law as "a bloated mass of beer and opium" and wondering "how Cookdom is to be saved from entire submergence". He did his typically generous best by making Ellen an annual allowance, but still had to face the unpleasantness caused by her using his name to secure trade credit. Brother George was by 1858 "at death's door with incipient phthisis", brought on it was thought by "extreme mental anxiety"; and, when he died in 1863, Tom had to sell his Royal Society Medal so that its value as gold could be used to clear up the mess in which George's affairs had been left. William, six years Tom's senior, was completely estranged from him for thirty years because of a family quarrel over George's marriage and, despite their both living in London, the brothers seem never again to have met. James, two years younger than William, qualified as a doctor and remained on excellent terms with George and Thomas, but by the time he was fifty-five he was "as near mad as a sane man can be". With his eldest sister

Eliza (always affectionately 'Lizzie' to him), Thomas had a very close emotional bond, and he once told her "of the surprising six people who sprang from our father & mother, you and I are the only two who seemed to be capable of fraternal love". Lizzie, at any rate, appears to have been a person of great stability, marrying a Dr Salt—who for some reason soon changed his name to Scott—and then bringing up a family happily and normally enough (with occasional financial help from Tom) in Tennessee. Rachel, the admirable mother, died of heart disease in 1852—but her husband suffered no shock because he was "nearly lost to . . . almost any other feeling beyond a vegetable existence". Soon he was "sunk in worse than childish imbecility of mind", and in 1855 he died under James's care at the Barming asylum. Beatrice Webb was presumably ignorant of this strange family history when, following a conversation with T. H. Huxley some thirty years later, she made a most percipient note in her diary: "Huxley, when not working, dreams strange things: carries on lengthy conversations between unknown persons living within his brain. There is a strain of madness in him."

But, if so, it was that thin strain to which great wits are near allied and from which Aristotle tells us no great soul is quite exempt. Reading Hutton's *Geology* in bed by candlelight as a lad of twelve, devouring Hamilton's *Logic*, learning German when he was supposed to be making hay on a Worcestershire farm, young Tom did not allow his education to cease with his departure from the school at Ealing. While Huxley was still a baby, Brougham founded his Society for the Diffusion of Useful Knowledge, and soon the intelligent self-educator could take his choice of innumerable encyclopædias and factual periodicals. Books of all sorts were becoming cheaper and more readily available, and the adolescent youngster soaked himself in printers' ink and thought about the world around him. At the age of twelve he would certainly have been excited by Queen Victoria's accession to the throne, he could not have missed the orgy of railroad

construction while he was in the Midlands, and he must have
heard much talk of the Charter in 1838 and the Anti-Corn
Law League a year later. In his adolescent journal *Thoughts
and Doings*, a miniature home-made affair which he kept
from 1840 to 1845, accounts of simple scientific experiments
jostle with immature philosophical speculations, a protest
against the treatment of dissenters is followed by a discussion
on the nature of the soul. Already in these pages his revolt
against narrow doctrine is foreshadowed by a note from
Lessing, "I hate all people who want to found sects";
already his wide interests come out in a plan of study which
includes German and Italian and Physics and Physiology;
already his philosophical bent appears in a youthful attempt
at the classification of all knowledge, with "doubt under
which head to put morality, for I cannot determine exactly
in my own mind whether morality can exist independent of
others, whether the idea of morality could ever have arisen
in the mind of an isolated being or not".

Unlike Newman, Huxley has left no self-regarding record
of his own mental development, but there is no doubt that in
these early days the dominant influence was Carlyle. From
him Huxley gained a hatred of humbug and sham, and *Sartor
Resartus* was long his standby. *Heroes and Hero-Worship* and
*The French Revolution* appealed to a personality early
conscious of its power, and many a quotation from Carlyle
went down in the miniature journal. In Carlyle, too, Huxley
found sanction for his own sympathy with the downtrodden,
and in his pages he came across German philosophers for
whom it seemed worth while to learn the tongue. As the years
went by, Huxley increasingly parted company with the sage's
prejudices and his exaltation of the great individual, but the
early imprint was indelible and the early debt never forgotten.
Towards the end of Carlyle's life, seeing him on the opposite
side of the street and taking pity on his solitariness, Huxley
crossed over to pass the time of day. Carlyle looked up,
peered into his face, said "You're Huxley, aren't you? the

man that says we are all descended from monkeys", and walked on. But even after this rebuff Huxley was glad to join in raising a memorial to his long-discarded mentor, for whose tonic influence on a young mind he remained ever grateful.

It was apparently from no special inclination that Huxley took up first medicine and then biology. His early wish was to be an engineer; but, with no family fortune to finance him and with two of his sisters married to doctors, it was almost inevitable that he should take up that profession. At the age of fifteen he migrated to London to begin his apprenticeship, and a period in the East End left him with vivid memories of poverty and squalor, so that he "used to wonder sometimes why these people did not sally forth in mass and get a few hours' eating and drinking and plunder to their hearts' content, before the police could stop and hang a few of them". Then, after working for a while under his brother-in-law Dr John Scott in North London, he managed in 1842 to secure a Free Scholarship for "young Gentlemen of respectable but unfortunate families", and his medical studies at Charing Cross Hospital began. He seems to have had no difficulty in carrying off prizes in chemistry and anatomy and physiology; and, if his name did not figure more prominently in the honours lists, it was doubtless because he spent a good deal of his time making caricatures of his teachers and a good deal of his energy in reading outside the prescribed fields of study. However, he was awarded a Gold Medal in the First Medical Examination of the University of London, and he had the satisfaction of seeing his first research paper published whilst yet a student. Then, since he needed to earn his living at some occupation which did not demand a high medical qualification, Huxley became an Assistant-Surgeon in the Royal Navy.

Fortunately, he failed to secure the resident hospital position which he had hoped for, and he was saved from a routine medical career by being posted to the 'donkey frigate' survey

ship HMS *Rattlesnake*. The vessel leaked at the seams and
swarmed with cockroaches, and Huxley's five-feet-eleven-
inches must have been most uncomfortable in his lower-deck
berth four-foot-ten in height, but there were more than com-
pensating advantages. The official naturalist, John Mac-
gillivray, was glad enough to have the assistance of a young
medico anxious to do research, and there was a tacit understanding that Huxley would be allowed to pursue his own
interests. The Captain of *Rattlesnake* was Owen Stanley,
brother of Dean Stanley and son of the Bishop of Norwich,
and he allowed the chart room to be used for books and
microscope. Leaving Spithead on the 3rd December 1846,
cruising inside the Great Barrier Reef and up through the
Torres Straits, Huxley worked away at the anatomy of marine
organisms and packeted back home research papers of peculiar brilliance. His devotion to marine life was not so exclusive
as to prevent his courting and engaging to marry a certain
Miss Heathorn of Sydney, but it was sufficient to ensure that
when he returned to England in 1850 there were many men of
science most anxious to make his acquaintance.

At a time when much was being taken on authority, and
not very reliable authority at that, Huxley had the great
advantage of studying biology thousands of miles away from
a university. A lesser man might have failed to make any
headway at all with no instructor and few books, but in his
case it was a benison to be thrown entirely on his own resources. With no teacher to tell him what he should see in the
specimens dredged up in his adapted wire-mesh meat cover,
he simply recorded what in fact he saw, and what he saw was
as novel as it was incontrovertible. Within a few months of
touching at Plymouth he was selected for Fellowship of the
Royal Society, and soon he was very much the young lion of
the scientific world. "I have taken a better position than I
could have expected among these grandees", he permitted
himself to boast to Lizzie, "and I find them all immensely
civil and ready to help me on."

What he most needed was time for research, and soon strings were being pulled to good effect. Sir Richard Owen * asked the First Lord of the Admiralty to relieve Huxley of normal naval duties, the Royal Society and the British Association added their weight, and on the 3rd December there came a nominal six months' appointment 'for special service' to HMS *Fisgard*, stationed at Woolwich as guard ship, with leave of absence from naval duties. This leave was extended for a further twelve months, then for another year and then another six months, and Huxley's researches went apace. Memoirs came out on the development of echinoderms, the morphology of ascidians and molluscs, the auditory organs of crustaceans and the anatomy of the rotifers; and still a great mass of work on the oceanic hydrozoa remained unpublished. Huxley took the view that, since his material had been collected on a naval voyage, the Admiralty should pay for its publication; but the Admiralty, sympathetic as it was to scientific research, did not share that view—perhaps understandably, since he had not even been the official naturalist on *Rattlesnake*. Some of his friends seem to have been a little alarmed by the way in which Huxley was pressing his claim (he wrote direct to the First Lord of the Admiralty and arranged for an intermediary to lay the matter before the Prime Minister), and when he was awarded the Royal Society's Gold Medal there was some trepidation about what he might say in his speech of acceptance. He promised a friend "I will 'roar you like any sucking dove' at the dinner", but unfortunately Huxley was never very strong on the habits of sucking doves. So, although he explained "I have been too long used to strict discipline to venture to criticise any act of my superiors", that did not prevent his making the acid remark that "The Government of this country, of this *great* country, has been two years debating

* Sir Richard Owen (1804–1892), who achieved enormous distinction as an anatomist, but made many enemies by reason of his vanity and jealousy. He was a very stubborn man and unwilling ever to admit an error, which proved to be his downfall when he came into conflict with Huxley.

whether it should grant the three hundred pounds necessary for the publication of these researches". But the Admiralty is not easily moved against its will, and no doubt it considered three years' leave of absence not ungenerous: at any rate, by January 1854 it would budge no further.

Neither would Huxley. The letters which passed between him and the Admiralty must surely be unique, and he must have been very confident about his standing in the world of science. On the 7th of the month further leave was refused, on the 1st February Huxley was posted to *Illustrious* at Portsmouth, six days later his application for cancellation of the posting was rejected, and on the 23rd the Admiralty sent an understandably acerbic inquiry why he had not joined his ship. The 1st March brought instructions to report immediately the reason for failing to obey the thrice-repeated order—and next day Huxley blandly explained that it was impossible for him to proceed to Portsmouth until the Admiralty had made up its mind about a grant in aid of publication. What nautical expletives may have accompanied the reading of this missive in Whitehall we can only guess, but on the 3rd March the Admiralty replied that, unless he immediately obeyed, his name would be removed from the Navy List. In those days, when Britannia really ruled the waves, expulsion from the Royal Navy was scarcely the best start to a young man's career in London—but Huxley never bluffed, and struck from the Navy List he was.

Prohibited from continuing his naval career (how fascinating a thought is that of Admiral Huxley!), he cast around for other employment and even contemplated emigrating to Australia and becoming a brewer. "To attempt to live by any scientific pursuit is a farce . . .", he had written despairingly to Miss Heathorn. "A man of science may earn great distinction, but not bread. He will get invitations to all sorts of dinners and conversaziones, but not enough income to pay his cab fare." Yet, although uncertain of what the future might hold, he seems never to have doubted that he would succeed in some field. "I will leave my mark somewhere," he told his sister Lizzie, "and it shall be clear and distinct T.H.H., his mark and free from the abominable blur of cant, humbug and self-seeking which surrounds this present world—that is to say, supposing that I am not already unconsciously tainted myself, a result of which I have a morbid dread."

The frequency and vigour with which Huxley declaimed against self-seeking imply an ambitious nature whose idealism feared its own ambition, but that does not make the idealism less real. By this time Huxley had been around the world and seen that poverty and squalor were not peculiar to London's East End, and the ruthlessness of men both black and white had made a deep impress on his mind. On the long sea voyages he had run into any number of petty jealousies and intrigues, he had found his towing-net hauled in with the excuse that it impeded the ship's passage, and he had known careful dissections thrown overboard before they could be drawn. The amused contempt of most of the officers for scientific pursuits had been a continual discouragement, and back in England he soon discovered that recognition depended as much on lobbying as on learning. So off he went to the British Association at Ipswich in 1851, confiding to his fiancée that "Anyone who conceives that I went down from any especial interest in the progress of science makes a great mistake. My journey was altogether a matter of policy". All the time his reputation was growing, and by the end of 1851 he was able to tell an Australian friend "When I last wrote I was but at the edge of the crush at the pit door at this great fools theatre—now I have worked my way into it, and through it, and I hope am not far from the check takers". Nothing came of a mooted Chair of Natural History at Sydney, a hoped-for appointment at Toronto went to a close relative of a Canadian politician, and applications at Aberdeen and Cork and King's College, London, met with no more success. Nevertheless, he told Miss Heathorn in the

C

summer of 1853, "My course in life is taken. I will *not* leave London—I *will* make myself a name and a position as well as an income by some kind of pursuit connected with science, which is the thing for which nature has fitted me if she has ever fitted any one for anything". Then, just in time to prevent his expulsion from the Royal Navy from being too catastrophic, he obtained a post as palæontologist and naturalist at the Government School of Mines in Jermyn Street. His fiancée set sail from Australia and reached England in the following May, and soon Huxley was writing triumphantly to Hooker * "I terminate my Baccalaureate and take my degree of M.A. trimony (isn't that atrocious?) on Saturday, July 21st".

It is evident from his dashing courtship and deep capacity for love that Huxley's resilience had preserved him from the emotional crippling which sometimes comes from an unhappy childhood, and somehow he managed to insulate his own marriage and family life from the sad failure of his father's. The toughness—the hardness, perhaps—which enabled him to do this had a Puritan quality not entirely free from self-righteousness, and it was probably developed in part as a protection against powerful sensual urges. We can only guess at the meaning of his reminiscence of schooldays, that "bullying was the least of the ill-practises current among us", and his confession that "few men have drunk more deeply of all kinds of sin than I" is an obvious exaggeration under the shock of bereavement, but statements like these at least imply an awareness of desires disciplined only with difficulty. Huxley seems to have accepted without question—and it is surprising in a man normally so sceptical of unsupported speculation—the naive notion that his lifelong tendency to dyspepsia and depression was due to some obscure poisoning in adolescence, and it is tempting to suppose that the true cause was a neurosis arising from repres-

* Sir Joseph Dalton Hooker (1817–1911), the famous systematic botanist, who was a lifelong friend of Huxley and who, with his father, largely built up the magnificent collections at Kew.

sion. But excursions into post-mortem psychoanalysis are rarely profitable, and Huxley's libido had best be left alone with the remark that he seems to have controlled it as efficiently as he did most things.

When *Rattlesnake* put into Mauritius in the May of 1847, Huxley assured his mother that the place was "a complete paradise, and if I had nothing better to do, I should pick up some pretty French Eve (and there are plenty) and turn Adam". But it was a few months later, when the young ladies of Sydney set out to entertain the company of the visiting frigate, that he really lost his heart. Miss Henrietta Anne Heathorn was about three months younger than the handsome assistant-surgeon who boldly came up and claimed a dance, and if it was not love at first sight it was something very like it. Nettie was fascinated by his keen sense of fun and ready wit and apparently boundless knowledge, and she waited anxiously for their next meeting. As for Hal (he was always Hal to her, not Tom), he could never quite make up his mind whether she was pretty or not, but he was head over heels in love. They met again at a ball at Government House, and a few days later Nettie saw him enter yet another ballroom: "O thought I there is that delightful doctor. What an evening of glamour it was. . . . Before we left he begged of me the red camellia I wore—which after my darling died I found preserved amongst his papers."

"God help me!", Huxley wrote in 1855, soon after their long separation was ended by Nettie's arrival in England, "I discover that I am as bad as any young fool who knows no better, and if the necessity for giving six lectures a week did not sternly interfere, I should be hanging about her ladyship's apron-strings all day." But her ladyship had fallen ill and been nearly killed by incompetent doctoring in Australia, and Huxley was so shocked by her appearance that he secured an honest opinion by presenting her to a leading London physician as if she were merely a patient in whom he had a professional interest. Nettie was given six months to live:

"Well, six months or not", announced Huxley to the indignation of the deceived consultant, "she is going to be my wife." They honeymooned at Tenby, where he had to carry her to and from the beach, but she recovered to bear him eight children and eventually outlive him.

It was during the Christmas of 1856 that Nettie presented her delighted husband with Noel, "a fair-haired, blue-eyed, stout little Trojan, very like his mother", and in the February of 1858 Jessie came along. They agreed to have no more, but a year later Marian arrived, and early in 1860 yet another was on its way. Then, in September, the sturdy young Noel was killed by scarlet fever, and Huxley had to control his own grief so as to bring the frantic mother back to her senses. For a long time she was really ill, and could not summon up much interest in her two young daughters, but when Leonard was born (and so called to contain the letters of their dead first-born's name) an aching gap was filled. During the next few years the family was reinforced by Rachel, Nettie, Henry and Ethel, and it became a by-word among their friends for its friendliness. As for Huxley himself, he was always advising his bachelor friends to marry and have children—making exception only of Herbert Spencer, whom he suspected would be incapable of selecting a suitable spouse.

It was perhaps not altogether good for Huxley's children to be quite so aware as Leonard was of the infallible rectitude of his moral judgements, but the household was by no means a paternal dictatorship. Probably Huxley was less indulgent with his own children than with grandson Julian, of whom he remarked "I like that chap! I like the way he looks you straight in the face and disobeys you", but the family was once described as "a Republic tempered by epigram". Certainly, his daughters were able to persuade him that there was no logical reason why, equally with their brothers, they might not smoke. His work kept him far too much from the children, but he often took them walking in St John's Wood and between the high hedges of West End Lane, while indoors they were delighted by his endless invention of funny drawings and his skill in carving animals from orange peel. As they grew older, he seems to have trusted them to behave sensibly in sexual matters and in the choice of marriage partners, although he was capable of giving shrewd enough advice on the characteristics of the sexes: "Men, my dear," he once wrote, "are very queer animals, a mixture of horse-nervousness, ass-stubbornness and camel-malice—with an angel bobbing about unexpectedly like the apple in the possett." At any rate, both Nettie and Harry felt confident enough to become engaged to people their parents had not yet met. "I am prepared to be the young lady's slave", Huxley wrote to his youngest son on hearing the news; "pray tell her that I am a model father-in-law, with my love. (By the way, you might mention her name; it is a miserable detail, I know, but would be interesting)." Jessie's marriage to F. W. Waller, Leonard's to Julia Arnold, Rachel's to W. A. Eckersley, Nettie's to J. H. Roller and Henry's to Sophy Stobart, seem to have been orthodox and uncomplicated affairs, but those of Marian and Ethel were tragically interconnected. If Huxley had favourites among his children they were these two, both of them brilliant personalities. Marian's marriage to Jack Collier, whose portrait of her father catches so fleetingly his peculiar melancholy, did not prevent her continuing with her own painting and being more than once hung in the Royal Academy, but after five years she was struck by a hopeless disease and in 1887 she died near Paris at the age of twenty-seven. Two years later her youngest sister Ethel, recently a proud prize-winner in modelling at the Slade School, decided to marry Marian's widower Jack, a thing not merely scandalous but illegal. But that was her decision, and her father accepted it without question. He went with them to Norway, where the marriage law was less archaic, and on his return approached Lord Hartington to see if the Upper House could not be persuaded to allow the passage of a reforming Bill for

England. (It is a remarkable coincidence that Ethel's first-born, Laurence, later became HM Ambassador to Norway.)

In a life always lived as fully outside the laboratory as in it, Huxley produced more than a hundred and fifty research papers, dealing with topics as varied as the morphology of the heteropoda and the hybridism of gentians, the classification of crayfish and the phylogeny of crocodiles, the physical anthropology of the Patagonians and the human remains from Neanderthal. In the five furious years following the appearance of Darwin's *Origin of Species*, Huxley's forty-six publications included nine important contributions to the evolution controversy and some scientific popularisation. Then, as the country turned its attention to the organisation of a national system of education, there followed two decades in which over a quarter of the 123 main items from his pen were devoted to one educational topic or another. Finally, in the last ten years of his life, philosophy and religion and public affairs accounted for most of his thirty-four major new publications. As one reads his writings on various aspects of education, on the nature of a university and on Descartes and Berkeley and Hume, on Aristotle's natural history and on Hebrew and Christian thought, one scarcely knows whether to admire the more his industry or his versatility—or, perhaps, whether not to regret his dispersion of effort. But, at least, one can understand why Huxley has not been more neatly docketed and catalogued in the cabinet of fame.

Certainly G. K. Chesterton exaggerated in describing him as "much more a literary than a scientific man", but Huxley was a master in the craft of letters. His palimpsest manuscripts shew how meticulously he corrected to achieve his crystalline prose, and it has been argued that his example was responsible for the happy clarity of Stevenson and later novelists. His elementary textbooks contain descriptions so lucid as to produce the effect of a piece of chalk in a skilful hand, and at

times one is almost inclined to accept H. L. Mencken's judgement that he was "perhaps the greatest virtuoso of plain
English who has ever lived". Huxley once told the readers of
*The Pall Mall Gazette* "I venture to doubt the wisdom of
attempting to mould one's style by any other process than
that of striving after the clear and forcible expression of
definite conceptions; in which process the Glassian precept,
'first catch your definite conceptions', is probably the most
difficult to obey", but there was more to his own style than
that. Aldous Huxley has submitted his grandfather's prose to
literary analysis, and has shewn how much of its merit is due
to its economy and lucidity, its skilful use of alliteration, its
neat antitheses, and its rhythm so reminiscent of the poetical
books of the Old Testament. But perhaps it was that stormy
petrel Ray Lankester * who really put his finger on the reason
for Huxley's extraordinary literary effectiveness: "In his
case more than in that of his contemporaries, it is true that
the style is the man . . . now he is gravely shaking his head,
now compressing the lips with emphasis, and from time to
time with a quiet twinkle of the eye making unexpected
apologies or protesting that he is of a modest and peace-
loving nature." And it was this power of projecting his personality on to the printed page which made his arguments
appear as a direct communication to each individual
reader.

Since his death there has crystallised a picture of *Huxley
Eikonoklastes*, joyful only in destruction, but this is less than
half the story. John Fiske † was not the only one to discover

---

* Sir Edwin Ray Lankester (1847–1929), who from childhood had been a
great admirer of Huxley and always sought his advice. In 1874 he resigned his
Fellowship of Exeter College, Oxford, to become Professor of Zoology and
Comparative Anatomy at University College, London, but returned to Oxford
in 1891 as Linacre Professor. He was the main founder of the Marine Biological Association and in 1898 became Director of the British Museum
(Natural History).

† John Fiske (1842–1901), the historian and philosopher who was an important populariser of evolution in America. A precocious youth, he could
read ten languages by the age of twenty, but his *alma mater* Harvard never
gave him a Chair.

with surprise that "the ruling characteristic in his nature was *tenderness*", and in his *Table Talk of Shirley* John Skelton * remarked "Huxley had probably the most trenchant intellect of the time; yet, on the emotional side he was extraordinarily tender and sympathetic—no woman more so". Yet, although we cannot discount his own confession to Lizzie, "I have a woman's element in me. I hate the incessant struggle and toil to cut another's throat among us men", there was undoubtedly in him much of the pugnacious Percy, 'the Hotspur of the north', who killed some six or seven dozens of Scots at a breakfast, washed his hands, and said to his wife, "Fie upon this quiet life! I want work". As a young man of twenty-five Huxley declared "if it should be necessary for me to find public expression to my thoughts on any matter I have clearly made up my mind to do so, without allowing myself to be influenced by hope of gain or weight of authority", and it was not merely theocratic authority that he rejected. Two years before his notorious clash with the Bishop of Oxford in 1860, he was already in the bad books of Owen for refusing to submit to the accepted doctrines of cranial structure; two years before his death he was still insisting that " 'Authorities', 'disciples', and 'schools' are the curse of science; and do more to interfere with the work of the scientific spirit than all its enemies".

It is, however, his controversies with the Christians which are commonly recalled, and the skill they display is immense. Today there is a tendency in some quarters to dismiss Huxley's carefully considered philosophy of agnosticism as an amateurish aberration, but his contemporaries never made that mistake. He was not one to enter into debate without being very sure of his ground, and his manuscript notes testify to careful study of the questions at issue. And so, when the Chancellor of St Paul's attempted a loosely argued justification of belief in Biblical miracles, he came in for a

---

* Sir John Skelton (1831–1897), the Edinburgh advocate, essayist and biographer.

dialectical dissection for which some of the tools had been sharpened by the medieval schoolmen. Similarly, when St George Mivart * argued that the idea of evolution would have been acceptable to the great Roman Catholic theologian Suarez, Huxley did not take long to dig out the learned Jesuit's Latin writings and "come out in the new character of a defender of Catholic orthodoxy, and upset Mivart out of the mouth of his own prophet". But Huxley was not a sceptic for lack of any sense of the numinous, and *The Quarterly Review* was percipient when it greeted the first volume of his collected essays with the salutation *O testimonium animae naturaliter Christianae!* The debates with Gladstone, of course, constituted a special case, for Huxley was so disgusted with what he considered the G.O.M.'s intellectual opportunism that he took particular pleasure in scalping him: he once compared Gladstone with "one of those spotted dogs who runs on in front, but is always turning round to see whether the carriage is coming".

Unfortunately, Huxley's reputation as a controversialist has somewhat obscured his effectiveness as a man of affairs. Yet, when one follows the ways in which, sometimes by dull plodding committee work and sometimes by lobbying and private string-pulling and sometimes by public campaigning, he succeeded so often in moving matters in the direction he desired, one is forced to agree with an American judgement that "As a political operative, Huxley was devastatingly efficient". More than one attempt was made to tempt him to Westminster, and Grant Duff † did not think that he would have been much behind Gladstone as a debater or Bright as an orator, but perhaps he would not have gone so far in

---

* St George Jackson Mivart (1827–1900), a distinguished, if erratic, biologist who lectured successively at St Mary's Hospital, a Roman Catholic College in Kensington, and Louvain. He was eventually excommunicated for the repudiation of ecclesiastical authority.

† Sir Mountstuart Elphinstone Grant Duff (1829–1906), who "was in the habit of meeting or corresponding with almost everyone of any eminence in social life in England, and with many similar persons abroad" (*DNB*) and whose fourteen-volume diary is a rich mine of Victorian lore. He preceded Huxley as Rector of Aberdeen University.

this direction as in many others—he had not the politician's dual requirements of *une bonne digestion et un mauvais coeur*. Yet, despite his recurrent dyspepsia, he managed to manœuvre the forces for scientific and technical education in such a way as to produce the great South Kensington College, he so reconciled conflicting interests as to clear the path for a teaching University of London, and by his dominant influence on the first London School Board he did as much as any man to sketch the pattern for England's first comprehensive system of elementary education.

Those of his contemporaries who knew the man himself in all his fullness shared Lord Avebury's* view, "The truth is that Huxley was one of those all-round men who would have succeeded in any walk of life". He could perhaps never have been more than a very minor poet, but his verses on the death of Tennyson have real merit; in art he was entirely untrained, but his sketches and paintings shew great talent and his scientific illustrations are also works of art; in music he had no executive ability, but his taste was discriminating and his enjoyment keen. It is scarcely an exaggeration to say that "Huxley had more talents than two lifetimes could have developed. He could think, draw, speak, write, inspire, lead, negotiate, and wage multifarious war against earth and heaven with the cool professional ease of an acrobat supporting nine people on his shoulders at once". And yet through all his wide-ranging activities there runs one strong thread. Whether in his professorial chair at the School of Mines or as Dean of the Normal School of Science or at the annual meetings of the British Association, whether in the pages of the quarterlies or in the correspondence columns of the daily papers, whether in committee or in cabal, from first to last his

---

* Sir John Lubbock, 1st Baron Avebury (1834–1913), the banker and distinguished amateur of science, whose home became a social centre for people of importance in many walks of life. An active Member of Parliament (remembered as the originator of August Bank Holiday), he also was Chairman of London County Council, Vice-Chancellor of the University of London and Rector of St Andrews University.

concern was with education. And, now that his scientific work has suffered the fate of all good research and been overlaid by its progeny, now that his controversial writings have become pieces to be admired for their elegant craftsmanship but no longer put to daily use, it is as an educator that T. H. Huxley has the greatest significance.

# CHAPTER II

# A Culture Adequate to the Age

> The modern world is full of artillery; and we turn out our
> children to do battle in it, equipped with the shield and sword
> of an ancient gladiator.
>
> *Lecture to teachers at South Kensington Museum, 1861*

LINKING MOST OF the cultural problems facing England a
century ago was the basic question of State intervention.
Nassau Senior spoke for many when he declared that "the
main, almost sole, duty of Government is to give protection",
and there were always those who opposed any national aid for
education as a matter of principle. During the first quarter of
the century a whole series of efforts at establishing a State-
supported system of schools had foundered on sectarian or
*laissez faire* opposition, and even when Parliament reluc-
tantly provided £20,000 for educational purposes in 1833—
after willingly voting £50,000 to improve the Royal stables—
it did so without any apparent awareness that a new principle
had in fact been ceded. By 1847 a Committee of the Privy
Council was distributing £100,000 *per annum* in school grants,
but still politicians spoke as if education were a purely private
matter or solely the concern of the Churches. During the 1850s
Acts of Parliament regulated the ancient universities, the Department of Science and Art began to exercise a powerful
influence on the schools, and the Newcastle Commission
investigated the possibility of providing a system of sound

22

and cheap elementary instruction. In the following decades the Clarendon and Devonshire Commissions examined a wide range of educational institutions—but still there was a sort of pretence that the State should not interfere with education. So, maintaining in theory a belief in non-intervention which was contravened in practice, refusing to plan any system as a whole but patching and building piecemeal as each new need appeared, England by 1870 had passed the point of no return. Throughout the length and breadth of the land, Matthew Arnold noted, there was a sense of weariness with the old organisations and a desire, vague and obscure as yet, for a general transformation. "It is in the fermenting mind of the nation," he declared, "and his is for the next twenty years the real influence who can address himself to this."

Like Arnold, Huxley saw clearly that the conditions of the age called for radical reform, but his emotional attitude to the need was quite different. Arnold, educated at Rugby and Oxford and entering by right of birth into London society, was always casting lingering glances over his shoulder to the halcyon days when the worthiest aristocracy in the world had set a high example of thought and behaviour. Huxley, winning what education he could by his own efforts and as a young man searching for inexpensive rooms in a London suburb, looked forward to the day when the new fermenting forces would make men nobler than the world had yet seen. For the one the *Zeitgeist* was a depressing thing and the modern situation blank and barren; for the other the spirit of the age was pregnant with exciting possibilities. Despite his egalitarian beliefs, the poet was always one of the governing class and never quite at ease in an increasingly democratic age; although sometimes autocratic in action, the biologist never forgot his humble origin and revelled in a society whose barriers were breaking down. So, while Arnold looked with longing at the more uniform and centralised cultures of continental Europe, Huxley was optimistic about the cultural potentialities of his own unruly but energetic countrymen. And, not surprisingly, he appreciated the emerging cultures of the new lands in a way that was quite impossible for Arnold.

The bustle and bounce of America Huxley found not offensive but exhilarating, and his comment in 1876 as he looked down at the busy little boats in New York harbour is illuminating. "If I were not a man," he told the correspondent of *The New-York Tribune*, "I think I should like to be a tug." When he noted that the river skyline was dominated by the tall buildings of a newspaper and a telegraph company, he had no nostalgia about the dreaming spires of Oxford: "Ah, that is interesting; that is American," he declared. "In the Old World the first things you see as you approach a great city are steeples; here you see, first, centres of intelligence." Pioneer improvisation did not worry him— after all, he had spent several years roughing it around the world—and strange speech and customs did not repel. So, where Arnold deplored the vulgarity and lack of culture in America, Huxley congratulated the assembled citizens of a little Tennessee town upon the admirable work of their crude frame schools. The truth is that Huxley himself was (in the better sense of that word) a little 'vulgar': his gentleness prevented abundant energy from degenerating into mere pushfulness, as his generosity made it impossible for acquisitiveness to become mere money-grubbing, but the hurly-burly of an expanding society suited his vigorous nature to perfection. It was because he not merely acknowledged the *Zeitgeist*, but was himself in harmony with it, that so often he seemed able to recognise the right moment and manner to bring educational issues to a head.

In this he was perhaps aided by a certain insularity. "Depend upon it . . .", he told Hooker in 1858, "when the English mind fully determines to work a thing out it will do it better than any other. I firmly believe in the advent of an English epoch in science & art which will lick the Augustan

. . . into fits." As a young man he wrote to his mother that Rio de Janeiro was a hot and stinking town, "the odours here being improved by a strong flavour of nigger from the slaves", and the Portuguese slave-masters he dismissed with the comment "there is not a more vile, ignorant, and besotted nation under the sun". Brought up not in an enlightened household like that of the Mills or the Amberleys, but among the philistine lower middle classes, Huxley had in his early days a fair share of prejudices of all kinds—what is striking is the extent to which he managed to discard them. As late as 1865 he still believed that the average Negro was inferior to the average White, and his writings were disfigured by such phrases as "our prognathous relative" and "our dusky cousins". But he was too warm-hearted to accept the arbitrary domination of any human being by another, and too clear-headed to overlook the moral damage which oppression does to the oppressor, so the American North had his support against the Southern States in whose army his sister Lizzie's son was serving. Then in 1866, when Governor Eyre of Jamaica secured the execution under martial law of a coloured agitator named Gordon, Huxley parted from friends like Tyndall * and Kingsley,† and from his early hero Carlyle, to join with those who sought Eyre's prosecution for murder. It was, he said, irrelevant whether Eyre acted from high motives or Gordon from low, for "English law does not permit good persons, as such, to strangle bad persons, as such", and he set himself solidly against the "hero-worshippers who believe that the world is to be governed by its great men, who are to lead the little ones, justly if they can; but if not, drive or kick them the right way". A year later, after examining the ethnological evidence thoroughly for himself, he had overcome his earlier prejudice to such an

---

* John Tyndall (1820–1893), the physicist who succeeded Faraday as Superintendent of the Royal Institution. Despite various political differences, he and Huxley remained the most intimate of friends.

† Charles Kingsley (1819–1875), perhaps best remembered for his satire *The Water Babies*. As a progressive clergyman and social reformer he had a considerable influence on the cultural development of his time.

extent as to assure the citizens of Birmingham that there was no reliable evidence for any ideas of innate racial superiority.

The same process of self-liberation from early prejudice took place in connexion with anti-semitism. In 1858 Huxley was capable of sending Hooker a rather nasty note about "a little Jew—of whom I know nothing and hate as I hate all the chosen peoplesh (*sic*)", but his regular reading of the Old Testament gave him a mounting admiration for the Hebrew spiritual genius and his study of history made him deeply appreciative of the great achievement of a persecuted people. "If I were a Jew," he declared in the last year of his life, "I should have the same contempt as he has for the Christian who acted in this way towards me, who took my ideas and scorned me for clinging to them." He once told Romanes * "the only religion that appeals to me is prophetic Judaism. Add to it something from the best Stoics and something from Spinoza and something from Goethe, and there is a religion for men"; and, after Oxford had removed its religious tests, he helped the brilliant Jew Sylvester † to secure the Savilian Chair of Geometry.

The position with regard to the Irish was rather different. Huxley once wrote disparagingly of "a pack of Hibernian jobbers", and in 1890 he told Hooker that the root of the Irish trouble was that they were all ingrained liars, but one suspects that such aspersions were not so much the expression of any real ethnic prejudice as a semi-jocular justification of his opposition to Home Rule. He found that he could not help admiring Parnell, whom he regarded as honest and clear-sighted and courageous, but he feared that any disturbance of British rule in Ireland would bring suffering and blood-shed. In the same way, it is doubtful if he really believed that

* George John Romanes (1848–1894), a wealthy Canadian who worked as a private student under Michael Foster at Cambridge and Burdon-Sanderson in London. In 1890 he moved to Oxford and in the following year founded the Lectureship there which bears his family name.

† James Joseph Sylvester (1814–1897), who was ranked as Second Wrangler at Cambridge in 1833, but as a Jew could not take a degree. He occupied Chairs at University College, London, the University of Virginia and Johns Hopkins University before moving to Oxford in 1883.

the Afghans were "a pack of disorderly treacherous blood-thirsty thieves and caterans", which was how he justified to his daughter Jessie the British suppression in 1878; but he was convinced that, although the Indian Empire was a curse to England, so long as it was held at all it must be held firmly. The family declared that he was becoming a Jingo, and perhaps the vigour of his language cloaks some inner doubt, but there was something to be said for his view that at that time real justice demanded the *Pax Britannica* in India. Certainly, despite his creditable extirpation of youthful prejudices against other peoples, Huxley retained to the end a considerable prejudice in favour of the English. Perhaps that made the more effective his criticisms of English attitudes and English institutions.

The extreme individualism of the times he regarded as "merely reasoned savagery, utter and unmitigated selfishness incompatible with social existence", and he declared that he would be ashamed to accept all the benefits which society gives and then object to paying a contribution towards the education of other men's children. When he stood for election to the London School Board in 1870, he made it quite clear that he had no intention of putting his constituents' pockets before the educational needs of the teeming children of the metropolis, and later in the century he favoured local taxation for technical education and State aid for the new university colleges of the provinces. Believing that all social and legal rights are the outcome of historical processes rather than of any hypothecated primeval 'social contract', Huxley saw no reason why private prerogatives and duties should not be altered as the public good demanded. He believed that the attainment of health and wisdom might be promoted or hindered to an almost indefinite extent by education, and in the conditions of his time he had no doubt that the establishment of a satisfactory system of education implied much more State intervention than most of his contemporaries were willing to contemplate. It was because

D

Gladstone's government was the first to insist, as a matter of national policy, that every citizen should receive some education, that Huxley agreed to speak in Liverpool at the unveiling of the statue to his favourite enemy outside St George's Hall.

Convinced by his own intimate experience of the workings of the Science and Art Department that private endeavour could not have achieved anything like the same great work, Huxley was impatient with those who assumed that governmental undertakings were necessarily inefficient. "The State lives in a glass house", he pointed out; "we see what it tries to do, and all its failures, partial or total, are made the most of. But private enterprise is sheltered under good opaque bricks and mortar. The public rarely knows what it tries to do, and only hears of failures when they are gross and patent to all the world." Moreover, he remarked, "If continental bureaucracy and centralisation be fraught with multitudinous evils, surely English beadleocracy and parochial obstruction are not altogether lovely". In 1884, when the House of Commons set up a Select Committee to consider the administration of its Votes for education, science and art, he testified that he would like to see "a sagacious and influential Minister, with a seat in the Cabinet, enabling him to give the greatest force to his views which a Minister can give". The Minister of Education, he thought, "would be very unwise if he attempted to meddle with the special regulations of each school, because they very often depend upon all sorts of local conditions", and "his business is not to interfere and reduce the whole educational system of the country to one dead level, but to correct abuses". Nevertheless, knowing that freedom might be interpreted by some local educational bodies as freedom to do nothing, he had no hesitation in saying that the Minister should "by distinct regulation occasionally, if necessary, force upon these bodies, if they would not initiate it voluntarily, a modification of their educational system in the desired direction". Sixty years later, the 1944 Education

Act provided just that balance of powers which he had recommended.

Huxley's support for universal education was in no way based upon any belief in innate equality. On the contrary, he believed that the native capacities of mankind vary no less than their opportunities, and it was with brutal frankness that he told a meeting of Working Men's Clubs "The great mass of mankind have neither the liking, nor the aptitude, for either literary, or scientific, or artistic pursuits; nor, indeed, for excellence of any sort". But the natural inequality of men was not a natural inequality of classes, and Huxley informed a Marylebone meeting "he did not believe that if 100 men were picked out of the highest aristocracy in the land and 100 out of the lowest class there would be any difference of capacity among them". He therefore had no sympathy with those who maintained that there was something improper about a working man's becoming discontented with his station in life, and to the Birmingham and Midland Institute he said so in scathing terms:

One hears this argument most frequently from the representatives of the well-to-do middle class; and, coming from them, it strikes me as peculiarly inconsistent, as the one thing they admire, strive after, and advise their own children to do, is to get on in the world, and, if possible, rise out of the class in which they were born into that above them. Society needs grocers and merchants as much as it needs coalheavers; but if a merchant accumulates wealth and works his way to a baronetcy, or if the son of a greengrocer becomes a lord chancellor, or an archbishop, or, as a successful soldier, wins a peerage, all the world admires them; and looks with pride upon the social system which renders such achievements possible. Nobody suggests that there is anything wrong in their being discontented with their station; or that, in their cases society suffers by men of ability reaching the positions for which Nature has fitted them.

A new-born infant, he remarked, does not come into the world labelled scavenger or shopkeeper or bishop or duke, but as a mass of red pulp very like another, and it is only by giving each child a decent education that one can discover what he is good for. "We have all known noble lords who would have been coachmen, or gamekeepers, or billiard-markers, if they had not been kept afloat by our social corks," he continued, and his regret was not that society should do its utmost to help capacity to ascend, but that it had no machinery to facilitate the descent of incapacity.

Among the many in his day who promoted popular education, Huxley had an important advantage: the workers accepted him as one of themselves. He was largely self-educated and they knew it, he was the prophet of science and they shared his vision, he was the hammer of the Establishment and they enjoyed the sound of his blows. He had no romantic illusions about the working classes; but, because he was unambiguously on their side in the struggle for equality of opportunity, they accepted from him plain speaking which would have damned most men in their eyes for ever. Unlike some angry young men of a century later, he never despised the common people, and they sensed it.

Huxley had been indelibly marked by his early experiences as apprentice to an East End doctor, when people came to him for medical aid who were really suffering from nothing but slow starvation:

> I have not forgotten—am not likely to forget so long as memory holds—a visit to a sick girl in a wretched garret where two or three other women, one a deformed woman, sister of my patient, were busy shirt-making. After due examination, even my small medical knowledge sufficed to show that my patient was merely in want of some better food than the bread and bad tea on which these people were living. I said so as gently as I could, and the sister turned on me with a kind of choking passion. Pulling out of her pocket a few pence and halfpence, and holding them out, "That is all I get for six-and-thirty hours' work, and you talk about giving her proper food".

In 1870 he was delighted to be driven about Liverpool in the Mayor's magnificent coach as befitted the President of the British Association, and he mixed smoothly enough with "a fashionable and brilliant assemblage of ladies and gentlemen" in the Philharmonic Hall, but between sessions he also explored the city slums—and he minced no words in recounting his experiences at a later gathering of the respectable:

He declared that it had been a shock to him, walking through Liverpool streets, to see unwashed, unkempt, brutal people side by side with indications of the greatest refinement and the greatest luxury. . . . The people who formed what are called the upper strata of society talked of political questions as if they were questions of Whig and Tory, of Conservative and heaven knows what; but beneath there was the greater question whether that prodigious misery which dogs the footsteps of modern civilisation should be allowed to exist. . . . He believed that was the great political question of the future.

It was no doubt as a result of this outburst that the Liverpool United Trades Council petitioned him to speak on their behalf, and in the following spring he lectured in Hope Hall to help the Operative Trades Committee to liquidate the debt on their meeting-place. A few months later he was asking a Birmingham audience "What gives force to the socialistic movement which is now stirring European society to its depths, but a determination on the part of the naturally able men among the proletariat, to put an end, somehow or other, to the misery and degradation in which a large proportion of their fellows are steeped?" Speaking again after the passage of sixteen years he was still pressing the point, and he warned a Manchester meeting to have a care that the sole prospect of a life of labour should not be an old age of penury: "any social condition in which the development of wealth involves the misery, the physical weakness, and the degradation of the worker, is absolutely and infallibly doomed to collapse. Your bayonets and cutlasses will break under your hand". No wonder that he received complaints that his words were being quoted by 'socialist agitators'!

Huxley was far from being a socialist, but he had a deep contempt for 'society' and its myrmidons. The proper reward of intellectual distinction, he held, was the regard of those best qualified to assess it, and "Newton and Cuvier lowered themselves when the one accepted an idle knighthood, and the other became a baron of the empire. The great men who went to their graves as Michael Faraday and George Grote seem to me to have understood the dignity of knowledge better when they declined all such meretricious trappings". For his own part, he wanted nothing of such affairs. "It was known that the only peerage I would accept was a spiritual one," he jokingly explained to Mrs Clifford, "and as H.M. shares the not unnatural prejudice which led her illustrious predecessor (now some time dead) to object to give a bishopric to Dean Swift, it was thought that she could not stand the promotion of Dean Huxley." In the June of 1887 the Prime Minister invited him to a private discussion on a "matter of some public interest", which turned out to be a query by Lord Salisbury about what form of public recognition would be acceptable to men of intellectual distinction, and the particular proposal was the institution of an analogue to the *Pour le Mérite*. As it turned out, Britain's Order of Merit was not to be established in Huxley's lifetime, and Salisbury explored another possibility: would a Privy Councillorship be acceptable? Since this was not a mere title but an office, and since it seemed to him very desirable that men of science and letters should have some advisory function in affairs of State, Huxley accepted. "The Archbishopric of Canterbury is the only object of ambition that remains to me," he told Hooker. "Come and be Suffragan; there is plenty of room at Lambeth and a capital garden!"

Huxley was never worried about what consequences might follow the emergence of the workers into positions of power. "Compare your average artisan and your average country squire," he suggested, "and I don't believe you will find a pin to choose between the two in point of ignorance, class feeling, or prejudice. . . . Why should we be worse off under one régime than under the other?" Some inborn plebeian blindness, he declared, prevented his seeing why pigeon-shooting at Hurlingham should be refined while rat-killing in Whitechapel was low, nor could he understand why "What a lark" was gutter-slang while "How awfully jolly" was the mark of a gentleman. He not only wished to help the workers, but had a high view of their moral rights and intellectual potentialities: "I believe in the fustian", he told Dyster,* "and can talk better to it than to any amount of gauze and Saxony." Nor was he content with talk: when he heard of a Southampton docker who spent his little spare cash in biological study, he saw to it that he was provided with a good microscope and plenty of encouragement.

Artisans across half the land heard Huxley from time to time, but it was among the men and women of the metropolis that his main work was done. Naturally, he helped Maurice † by lecturing occasionally at the Working Men's College which a group of Christian Socialists had founded in 1854, but his special pride was his own South London Working Men's College on the other side of the Thames. The moving spirit in this intriguing but largely forgotten institution was a certain William Rossiter, a portmanteau worker who had joined Maurice's College in its first term and thereafter become a teacher. Huxley agreed to act as Principal of the College, at whose opening in Southwark he delivered his much-quoted 1868 address 'A Liberal Education and Where to Find It'. The collegiate classes ranged widely over literature and languages, mathematics and the sciences, and various commercial and industrial subjects, and in addition there grew up an evening adult school for women and a day school for boys and girls. Most of the donkey work was done by Rossiter, but the Principal delivered occasional lectures, secured well-known speakers like Palgrave ‡ and Conway §

* Frederick Daniel Dyster (1810–1893), with whom Huxley often stayed at Tenby when examining coastal organisms.
† Frederick Denison Maurice (1805–1872), who had to vacate his Chair at King's College, London, following the publication of his *Theological Essays* in 1853. He took an active part in the promotion of education for women and workers and, even after becoming Professor of Moral Theology at Cambridge in 1866, maintained his connexion with the Working Men's College.
‡ Francis Turner Palgrave (1824–1897), the poet and critic, best remembered for his *Golden Treasury* series.
§ Moncure Daniel Conway (1832–1907), the Unitarian clergyman who came to England from America in 1863 and became 'Minister' of the South Place Ethical Society. His name is perpetuated in Conway Hall, Red Lion Square.

and Payne,* and performed conscientiously the ceremonial duties of presiding at meetings and presenting certificates to students. As the years went by the College gathered strength and opened the first free library in South London, and in 1878 it migrated to fresh premises in Upper Kennington Lane. But Huxley found it increasingly difficult to devote much time to the institution, and at the end of 1880 he resigned his Principalship. The flourishing library soon blossomed out into branches and also opened an art gallery, but after 1884 the College side of the venture seems to have given way completely to its sturdy offspring. All over South London there are now free libraries, the Camberwell School of Arts and Crafts continues under the London County Council, and in Peckham Road the South London Art Gallery still dates its foundation from that January of 1868 when Huxley opened his Working Men's College. It is somehow fitting that a man of so catholic a mind should be remembered by a group of institutions of the arts in South London as well as by the great group of science schools in South Kensington.

Although he was never in any doubt about the intellectual potential of the English worker, Huxley's early attitude to the women of England was somewhat ambiguous. In 1860, for example, he refused to support Lyell's suggestion that females might be admitted to the Geological Society and, seven years later, Kate Lady Amberley noted in her journal that he did not believe women would ever equal men in power or capacity. Perhaps, however, Kate failed to distinguish between his view of the existing state of the female mind and his estimate of its potentialities, and certainly his reluctance to admit women to the Geological Society arose from the fact that it was not a place for the education of students but a place for discussion by experts. Nine-tenths

---

* Joseph Payne (1808–1876), a progressive schoolmaster who occupied at the College of Preceptors the first Chair of Education in England.

of women at that time, he told Lyell,\* were sunk in mere
ignorant parsonese superstition, and no permanent advancement could come until the female half of the race had been
emancipated. The idea that a woman should learn only so
much as would enable her to sympathise with her husband's
pleasures and those of his best friends, harboured even by
a progressive thinker like Ruskin, was entirely alien to
Huxley:

> Granting the alleged defects of women, is it not somewhat absurd to
> sanction and maintain a system of education which would seem to have
> been specially contrived to exaggerate all these defects? . . . With few
> insignificant exceptions, girls have been educated either to be drudges,
> or toys, beneath man; or a sort of angels above him. . . . The possibility
> that the ideal of woman-kind lies neither in the fair saint, nor in the fair
> sinner . . . that women are meant neither to be men's guides nor their
> playthings, but their comrades, their fellows, and their equals, so far as
> Nature puts no bar on that equality, does not seem to have entered into
> the minds of those who have had the conduct of the education of girls.

So far as his own daughters were concerned, he was quite
clear that "They at any rate shall not be got up as mantraps
for the matrimonial market", and the blatant injustices to
which women were subjected brought him over firmly to the
support of female education. Already in 1861 he was helping
Elizabeth Garrett † with her physiological studies, and when
all medical schools were closed against her he gave admission
to his lectures at South Kensington. In 1874, when Sophia
Jex-Blake ‡ sought his support against various obstacles which
were being placed in the way of women medical students at
Edinburgh, he refused to condemn those professors who objected to teaching anatomy and physiology to mixed classes,
but he wrote to *The Times* "I am at a loss to understand on
what grounds of justice or public policy a career which is

* Sir Charles Lyell (1797–1875), the eminent geologist who taught people to
think in terms of millions of years and so did much to prepare the public mind
for Darwin's theory.
† Elizabeth Garrett Anderson (1836–1917), a pioneer woman doctor and an
early suffragist. She was a member of the first London School Board.
‡ Sophia Louisa Jex-Blake (1840–1912), who was the main founder of the
London Medical School for Women.

open to the weakest and most foolish of the male sex should be forcibly closed to women of vigour and capacity". By this time he had sufficiently overcome his own prejudices to admit females to his ordinary classes and even to have a 'demonstratrix' in physiology, and in the following year he said that if it depended on him women would be examined in Aberdeen University the next day. He had become convinced that many of the alleged disabilities of females were the product of their mode of life, and his 1865 lecture, 'Emancipation—Black and White', answered those who asked what could be done to bring about a better state of things:

> We reply, emancipate girls. Recognise the fact that they share the senses, perceptions, feelings, reasoning powers, emotions, of boys, and that the mind of the average girl is less different from that of the average boy, than the mind of one boy is from that of another; so that whatever argument justifies a given education for boys, justifies its application to girls as well. So far from imposing artificial restrictions upon the acquirement of knowledge by women, throw every facility in their way. . . . Let us have "sweet girl graduates" by all means. They will be none the less sweet for a little wisdom; and the "golden hair" will not curl less gracefully outside the head by reason of there being brains within.

Huxley seems to have retained a belief that the inevitable distinction of biological function between men and women would in general ensure that men maintained an advantage in the struggle for the prizes of life, but he saw no reason why social injustice should be added to biological handicap. His own experience on Royal Commissions, he once told Jowett, was that "no witness is so dishonest as a really good woman with a cause to serve", but he was still prepared to serve their causes. So we find him supporting Emily Davies * in the foundation of Girton College and Maria Grey † in promoting the National Society for the Improvement of Women's

* Sarah Emily Davies (1830–1921), the founder of Girton College, Cambridge, originally opened at Hitchin.
† Maria Georgina Grey (1816–1906), main founder of the Girls' Public Day School Company (now Trust), after whom is named a college for teachers in London.

Education; we find him taking the chair at the public meeting which led to the establishment of the South Hampstead High School for Girls and serving on the Education Committee of the Princess Helena College for Girls at Ealing; and—mercifully unsuspecting that nearly seventy years would elapse before the demand was granted—Huxley was one of those who in 1880 petitioned Cambridge University to open its degrees to women.

As England slowly organised its system of education, and increasingly set its face against nepotic place-filling, examinations of all kinds proliferated. For entry into the civil service, for scholarships and Fellowships at the ancient universities, for earning school grants from the government, examination success became the great essential. Already by 1863 Kingsley was complaining about "the Isle of Tomtoddies, all heads and no bodies", where the children sang morning and evening to their great idol Examination, and as the years went by the disadvantages of the system became more obvious. In his 1874 Rectorial Address at Aberdeen Huxley spoke of students who "work to pass, not to know; and outraged science takes her revenge. They do pass, and they don't know". Three years later he told a meeting at the Society of Arts "The educational abomination of desolation of the day is the excessive stimulation of young people to work at high pressure by incessant competitive examinations", and he deplored the destruction of youthful freshness by what he called "precocious mental debauchery . . . book gluttony and lesson bibbing". Nevertheless, he did not see how examinations could be dispensed with, so he concentrated on using them as a check to the sham teaching he so much deplored.

Many of those who had faith in examinations were fortified by a belief in the transfer of training from a school subject to the affairs of everyday life, and this belief was commonly associated with the idea that the mind consisted of a group of 'faculties'—of memory, observation, and so on. Huxley, as a man of his time, often used the psychological jargon of the time, but the usage did not commit him to any particular view of mental structure:

> In the language of common life, the "mind" is spoken of as an entity, independent of the body, though resident in and closely connected with it, and endowed with numerous "faculties". . . . The popular classification and terminology of the phenomena of consciousness, however, are . . . a legacy, and, in many respects, a sufficiently *damnosa hœreditas*, of ancient philosophy, more or less leavened by theology. . . . Very little attention to what passes in the mind is sufficient to show, that these conceptions involve assumptions of an extremely hypothetical character. And the first business of the student of psychology is to get rid of such prepossessions.

But, whether or not observation and reasoning are 'faculties', Huxley had no doubt that they could be developed by education and that it was the teacher's job to develop them.

It was largely because he believed that science was a peculiarly valuable means of mental training that Huxley so strongly advocated its teaching, but it was only if science were taught in a certain way that he made any claims for it at all. He would not have demurred from Moberley's * complaint to the Clarendon Commission, that a scientific fact is "simply a barren fact" which becomes forgotten and is perfectly unfruitful; but he would have added that the same is true of a grammatical fact, and that in either case the fact might be so taught as to germinate in the mind and produce intellectual fruit. He believed that "those who refuse to go beyond fact, rarely get as far as fact", but that was no reason for closing the mind against the facts of science or for failing to make them a normal part of schooling.

In the introduction to his *Collected Essays* Huxley spoke of "the conviction which has grown with my growth and strengthened with my strength, that there is no alleviation for the sufferings of mankind except veracity of thought and action, and the resolute facing of the world as it is when the

---

* William Moberley (1803–1885), the elegant Latinist who was Headmaster of Winchester College and later became Bishop of Salisbury.

garment of make-believe by which pious hands have hidden its uglier features is stripped off", and one of the things that attracted him so greatly to Goethe was the poet's courageous facing of fact. While he was waiting in 1856 for the birth of his first child, Huxley jotted down these lines in his notebook:

> Willst du dir ein hübsch Leben zimmern,
> Musst dich ans Vergangene nicht bekümmern;
> Und wäre dir auch was Verloren,
> Musst immer thun wie neugeboren.
> Was jeder Tag will, sollst du fragen;
> Was jeder Tag will, wird er sagen.
> Musst dich an eigenem Thun ergötzen;
> Was andere thun, das wirst du schätzen.
> Besonders keinen Menschen hassen
> Und das Übrige Gott überlassen.*

The verse expresses perfectly his own scientific calvinism. In one of his earliest lectures he pointed out that a proportion of pain was present even at the lowest level of the animal creation, and what was inevitable must be borne. Of moral purpose and beneficence he saw no trace in the universe except that which was of human making, and the world had to be seen as it was before it could be improved.

Huxley repeatedly declared his allegiance to Goethe's *thätige skepsis*, and there is wryly amused self-knowledge in his remark "Why I was christened Thomas Henry I do not know; but it is a curious chance that my parents should have fixed for my usual denomination upon the name of that particular Apostle with whom I have always felt most sympathy". He once spoke to Mivart of "the sin of faith", and it

---

\* If you wish a noble life to make,
  All grief o'er what's gone by forsake;
  And whatso may be lost to you,
  Act as if you're born anew;
  What each day wills, that shall you bear;
  What each day wills, it will declare.
  To your own task devote your days;
  Let others' work receive your praise;
  Above all else, bear no man hate
    —The rest to God renunciate.

was largely because good science teaching encourages the habit of questioning authority that he so strongly advocated it:

In the world of letters, learning and knowledge are one, and books are the source of both; whereas in science, as in life, learning and knowledge are distinct and the study of things, and not of books, is the source of the latter . . . the great benefit which a scientific education bestows, whether as training or as knowledge, is dependent upon the extent to which the mind of the student is brought into immediate contact with facts—upon the degree to which he learns the habit of appealing directly to Nature.

His advocacy, moreover, had no bias towards scientific authority, and he wanted school teaching to lay "a firm foundation for the further knowledge which is needed for the critical examination of the dogmas, whether scientific or anti-scientific, which are presented to the adult mind".

It is possible to select from Huxley's writings passages which seem to imply that an education in science would automatically produce keen observation and clear thought, but he was engaged in an offensive against heavily defended pedagogical positions and to take his battle-cries as judicial statements is absurd. Considered as a whole, his published writings concur with his correspondence and his own practice to demonstrate an acute awareness that the virtues of science teaching depend entirely on its method. Distributing the prizes at the Liverpool Institute School in 1883, he condemned those detestable books which answered the question "What is a horse?" by a mere scholastic formula, "The horse is termed *Equus caballus*; belongs to the class Mammalia; order, Pachydermata; family Solidungula", and he laid down four conditions if science teaching were to be of any good at all, if it were not to be less than no good, if it were to take the place of that which was already of some good. These conditions were that the topics should be carefully selected, that the teaching should be practical and bring the children into direct contact with facts, that the teacher should himself have a real mastery of his matter, and that sufficient time should be devoted to the subject to allow of thorough study. He admitted to a Manchester audience in 1871 that there was a good deal of science teaching which was inferior as an educational instrument to the ordinary school work at Latin grammar, and unless science were so taught as to take advantage of its peculiar virtues he would prefer it not to be taught at all.

Recognising that the whole of modern thought is steeped in science and that even those who affect to ignore or despise it are unconsciously impregnated with its spirit, Huxley did not see how anyone could claim to be educated without a considerable knowledge of its subject matter and a clear understanding of its methods. Yet he had no desire for a narrow curriculum, and at the opening of Sir Josiah Mason's Science College in Birmingham he issued a warning that an exclusively scientific training would bring about a mental twist as surely as an exclusively literary training. "The value of the cargo", he remarked, "does not compensate for the ship's being out of trim." When he came to give evidence to the 1884 Select Committee on Education in Science and Art, he said "I do not disguise my conviction that the whole theory on which our present educational system is based, is wrong from top to bottom; that the subjects which are now put down as essential . . . are luxuries, so to speak; and that those which are regarded as comparatively unessential and as luxuries are the essentials". In advocating a complete *boule-versement* of the existing system, he looked upon English literature and history and political economy as having the same claims as natural science, and these four subjects he would make the common foundation of all education.

If Huxley was right in believing that a man of average mind may be trained in one direction to literature or in another direction to science, our present problem of the shortage of scientists may not be so intractable as it sometimes appears, but perhaps he was generalising from his own wide tastes and abilities. The very flavour of his writing tells of his love for Milton, and his urge to read the *Divina Commedia* in Dante's own tongue was strong enough to make him learn Italian as a young man. Wordsworth and Shelley never much appealed to him, but for Tennyson and Spenser and Keats he had a strong affection, as for much of the early Browning. Always he was returning to his favourite, Meredith's *Modern Love*, and his library was rich in prose literature of all kinds. His diaries shew him attending the Rabelais Club and the Garrick Club and the Literary Society, and in his younger days he went regularly to operas and concerts. Year by year he managed to find time for art exhibitions, and it was not entirely in jest that he spoke at the Royal Academy dinner in 1876:

> The recent progress of biological speculation leads to the conclusion that the scale of being may be thus stated—minerals, plants, animals, men who cannot draw—artists. . . . We have long been seeking, as you may be aware, for a distinction between men and animals. The old barriers have long broken away. Other things walk on two legs and have no feathers, caterpillars make themselves clothes, kangaroos have pockets. If I am not to believe that my dog reasons, loves and hates, how am I to be sure that my neighbour does? Parrots, again, talk what deserves the name of sense as much as a great deal which it would be rude to call nonsense. Again, beavers and ants engineer as well as the members of the noblest of professions. But . . . man alone can draw or make unto himself a likeness. This then, is the great distinction of humanity, and it follows that the most pre-eminently human of creatures are those who possess this distinction in the highest degree.

Nevertheless, it was the sciences which were Huxley's special love, and he believed that they could be a highly moralising study. At times, indeed, his passion for a moral outcome of education led him into strangely uncritical remarks, as when he told a meeting at St Martin's Hall "I cannot but think that he who finds a certain proportion of pain and evil inseparably woven up in the life of the very worms, will bear his own share with more courage and submission". In assessing Huxley's claims for science teaching,

**THE ASSISTANT-SURGEON**
*'I will leave my mark somewhere, and it shall be clear and distinct'* (p. 11)

**THE YOUNG EAGLE**

'*I am sharpening up my claws and beak in readiness*'  p. 68)

however, it is important to remember that he included under that term not only the experimental sciences but also the social sciences and whatever ethical principles could be rationally established. He told Lord Farrer * in 1894 that the so-called 'sociology' of the time was riddled with *a priori* assumptions, which were as much an anachronism in the study of social life as they would be in hydrostatics, and that what was necessary was an objective study of the different ways in which humans would in fact behave under different circumstances. "The Political Economists have gone the right way to work ...", he declared, "by tracing out the effects of one great cause of human action, the desire of wealth, supposing it to be unchecked. If they, or other people, have forgotten that there are other potent causes of action which may interfere with this, it is no fault of scientific method, but only their own stupidity." There was, he believed, much need for someone to do the same sort of thing for ethics, "Settle the question of what will be done under the unchecked action of certain motives, and leave the problem of 'ought' for subsequent consideration". And, in the meanwhile, until this desired science of 'eubiotics' should be constructed, he would have all children instructed in those ethical principles which appeared to lead to communal well-being and in those facts of social existence which had ethical implications.

"That which I mean by 'Science'," he wrote to Charles Kingsley, "is not mere physical science but all the results of exact methods of thought whatever be the subject matter to which they are applied ... people fancy that mathematics or physics or biology are exclusively 'Science'—and value the clothes of science more than the goddess herself." It was to the cult of this goddess, she of all-pervading honesty, that Huxley devoted his many-sided life. And honesty, too, was a word with wide significance for him. There was intellectual honesty and artistic honesty and moral honesty, and all were

* Sir Thomas Henry Farrer, 1st Baron (1819–1899), who as Permanent Secretary of the Board of Trade for some twenty years exercised considerable influence on English legislation.

E

necessary to the complete man. Science was to be taught not by itself or for itself, but as an integral part of that liberal education which he defined at his Working Men's College in these words:

That man, I think, has had a liberal education who has been so trained in youth that his body is the ready servant of his will, and does with ease and pleasure all the work that, as a mechanism, it is capable of; whose intellect is a clear, cold, logic engine, with all its parts of equal strength, and in smooth working order; ready, like a steam engine, to be turned to any kind of work, and spin the gossamers as well as forge the anchors of the mind; whose mind is stored with a knowledge of the great and fundamental truths of Nature and of the laws of her operations; one who, no stunted ascetic, is full of life and fire, but whose passions are trained to come to heel by a vigorous will, the servant of a tender conscience; who has learned to love all beauty, whether of Nature or of art, to hate all vileness, and to respect others as himself.

Such an one and no other, I conceive, has had a liberal education; for he is, as completely as a man can be, in harmony with Nature.

# CHAPTER III

# Morality and Metaphysics

I wish not to be in any way confounded with the cynics who delight in degrading man—or with the common run of materialists—who think mind is any the lower for being a function of matter. I dislike them even more than I do the pietists.

*Letter to J. D. Hooker, 6 January 1861*

TOWARDS THE END of his days Huxley recalled how, as a child, he had turned his pinafore wrong side forwards to represent a surplice and then delivered a sermon in the kitchen in imitation of the local vicar. "That", he declared, "is the earliest indication I can call to mind of the strong clerical affinities which my friend Mr Herbert Spencer has always ascribed to me," and Spencer was not alone in this ascription. Favourably referred to by John Skelton as 'the John Knox of Agnosticism' and unfavourably by *The Spectator* as 'Pope Huxley', from time to time jokingly addressed by friends as 'Reverend Sir' or 'Honoured Episcopus', Huxley had the amused self-knowledge to sign a letter on one occasion as his scientific correspondent's "right reverend father in worms and Bishop of Annelidae".

Yet, although there was something of the prelate in Huxley's proud nature, there was more of the prophet, foreseeing the future and under compulsion to proclaim his vision boldly. "The longer I live," he declared, "the more obvious it is to me that the most sacred act of a man's life is to say and to feel 'I believe such and such to be true' ". As is the way with prophets, his tenacity at times amounted almost to pig-headedness and his moral certitude almost to priggishness, and such men can be uncomfortable companions. But when the prophet has also a tender soul and an impish sense of humour, he can be a joy to all around him. "It was worth being born to have known Huxley", declared Edward Clodd,* and it was because their master saw science as a holy quest for truth that Huxley's pupils were infected by his moral fervour and became his devoted disciples.

In his *Rattlesnake* diary the young assistant-surgeon had written "*Gott hilfe mir!* Morals and religion are one wild whirl to me", but throughout his life they were to remain major preoccupations. Hundreds of folios of notes bear witness to the seriousness with which he studied theology and philosophy, and he not only planned but actually started writing a comprehensive History of Christianity. Very soon his intellect drove him to agnosticism, but the quality of reverence in his large and generous nature comes out in the verses he wrote on the death of Tennyson, of which one stanza must here suffice:

> And oh! sad wedded mourner seeking still
> For vanished hand-clasp, drinking in thy fill
> Of holy grief; forgive, that pious theft
> Robs thee of all, save memories left:
> Not thine to kneel beside the grassy mound
> While dies the western glow; and all around
> Is silence: and the shadows closer creep
> And whisper softly: All must fall asleep.

Huxley's morality had a strongly calvinistic streak, and he once told the Cambridge Young Men's Christian Association that "if some great Power would agree to make me always think what is true and do what is right, on condition of being turned into a sort of clock and wound up every morning

---

* Edward Clodd (1840–1930), friend of many Victorian intellectuals, who lectured at the Royal Institution as recently as 1921 and surprisingly spans the pre-Darwinian and the immediately pre-Atomic ages.

before I got out of bed, I should instantly close with the offer". Ten months before Darwin's *Origin of Species* appeared in print, his bulldog was already considering the moral implications of the theory of evolution, and he saw nothing in it to degrade mankind. "After all," he assured Dyster, "it is as respectable to be modified monkey as to be modified dirt", and two years later he used the first number of *The Natural History Review* to scotch the idea that a belief in evolution warranted any diminution of morality:

> The proof of his claim to independent parentage will not change the brutishness of man's lower nature; nor, except to those varlet souls who cannot see greatness in their fellow because his father was a cobbler, will the demonstration of a pithecoid pedigree one whit diminish man's divine right of kingship over nature; nor lower the great and princely dignity of perfect manhood, which is an order of nobility, not inherited, but to be won by each of us, so far as he consciously seeks good and avoids evil, and puts the faculties with which he is endowed to their fittest use.

Anxious as he was to avoid the undermining of any institution which might promote morality, Huxley did his best to co-operate with those liberally disposed churchmen who sought to cleanse religion of inessential accretions and bring it into harmony with scientific fact. But not many of the clergy were as open-minded as 'Hang-theology Rogers' * or Charles Kingsley or Dean Farrar †; and, when Huxley spoke in 1867 at Sion College, the City's ancient centre of theological study, his temperate address met with the most intemperate opposition. One future bishop wrote immediately after the meeting to apologise "that you should have been met by some of my brethren with a rudeness & roughness

---

* William Rogers (1819–1896), the very liberal Rector of Bishopsgate who built up a whole network of church schools and in 1870 was elected one of the first members of the London School Board.

† Frederick William Farrar (1831–1903), who had taught at Marlborough and Harrow before returning to Marlborough as headmaster. He became Chaplain to the Queen and to the Speaker of the House of Commons, as well as Canon of Westminster and later Dean of Canterbury, and his progressiveness in both theology and pedagogy did much to help in the reorientation of English education.

which stood in painful contrast with the calm dignity, &
gentlemanly quietness of your own manner", and thirty
years later Farrar was still furious at the bad behaviour of the
clergy. "I remember the meeting well . . .", he told Leonard
Huxley. "Your father made one of his powerful and exquisitely lucid speeches furnishing the most decisive geological & archæological proofs of the vast antiquity of the
world, & of man. . . . The meeting made me very angry &
was a melancholy exhibition of clerical intolerance." Farrar
himself, although impressed by the earnest and delightful
conversations which he had with Huxley on religious subjects, complained that his conceptions of what the clergy
were bound to believe were exceedingly wide of the mark.
But, when he was told at Sion College that even bishops and
archbishops had abandoned many of the traditional beliefs,
Huxley had a simple retort: "Why, then, do you not teach
these things to your congregations?"

In a notebook of aphorisms Huxley made a jotting which
reflects very clearly his general view of religion:

Religions rise because they satisfy the many and fall because they
cease to satisfy the few.

They have been the day dreams of mankind and each in turn has
become a nightmare from which a gleam of knowledge has waked the
dreamer.

The religion which will endure is such a day dream as may still be
dreamed in the noon tide glare of science.

He declared that he had a great respect for all the old
bottles, and that if the new wine could be contained without
bursting them he would be very glad, but he confessed that
he could not see how that could be done. "It is clear to me",
he told Kingsley, "that if that great and powerful influence
for good or evil, the Church of England, is to be saved from
being shivered into fragments by the advancing tide of science
—an event I should be very sorry to witness . . . it must be
by the efforts of men who, like yourself, see your way to the
combination of the practice of the Church with the spirit of

science." However, although he continued in close friendship with many clergymen, the continued hostility of others gradually convinced him that no reconciliation was possible. And, in any event, he saw as the century proceeded that science was less in danger of suppression by clerical obscurantism than of distortion by social self-delusion.

As its economy expanded and its wonderful machines gained ever new triumphs, Victorian England increasingly extracted from Darwin's theory an apparently scientific sanction for its belief in inevitable progress. For people who were demonstrably doing extremely well in the struggle for existence, it was gratifying to believe that this was due to biological superiority, and sensitive souls who were appalled by social squalor found comfort in the thought that cut-throat competition led ultimately to the survival of the fittest. From the start Huxley had set himself against such pseudo-science, and he maintained that "So far from any gradual progress forming any necessary part of the Darwinian creed, it appears to us that it is perfectly consistent with indefinite persistence in one state, or with a gradual retrogression". He at least cannot have been surprised that Tom the Water Baby, following the history of the great and famous nation of the Doasyoulikes (who lived by the Happy-golucky Mountains where flapdoodle grew wild), saw a highly cultured people gradually change into ape-like savages.

In essays and addresses through the years, Huxley urged that the struggle of animal nature was one thing and the organisation of human society another, and he indicated the fallacy of all forms of Panglossism based on their confusion. In 1888 he produced for *The Nineteenth Century* a paper on 'The Struggle for Existence in Human Society', which led, as he had realised it would, to a quarrel with Herbert Spencer, who held the comfortable belief that poverty was no longer much of a problem in England and that in any case the State should not interfere. "Great is humbug, and it will prevail", Huxley told the editor, "unless the people who do not like it will hit hard. The beast has no brains, but you can knock the heart out of him." From the point of view of the moralist, his article maintained, the animal world is on about the same level as a gladiators' show, and he insisted that the facts of nature give no support to the optimistic dogma that this is the best of all possible worlds. As for the argument that the terrible struggle for existence tends to final good, he commented sardonically that it is not clear what compensation *Eohippus* got for its sorrows in the fact that some millions of years later one of his descendants was to win the Derby. In fact, he concluded, "the course shaped by the ethical man— the member of society or citizen—necessarily runs counter to that which the non-ethical man—the primitive savage, or man as a mere member of the animal kingdom—tends to adopt. The latter fights out the struggle for existence to the bitter end, like any other animal; the former devotes his best energies to the object of setting limits to the struggle".

This of course was the great theme of Huxley's Romanes Lecture on 'Evolution and Ethics', delivered at Oxford in 1893. Prohibited by the terms of his invitation from dealing with politics or religion, he managed to say a good deal about both. "There is no allusion to politics in my lecture, nor to any religion except Buddhism . . .", he wrote after preparing his draft. "If people apply anything I say . . . to modern philosophies . . . and religions, that is not my affair. To be honest, however, unless I thought they would, I should never have taken all the pains I have bestowed on these 36 pages." Huxley was ailing and his voice was feeble, but *The Oxford Magazine* was enthusiastic: "We can only express our humble admiration of the masculine vigour of Professor Huxley's thought and of the language in which it is clothed. A more exquisitely finished academic discourse was never placed before any audience in any language."

Tracing the progression of mankind from primitive conditions and analysing the rôles played by self-assertion, cunning, curiosity, imitativeness and ruthlessness, the Romanes

Lecture also shewed how social advance had depended on the development of the ideas of justice and law and ethical obligation. Huxley agreed with people like Herbert Spencer that our ideas of morality have in fact evolved, but he denied that the evolutionary process provided any criterion of morality. He decried "the fanatical individualism of our time [which] attempts to apply the analogy of cosmic nature to society" and concluded that the ethical progress of society depends, not on imitating the cosmic process, still less on running away from it, but on combating it. There was nothing especially novel in all this, but many of those who had claimed scientific sanction for their political prejudices were resentful of a blast from this quarter. "Don't you know that I am become a reactionary and secret friend of the clerics?" Huxley gleefully asked Lord Farrer. "My lecture is really an effort to put the Christian doctrine that Satan is Prince of this world upon a scientific foundation."

Why the Romanes Lecture caused surprise is difficult to understand, for it had been clearly foreshadowed in Huxley's address on 'Administrative Nihilism' more than twenty years earlier. Speaking at the Birmingham and Midland Institute in 1871, at a time when the *laissez faire* extremists were decrying the provisions of Forster's Education Act, he had vigorously opposed the view that the sole proper function of the State was that of keeping order, which he decried as advocating "neither a monarchy, an aristocracy, nor a democracy, but an *astynomocracy*, or police government". There is no evidence that Huxley ever read Marx, but there is an unmistakable flavour of historical materialism about his sardonic remark that "men have become largely absorbed in the mere accumulation of wealth; and as this is a matter in which the plainest and strongest form of self-interest is intensely concerned, science (in the shape of Political Economy) has readily demonstrated that self-interest may be safely left to find the best way of attaining its ends". And, whatever political economy might have to say, he was not going to allow biology to be abused to the same end. The facile and then favourite analogy between the body politic and the body physiological, upon which Herbert Spencer had relied in his essay 'The Social Organism', he shewed to be quite fallacious —indeed, he remarked, if the analogy had any validity at all it favoured more rather than less State intervention: "Even the blood-corpuscles can't hold a public meeting without being accused of 'congestion'—and the brain, like other despots whom we have known, calls out at once for the use of sharp steel against them."

As suspicious of *a priori* argument in politics as in science or in religion, Huxley produced in 1890 a series of highly critical articles for *The Nineteenth Century*. His essay 'On the Natural Inequality of Men' shot holes in Rousseau's derivation of egalitarianism from a postulated 'state of nature'; 'Natural Rights and Political Rights' demonstrated that, if each Londoner has a 'natural right' to a share in the property of the Duke of Westminster, so have the millions of Asia and Africa to the property of all Englishmen; 'Capital—the Mother of Labour' had great fun with the fallacies of Henry George. It was all extremely clever, and it is difficult to put a finger on any logical flaw in these essays, but they emit a mild aroma of conservative prejudice. Twenty years earlier Huxley had argued that, if the abolition of private ownership could be shewn to promote the good of the people, the State would have the same justification for abolishing property as it had hitherto had for maintaining it, but now the sharper edge of his dialectical sword seemed to be turned more often on the left than on the right. The balance was somewhat redressed by 'Government: Anarchy or Regimentation', which attacked extreme individualism equally with regimental socialism and emphasised that the great political problem of the future would be that of over-population, but it is difficult not to conclude that a limit had been set to Huxley's radicalism by his increasing stake in society. As a young man in the 1850s, casting about for a scientific competence in London, Huxley could scarcely produce his cab fares and did not see how he could possibly afford to marry. But in 1864 he was earning £950 in a year apart from royalties, in 1871 his literary and miscellaneous earnings were over £1000 and his total income some £2100, in 1876 when the income tax was a mere threepence in the pound he earned about £3000, and in 1893 he noted total assets of over £14,000. Even with earnings like these his generosity sometimes left him financially embarrassed, and certainly he never lost his intense awareness of the pauperism of the people or his moral indignation at it, but few men could be entirely unaffected by such a change in personal fortune. Genuine regard for the workers Huxley had in plenty, intense contempt for the trappings of aristocracy and the apologists of privilege, but in the last resort he came down on the side of property.

Darwin and Hooker both declared that in comparison with Huxley they felt quite infantile in intellect, and Wallace * experienced in his presence a feeling of awe and inferiority which neither Darwin nor Lyell produced, but the wide-ranging restlessness of his mind caused great concern to his scientific friends. In 1861 Hooker urged him "Do take the counsel of a quiet looker on and withdraw to your books and studies in pure Natural History; let modes of thought alone. You may make a very good naturalist, or a very good meta-physician (of that I know nothing, don't despise me), but you have neither time nor place for both". The strain of his many activities told on Huxley—two years later he was complaining to Darwin "I wake up in the morning with somebody saying in my ear, 'A is not done, and B is not done, and C is not done, and D is not done', etc., and a feeling like a fellow whose duns are all in the street waiting for him"—but the pleasure he took in poking his finger into so many pies comes clearly through the complaints. In 1871 Hooker grumbled to

* Alfred Russel Wallace (1823–1913), the co-author with Darwin of the theory of evolution by natural selection. In his later years he became absorbed in somewhat eccentric spiritualist and anti-vaccination activities.

Darwin that Huxley's love of exercising his marvellous intellectual power over men was leading him "on—and on—and on—God knows to where", but he knew by then that a laboratory was not large enough to contain his friend. Within a few months Huxley was gloating to Michael Foster * "I have been pounding Mivart & the Quarterly Reviewer as you will see in Contemporary for November—Also discussing functions of Government vide Fortnightly for November; also discussing Ritualism see Quarterly for January; also an article on Lord Russell & Lord Somers see Edinburgh for ditto: with a paper on the distinctive character of the eloquence of the Revd. Morley Punshon in the Nonconformist for December": what could his friends do with such a man?

With his wide interests, his deep culture and his moral earnestness, Huxley was clearly marked out for the Metaphysical Society founded by Knowles † in 1869—he and Mivart, indeed, had discussed the possibility of forming a 'Verulam Club' with similar intent three years earlier. What a constellation of intellectual stars that Society composed! Dean Stanley and Dean Alford from the established Church, Cardinal Manning and Father Dalgairns and W. G. Ward to represent re-emergent Rome, Huxley and Tyndall for the natural sciences, Gladstone and Tennyson and Froude, Mark Pattison and James Martineau and Frederic Harrison—all through a decade meeting nine times a year to probe the foundations of their beliefs. The delightful story, that an absentee from one of the meetings later inquired anxiously "Well, is there a God?" and was told "Yes, we had a good majority", sounds somewhat apocryphal; but many accounts confirm that these men debated the most explosive questions

* Sir Michael Foster (1836–1907), one of Huxley's closest friends, who in 1870 became Praelector in Physiology at Trinity College, Cambridge, and in 1883 the university's first Professor of that subject.
† Sir James Thomas Knowles (1831–1908), an architect who 'dined everywhere' and 'knew everyone' in Victorian England. From 1870–1877 he edited *The Contemporary Review*, and then founded *The Nineteenth Century*, from which he made a fortune.

with a mutual respect and toleration which it would be difficult to match today.

Huxley was a regular attender at the Metaphysical Society and frequently took the chair at its meetings. His first paper, 'The Views of Hume, Kant and Whately upon the Logical Basis of the Doctrine of the Immortality of the Soul', was also the first to be printed and distributed to members; his second, provocatively entitled 'Has a Frog a Soul, and of what Nature is That Soul, Supposing it to Exist?', developed the same theme in a somewhat ironic fashion—and it says much for the members' urbanity that they seem to have discussed both papers without acrimony. Huxley's third contribution, 'The Evidence of the Miracle of the Resurrection', has been described by the Society's historian as "the most notorious paper ever presented to the Society and the only one to which an additional evening was devoted for further discussion", and John Morley * was so alarmed by this attack on "the arch-miracle which is the basis of their whole system of belief" that he dissuaded Huxley from publishing it. As for Newman, he was so appalled at the idea of Manning's allowing the paper to be read in his presence that he thanked his stars he was not a member—comforting himself only with the thought "Perhaps it is a ruse of the Cardinal to bring the Professor into the clutches of the Inquisition".

One regrets that a society so scintillating could not have gone on for ever, but the conditions of its success were transient. During those ten years, political passions had been sharpened by the Franco-Prussian war and theological boundaries hardened by the dogma of papal infallibility, in a decade of industrious discussion the members had delineated their grounds and defined their terms, and further argument became either sterile or superfluous. On 16 November 1880 the Metaphysical Society was formally dissolved, and we

* John Morley, 1st Viscount (1838–1923), who made *The Fortnightly Review* into a powerful organ of liberal opinion. In Parliament from 1883, he consistently opposed imperialism and resigned from the Cabinet with John Burns in 1914.

shall be lucky if we see its like again. Let Knowles, the founder, recall in his letter to Leonard Huxley the atmosphere of this impressive institution:

> On all sides there was a wonderfully genial & kindly tone about the Metaphysical Society which was very largely owing to your Father & to Dr. Ward—who habitually hit each other at the hardest—but never with a touch of lost temper or lost courtesy. Your Father & Manning usually concluded our discussions—(or at any rate *very* frequently) with a lively but most friendly duel—and as one of the Bishops said— "at any rate this Society has taught us that we haven't all got horns & hoofs".

This, perhaps, epitomises Huxley's contribution to the cause of rational morality. At a time when Darwinism seemed to many minds to blur the distinction between virtue and vice, Darwin's bulldog was patently a man of almost puritanical uprightness. Publicly and unambiguously rejecting traditional beliefs, he demonstrated in his daily life that an unbeliever may be virtuous. Before Huxley there had been many upper-class sceptics who, taking advantage of the latitude which an undemocratic era allows to the governing group, had expressed in their own social circle views which would have landed an artisan in jail. In his own day there were many highly respectable men who kept fairly quiet about their disbelief and many who proclaimed their infidelity but were not very respectable. But here was a devoted husband whose wife took the children regularly to church, who was hardworking and frugal, who objected to 'strong language' on the golf course at St Andrews, who was Senator of one university and Rector of another and Governor of Eton and member of Her Majesty's Most Honourable Privy Council—and yet who was as unabashed by presbyters at Edinburgh as by prelates at Oxford, who attacked superstition and asserted intellectual freedom, who coined the word 'agnostic'. What further proof could be needed that loss of belief need not imply loss of morality or respectability?

Unlike Darwin, whose religious beliefs atrophied unnoticed and eventually died from disuse, Huxley deliberately excised what his intellect told him were obstructive vestigial bodies, and it is possible to trace the progress of the operation. His adolescent distaste for sectarianism came from generosity of spirit rather than theological doubt, and at the age of twenty-five he wrote to his sister "God bless you, dearest Lizzie" as if he really meant it. Two years later, on their mother's death, he had to admit "I offer you no consolation, my dearest sister, for I know of none"; but, following a cynical remark to his fiancée about the praise of eminent scientists, he uttered the prayer "God forgive me if I do them any great wrong". In 1854 he remarked in a lecture "I take it that all will admit there is a definite Government of this universe", but it is noticeable that invocations in his letters increasingly tend from this time to address 'the gods' rather than 'God'. It seems that in his later twenties and early thirties Huxley was hovering between a vague deism and an equally vague pantheism, and was certainly already no Christian, but he had not yet decided against some sort of divinity. In 1856, for example, he declared at the Royal Institution that "man, looking from the heights of science into the surrounding universe, is as a traveller who has ascended the Brocken and sees, in the clouds, a vast image, dim and awful, and yet in its essential lineaments resembling himself"—but he could see no sort of evidence that the shadow was a benevolent one as Christianity asserts. He did, however, make the interesting comments that "living nature is not a mechanism but a poem" and that "the æsthetic faculties of the human soul have . . . been foreshadowed in the Infinite mind". In the winter of 1858–1859 he gave a series of lectures at Jermyn Street to working men on 'Objects of Interest in the Collection of Fossils', and a similar attitude appeared:

In science, faith is based solely on the assent of the intellect; and the most complete submission to ascertained truth is wholly voluntary, because it is accompanied by perfect freedom, nay, by every encouragement, to test and try that truth to the uttermost.

I have said that our faith in the results of the right working of the human mind rests on no mere testimony. But there is *One* that bears witness to it, and He the Highest. . . . Donati's comet lately blazing in the heavens above us at its appointed time . . . and hundreds of other like cases which I might cite, are to my mind so many signs and wonders, whereby the Divine Governor signifies his approbation of the trust of poor and weak humanity, in the guide which he has given it.

True science and true religion are twin-sisters, and the separation of either from the other is sure to prove the death of both. Science prospers exactly in proportion as it is religious; and religion flourishes in exact proportion to the scientific depth and firmness of its bases.

Before long the twin sisters were pulling each other's hair at Oxford, but the crystallisation of Huxley's doubts seems to have been caused less by what he called 'the Sammy fight' than by Mansel's 1858 Bampton Lectures on 'The Limits of Religious Thought'. He greatly admired the theologian's clear and forceful reasoning, and begged Sir Charles Lyell to read the lectures—although, he added, "regarding the author as a churchman, you will probably compare him, as I did, to the drunken fellow in Hogarth's contested election, who is sawing through the signpost at the other party's public-house, forgetting he is sitting at the other end of it". Certainly by the autumn of 1860, distraught and nearly broken by the death of his first-born infant Noel, he saw quite clearly that he had no religious conviction which could bring him any comfort.

Charles Kingsley, with characteristic kindness, had sought to soften the blow in a letter of conspicuous charity, but Huxley's reply rejected what his feelings craved but his intellect could not accept:

My convictions, positive and negative, on all the matters of which you speak, are of long and slow growth and are firmly rooted. But the great blow which fell upon me seemed to stir them to their foundation, and had I lived a couple of centuries earlier I could have fancied a devil scoffing at me and them—and asking me what profit it was to have stripped myself of the hopes and consolations of the mass of mankind? To which my only reply was and is—Oh devil! truth is better than much

THE COMMITTEE MAN

*'Believe I am reckoned a good chairman of a meeting'* (p. xxii)

profit. I have searched over the grounds of my belief, and if wife and child and name and fame were all to be lost to me one after the other as the penalty, still I will not lie.

He had, he explained, no *a priori* objection to the doctrine of immortality ("Give me such evidence as would justify me in believing anything else, and I will believe that. Why should I not? It is not half so wonderful as the conservation of force, or the indestructibility of matter"), but he would not base convictions on mere analogies and probabilities and aspirations. He did not doubt the existence of human personality or the supremacy of man over beast, but none of this seemed to him to be evidence for immortality. As for the argument that the promise of eternal reward was necessary to morality, he rejected it as both untrue and unworthy:

As I stood behind the coffin of my little son the other day, with my mind bent on anything but disputation, the officiating minister read, as part of his duty, the words, "If the dead rise not again, let us eat and drink, for tomorrow we die". I cannot tell you how inexpressibly they shocked me. Paul had neither wife nor child, or he must have known that his alternative involved a blasphemy against all that was best and noblest in human nature. I could have laughed with scorn. What! because I am face to face with irreparable loss, because I have given back to the source from whence it came, the cause of a great happiness, still retaining through all my life the blessings which have sprung and will spring from that cause, I am to renounce my manhood, and, howling, grovel in bestiality? Why, the very apes know better, and if you shoot their young, the poor brutes grieve their grief out and do not immediately seek distraction in a gorge.

Carlyle, he declared, had taught him that a deep sense of religion was compatible with entire absence of theology, science and its methods had given him a resting-place independent of authority and tradition, and love had opened up to him a view of the sanctity of human nature, but he had no belief in an immortal soul. He accepted with some bitterness that "As our law stands, if the lowest thief steals my coat, my evidence (my opinion being known) would not be

F

received against him", and he was ready to be called atheist and infidel and other hard names; but, he concluded, "One thing people shall not call me with justice and that is—a liar".

Huxley coined the word 'agnostic', he tells us, because tolerably early in life he discovered that one of the unpardonable sins was for a man to presume to go about unlabelled. "The world regards such a person as the police do an unmuzzled dog, not under proper control. I could find no label to suit me, so, in my desire to range myself and be respectable, I invented one; and, as the chief thing I was sure of was that I did not know a great many things that the —ists and the —ites about me professed to be familiar with, I called myself an Agnostic." Fearing that many of those who had adopted his label were tending to deny rather than to doubt, he emphasised in *The Agnostic Annual* that any assertion of the impossibility of miracles, on the ground that the order of nature was uniform, begged the whole question under discussion. As he had much earlier explained to Kingsley, "I know nothing of Necessity, abominate the word Law (except as meaning that we know nothing to the contrary), and am quite ready to admit that there may be some place, 'other side of nowhere', *par exemple*, where $2 + 2 = 5$, and all bodies naturally repel one another instead of gravitating together. I don't know whether Matter is anything distinct from Force. I don't know that atoms are anything but pure myths. . . . In other words, I believe in Hamilton, Mansel and Herbert Spencer so long as they are destructive, and I laugh at their beards as soon as they try to spin their own cobwebs". Not surprisingly, he feared that if there were a General Council of the Church Agnostic he would probably be condemned as a heretic.

Early in 1886 Frank Harris * begged Huxley to write an

---

* Frank Harris (1856–1937), the extraordinarily gifted *confidante* of so many in the 1890s, whose repulsive and fascinating and unreliable autobiography, *My Life and Loves*, casts an illuminating if excessively lurid light on many personalities of the time.

article for *The Fortnightly* on the scientific basis of morality, but repeated illness sent him to moor and mountain in search of health. Then, in November, W. S. Lilley produced his article 'Materialism and Morality', stating that Huxley was a materialist and implying that therefore he could not be moral, and this provided the needed tonic. From Ilkley he sent Harris his 'Science and Morals', a hard-hitting defence of his philosophical and ethical position. "My creed may be an ill-favoured thing," he wrote, "but it is mine own, as Touchstone says of his lady-love; and I have so high an opinion of the solid virtues of the object of my affections that I cannot calmly see her personated by a wench who is much uglier and has no virtue worth speaking of." He insisted strongly that morality has no necessary connexion with religious belief; and, as for putting the blame for modern wickedness on poor Cinderella Science, he suggested that her much older sisters Philosophy and Theology had more to answer for. "Cinderella . . . lights the fire, sweeps the house, and provides the dinner; and is rewarded by being told that she is a base creature. But in her garret she has fairy visions out of the ken of the pair of shrews who are quarrelling downstairs. She sees the order which pervades the seeming disorder of the world . . . and she learns . . . that the foundation of morality is to have done, once and for all, with lying." It was with evident relish that he asked his wife "Have you read the Fortnightly? How does my painting of the Lilley look?"

Although Huxley had told Kingsley in 1863 that he could see no sort of evidence that the great unknown underlying the phenomena of the universe stands to us in the relation of a loving Father as Christianity asserts, another passage in this intriguing correspondence shews how far he was from rejecting all that a liberal theology might imply:

Science seems to me to teach in the highest and strongest manner the great truth which is embodied in the Christian conception of entire surrender to the will of God. Sit down before fact as a little child, be prepared to give up every preconceived notion, follow humbly wherever and to whatever abysses nature leads, or you shall learn nothing. I have only begun to learn content and peace of mind since I have resolved at all risks to do this.

When *The Water Babies* appeared, with its "one true, orthodox, rational, philosophical, logical, irrefragable, nominalistic, realistic, inductive, deductive, seductive, productive, salutary, comfortable, and on-all-accounts-to-be-received doctrine . . . that your soul makes your body, just as a snail makes his shell", Huxley assured its author that he was as ready to believe that doctrine as its converse, because it was impossible to obtain any evidence as to the truth of either. His fundamental axiom of speculative philosophy, he declared, was that it is absurd to imagine that we know anything with certainty about either spirit or matter. He found it simplest to suppose that both physical and mental phenomena are manifestations of the same essential substratum, but he was ready to admit that there were other possibilities:

If you are of a different opinion, and find it more convenient to call the $x$ which underlies (hypothetically) mental phenomena, Soul, and the $x$ which underlies (hypothetically) physical phenomena, Body, well and good. The two-fluid theory and the one-fluid theory of electricity both accounted for the phenomena up to a certain extent, and both were probably wrong. So it may be with the theories that there is only one $x$ in nature or two $x$'s or three $x$'s.

For, if you will think upon it, there are only four ontological hypotheses now that Polytheism is dead.

I. There is no $x$ = Atheism on Berkeleyan principles.
II. There is only one $x$ = Materialism or Pantheism, according as you turn it heads or tails.
III. There are two $x$'s } = Speculators *incertae sedis*.
    Spirit and Matter
IV. There are three $x$'s } = Orthodox Theologians.
    God, Souls, Matter

To say that I adopt any one of these hypotheses, as a representation of fact, would to my mind be absurd; but No. 2 is the one I can work with best.

Although Huxley always asserted the impossibility of answering the ultimate questions of existence, his strict theoretical agnosticism does not hide a practical conviction that ideas express material realities. During the 1870s he made a series of utterances with metaphysical implications—the address on Descartes to the Cambridge YMCA, the essay on Bishop Berkeley in *Macmillan's*, the British Association address at Belfast on animal automatism, the admirably lucid little volume on Hume, and the discourse at the Royal Institution on sensation and the sensiferous organs—and in all of them the formal argument impartial between materialism and idealism is accompanied by incidental indications of a belief in the reality of the material world. Lenin was right when he remarked "Huxley's philosophy is as much a mixture of Hume and Berkeley as is Mach's philosophy. But in Huxley's case the Berkeleian streaks are incidental, and agnosticism serves as a fig-leaf for materialism".

After his retirement in 1885, Huxley began once again to take up the theologico–philosophical questions which had been with him all his life but which the heavy calls of official duties had forced him latterly to neglect. Early in 1886 his scientific and religious interests were most fruitfully combined in 'The Evolution of Theology: an Anthropological Study', which traced the course of religious beliefs from animism through monolatry to the refined monotheism of the Hebrew prophets. The extent to which he anticipated the great theme of Frazer's *Golden Bough* is remarkable (although he had himself been in some sense anticipated by Newman's 'Essay on Development'), and this work gives some indication of his constructive ability when he was not concerned to demolish an opponent. His temperament was admirably suited to the theological mode of thought, and it was not a slip of the pen which caused Bishop Thirlwall to inform a friend that two of the contributors to the discussions of the Metaphysical Society were "Archbishop Huxley and Professor Manning". "What a Paley was in Huxley lost!", lamented *The Quarterly Review*.

Towards the end of 1886, lazily convalescing in Yorkshire, Huxley read a sermon preached in St Paul's by its Chancellor, Dr Liddon, who argued that the surprising and catastrophic events chronicled in the Scriptures could be explained as the suspension of the lower laws of nature by a higher law. This led Huxley to consider the meaning of the word 'law' in science, and the outcome was his vivacious article 'Scientific and Pseudo-scientific Realism'. The idea that the laws of nature are efficient causes rather than convenient summaries of observed fact, he remarked, was a deplorable relic of medieval realism, and he objected to the saddling of science with scholastic universals. He paid high tribute to the dialectical skill of the schoolmen (observing in passing that "When a logical blunder may ensure combustion, not only in the next world but in this, the construction of syllogisms acquires a peculiar interest"), and he admired their devotion to exact thought. Even if his tribute to the early theologians seemed suspiciously like a rebuke to their modern successors, he carefully refrained in this essay from any sort of personal attack on Liddon; but, when the Duke of Argyll * entered the fray with his 'Professor Huxley on Canon Liddon', and complained of the unfairness of criticising a preacher whose calling debarred him from disputation, the temperature rose considerably. Replying with 'Science and Pseudo-Science' in *The Nineteenth Century* for April, Huxley wondered whether his Grace ever read the religious newspapers with their continual controversies, and scathingly commented "Nothing has done more harm to the clergy than the practice, too common among laymen, of regarding them, when in the pulpit, as a sort of chartered libertines, whose divagations are not to be taken seriously". "So much", he concluded his introduction, "for the lecture on propriety." When the editor received the manuscript of this paper he gave "one gasp of

* George Douglas Campbell, 8th Duke of Argyll (1823–1900), a prominent Whig of the day. He became Chancellor of St Andrews and Rector of Glasgow, and had some considerable learning, but Huxley could not stomach what he regarded as his intellectual evasiveness.

delight", and Holyoake * told Huxley that it ought to have been entitled 'The Ignorance of the Duke of Argyll'. But, if he was nothing else, Argyll was persistent and, coming out of his corner with 'A Great Lesson', he painted a picture of a scientific world terrorised by the massive reputation of the dead Darwin and the overwhelming authority of the very living Huxley. No doubt the Duke deserved the demolition to which he was then subjected in 'Science and the Bishops', but perhaps it was unnecessarily unkind.

Despite his archiepiscopal tendencies, Huxley was much offended by the "effete and idolatrous sacerdotalism" whose growth seemed to him the saddest spectacle which his generation of Englishmen had witnessed, and he was not much more favourably inclined towards that "incongruous mixture of bad science with eviscerated papistry" which was Positivism. It was in 1868, in a 'lay sermon' at Edinburgh, that he produced his brilliant definition of the system of Auguste Comte as "Catholicism *minus* Christianity". He had read both the *Philosophie* and the *Politique* some sixteen years earlier, and had formed as low an opinion of their author's intellectual rigour as of his treatment of his wife. Naturally, he approved of the proposal to reform society *sans ni dieu ni roi*, but he was repelled both by Comte's later authoritarianism and by what he considered the sham pietism of his followers, and his article on 'Scientific Aspects of Positivism' in *The Fortnightly* was biting.

In the autumn of 1888, the opportunity occurred to deal with Christianity and the Religion of Humanity together. Addressing an enthusiastic Church Congress meeting in Manchester, the Principal of King's College, London, declared that those who called themselves agnostics were really infidels, and implied that Huxley lacked the courage to use that hard name. Huxley's reply was delayed by convalescence

* George Jacob Holyoake (1817–1906), the Co-operative leader and secularist who was imprisoned for blasphemy. He and Huxley were never close friends, but they corresponded and met occasionally and Huxley contributed to the support of the Leicester Secular Hall.

in the Engadine, but in the following February *The Nineteenth Century* carried his essay, 'Agnosticism', which answered both Dr Wace and a recent criticism of agnosticism by the Positivist leader, Frederic Harrison.* Wace hit back with 'Agnosticism: a Reply'; Huxley replied with 'Agnosticism: a Rejoinder'; back came Wace with 'Christianity and Agnosticism'; and finally there was Huxley's 'Agnosticism and Christianity'. Knowing something of Huxley's capacity for abstract thought, one might have hoped for valuable metaphysical discourse in these three papers on agnosticism, but in the main such hopes are disappointed.

When he had completed the last of the trilogy, Huxley wrote to his friend Hooker "I want you to enjoy my wind-up with Wace in this month's XIX. . . . It's as full of malice as an egg is full of meat—and my satisfaction in making Newman my accomplice has been unutterable". And that, no doubt, explains the disappointment. Huxley was capable of shedding light, but he too much enjoyed engendering heat; he could construct a consistent ideology, but he preferred to demolish the shaky structures erected by his opponents. It was his 'agnosticism' which provided the unifying idea for many ancient strands of sceptical criticism, but for a substantial study of the wider implications of the agnostic approach one has to go to Leslie Stephen. Yet, in the conditions of his time, Huxley was perhaps justified by his comment in another context:

There is a prevalent idea that the constructive genius is in itself something grander than the critical, even though the former turns out to have merely made a symmetrical rubbish heap in the middle of the road of science, which the latter has to clear away before anybody can get forward. The critic is told: It is all very well to show that this, that or the other is wrong; what we want to know is, what is right?

Now, I submit that it is unjust to require a crossing sweeper in Piccadilly to tell you the road to Highgate; he has earned his copper if he has done all he professes to do and cleaned up your immediate path.

* Frederic Harrison (1831–1923), the lawyer and philosopher who founded *The Positivist Review*.

# CHAPTER IV

# Smiting the Amalekites

It is assuredly of no great use to tear ones life to pieces before one is fifty—But the alternative, for men, constructed on the high pressure tubular boiler principle, like ourselves—is to lie still & let the devil have his own way—And I will be torn to pieces before I am forty sooner than see that.

*Letter to J. D. Hooker, 19 December 1860*

IN 1887, WHEN the Bishop of Ripon sought Huxley's advice about a scientific reference in the Jubilee sermon he was to preach to the House of Commons, the recently retired biologist told him "in part from force of circumstance & in part from a conviction that I would be of more use in that way I have played the part of something between maid of all work and gladiator-general for science". But, willing as he ever was to perform the daily chores of the maid-of-all-work, it was in the rôle of gladiator-general that he really revelled. He once admitted to John Skelton that an article of Gladstone's "caused such a flow of bile that I have been the better for it ever since", and he commonly found controversy admirably cholagogic. "Where there was strife, there was Huxley", Justin McCarthy recalled, and Lecky expressed a common view when he wrote sarcastically "What an unfortunate man you are! With your 'deep sense of the blessedness of peace' engaged, I believe, in no less than 3 fairly vehement controversies!" It comes as something of a palinode to find Huxley telling his protégé Ray Lankester that "battles, like hypotheses, are not to be multiplied beyond necessity", yet there was justice in the remark "No use to *tu quoque* me. Under the circumstances of the time, warfare has been my business and duty". That it was also his pleasure does not affect the main issue.

In one of his notebooks Huxley copied out from *Piers Plowman* the apophthegm "whan alle tresores ben tryed treuth is the beste", and it was because he believed that the Bishop of Oxford * had offended against the ploughman's vision that he trounced him so unmercifully in 1860. Yet the famous clash at the British Association meeting was not of Huxley's choosing. He had warned Darwin in the previous autumn that his *Origin of Species* would be greeted with considerable abuse and misrepresentation, and had assured him "I am sharpening up my claws and beak in readiness", but he had no intention of making the fur fly in Oxford. When the university's Professor of Botany presented a paper on 28th June to Section D, 'On the final causes of the sexuality of plants, with particular reference to Mr. Darwin's work on *The Origin of Species*', Huxley declined an invitation to take part in the discussion, for he felt that the audience was one which would allow sentiment to interfere unduly with reason. And, even when Sir Richard Owen made misstatements about the comparative anatomy of man and gorilla, he contented himself with a direct contradiction and a promise to produce his evidence later. But soon the university grapevine was saying that the Bishop would settle the heretics' hash on the last day of the month, and Huxley could not withstand the pressure from his friends to postpone his departure from Oxford until after the meeting. So, while Dr Draper of New York droned out his lecture 'On the intellectual development of Europe considered with reference to the views of Mr. Darwin', Wilberforce and Huxley sat not far from each other on the platform.

* Samuel Wilberforce (1805–1873), Bishop of Oxford from 1845 to 1869 and thereafter Bishop of Winchester. A brilliant scholar and Fellow of All Souls, his memory is perhaps unduly clouded by the 1860 episode.

Attracted by the prospect of episcopal pyrotechnics, an audience of some seven hundred arrived at the Museum and the meeting was transferred to a larger hall. Massed in the middle of the room were the clergy, in one corner sat a small knot of pro-Darwin undergraduates, and down the length of one side the ladies waited and fluttered their handkerchiefs. After the lecture two or three members discussed Dr Draper's paper for a few minutes, but the crowd soon tired of the grape-shot and called out for the heavy artillery. Bland and jovial, aware of his brilliance and comfortable in the knowledge that the audience was with him, 'Soapy Sam' spoke "for full half an hour with inimitable spirit, emptiness and unfairness". And he made the fatal error of an offensive personal inquiry about Huxley's own simian ancestry. "The Lord hath delivered him into mine hands", the young biologist muttered to his neighbour, and he proceeded to enlist against his adversary the Victorians' high regard for truthfulness and good taste. His quiet gravity contrasting with the Bishop's smiling insolence, Huxley triumphed completely. The many accounts of the episode differ in detail, but nothing conflicts with that which Huxley himself sent to his friend Dyster in South Wales:

Samuel thought it was a fine opportunity for chaffing a savan—However he performed the operation vulgarly & I determined to punish him—partly on that account and partly because he talked pretentious nonsense.

So when I got up I spoke pretty much to the effect—that I had listened with great attention to the Lord Bishops speech but had been unable to discover either a new fact or a new argument in it—except indeed the question raised as to my personal predilections in the matter of ancestry—That it would not have occurred to me to bring forward such a topic as that for discussion myself, but that I was quite ready to meet the Right Revd. prelate even on that ground—If then, said I the question is put to me would I rather have a miserable ape for a grandfather or a man highly endowed by nature and possessed of great means of influence & yet who employs those faculties & that influence for the mere purpose of introducing ridicule into a grave scientific discussion—I unhesitatingly affirm my preference for the ape.

Whereupon there was inextinguishable laughter among the people—

and they listened to the rest of my argument with the greatest attention.
. . . I think Samuel will think twice before he tries a fall with men of
science again. . . . I believe I was the most popular man in Oxford for
full four & twenty hours afterwards.

Science had served notice on Theology that she would be no
longer subservient, and one lady fainted at the declaration of
independence. In his quiet country retreat, far from the fray,
Darwin received the news with nervous chuckles of delight:
"how durst you attack a live bishop in that fashion? I am
quite ashamed of you! Have you no respect for fine lawn
sleeves? By Jove, you seem to have done it well!"

Yet Huxley's devastating speech was not primarily an
attack on the Church, and the view of him as *sacerdos semper
ubique et omnibus inimicus* is quite false. The essential enemy
was intellectual dishonesty wherever it might be found, and
only the peculiar conditions of the time led Huxley to cross
swords so often with the clergy. In 1886, writing a chapter for
Darwin's biography, Huxley recalled that in the 1850s he
was by no means an uncritical evolutionist and, "reversing
the apostolic precept to be all things to all men, I usually
defended the tenability of the received doctrines when I had
to do with the transmutationists; and stood up for the
possibility of transmutation among the orthodox". One of
the privileged few to be admitted to Darwin's thoughts before
his theory appeared in print, Huxley had from the start
maintained that there were serious gaps in the evidence
which had been marshalled. "I by no means suppose that the
transmutation hypothesis is proved or anything like it—", he
told Lyell in 1859, "but I view it as a powerful instrument of
research—Follow it out & it will lead us somewhere—while
the other notion is like all the modifications of 'final causa-
tion' a 'barren virgin'." Darwin's theory he believed to be
not only a *possible* explanation of the biological facts; but,
more important, a possible *explanation*. The current theologico–scientific views seemed to him to be not explanations
at all, but merely discreditable attempts to satisfy both

science and religion by means of ambiguity; and, although he had no *a priori* objection to the Genesis account of creation, he felt entitled to demand some particle of evidence for a statement which seemed to him to be highly improbable. Therefore, he declared, "The only rational course for those who had no other object than the attainment of truth was to accept 'Darwinism' as a working hypothesis and see what could be made of it. Either it would prove its capacity to elucidate the facts of organic life, or it would break down under the strain". What he was not prepared to allow was the smothering of Darwin's theory by prejudice and abuse, and he set himself to secure a fair hearing. When Darwin subscribed a letter in 1859 with the words "Farewell my good & admirable agent for the promulgation of damnable heresies", he already knew what a valiant ally he had found.

It is interesting that, not very long after his marriage, Huxley had himself settled on 1860 as the year of decision in his life. Shortly before midnight on the last day of 1856, sitting in the little room he used as a study and waiting for his wife to be delivered of their first child, he made an addition to his adolescent journal:

1856–7–8 must still be "Lehrjahre" to complete training in principles of Histology, Morphology, Physiology, Zoology, and Geology by *Monographic Work* in each Department. 1860 will then see me well grounded and ready for any special pursuits in either of these branches. . . . In 1860 I may fairly look forward to fifteen or twenty years "Meisterjahre". . . .

To smite all humbugs, however big; to give a nobler tone to science; to set an example of abstinence from petty personal controversies, and of toleration for everything but lying; to be indifferent as to whether the work is recognised as mine or not, so long as it is done;—are these my aims? 1860 will show.

It was a man conscious of his matured power whom Wilberforce had crossed, and before the summer was out Huxley was enjoining Hooker "take care of yourself, there's a good fellow. . . . We have a devil of a lot to do in the way of smiting the Amalekites".

Huxley's first Amalekite, as a matter of fact, had been not the Bishop of Oxford but the Archbishop of Comparative Anatomy. Sir Richard Owen, Director of the Hunterian and later of the British Museum, and sometimes called 'the British Cuvier', was a person of immense prestige and equal vanity and arrogance. His influence with the Admiralty after Huxley had been paid off from *Rattlesnake* was invaluable to the young assistant-surgeon, but the condescension with which he granted a request for a testimonial in 1852 was such that Huxley felt like knocking him down. Earlier in the year the younger man had feared that his powerful senior might allow jealousy to impede the publication of his Royal Society memoir, 'On the Morphology of the Cephalous Mollusca', but he managed to manœuvre the paper into print—at the same time assuring his fiancée "On my own subjects I am his master, and am quite ready to fight half a dozen dragons". Things were made no better in 1856, when Owen took advantage of facilities provided at Jermyn Street to arrogate to himself Huxley's title as Professor of Palæontology in the School of Mines. Further feeling was generated when Huxley's 1858 Croonian Lecture, 'On the Theory of the Vertebrate Skull' (delivered at the Royal Society with Sir Richard himself in the chair), dared to demolish Owen's claim that the skullbones were modified vertebræ, and Huxley was unkind enough to write to Hooker that the British Cuvier stood in precisely the same relation to the French as British brandy to cognac. With pomposity and jealousy on the one side, and boundless vigour and missionary zeal on the other, it is not surprising that the final clash between Owen and Huxley was a resounding one.

Huxley's reply to Owen's assertion at Oxford, that the brain of the gorilla differed more from the brain of man than it did from the brains of the very lowest quadrumana, appeared in January 1861 in the first number of *The Natural History Review*, and Wilberforce was not left long in ignorance of the undermining of his scientific adviser:

The Athenaeum
Jany 3rd, 1861

Professor Huxley presents his compliments to the Lord Bishop of Oxford—Believing that his Lordship has as great an interest in the ascertainment of the truth as himself, Professor Huxley ventures to draw the attention of the Bishop to a paper in the accompanying number of the *Natural History Review* "On the Zoological relations of Man with the Lower Animals".

The Bishop of Oxford will find therein full justification for the diametrical contradiction with which he heard Prof. Huxley meet certain anatomical statements put forth at the first meeting of Section D, during the late session of the British Association at Oxford.

Owen had declared unambiguously that the structure known to anatomists as the *hippocampus minor* occurred only in the human brain, and unambiguously he was wrong. "The fact is", Huxley commented, "he made a prodigious blunder in commencing the attack, and now his only chance is to be silent and let people forget the exposure." But Owen would not keep quiet, and the dispute was brought to the *Punch*-reading public in a series of comic verses. One, headed THE GORILLA'S DILEMMA, had this touching first stanza:

> Say am I a man and a brother,
> Or only an anthropoid ape?
> Your judgment, be't one way or t'other,
> *Do* put into positive shape.
> Must I humbly take rank as quadruman
> As OWEN maintains that I ought:
> Or rise into brotherhood human,
> As HUXLEY has flatt'ringly taught?

Another, headed MONKEYANA and contributed by 'Gorilla' from the Zoological Gardens, delighted in the contest:

> Then HUXLEY and OWEN,
> With rivalry glowing,
> With pen and ink rush to the scratch;
> 'Tis Brain *versus* Brain,
> Till one of them's slain;
> By Jove! it will be a good match!

Its final two stanzas left no doubt about which contestant had been slain:

> Next HUXLEY replies
> That OWEN he lies
> And garbles his Latin quotation;
> That his facts are not new,
> His mistakes not a few,
> Detrimental to his reputation.
>
> To twice slay the slain
> By dint of the Brain
> (Thus HUXLEY concludes his review),
> Is but labour in vain,
> Unproductive of gain,
> And so I shall bid you "Adieu!"

For the less sophisticated there appeared in 1863 a burlesque eight-page pamphlet, *A Report of a Sad Case . . . Owen versus Huxley*, recounting how the two biologists had caused a breach of the peace:

> *Policeman X*—"Well, your Worship, Huxley called Owen a lying Orthognathous Brachycephalic Bimanous Pithecus; and Owen told him he was nothing but a thorough Archencephalic Primate."
> *Lord Mayor*—"Are you sure you heard this awful language?"

Even the nurseries of England heard obscure echoes of the clash, for many a nanny must have read to her charges the passage in *The Water Babies* describing how "The Professor . . . got up once at the British Association, and declared that apes had hippopotamus majors in their brains just as men have. Which was a shocking thing to say; for, if it were so, what would become of the faith, hope, and charity of immortal millions?"

It was not because Wilberforce and Owen differed from him that Huxley set about them so sharply. He was capable, when he regarded a scientist as worthy and painstaking, of going out of his way to avoid any hurt while correcting his scientific views. And, where a clergyman seemed to be conscientiously trying to take account of the new knowledge, Huxley would be patient and considerate and tolerant. But

# A Report

OF

# A SAD CASE,

Recently tried before the Lord Mayor,

# OWEN *versus* HUXLEY,

*In which will be found fully given the*
*Merits of the great Recent*

# BONE CASE

~~~~~~~~~~

LONDON.

———

1863.

*Policeman X*—He behaved uncommon plucky, though his heart seemed broke. He tried to give Huxley as good as he gave, but he could not, and some people cried "Shame," and "he's had enough," and so on. Never saw a man so mauled before. 'Twas the monkey that worrited him, and Huxley's crying out, "There they are—bone for bone, tooth for tooth, foot for foot, and their brains one as good as t'other."

Lord Mayor—That was certainly a great insult.

Huxley—So they are, my lord, I can show——

Here a scene of indescrible confusion occurred. Owen loudly contradicted Huxley; the lie was given from one to the other; each tried to talk the other down; the order 'Silence' was unheeded; and for a time nothing could be heard but intemperate language, mingled with shouts of "Posterior Cornu," "Hippocampus," "Third Lobe," &c., &c. When order was restored, the Lord Mayor stated that, in all his experience, he had never witnessed such virulent animosity among costermongers.

The Lord Mayor here asked whether either party were known to the police?

*Policeman X*—Huxley, your Worship, I take to be a young hand, but very vicious; but Owen I have seen before. He got into trouble with an old bone man, called Mantell, who never could be off complaining as Owen prigged his bones. People did say that the old man never got over it, and Owen worritted him to death; but I don't think it was so bad as that. Hears as Owen takes the chair at a crib in Bloomsbury. I don't think it be a harmonic meeting altogether. And Huxley hangs out in Jermyn Street.

Lord Mayor—Do you know any of their associates?

*Policeman X*—I have heard that Hooker, who travels in the green and vegetable line, pats Huxley on the back a good deal; and Lyell, the resurrectionist, and some others, who keep dark at present, are pals of Huxley's.

Lord Mayor—Lyell, Lyell; surely I have heard that name before.

*Policeman X*—Very like you may, your Worship; there's a fight getting up between him and Falconer, the old bone-man, with Prestwitch, the gravel sifter, for backer.

Owen—He's as bad as any of 'em, my lord. I thought he was a friend of mine, but he's been saying things of me as I don't like; but I'll be even with him some day.

Lord Mayor—Silence! Have you seen the prisoners in the company of any ticket-of-leave men?

cleric and layman alike felt his lash if they tried to suffocate intellectual freedom by the weight of traditional authority. "We are in the midst of a gigantic movement greater than that which preceded and produced the Reformation, and really only the continuation of that movement . . .", he wrote to his wife in 1873, "nor is any reconcilement possible between free thought and traditional authority. One or other will have to succumb after a struggle of unknown duration, which will have as side issues vast political and social troubles." And, he concluded, the movement will be furthered most by "those who teach men to rest in no lie, and to rest in no verbal delusions. I may be able to help a little in this direction—perhaps I may have helped already". *Magna est veritas et prevalebit* was his deepest conviction, and in one of his notebooks he jotted down the stages by which victory was to come:

### The Four Stages of Public Opinion

#### I (Just after publication)

The Novelty is absurd and subversive of Religion & Morality. The propounder both fool & knave.

#### II (Twenty years later)

The Novelty is absolute Truth and will yield a full & satisfactory explanation of things in general—The propounder man of sublime genius & perfect virtue.

#### III (Forty years later)

The Novelty won't explain things in general after all and therefore is a wretched failure. The propounder a very ordinary person advertised by a clique.

#### IV (A century later)

The Novelty a mixture of truth & error. Explains as much as could reasonably be expected.

The propounder worthy of all honour in spite of his share of human frailties, as one who has added to the permanent possessions of science.

Confident as he was in the ultimate victory of truth, Huxley saw no reason why he should not speed up the process, and Wilberforce and Owen were not the only Amalekites in need of smiting. In 1862, unexpectedly called upon to deliver the anniversary address to the Geological Society owing to the illness of the President, he decided to make a critical examination of the state of geological knowledge. "I am going to criticise Palaeontological doctrines in general", he told Hooker, "in a way that will flutter their nerves considerably. . . . I mean to turn round and ask, 'Now, Messieurs les Palaeontologues, what the devil *do* you really know?'" In his address he excused his procedure "because it was useful to look into the cellars and see how much gold was there, and whether the quantity of bullion justified such an enormous circulation of paper", and it is scarcely surprising that after the meeting there were some protests at his boldness. Seven years later, by then himself President, he once again gave the anniversary address to the Geological Society, and this time emphasised the considerable assumptions made in eminent scientists' calculations of the age of the earth. "If I were in your shoes", declared a deliciously titillated Darwin, "I should tremble for my life." The one thing which annoyed Huxley more than unwarranted assumptions by clerics was unwarranted assumptions by scientists and, when the occasion was not opportune to act himself, he did his best to secure a surrogate. "I wonder if you are going to take the line of showing up the superstitions of men of science", he asked Kingsley before a lecture at the Royal Institution. "Their name is legion and the exploit would be a telling one. I would do it myself only I think I am already sufficiently isolated and unpopular."

Usually, however, Huxley was ready to do his own smiting, and most often the Amalekites were men who opposed the theory of evolution. The readiness with which he always sprang to the defence of Darwin is so striking as to require further explanation than is provided by regard for scientific truth: there was a deep emotional attachment, too, and the way in which the younger man took on the protective part of elder brother is at times quite touching. So soon as *The Origin* appeared Huxley arranged for a review by himself to be printed in the leading daily as if by a staff writer: "the educated mob who derive their ideas from the *Times* . . .", he declared, "*shall* respect Darwin & be d——d to them." Repeatedly the devoted disciple advised Darwin to keep quiet and leave the wrestling to him, and as often the meek master expressed gratitude for this eminently satisfactory arrangement. "You ought to be like one of the blessed gods of Elysium," Huxley wrote, "and let the inferior deities do battle with the infernal powers": Darwin enjoyed receiving protection, Huxley enjoyed giving it, and both were happy.

The autumn of 1864 provided two occasions for the functioning of this strange symbiosis. Criticisms of Darwin's theory were published by the German histologist Rudolf von Kölliker and by the French physiologist M. J. P. Flourens, and in each case the criticism was misconceived. Darwin was as usual delighted with Huxley's demolition of his opponents, and Huxley as usual gratified by Darwin's delight. "If I do not pour out my admiration . . . I shall explode" came the chortle from Down; "Hang the two scalps up in your wigwam!" came the contented crow from Jermyn Street. Two months later, when the Royal Society sufficiently overcame its conservatism to award Darwin its Copley Medal, there came another opportunity to deal with attempted denigration —Darwin, as usual, staying in his rural retreat while the ructions proceeded. Colonel Sabine, the President, managed to insinuate into his address that the medal was for the recipient's general biological achievement but not for his work on evolution, and of course this brought Huxley to his feet to demand that the relevant Minute of Council be read to the meeting—"Sabine didn't exactly like it, I believe", he told the honoured absentee.

It was more than a decade before Darwin's own university honoured him with a doctorate, and, while he dined quietly with his wife, his bulldog barked on his behalf at the Cambridge Philosophical Society's dinner in Clare:

Mr. Darwin's work had fully earned the distinction you have today conferred upon him four and twenty years ago; but I doubt not that he would have found in that circumstance an exemplification of the wise foresight of his revered intellectual mother. Instead of offering her honours when they ran a chance of being crushed beneath the accumulated marks of appreciation of the whole civilised world, the University has waited until the trophy was finished, and has crowned the edifice with the delicate wreath of academic appreciation.

True, Darwin was later assured that "There was only a little touch of the whip at starting, and it was so tied round with ribbons that it took them some time to find out where the flick had hit", but it is difficult to believe that all Cambridge hides were so insensitive.

A few months after flicking the whip at Cambridge, Huxley was telling John Morley "Controversy is as abhorrent to me as gin to a reclaimed drunkard", and certainly for a while he was comparatively quiet. The idea of evolution was now fairly widely accepted and Darwin had little need of an agent-general, the promotion of technical education took up a good deal of time and effort, and the new Normal School of Science at South Kensington needed putting on its feet. Between 1880 and 1885, some of Huxley's time was also taken for his duties as Inspector of Salmon Fisheries, Governor of Eton, Crown Fellow and Senator of the University of London, Trustee of the British Museum, President of the Royal Society and member of two Royal Commissions, and always his health was uncertain. During the British Association meetings at Dublin in 1878 one woman was overheard remarking to another "Oh, there comes Professor Huxley; faded, but still fascinating", and for a few years it looked as if the fading might be permanent. Left lethargic by recurrent dyspepsia and depression, deprived of the comfort of his pipe by the extraction of all his teeth in 1884, Huxley seemed for a while to have become not merely a drunkard reclaimed but one who had lost the capacity to drink.

It was towards the end of 1885, when freedom from the

daily cares of a full-time post was beginning to bring fresh vigour to a body nearly broken, that the decisive mental tonic was administered by Gladstone. The Grand Old Man had always been a favourite target (Huxley once remarked "Some of these days he will turn inside out like a blessed Hydra—and I dare say he will talk just as well in that state as in his normal condition. I have never heard or read of any body with such a severely copious chronic glossorrhoea"), and now in the November *Nineteenth Century* he provided a magnificent object for dissection. Asserting in his article 'The Dawn of Creation and Worship' that the order of events adumbrated in Genesis was in harmony with the findings of Science, Gladstone set off an heroic conflict which was to continue intermittently for the best part of a decade.

A quarter of a century earlier, when *The Origin of Species* first appeared, most Christians had felt confident enough to set themselves in unambiguous opposition. They could, after all, count on the support of many eminent scientists, and Huxley himself admitted that the palæontological evidence at that time was far from decisive. After another ten years of geological research there was a clear balance in favour o f evolution, by 1876 an immense variety of American fossils had provided detailed information about the stages through which certain forms of animal life had passed, and by 1881 Huxley regarded the evidence of the fossil record as so un-equivocal that if biology had not already provided a theory of evolution geology would have had to do so. Nor was it any longer possible for the Church to rely on the great force of educated ignorance, for right across the land geology had become a favourite hobby of country clergymen and the evidence for evolution could be denied only by those willing to deny their own eyes. The ideological status of science had risen to a new peak, and it was clearly necessary for theology to come to terms. Gladstone, a leader in both Church and State, was very conscious of this need, and in 1877 he had gone with Huxley and others to visit Darwin at Down. Now, when the French theologian Réville presented the Genesis story of creation as merely a charming primitive tradition, Gladstone claimed that its account of the serial production of the earth and its various orders of living things was affirmed by science itself. Unfortunately for Gladstone, his knowledge of geology was markedly inferior to Huxley's knowledge of Biblical exegesis, and the contest was too uneven.

Beneath the conventional courtesies of Huxley's reply there was a good deal of venom. As President of the Royal Society he had felt that good taste demanded a certain restraint on his part, but Gladstone's article sent him "blaspheming about the house with the first healthy expression of wrath known for a couple of years"; and, having recently resigned the Presidency, he was now a free man. 'The Interpreters of Genesis and the Interpreters of Nature' was a hard-hitting rebuttal of Gladstone's arguments: "Do read my polishing off of the G.O.M.," Huxley begged Herbert Spencer, "I am proud of it as a work of art, and as evidence that the volcano is not yet exhausted." Gladstone had perhaps not expected Huxley to intervene so effectively in his dispute with Réville, but even after being rebutted he was not wise enough to leave well alone. His 'Proem to Genesis' in January's *Nineteenth* ceded some of Huxley's points but failed to admit other errors, and soon his opponent was telling Farrer "the extreme shiftiness of my antagonist provoked me, and I was tempted to pin him and dissect him as an anatomico-psychological exercise".

When Knowles received the manuscript of 'Mr. Gladstone and Genesis' he was moved to write "may I take my courage in both hands—& ask you to be a little less fierce & more good humoured about your vivisection?". Next day Huxley returned his 'wild cat' to Knowles with the assurance "He is now castrated; his teeth are filed; his claws are cut; he is taught to swear like a 'mieu'; and to spit like a cough; and

when he is turned out of the bag you won't know him from a
tame rabbit"—but the rabbit, if tame, was crafty. Huxley had
at his disposal all the arts of advocacy, and in this essay they
were used with devastating skill. Setting himself up in mock
humility as "a simple-minded person, wholly devoid of
subtlety of intellect", and so unable to fathom the depths of
alternative meaning in Gladstone's propositions, he proceeded to demonstrate how probing his plummet could be.
Identifying himself with "my respected clients, the people of
average opinion and capacity", and getting in a side-blow at
the G.O.M. by remarking that "a representative of average
opinion . . . appears to be the modern ideal of a leader of
men", he went on to display a far from average knowledge
both of palæontology and of textual criticism. Humbly admitting that it would be presumptuous to instruct his adversary on Indian and Greek philosophy, he nevertheless managed to suggest that Mr Gladstone could with benefit consult
"that most excellent and by no means recondite source of
information, the 'Encyclopaedia Britannica'." And, all in all,
he managed to make the Prime Minister look something of a
fool.

It is easy today to conclude that two great minds might well
have found something more important to debate than the details of pentateuchal cosmogony, but it is not difficult to
understand why the clash was so sensational and led to such
a vast subsidiary correspondence in the daily and periodical
Press. The issue was at that time a major one: Gladstone
sought to prove that the ground which science had made its
own was of no strategic importance to religion, which indeed
had prepared the way for the advance; Huxley replied that the
Church was slyly seeking to cover an important retreat by a
glossographic smokescreen. Those who admitted that Genesis
was in conflict with science Huxley regarded as honest and
enlightened, those who maintained the literal infallibility of
scripture he regarded as honest if impervious to argument,
but those who tried to keep a foot in both camps he held in

contempt. In one of his notebooks he jotted down a satirical verse on a Church Congress:

> Benevolent maunderers stand up and say
> That black and white are but extreme shades of grey:
> Stir up the black creed with the white,
> The grey they make will be just right.

These few lines express perfectly his deep disgust with all double-speak.

When Canon Liddon, the Chancellor of St Paul's, preached towards the end of 1889 a sermon on 'The Worth of the Old Testament', and sought to counter the modernists of *Lux Mundi* with the assertion that the trustworthiness of the Old Testament is, in fact, inseparable from the trustworthiness of our Lord Jesus Christ, Huxley produced a reply which was entirely polite. The opportunity to have fun with Lot's wife and Jonah and the whale was too good to miss, and 'The Lights of the Church and the Light of Science' was perhaps a little unkind, but there was not much acid in the article. A year later, when Gladstone paraded a pony out of the same stable, he was treated in a very different manner. Huxley's trip to the Canaries in the spring of 1890 had given him a prodigious appetite and a new zest; and, when he read in *Good Words* an attack on one of his earlier essays, he whooped joyfully "Yes—Mr. Gladstone has dug up the hatchet. We shall see who gets the scalp".

Huxley's essay 'Agnosticism', written in reply to Dr Wace, had remarked that the wanton destruction of other people's property in the story of the Gadarene swine was clearly a misdemeanour, and this was the point of Gladstone's attack. Quite ignoring the fact that Huxley had denied credence to the story, and thus converting the remark into an attack on Jesus's personal character, he managed to generate in his article a good deal of *odium theologicum*. Angrier than he had been for a long time, Huxley produced in 'The Keepers of the Herd of Swine' as hard-hitting an essay as one may have the fortune to read, and space must be spared for its opening paragraph:

I had fondly hoped that Mr. Gladstone and I had come to an end of disputation, and that the hatchet of war was finally superseded by the calumet, which, as Mr. Gladstone, I believe, objects to tobacco, I was quite willing to smoke for both. But I have had, once again, to discover that the adage that whoso seeks peace will ensue it, is a somewhat hasty generalisation. The renowned warrior with whom it is my misfortune to be opposed in most things has dug up the axe and is on the war-path once more. The weapon has been wielded with all the dexterity which long practice has conferred on a past master in craft, whether of wood or state. And I have reason to believe that the simpler sort of the great tribe which he heads, imagine that my scalp is already on its way to adorn their big chief's wigwam. I am glad therefore to be able to relieve any anxieties which my friends may entertain without delay. I assure them that my skull retains its normal covering, and that though, naturally, I may have felt alarmed, nothing serious has happened. My doughty adversary has merely performed a war dance, and his blows have for the most part cut the air. I regret to add, however, that by misadventure, and I am afraid I must say carelessness, he has inflicted one or two severe contusions on himself.

After this light-hearted introduction, Huxley proceeded to hurl massive and well-digested learning at Gladstone's head with elegant and almost contemptuous ease. Marshalling the evidence that Gadara was a Gentile rather than a Jewish city ("And I may remark that, if my co-trustee of the British Museum had taken the trouble to visit the splendid numismatic collection under our charge, he might have seen two coins of Gadara"), displaying an intimate knowledge of the works of Josephus and of recent Biblical scholars, he soon made hay of Gladstone's assertion that the Mosaic Law forbade Gadarenes to keep pigs; and the other points at issue were disposed of with equal dexterity. Whether it was worth doing may perhaps be doubted, but it was done supremely well.

When Gladstone incorporated his *Good Words* articles in a separate volume, *The Impregnable Rock of Holy Scripture*, Huxley replied with 'Illustrations of Mr. Gladstone's Controversial Methods', and he defended the devotion of so much attention to this story of the swine. The question at issue, he declared, was "whether the men of the nineteenth century are to adopt the demonology of the men of the first century, as divinely revealed truth, or to reject it, as degrading falsity. . . . Whether the twentieth century shall see a recrudescence of mediæval papistry, or whether it shall witness the severance of the living body of the ethical ideal of prophetic Israel from the carcase, foul with savage superstitions and cankered with false philosophy, to which the theologians have bound it". There is no doubt about the depth and sincerity of Huxley's conviction; nor need one question his assertion that "My object has been to stir up my countrymen to think about these things; and the only use of controversy is that it appeals to their love of fighting, and secures their attention". Yet, one fears, there were other and somewhat less worthy motives. To his intimate Hooker, Huxley wrote "Why the fools go on giving me the opportunity of saying the most offensive things to their beloved 'Christianity', under the guise of justifiable self-defence it is hard to say—Except that they are fools—of the worst sort to wit, clever fools". To his son Leonard he later remarked "As to Gladstone and his Impregnable Rock, it wasn't worth attacking them for themselves; but it was important at that moment to shake him in the minds of sensible men": the moment was one in which Gladstone's whole Irish policy was at a crisis following Parnell's adultery with Kitty O'Shea.

Grant Duff told Leonard Huxley that when his father crossed words with Gladstone "the contest was like nothing that has happened in our times save the struggle at Omdurman. It was not so much a battle as a massacre", and certainly Huxley's adversaries commonly came out of these contests looking uncommonly slashed about. Mostly this was the inevitable result of getting in the way of one unsurpassed in the skills of controversy, but Huxley had another advantage of which his opponents were presumably unaware: the *Nineteenth*'s editor was on his side. When it was not possible to provide proofs of Gladstone's and Argyll's articles, Knowles sent advance copies of the periodical at the earliest possible moment, and he was very ready to allow Huxley to have the last word with Wace. In part, no doubt, this partiality was due to personal regard for Huxley, in part to general approval of his line; but Knowles was an extremely shrewd business man, and he naturally went out of his way to humour a contributor whose writings repeatedly sent his journal into second or several editions.

But for this prince of controversialists the end was drawing near and, appropriately enough, it was in the middle of a controversy that he died. On the Boxing Day of 1889 he had told Tennyson "I envy your vigour, and am ashamed of myself beside you for being turned out to grass. I kick up my heels now and then, and have a gallop round the paddock, but it does not come to much", and within the year he had moved to a more remote paddock at Eastbourne. A leisurely seaside life did him good, and he saw Tennyson buried in Westminster Abbey in 1892, but in the following year he barely found the strength to deliver his Romanes lecture at Oxford. A summer visit to Maloja set him up sufficiently to stand the winter, he managed to struggle through 1894 against influenza and miscellaneous minor ailments, and then the February of 1895 brought a fillip in the form of *The Foundations of Belief*, by A. J. Balfour.* Knowles complained to Huxley "Since you have forsaken the constable's beat the loose characters of thought have plucked up too much courage", and begged him to review the book. Wilfrid Ward † has related how, a few days later, Huxley called on him in high spirits and declared "Mr. Balfour has acted like the French in 1870: he has gone to war without any ordnance maps, and without having

---

* Arthur James Balfour (1848–1930), the eminent politician and elder brother of Huxley's protégé F. M. Balfour, the biologist. He was Vice-President of the Council of Education for Scotland, Rector of St Andrews and of Glasgow, Chancellor of Edinburgh and Senator of London University.

† Wilfrid Philip Ward (1856–1916), second son of W. G. Ward. After studying at the Gregorian University in Rome he became a leading apologist of Roman Catholicism and is best remembered for his life of Newman.

surveyed the scene of the campaign", and the following morning the first half of his review-article was in the post. Knowles speeded things up with a special messenger to carry proofs down to Eastbourne, and 'Mr. Balfour's Attack on Agnosticism' appeared in the March number. "I think the cavalry charge in this month's *Nineteenth* will amuse you", Huxley wrote to one of his daughters. "The heavy artillery and the bayonets will be brought into play next month." But next month Huxley was on his back in bed with influenza, before the end of June he was dead, and his wife refused all urgings to allow the posthumous publication of her husband's last article. For once, Huxley did not have the final word.

# CHAPTER V

# Science for the Citizen

I have said that the man of science is the sworn interpreter
of nature in the high court of reason. But of what avail is his
honest speech, if ignorance is the assessor of the judge, and
prejudice the foreman of the jury? I hardly know of a great
physical truth, whose universal reception has not been preceded by an epoch in which most estimable persons have
maintained that the phenomena investigated were directly dependent on the Divine Will, and that the attempt to investigate
them was not only futile, but blasphemous. And there is
wonderful tenacity of life about this sort of opposition to
physical science. Crushed and maimed in every battle, it yet
seems never to be slain; and after a hundred defeats it is at
this day as rampant, though happily not so mischievous, as
in the time of Galileo.

*Lecture at Royal Institution, 10 February 1860*

ALTHOUGH HUXLEY IS so well remembered for his major
controversial battles, these were of less importance than the
long slow campaign of attrition which he waged against
educated ignorance. A public speaker of outstanding brilliance, he was fortunate to build his public career at a time of
rapidly mounting interest in science, when people would willingly forgo an evening of mysterious illusions by Maskelyne
and Cook, or of impersonations by the great Maccabe, in
order to see and hear an eminent scientist.

The first lecture Huxley ever gave in his life was 'On Animal
Individuality', delivered on 30 April 1852 as a Friday Evening

Discourse at the Royal Institution, whither the fashionable intelligentsia of the metropolis would repair periodically for scientific instruction seasoned with social intercourse. Standing as a tyro in the place of Faraday, before the 'best' audience in London, the young biologist was understandably nervous. Yet, although it was only by careful study that he perfected his public speaking, his lectures were from the start sufficiently impressive to make him a regular star performer at the Royal Institution. Altogether he gave twenty-two of these Friday evening discourses, which during his first six years ranged over a fairly wide biological field. In the June of 1859, with Darwin's *Origin* about to come off the press, Huxley flew a kite in his lecture, 'On the Persistent Types of Animal Life', in which he argued that the theory of evolution was quite consistent with the continuance of some types unaltered over long periods. It was in his 1860 lecture, 'On Species and Races, and Their Origin', that he made his striking claim that science should appear before a knowledgeable judge and an unbiased jury, and for many a year to come he was to be Britain's most popular scientific preceptor.

During the 1860s and 1870s Huxley's Royal Institution lectures dealt with embryology and human palæontology, ethnology and comparative morphology, evolution and psycho-neurology, and the public seems to have lapped it all up. Then, in 1880, with the idea of evolution generally accepted, came a triumphant lecture 'On the Coming of Age of "The Origin of Species"'. It is a tribute to his devotion to the spirit of science that, on this jubilant occasion, he paused to urge caution on the enthusiastic votaries of Darwinism:

History warns us . . . that it is the customary fate of new truths to begin as heresies and to end as superstitions; and, as matters now stand, it is hardly rash to anticipate that, in another twenty years, the new generation . . . will be in danger of accepting the main doctrines of the "Origin of Species", with as little reflection, and it may be with as little justification, as so many of our contemporaries, twenty years ago, rejected them.

What the Royal Institution was to the West End, the London Institution was in some sort to the City, and there the office workers flocked to hear Huxley deliver lectures singly and in series. Whatever the ostensible subject, whether animal motion or the pedigree of the horse or the elements of psychology, the real subject was always the same: the necessity to base beliefs on adequate data and honest thinking. Other sections of London's public crowded out the lecture room at the Zoological Gardens to hear Huxley on starfish or on snakes or on squids; yet others repaired year by year to Jermyn Street for his winter courses of evening lectures; and the total effect of all this on the upper and middle classes of London must have been immense.

There was no radio or television in those days to carry the words of the wise men of the metropolis into every provincial parlour, but all over the country there were flourishing literary and philosophical societies able to attract to their meetings speakers of the highest reputation. And, with the very full reporting commonly given by the virile local Press, such speakers had an educational influence radiating far beyond the ranks of those who actually heard them. Huxley once refused an invitation with the explanation that he "did not care to address a *dilettante* audience such as Leamington was likely to afford", but through the years he spoke in most of the important regional centres. In 1862 he gave the Edinburgh Philosophical Institution two lectures on the relation of man to the lower animals, based on a series which he had already given to working men in London. "Fancy unco guid Edinburgh requiring illumination on the subject!", he wrote to his wife. "They know my views, so if they do not like what I shall have to tell them it is their own fault." Whereas Darwin in his *Origin* largely evaded the question of human evolution, contenting himself with the bland remark, "Light will be thrown on the origin of man and his history", Huxley at Edinburgh "told them in so many words that I entertain no doubt of the origin of man from the same stock as the apes". The

H

Presbyterian *Witness* came out with a furious attack on the audience for applauding this "blasphemous contradiction to biblical narrative and doctrine . . . the vilest and beastliest paradox ever vented in ancient [or] modern times amongst Pagans or Christians", and in fine sarcasm it expressed surprise that the meeting had not resolved itself into a Gorilla Emancipation Society. When Lyell saw some of the proofs of Huxley's little volume *Evidences as to Man's Place in Nature*, incorporating the substance of these Edinburgh lectures, he wrote "I hope you send none of these *dangerous* sheets to press without Mrs. Huxley's imprimatur". But the book went to press and quickly needed reprinting, was published in America and soon translated into German, and Darwin's muted cat was out of the bag with a loud squall.

Six years later, invited by an unorthodox clergyman to deliver a Sunday evening 'lay sermon' which would shame the liberal thinkers of Edinburgh out of their moral cowardice, Huxley returned to the northern capital. The theme of his lecture, 'On the Physical Basis of Life', was the essential unity of all living things, both plant and animal, and his bold generalisations so held the audience that they seemed almost to cease to breathe. Today, when any schoolchild may be taught about the common protoplasmic basis of life, it is difficult to understand why the lecture should have been greeted as gross and brutal materialism, but we have John Morley's word for it that "No article that has appeared in any periodical for a generation back (unless it be Deutsch's article on the Talmud in the *Quarterly* of 1867) excited so profound a sensation as Huxley's memorable paper On the Physical Basis of Life (1869). The stir was like the stir that in a political epoch was made by Swift's *Conduct of the Allies*, or Burke's *French Revolution*".

In the year before his Edinburgh 'lay sermon', Huxley had given two lectures on 'The Character, Distribution and Origin of the Principal Modifications of Mankind' to the Birmingham and Midland Institute. In a sentence which has a remarkably modern ring, he pointed out to his audience "They would perceive that he was very careful not to use races, species, varieties, or any such phrases; for all those words were simply theories and hypotheses", and he adjured those present to put out of mind their prejudices and passions. The English, he remarked, would have seemed to the Romans 2000 years ago as uncivilised as the nineteenth-century natives of New Zealand appeared to the English, and one could not assume that primitive peoples were incapable of advancement. Going straight to the sexual centre of racial prejudice, he gave examples to shew that the results of miscegenation depend markedly upon the social setting, and he concluded that a fair study of the facts would not support any assumption that the peoples of Europe were biologically more advanced than those of Africa. Finally, for good measure, he declared that he knew an Australian 'blackfellow' who was as intelligent and good a man as one half of the British Philistines, "and he supposed that even Mr. Matthew Arnold did not regard the British Philistine as a distinct species of animal".

Returning to Birmingham in 1868 to lecture on the lowest forms of animal life, in 1870 to describe the recently discovered fossils intermediate between birds and reptiles, in 1871 to deliver his Presidential Address to the Institute, and in 1874 to unveil the city's statue to Joseph Priestley, Huxley kept reminding the Midlands that scientific advance depended above all on freedom of thought and intellectual integrity. During the 1860s Hull's Royal Institution was told about the methods of palæontology, Liverpool's Philomathic Society heard the much-quoted address on scientific education, the Leeds Philosophical and Literary Society was impressed with the ethnic diversity of England's expanding Indian domains, and the Bradford Philosophical Society was shewn how much could be learned from a lump of coal. And so the tale continues from year to year, in one centre of population or another, with Huxley using whatever was his own current research interest as the text for a sermon on science and its methods.

In addition to hearing individual lectures by eminent scientists, the provincial towns entertained in turn the annual circus of the British Association for the Advancement of Science. Each year, from its foundation in 1831, the 'British Ass' brought the leading lights of science together for a week or so, and in those days the meetings received countrywide newspaper publicity beyond the dreams of the Association's Press officials today. The 1860 clash with the Bishop of Oxford brought Huxley right into the limelight and, from that time forward, his British Association speeches were powerful magnets for reporters and editorial writers. At the Cambridge meetings in 1862 he was President of the Biology section and was practically nominating all the officers in that section and in Physiology and Anthropology; at Norwich in 1868 the 'blasphemy' which was uttered in the city produced a meeting of protest by the clergy; at Exeter the following year a veritable gale of declamatory appeal to orthodoxy blew through the Anthropology section—and naturally attracted to its centre the recently elected President of the Ethnological Society.

For the Liverpool meetings of 1870, Huxley was President of the Association, and it was in this capacity that he delivered his memorable address on 'Biogenesis and Abiogenesis'. Thousands were still dying yearly of infectious diseases spread in ignorance of their mode of communication, and it was of vital importance that the people should accept the newfangled 'germ theory'. Admitting that, on the face of it, it seemed absurd to suppose that the air contained millions of minute living organisms, Huxley emphasised that science digs below surface appearances, and he gave his listeners precise directions for the performance of some simple experiments by which they could prove to their own satisfaction that the apparent absurdity was veritable truth. So far his thesis, though at that time still disputed, had no objectionable theological implications, but he went on to complete the trilogy of which the first two parts had been delivered in Edinburgh in 1862 and 1868. Having on the first occasion asserted his conviction that man as much as other animals had been produced by the process of evolution, and on the second that all living things both animal and vegetable had a common material basis, he now declared that "if it were given to me to look beyond the abyss of geologically recorded time . . . I should expect to be a witness of the evolution of living proto-plasm from not living matter". But 1870 was not 1860, and a decade of strenuous endeavour in the scientific education of the British public had produced its effect: the Earl of Derby congratulated Huxley on the temperate spirit of his address, and *The Liverpool Mercury* breathed not a word of abuse.

Across the Irish Sea four years later, at the British Associa-tion's Belfast meetings, Huxley delivered his paper 'On the Hypothesis that Animals are Automata, and its History', and received in the local newspapers as many encomia as re-proofs. By this time he was a familiar figure to wide sections of the public, and it was no longer possible for him to be pre-sented as anything other than an honest, well-meaning and entirely charming mortal. The citizens of Ulster, reading accounts of the dinner of the Red Lion Club in the Linenhall Hotel, must have felt that these scientists who held such dread-ful opinions were not, after all, such dreadful people. Meeting each year to feed on beef and ale and to provide a social even-ing for a group of progressive scientists who found the official Association dinners either too expensive or too dull or both, the club conducted itself with a vigorous and somewhat juve-nile jocosity which one can only envy in these more sophis-ticated and self-conscious days. Its crest was a red lion regardant, holding a tankard in one paw and a churchwarden pipe in the other, and its motto was *Dulce et decorum est desipere in loco*. The Lion-King (the chairman) wore at each meeting a velvet cap emblazoned with red lions rampant, and the Lion-Chaplain preceded meat with the grace, "Brother Lions, let us prey". The waiters were understandably alarmed when each service was acknowledged not by "Thank you" but by a growl or a snap, and the savants greeted each speech or song not by clapping their hands but by wagging their tails. Unfortunately we do not have the text of Tyndall's after-dinner communication 'On the Fortuitous Concourse of Atoms, with Special Reference to the First Chapter of Genesis', nor of Carpenter's paper, 'On Huxleyism, and the Abnormal Exercise of the Critical Function', but they seem to have been well received.

When the British Association was first founded, its appeal was especially to the middle and upper class intelligentsia, and for many years it made no effort to reach the manual worker. In 1866, however, it was resolved that in future there should be given each year a popular lecture for the benefit of the artisan classes, and Huxley undertook to explain the scheme to a meeting of workers gathered together at a few hours' notice. Despite the inadequate warning, a large number attended in the Drill Room of Nottingham Castle, and they may be forgiven the impatience which developed as they waited a full hour for the platform party. The mayor made things no better by explaining to the not-too-well-fed audience that the delay was due to an exceptional prolongation of the official banquet in the Exchange Hall, but Huxley's exposition of the Association's plan was greeted with loud cheers. His own contribution to the series, 'On a Piece of Chalk', was given to the working men of Norwich on a miserable day in the August of 1868, and is a brilliant piece of scientific popularisation. Even the dyspeptic *Norwich Argus*, which made an editorial attack on Huxley while he was in the city, had to admit that his working men's lecture was a great success, "Notwithstanding the moisture of the atmosphere and the dryness of the subject".

In his full-time courses at South Kensington Huxley always refrained as far as possible from propounding his own theological and cosmological opinions, for he was anxious that his students should form their own competent conclusions from the facts, but in the case of occasional public lectures the position was quite different. Father Hahn, a Jesuit priest who had studied biology under him, once asked why he always proclaimed himself an evolutionist in public but scarcely mentioned evolution to his regular students, and Huxley's reply is instructive. "Here in my teaching lectures", he explained, "I have time to put the facts fully before a trained audience. In my public lectures I am obliged to pass rapidly over the facts, and I put forward my personal convictions. And it is for this that people come to hear me."

In 1870 an audience of more than a thousand arrived at Hulme Town Hall to hear Huxley 'On Coral and Coral Reefs', and a year later the organisers of Manchester's 'Science Lectures for the People' took the Free Trade Hall for his talk on 'Yeast'. Lecturing to artisans up and down the land, Huxley put his scientific knowledge at the disposal of men much more eager for it than their social superiors. "The English nation will not take science from above," he once told Hooker, "so it must get it from below—We the doctors, who know what is good for it, if we cannot get it to take pills, must administer our remedies *par derrière*." But, although he was always prepared to perambulate the country in a good cause, it was London that really held his heart, and it was London's workers who had the greatest opportunity to see and hear him.

The Government School of Mines provided each winter at Jermyn Street several series of evening lectures for artisans, and the finely paternal suggestion of the Office of Works, that "The respectability of these persons should be vouched for by their employers", did not keep out Karl Marx when he wanted to learn sufficient science to write the section on machinery in *Das Kapital*. After his appointment to the School in 1854, Huxley naturally participated in this evening programme, and his respect for the workers ensured that their lectures were as meticulously prepared as any others that he gave. "I am sick of the dilettante middle classes", he told Dyster when sending a copy of the prospectus for his first course, "& mean to see what I can do with these hard handed fellows who live among facts." After the first three meetings he declared that the working men "are as attentive and as intelligent as the best audience I ever lectured to. In fact they *are* the best audience I ever had & they react upon me so that I talk to them with a will. . . . I have studiously avoided the impertinence of talking *down* to them".

Year by year Huxley kept the artisan students informed of the progress of his own and other researches, and the 600 seats of the lecture theatre were usually crammed full. "Feeling anxious to hear how Dr. Huxley will make the complex phenomena of nerve action clear to his auditors", Bernard Becker wended his way one evening through rain and hail to Jermyn Street, and found the hall crowded despite the weather. "It wants twenty minutes to the appointed hour," he continues, "and the happy possessors of tickets are arriving in great strength . . . the benches appear to possess a certain elastic property, and every corner is occupied. . . . I look around me at the audience and am content. Here he is, this working man, whom I have so often sought and found not. His place is not usurped by smug clerks and dandy shopmen." True, there were some who were prepared to pose as proletarians in order to secure entry (one clergyman wrote to beg a ticket, and promised that if admitted he would not dress up like an amateur casual and leave his brougham at the corner), but Huxley's Jermyn Street audiences were so genuinely artisan that Frederic Harrison wrote to a friend "The intimate alliance foretold by Comte between philosophers and the Proletariat has commenced".

In the early spring of 1861, fresh from his encounter with Wilberforce at Oxford, Huxley gave a course of lectures 'On the Relations of Man and the Rest of the Animal Kingdom', which prepared the ground for the Edinburgh address so anathematised by *The Witness* the following year. After a few lectures he was telling his wife "My working men stick by me wonderfully, the house being fuller than ever last night. By next Friday evening they will all be convinced that they are monkeys", and Lyell was astonished by the size and atten- tiveness of the audience. During the winter of 1862 Huxley spoke to his artisans 'On Our Knowledge of the Causes of the Phenomena of Organic Nature' and, since his lectures con- tained nothing new but were merely a restatement of Darwin's *Origin*, he had no intention of publishing them. However, he agreed to their being taken down in shorthand and printed for the use of his auditors, and before long they were adver- tised everywhere and sold in large numbers—with Huxley re- gretting that he had not turned an honest penny by publishing them himself. When the book reached the other side of the Atlantic, Youmans * described it as "the most perfect little gem of a book I have met with. . . . Huxley beats Hugh Miller † out of sight in lucidity", and Darwin inquired "What is the good of writing a thundering big book when everything is in this little green book, so despicable for its size? In the name of all that is good and bad, I may as well shut up shop altogether".

None of Huxley's other Jermyn Street lectures to working men—on human races, on bodily motion, on the crayfish and the dog and the oyster—had quite the impact of those of 1862, but through the years their cumulative effect was very great. The *rapport* between Huxley and his artisan audiences was by all accounts quite exceptional, and perhaps part of the explanation is that they respected him not merely as a man of learning but also as one in contact with the sort of reality which constituted their own daily lives. They recognised, in fact, the claim which he once staked for himself:

I am, and have been, any time these thirty years, a man who works with his hands—a handicraftsman. I do not say this in the broadly metaphorical sense in which fine gentlemen, with all the delicacy of Agag about them, trip to the hustings about election time, and protest that they too are working men. I really mean my words to be taken in

* Edward Livingston Youmans (1821–1887), the American chemist and educationist, who was a friend of Huxley, Spencer, Tyndall and many leading British scientists.
† Hugh Miller (1802–1856), whose *Old Red Sandstone* and *Footprints of the Creator* did much to arouse popular interest in geology.

their direct, literal, and straightforward sense. In fact, if the most nimble-fingered watch-maker among you will come to my workshop, he may set me to put a watch together, and I will set him to dissect, say, a blackbeetle's nerves. I do not wish to vaunt, but I am inclined to think that I shall manage my job to his satisfaction sooner than he will do his piece to mine.

These were days when the workers, inheritors of a radical anti-clerical tradition and resentful of the power and privilege of the Church, were hungry for the scientific knowledge which they believed would help them to better their lot. Huxley not only fortified their tradition, but also assuaged their hunger. "It will be something to show my mates and keep for my children", explained an Eastbourne working man when begging a used envelope bearing Huxley's signature. "He have done me and my like a lot of good; no man more."

It would be tedious to continue with accounts of Huxley's many other addresses to different sections of the general public—a course on physiography to three hundred women in 1869 and a course on elementary biology in 1871, an 1866 series of 'Sunday Evenings for the People' for those who did not attend places of worship but wished to listen to discourses on the wonders of the universe, lectures here and lectures there on this scientific topic and on that. Many of these addresses reached a very wide reading public, and the generality also bought up books produced primarily for the educational market. *Lessons in Elementary Physiology*, greeted by Kay-Shuttleworth * on its appearance in 1866 as a model of simplicity and clarity, was read by Elliot Smith † in far-away Australia and determined him on a scientific career, and in England it went through thirty printings in as many years. An edition of 10,000 of *Coral and Coral Reefs* quickly sold out on publication in 1871, and when *Physiography* came out in 1877 over 3000 copies went in a few weeks. Two separate

* Sir James Phillips Kay-Shuttleworth (1804–1877), the first Secretary to the Committee of Council on Education, and well called "the founder of English popular education".
† Sir Grafton Elliot Smith (1871–1937), the anatomist and pioneer ethnologist.

Russian translations of *Man's Place in Nature* appeared the year after the first English printing; others of Huxley's scientific books were quickly translated into French and German and Polish and Hungarian. Never has there been such a potent purveyor of science for the citizen.

In 1894 Andrew Lang * remarked "In England when people say 'science' they commonly mean an article by Professor Huxley in the *Nineteenth Century*", but Huxley was busy with scientific journalism long before then. Initially, his interest was frankly financial—when he was invited in 1853 to write for *The Westminster Review* he made of the editor "one most base & mechanical preliminary inquiry to wit: What's the pay?"—but he soon came to take delight in the hectic business of keeping the compositors busy. By 1858 he was discussing with Hooker and Tyndall the possibility of starting a review to do for science what *The Quarterly* and *The Westminster* did for letters, and in the meanwhile he marshalled the scientists of the metropolis to produce an article each fortnight for *The Saturday Review* with a guarantee that there would be no editorial alterations.

Then, in 1860, it was suggested that the Irish *Natural History Review* should be published in England, and Huxley exuberantly told Hooker "if I chose to join as one of the Editors the effectual control would be pretty much in my hands". His friends were horrified at the thought of his taking on this extra burden, but the combined admonitions of Darwin and Hooker and Lyell proved ineffective. No doubt attracted by the prospect that, as he put it, "The tone of the Review will be mildly episcopophagous", Huxley threw himself into the venture with enormous energy and meticulous attention to detail. The first number appeared in the January of 1861 with the motto *E Pur Si Muove*, and Huxley was hopeful for the future, but he was soon to find that his friends' forebodings had been justified. "It is no use letting other people look after the journal", he was complaining before

* Andrew Lang (1844–1912), the folk-lorist and man of letters.

long, "I find unless I revise every page of it, it goes wrong", and even the appointment of paid editors did not put things right. For a while the review struggled on, but in 1865 this first venture of its kind came to an untimely end. The same year saw the failure of *The Reader*, started in 1863 by Tom Hughes * and J. M. Ludlow † as a 'Review of Literature, Science and Art', and it seemed that England was not yet ready for a semi-popular periodical dealing with science. Soon, however, the House of Macmillan was flexing its vigorous young muscles to this end, and in the November of 1869 Huxley had the satisfaction of introducing the first number of *Nature*. The prime object of the new publication was "to place before the general public the grand results of Scientific Work and Scientific Discovery, and to urge the claims of Science to a more general recognition in Education and in Daily Life", and for many years Huxley took a god-fatherly interest in its editing. What he would think of the *Nature* of today, as unlikely to appeal to the general public as any periodical that ever came off the press, we can only guess.

This was a period of feverish activity in the publication of new periodicals and, although the majority soon failed, there were some which were destined to play a great part in the moulding of informed opinion. The application of steam power to printing made it possible for large editions to come off the press quickly and cheaply, and there were hundreds of thousands of homes which looked to the quarterlies and monthlies as their main source of serious instruction and ideas. Each periodical had its own peculiar confraternity of readers, ranging from the literate artisan in some cases to the high academic in others, and each new issue was awaited with an eagerness which our generation does not know. The

* Thomas Hughes (1822–1896), the author of *Tom Brown's Schooldays* and an energetic Christian Socialist, who was for a while Principal of the Working Men's College.
† John Malcolm Forbes Ludlow (1821–1911), who is sometimes claimed to have been the real founder of the Working Men's College.

earlier reviews, like *The Edinburgh* and *The Quarterly*, catered for a comparatively small cultivated audience and followed the tradition of anonymous authorship, but the later journals went over to signed articles and the more successful writers had a popular following like that of today's television 'personalities'. Founded in the November of 1859, and edited first by David Masson and later by George Grove and John Morley, *Macmillan's* provided each month a not too controversial miscellany of serialised fiction, travel, history, politics and popular science, and at times its issues went into a hundred thousand respectable homes. The second number carried Huxley's 'Time and Life', an early salvo in the Darwinian battle, and later issues took to a wide readership his South London address 'A Liberal Education and Where to Find it', his Norwich lecture 'On a Piece of Chalk', his after-dinner speech to the Liverpool Philomathic Society on 'Scientific Education', his address to the Cambridge YMCA on Descartes, his 'Bishop Berkeley on the Metaphysics of Sensation', and his Royal Institution lecture on the border territory between animals and plants.

*The Fortnightly Review*, founded in 1865 on the model of the *Revue des Deux Mondes* and despite its title very soon a monthly, became in the capable hands of Morley the most talked-about journal in England. As the principal organ of mid-Victorian progressive and rationalist thought, and with a readership much in excess of its circulation, *The Fortnightly* provided an excellent medium for Huxley's papers 'On the Methods and Results of Ethnology', 'On the Adviseableness of Improving Natural Knowledge', 'The Scientific Aspects of Positivism', 'Administrative Nihilism', 'Science and Morals' and 'An Apologetic Irenicon'. His essay 'The Physical Basis of Life' sent the February 1869 number into seven editions, and Morley was understandably anxious not to lose such an author to other journals. However, when Knowles took over *The Contemporary Review* from Dean Alford in 1870, he became a serious competitor. *The Contemporary* had been founded by Alexander Strahan in 1866 to cater for those Christians who were not afraid of collision with modern thought, and its solid learning and quiet fervour appealed greatly to the increasing number of liberal clergy interested in anything from art and music and literature to science and theology and women's education. Huxley gave Knowles 'Some Fixed Points in British Ethnology', his 'School Boards' and 'Mr. Darwin's Critics', his Bradford address 'On the Formation of Coal', his Manchester lecture 'Yeast', and his 'Universities: Actual and Ideal'. By 1874 Morley was seriously worried by the competition: "Anything from you will always be a powerful help to the Review—," he wrote, "and I hope that you will remember it as often as you can." But he had to be content with Huxley's assurance, "I am becoming as spoiled as a maiden with many wooers. However, as far as the Fortnightly, which is my old love, and the Contemporary which is my new, are concerned, I hope to remain as constant as a persistent bigamist can be said to be".

This was a gratifying position, no doubt, for the bashful maiden, but less so for the ardent suitors: "Knowles and I are going about like ravening lions . . .," wrote Morley three years later, "and I am eager for all you will throw me." But by this time Knowles had started his immensely successful *Nineteenth Century*, to which he attracted the varied talents of the Metaphysical Society, and increasingly he was to secure the lion's share. Several times each year, and quite apart from his controversial essays, Huxley edited an extensive 'Recent Science' section, and thus had his rostrum in a journal so widely read and influential as to be called "the fourth estate of Britain". Ever in demand and able to pick whatever periodical best suited his particular purpose, on occasion writing for little-known magazines like *Youth's Companion*, and with a style such that "The plainest of plain folk can read him with instruction; the finest of lettered folk can read him with delight", he was able to bring a better understanding of science and its methods to great numbers of all classes.

Whenever he spoke about science, wherever he wrote, Huxley urged that the great essential was to dig below words to things, and it is not surprising that he had a high view of the educational potential of museums. He had not been long at Jermyn Street before he realised that the sort of arrangement and cataloguing of specimens which suited the research worker was quite useless for the education of the general public, and he sent the Director a memorandum advising the preparation of a popular catalogue. In less than three years he had rearranged the specimens and written simple introductions to the various sections, and the Museum of Practical Geology became an instrument capable of popular scientific education.

This was a time when museums were being developed not only in the great cities, but also in small towns all over the country. The Warwickshire Natural History and Archæological Society was wise enough to seek Huxley's advice, and he urged that a modest local museum should not seek to emulate a great collection, but should concentrate on providing a truly educational conspectus of the locality. Chester received the same advice, and a century later one can only regret that dozens of other small museums were not warned against "the ordinary lumber-room of clubs from New Zealand, Hindoo idols, sharks' teeth, mangy monkeys, scorpions, and conch shells—who shall describe the weary inutility of it?" Such a collection, Huxley believed, merely led the unwary to look for scientific objects elsewhere than under their noses, when they should realise that, as William Meister had it, their America is here.

In the case of a larger museum it was possible to be more ambitious, but it was equally important for ambition to be intelligently regulated and to look for maximum utility rather than superficial impressiveness. When the Commissioners who were planning a Natural History Museum for Manchester sought Huxley's advice in 1868, he laid down six principles of museum management as valid today as then:

1. The public exhibition of a collection of specimens large enough to illustrate all the most important truths of Natural History, but not so extensive as to weary and confuse ordinary visitors.

2. The accessibility of this collection to the public.

3. The conservation of all specimens not necessary for the purpose defined in (1) in a place apart.

4. The accessibility of all objects contained in the museum to the curator and to scientific students, without interference with the public or by the public.

5. Thorough exclusion of dust and dirt from the specimens.

6. A provision of space for workrooms, and, if need be, for lecture-rooms.

Nearly twenty years later he was advising on a new museum in Cambridge, and again urged the importance of a rational organisation to meet the quite distinct needs of the specialist engaged in research and the non-specialist looking for some general scientific education. "On the present plan or no plan," he pointed out, "Museums are built at great cost, and in a few years are choked for want of room."

In the great British Museum itself, then containing the scientific as well as other exhibits, there was the same failure in arrangement, and Huxley complained that "people stroll through the enormous collections . . . but the sole result is that they are dazzled and confused by the multiplicity of un-explained objects, and the man of science is deprived . . . of the means of advancing knowledge". By 1858 it was clear that the biological section could not be properly displayed in the Bloomsbury building, and a considerable debate developed about what should be done. Darwin had so low an opinion of the governing classes' interest in science that he thought it wise to "stick to the mummies and Assyrian Gods &c." as long as possible, and other biologists were divided among themselves. Some wanted to move the whole collection to South Kensington, some wanted to transfer the herbarium to Kew, and Huxley had the notion of sending a representative selection to South Kensington for public display and housing the remainder near enough to Regent's Park for them to be studied side by side with the living animals in the Zoo. He canvassed men of influence, including the Prince Consort himself, but a decade elapsed before any decisive step was taken. Then, in 1870, Henry Cole * sent Huxley a confidential note asking his views about a Natural History Museum at South Kensington, then another note asking him to inspect a possible site for "a Huxley-sized Museum", and the great new venture was under way. As early as 1863 Robert Lowe † had said that Huxley was the only man fit to be at the head of the nation's natural history collections, and later he was offered the post, but instead he nominated William Flower.‡ He became a trustee of the British Museum in 1884, but had neither the time nor the energy to do anything at all revolutionary. One can imagine how much more effective instruments of popular education our museums would have been had they developed as Huxley wished, and it may be a long time before such great opportunities are with us again.

Herbert Spencer once described Huxley as "about the last man I should think of as likely to give up the point in argument, or be persuaded to abandon a course he had decided on". But, he continued, "Nevertheless, there is a sense in which he is . . . too yielding. For if he is asked to undertake anything, either for the benefit of an individual or with a view to public benefit, he has difficulty in saying no". The public benefit required that Huxley should devote a large share of his time and energy to the scientific education of the people; and, if this means that we have fewer of his beautiful research papers than would otherwise have been the case, who is to say they are not well lost?

* Sir Henry Cole (1803–1882), Secretary of the Department of Science and Art. Cole was a man of extraordinarily varied interests and talents, ranging from the utilisation of sewage to the designing of tea services, and he was the main organiser of the 1851 exhibition.

† Robert Lowe, 1st Viscount Sherbrooke (1811–1892), who was Vice-President of the Committee of Council on Education from 1859–1864, Chancellor of the Exchequer from 1868–1873, and Home Secretary 1873–1874. As a young man he had gone to practise law in Australia, and was there during the visit of *Rattlesnake*.

‡ Sir William Henry Flower (1831–1899), whose *Observations on the Posterior Lobes of the Quadrumana* decisively vindicated Huxley against Owen.

I

CHAPTER VI

# Building a School of Science

To speak nautically, I have been there long enough to "know the ropes"—and I shall take pleasure in working the place into what I think it ought to be.

*Letter to F. D. Dyster, 18 August 1858*

ON THE 9th November 1850, when Huxley was paid off at Chatham from *Rattlesnake*, the Crystal Palace was rising in Hyde Park and everyone was talking about the next year's Great Exhibition. British railway engineers were at work across half the world, a submarine cable had been laid under the English Channel, and industry and commerce were about to experience an unprecedented expansion. Prices were soon to drop and living standards to rise, everywhere there was the throbbing of a mighty economic machine slipping into high gear, and England was all set for a period of remarkable social stability. Well might it be said that of all decades in our history a wise man would choose the 1850s to be young in.

During the three years while Huxley had leave of absence to work on his *Rattlesnake* material, the Government School of Mines was still trying to settle its purpose. It was in 1835 that the Geological Survey had been founded as a branch of the Ordnance Survey, with small offices in Craig's Court off Whitehall, and in 1841 the Museum of Practical Geology was opened to the public. The people flocked in their thousands to inspect the great collection of mining models and railway sections and building materials, including the considerable range of stones accumulated for the Commission advising on the rebuilding of the Houses of Parliament, and new premises were provided in Jermyn Street in time for the 1851 exhibition. Performing a triple task as technical school of mining, geological museum, and centre for the scientific instruction of the general public, the School of Mines was for many a year to be pulled this way and that by rival enthusiasts.

In 1854 the School's palæontologist migrated to Edinburgh to become Professor of Natural History there, and the lectures which Forbes * was due to give at Jermyn Street were taken over by Huxley at short notice in May. In July he received a half-lectureship in palæontology at £100 per annum (soon to be doubled in both scope and salary), in August he was commissioned on fee to make a coastal survey, and in the following April he was also appointed Naturalist at a salary of £200 rising to £600. Settled down at the School with which he was to spend his whole working life, Huxley's letters to Lizzie took on a confident and well-satisfied tone:

I'll tell you how many irons I have in the fire at this present moment: (1) a manual of Comparative Anatomy for Churchill: (2) my "Grant" book: (3) a book for the British Museum people (half done): (4) an article for Todd's *Cyclopaedia* (half done): (5) sundry memoirs on Science: (6) a regular Quarterly article in the *Westminster*: (7) Lectures at Jermyn Street in the School of Mines: (8) lectures at the School of Art, Marlborough House: (9) lectures at the London Institution, and odds and ends.

Already he was becoming what Herbert Spencer later called him, a man who was continually taking two irons out of the fire and putting three in.

Characteristically, Huxley gave at Jermyn Street twice as many lectures as he was obliged to deliver, and brilliant

* Edward Forbes (1815–1854), a Manxman whose early death cut short a career of great promise. He was by all accounts the most charming and witty of men and was always in demand for after-dinner entertainment at scientific gatherings.

lectures they seem to have been. He often maintained that he found public speaking difficult, but if he had difficulties his auditors were unaware of them. "As a class lecturer," wrote G. B. Howes,* "Huxley was *facile princeps*, and only those who were privileged to sit under him can form a conception of their delivery. Clear, deliberate, never hesitant or unduly emphatic, never repetitional, always logical, his every word told." A student remembers "that rich fund of humour ever ready to swell forth when occasion permitted, sometimes accompanied with an extra gleam in his bright dark eyes, sometimes expressed with a dryness and gravity of look which gave it a double zest"; another recalls that "As one listened to him one felt that comparative anatomy was indeed worthy of the devotion of a life, and that to solve a morphological problem was as fine a thing as to win a battle"; yet another tells how he "sat in face of his blackboard and watched him embroider it most exquisitely with chalks of varied hue; the while he talked like a book; with absolute precision, in chosen words". This last, it is true, feared that Huxley's basilisk artistry might hypnotise students into merely imagining that they were learning, but few others ever qualified their admiration.

Huxley himself was never sure how much students benefited from any lecture course (although he was in no doubt about the benefit to himself in the necessary preparation), and mere book learning in science he regarded as a sham and a delusion. He recalled an occasion when an instructor in physiology for the Science and Art Department, seeing a drop of blood under a microscope for the first time, exclaimed "Dear me! it's just like the picture in Huxley's *Physiology*"; and such dependence on the authority of print it was important to demolish. Unfortunately, the building in Jermyn Street had no adequate laboratory facilities for a thorough practical course, and for some years he had to content himself with the next best thing

---

* George Bond Howes (1853–1905), who went to the School of Mines in 1874 to help Huxley in the development of practical biological teaching.

—"namely, as full an exposition as I could give, of the character of certain plants and animals, selected as types of vegetable and animal organisation".

This 'type system', by which the student learned about yeast and fern and flowering plant, about amœba and earthworm and crayfish, about cockroach and frog and rabbit, spread right across the world and still remains the common mode of biological teaching. In the hands of succeeding generations of pedants it has become a by-word for unimaginative instruction, but Huxley is not to blame for that. As soon as he got an adequate laboratory he made his students observe each type for themselves, and that in itself was a revolution. Patrick Geddes * relates how, instructed by Huxley to examine the radula of a whelk, he found that the mechanism was different from that described by his master. Huxley told him to look again, then looked again himself and slapped his student's shoulder in delight: "'Pon my word, you're right!", he declared. "You've got me! I was wrong! Capital! I must publish this for you!"—and had the discovery published by Geddes in the Zoological Society's *Transactions* explicitly as a correction of his own work. Today, when every secondary school and college has a biological laboratory in direct descent from the one which Huxley devised for his students, it is difficult to remember that things have not always been so. "It was a real stroke of genius to think of such a plan", wrote Darwin. "Lord, how I wish that I had gone through such a course." In Huxley's hands, Jeffery Parker † assures us, the type specimens were not treated as the isolated things they necessarily appear in a laboratory manual or an examination syllabus, but took their places as examples of different grades

* Sir Patrick Geddes (1854–1932), the pioneer of town planning and community development, who studied biology at the School of Mines and later taught science and sociology at several universities, being especially remembered at Edinburgh.

† Thomas Jeffery Parker (1855–1897), a student of Huxley's who later became his demonstrator and then went to New Zealand as the first Professor of Natural History in the University of Otago. 'Parker and Haswell' is still in its most recent edition a standard textbook of zoology.

of organisation in a biological course which included a good deal of work of a more general character.

His contemporaries knew of Huxley's brilliance as a lecturer, and most biologists today know that it was he who really established the practical teaching of their subject, but one must go to the Council Minutes of the School of Mines to appreciate his part in promoting what was eventually to become England's first university of science and technology. At the time of Huxley's appointment in 1854, De La Beche* and most of his colleagues were determined that the School of Mines should be a technical school of mining. To Huxley, on the other hand, any move which might convert the School to a general college of science was welcome, and for many years the tug-of-war was to continue. Within a year of Huxley's appointment De La Beche died, and Murchison,† the new Director, recognised from the start the power in the personality of the junior lecturer. In his second session at Jermyn Street, Huxley arranged to go north for some field work on Arran at the time of an inter-staff dispute, and the Director's comment is a striking tribute to the place which the newcomer had already made for himself: "How we are to get the whole machine in the right working order is not yet quite clear to me. If you were present all would go right; but in your absence the two rivals cannot be made to cooperate for the good of the Establishment."

For his part, Huxley regarded Murchison as "a very trying old party", and he himself cannot have been an amenable underling. In 1856 the Director received an inquiry from the President of the Board of Trade, why an evening course of lectures to the general public had not been delivered during the session, and Huxley provided the laconic explanation that "he did not find it convenient to repeat his course". Thus encouraged by their newest colleague, the professors went on to

---

* Sir Thomas Henry De La Beche (1798–1855), one of the leading geologists of his day and the first Director of the Geological Survey.
† Sir Roderick Impey Murchison (1792–1871), the field geologist who founded the three great divisions of Silurian, Permian and Devonian rocks.

resolve that, if asked to give lectures outside their normal School of Mines commitments, "they must be the subject of a new engagement which they are individually at liberty to accept or decline". Before he had been in the place a year, Huxley was elected to be one of the two professors who audited accounts prior to the distribution of students' fees among them; he soon became one of the few authorised to sign cheques on behalf of the School; he and Smyth * were deputed to arrange the recataloguing of the scientific collections; and in general the Minutes indicate that almost from the day of his appointment influence gravitated into Huxley's hands. By 1859 he was arranging for the Chair of Physics to be offered to his friend and educational ally Tyndall; in 1860 he was asked by his colleagues to undertake the complete recasting of the Prospectus; in 1861 he and Smyth and Ramsay † were invited to consider both the matriculation of students and the type of certificate which they should receive. Why a junior member of staff, without any of the wealth or family influence which often explains so much, should have immediately become so influential in the School of Mines is an interesting question. Yet, given his energy, his decisiveness, his confidence and his immense personal charm, and adding to these the wide divisions of opinion among his senior colleagues and his own sixth sense for the underswell of social change, could it have been otherwise? There is no missing the note of self-satisfaction in a letter of 1858 to sister Lizzie, but perhaps he may be forgiven a little vaunting within the family circle:

You want to know what I am and where I am—well, here's a list of titles. T.H.H., Professor of Natural History, Government School of Mines, Jermyn Street; Naturalist to the Geological Survey; Curator to the Palaeontological Collections (*non-official* maid-of-all-work in Natural Science to the Government); Examiner in Physiology and

* Sir Warington Wilkinson Smyth (1817–1890), Professor of Mineralogy at the School of Mines and later also Inspector of Crown Minerals.

† Andrew Crombie Ramsay (1814–1891), the best field geologist of the day, who in 1871 became Director-General of the Survey on the death of Murchison.

Comparative Anatomy to the University of London; Fullerian Professor of Physiology to the Royal Institution (but that's just over); F.R.S., F.G.S., etc. Member of a lot of Societies and Clubs, all of which cost him a mint of money.

Three times in a decade the School of Mines was subjected to examination by commissions recommending as to its future, and it is gratifying that this repeated uprooting for inspection did not lead to complete wilting. The first inquiry was made in 1861 under the chairmanship of Lord Granville,* and Huxley and Smyth were deputed by the School's Council to report on the commissioners' proposals: perhaps his colleagues were unaware that Huxley had already sent Granville a long letter of seven foolscap pages, and thus ensured that his own personal views were fully considered. He urged the appointment of additional staff and argued that students in their first year should pursue a wide scientific course in common, specialising in mining or metallurgy or geology only in their second year, and he wanted external as well as internal examiners. The evening lectures for working men and general audiences he would continue, and he urged that the museum should provide adequately for the public as well as for students. Otherwise, he wanted as little outside control as possible: "the Professors, the due discharge of their duties being provided for . . . should be allowed to develope [sic] the resources of the Institution in any way that may seem advisable."

The second inquiry, by the 1868 Select Committee on Scientific Instruction, came at a time when the School of Mines was being heavily criticised for the small number of qualified students produced in return for the public money provided. In his evidence, Huxley counter-attacked strongly:

I must take leave to deny that the School of Mines has been a failure. It is very true that the number of students who have been turned out of that School is comparatively small, especially if it is looked at as a mere

---

* Granville George Leveson-Gower, 2nd Earl Granville (1815–1891), twice Lord President of the Council and for many years Chancellor of the University of London.

matter of arithmetic in relation to expenditure, but those persons who have taken the associateship of the School of Mines are instructed men, most of them have filled and are filling important positions, and act as centres for the diffusion of science throughout this country, and the Colonies; and more than that, they have been of great value as leading people everywhere, though slowly, to admit the importance of professional training.

He laid the blame for the paucity of students at the door of the country's manufacturers, who failed to recognise the need for the higher technical training of senior staff, and again he urged that the School needed more teachers. In particular, he desired the addition of professors of botany and mathematics, and advocated that the Royal College of Chemistry in Oxford Street should be physically integrated with the School and a great central college of science developed. He took the opportunity to point out that he could not teach his own branch of science properly because he had no adequate laboratory, and —presumably a well-timed piece of string-pulling—a complaint about "Professor Huxley's anatomical preparations [having to be made] in a dark closet about eight feet square" was aired at just the right moment in Parliament. As to the academic autonomy of the teaching staff (it is a remarkable thing that it was so long preserved in an institution under direct government control), his position was unambiguous: "I am not aware that there would be any utility in having a governing body at the college; important educational bodies are managed by a council of professors, represented by a dean of faculty, and I think there is no need for anybody else." The Select Committee reported in terms very favourable to his views, but major changes were not to come yet awhile.

When the third inquiry took place, by the Duke of Devonshire's Commission on Scientific Instruction appointed in 1870, Huxley was in the comfortable position of being himself one of the commissioners. His ally Tyndall had left for the Royal Institution in 1868, and most of the senior professors were content (or insistent) that the School of Mines should remain in Jermyn Street as an adjunct to the Geological Survey. On the 22nd April 1871 Murchison, Ramsay, Smyth, Percy * and Hunt † combined in a memorial urging that the School remain in close connexion with the Mining Record Office and the Museum of Practical Geology: presumably they did not know that, two days earlier, their junior colleague Huxley had told a friend "Of course, *I* do not want to examine Percy or Smyth or Ramsay—and I shall have no questions to put if they come. But . . . I think it will be very desirable to put on record all that the opposition has to say. . . . I think they are fools for their pains, but that is their business". When the Commission reported in favour of moving the whole School to a large site in South Kensington *The Times* thundered out against the plan:

> A Royal Commission, on which Professor HUXLEY has occupied a prominent place . . . suggests the amalgamation of the School of Mines with a general School of Science at South Kensington. . . . We express no opinion here of Professor HUXLEY'S plan for founding an imposing National College of Science, but there is really no reason why the practical branches of instruction should be removed from their present most commodious and accessible position only that they may follow in the wake of biology, chemistry, and mathematics down to the all-absorbing suburb.

Huxley wrote a letter protesting that, although as one of the signatories of the Report he accepted its recommendations, he should not be singled out as peculiarly responsible for the plan. One may feel that perhaps he protested too much.

In 1871 Murchison died, Ramsay became Director-General of the Survey, and the School was placed under separate management. This management, laid down in a letter from the Science and Art Department, was of a kind to Huxley's liking:

> My Lords direct that pending the consideration of the Report of the Royal Commission on Scientific Instruction the Royal School of Mines

* John Percy (1817–1889), Professor of Metallurgy.
† Robert Hunt (1807–1887), Keeper of Mining Records.

shall be administered by a Committee composed of its Professors. The Senior Professor will act as Chairman.

Now Huxley and two others who wished to move to South Kensington found themselves opposed on a major matter of policy by most of the senior professors, including Smyth, the new Chairman of the Council; and so, discontented with their constricted conditions of work, they "got up a little sort of pronunciamento to say that we really could not go on teaching in that way any longer". In the July of 1872, no doubt after much debate, the Council resolved to transfer the instruction in Chemistry, Physics and Natural History to new buildings in South Kensington, and at last the great move got under way. Superficially honours were even, for the three professors who wished to move, moved, while those who wished to stay, stayed. But, in fact, the issue was decided: the times called for a great expansion of the School, and expansion was impossible in Jermyn Street. Geology, Metallurgy and Mining eventually migrated, and the dream of a great central school of science at South Kensington became a reality.

Since first going to Jermyn Street in 1854, Huxley had become a great power. By 1872 he had served as President of the British Association and of several scientific societies, he had become Secretary of the Royal Society and received honorary degrees at home and abroad, he had been a member of six Commissions and of the first London School Board, he had been appointed Governor of Owens College, and he was on the point of being elected Rector of Aberdeen University. Up and down the land he had lectured to local audiences, his fluent pen had made his name a household word, and he was on intimate terms with many of that close-knit circle which then administered England. At this time Huxley appears to have occupied *de jure* no special position in the School, but that did not prevent his acting as its *de facto* chief. Throughout the whole period 1872–1880 the permanent future of the School was still under governmental consideration, and such a situation of flux was favourable to a determined man who knew his own mind. In 1873 Donnelly * wrote from the Department of Science and Art to tell him that Lord Aberdare,† the new President of the Council, was "very nice and all that but scarcely vertebrate. Nothing is settled as to this place. . . . We are just told to drift on as well as we can", and while others drifted Huxley set sail. It had once been suggested that he should become the Department's Director of Science, but he had preferred to support Donnelly—and it must have been greatly fortifying to know that he was working under an official chief whom he himself had recommended for appointment. Those professors who opposed the plan to widen the scope of the School of Mines still spoke out in public with a freedom of language which rebukes our modern reticence, but there was now no doubt about who was in the saddle.

By 1880, as Donnelly pointed out in an official memorandum, the School of Mines had become "a place where a few persons connected with the mining industry are educated in science, and where a much larger number attracted by the eminence of the professors, and disregarding the name of the School . . . go through its curriculum". Huxley, always vividly aware that the key to further advance in science was the production of a sufficient number of good teachers, seized the opportunity to press for a change in the nature of the School. He told the Department that "the teaching of science in the existing training colleges is so bad that it would be absurd to look to them to provide elementary science teachers", and he regarded the institution of a Normal School of Science as the necessary crowning of the educational edifice. Other professors sent letters criticising the proposal, but Huxley advised that "hostile criticism is like physic—one may

* Sir John Fretchfield Dykes Donnelly (1834–1902), a Royal Engineers officer who eventually became Secretary of the Department of Science and Art.

† Henry Austin Bruce, 1st Baron Aberdare (1815–1895), Vice-President of the Committee of Council from 1864 to 1866, Home Secretary from 1868 to 1873, and Lord President of the Council from 1873 to 1874.

as well take a good dose while one is about it". On the 19th March 1881, the Vice-President of the Committee of Council communicated officially with the Secretary to the Treasury:

Their Lordships are . . . clearly of opinion that all such steps should be taken as are possible to bring back the School to its object as defined in 1853, and to make it a Metropolitan School or College of Science, not specially devoted to Mining but to all Science applicable to Industry, and with a special organization as a Training College for Teachers.

The Treasury concurred and the metamorphosis was effected.

Now the *éminence grise* stepped out into the forefront as formal head of the reconstituted 'Normal School of Science and Royal School of Mines'. It was during the summer vacation that he received the official invitation:

Spencer House,<br>
St. James' Place, S.W.<br>
18 August 81

My dear Mr. Huxley,

We are organizing the new Normal School of Science at South Kensington, and we are to have a Dean at the head of the Professors.

It would be of great advantage, if you would consent to accept this Post.

You are in every way the right man for it.

You would bring distinction to the office, and we should like to mark by this Honorary appointment our sense of the services which you have already rendered to our Science Schools.

Yrs scly,<br>
Spencer *

Professor Huxley.

Within the week Huxley was amusedly rebuking Donnelly, his official chief: "I am astonished that you don't know that a letter to a Dean ought to be addressed 'The Very Revd.'. I don't generally stand much upon etiquette, but when my

---

* John Poyntz Spencer, 5th Earl (1835–1910), who served two terms as Viceroy of Ireland and was at this time Lord President of the Council. He later became Chancellor of the Victoria University of Manchester.

sacred character is touched, I draw the line", and he was not the only one who found the title somewhat incongruous. However, it had its advantages—H. G. Wells, an early student at the Normal School, tells us that his mother, fearful of her son's contamination by a notoriously irreligious man, was reassured when he explained that Huxley was a Dean.

'The General', as he was usually called by his colleagues, could be rather stern and exacting to a new subordinate; but, once convinced that confidence was justified, he practically let him take his own course and never interfered in matters of detail. His conviction that it was mere ruin to any service to let seniority interfere with the promotion of men of marked superiority led him at times into a certain ruthlessness, but he took disciplinary action only after the fullest investigation and he was prepared when necessary to defend his subordinates with all his considerable stubbornness. During the four years of his full-time Deanship, Huxley had many other public commitments and his health was deteriorating, but it proved possible to get the new institution firmly on its feet. The library and collections of specimens were reorganised, the Associateship of the School was opened to women, research facilities were provided free of charge to students of proved ability, and in the June of 1885 there came a new scheme of instruction with that common course in the first year and elective courses in the second which Huxley had so long wanted.

But by this time his health was failing badly, and after thirty years at the School he felt it was time to retire: in the September of 1884 he wrote to Donnelly "Surely I may sing my *nunc dimittis* with a good conscience". Donnelly replied, "*Very very sorry*—not the less so that I knew it would come and must come—you are so extravagant of your vis viva", but he did his best to delay the resignation. Huxley was urged to go on leave for two months to get his liver and lights in order, and soon the wheels were turning to extend the leave.

"I am sure this will be a *true economy*", Mundella * wrote from the Privy Council Office to Donnelly, and soon Donnelly was writing to tell Huxley "We decided you ought not to come home till after Easter—devilish good natured, wasn't it? Gave you no trouble of saying yes or no". He had to add, "Home Office—that's the bogey", so the Home Secretary was approached personally to remove all difficulties, and until April the convalescence continued in Naples, Florence, Rome, Venice and San Remo. But even this prolonged holiday could not restore full health and, on 11 May 1885, Huxley gave formal notice of resignation. How his services had been appreciated appears in a letter from the Vice-President of the Committee of Council, enclosing a Treasury decision that his superannuation would be £1200 per annum—a sum which, with a Civil List Pension of £300, meant that he retired on full salary:

*Confidential.*

House of Commons.
June 19, '85.

My dear Huxley,

The enclosed will give you the final decision of the Treasury in your case. I know it has been *twice* before the Prime Minister and I have done all I could to get the largest possible sum. I hope the amount fixed will be satisfactory to you.

Always faithfully yours,
A. J. Mundella.

Even then the School would not let him go completely. An official memorandum by Donnelly pointed out that "Mr. Huxley has developed in the Normal School a systematic course which is now being adopted generally by the Universities and other places of instruction in this country and has extended to America and the Colonies", and the memorandum went on to urge that at least part of his services should be retained:

* Anthony John Mundella (1825–1897), the son of an Italian political refugee, who was Vice-President of the Committee of Council from 1880 to 1885 and after whom Nottingham's Mundella School is named.

It is of the very highest importance to the Normal School of Science that, if it be possible so to arrange it, he should continue to act as Dean, and to retain a general charge of and control over the biological section of that recently formed School. The eminence of his position as a Man of Science renders his connection with it in any capacity of the greatest service for the prestige it gains and that position combined with his sound judgment and business capacity enables him to fill the office of Dean with an efficiency which no one else that I know of could approach.

The Treasury was at first reluctant to agree, but by August everything had been arranged and Huxley continued in the rôle of Grand Old Man, called in for occasional consultation—and for the settling of disputes between what Donnelly in a moment of indignation called "the respective functions of the God Almighty Professor and the black beetle official". In 1889 he moved to Eastbourne and gave his biological library to the institution he had served so long and so well, and a year later the Normal School became the Royal College of Science. There were those who had never forgiven him for converting a mining school into a general school of science, but the students at South Kensington knew what had been gained. "We are now part of what will in time become a great Science University;" their magazine proudly proclaimed, "the Royal College of Science as a nucleus, teaching pure science, laying the foundation for the special knowledge to be acquired afterwards in a chain of technical schools with which it will be surrounded." The great science university which is now the Imperial College of Science and Technology is an impressive memorial to its chief builder.

# CHAPTER VII

# Technical and Professional Education

There is a well-worn adage that those who set out upon a great enterprise would do well to count the cost. I am not sure that this is always true. I think that some of the very greatest enterprises in this world have been carried out successfully simply because the people who undertook them did not count the cost; and I am much of the opinion that, in this very case, the most instructive consideration for us is the cost of doing nothing.

*Address on behalf of the National Association for the Promotion of Technical Education, 29 November 1887*

IN 1851 ENGLAND had twice as many domestic servants as cotton workers, and agriculture was still the greatest industry, but the population had doubled in half a century and a huge urban proletariat was already established. It was apparent that the country's rapidly developing industry would need large numbers of men with all sorts of technical skills, and many of the Mechanics' Institutes founded earlier in the century made noble efforts to fill the gap. At the university level, both University College and King's College in London had Professors of Engineering, and in 1855 a Regius Chair of Technology was established at Edinburgh, but few students studied these subjects. There was as yet no adequate basis of elementary education to support such endeavours, but a band of far-sighted men went on planning the system of technical education which was to be built in the last decades of the century.

It was in 1853, following the immensely successful Great Exhibition, that the Department of Science and Art was founded, with Henry Cole as Secretary for Art and Lyon Playfair * as Secretary for Science. Formed initially under the Board of Trade, the Science and Art Department at first directed its efforts mainly towards adult workers in industry, but after coordination with the Education Department in 1856 it became a powerful engine for the promotion of practical teaching in the schools. As early as 1854 Huxley was lecturing for the Department at Marlborough House and, even if at first his interest was at least as much financial as educational, he soon became convinced of the great value of the work. He was convinced, too, that in the conditions of his time thorough and searching testing was an indispensable accompaniment of teaching, so he gave much time and effort to the nation-wide system of examinations built up by the Department. Huxley was not blind to the defects and dangers of written examinations, which he regarded as an imperfect test of knowledge and an even poorer test of capacity, but he considered them to be the only practicable check upon the sham teaching which was encouraged by the system of 'payment by results'. He therefore tried to make the check an effective one, and his correspondence reflects an acute concern that the questions should be carefully considered and the answers meticulously marked.

"It is commonly supposed", Huxley pointed out at Aberdeen, "that any one who knows a subject is competent to teach it; and no one seems to doubt that any one who knows a subject is competent to examine in it. I believe both these opinions to be serious mistakes." He regarded examining as an art, and a difficult one, which like any other art had to be

* Sir Lyon Playfair, 1st Baron (1818–1898), who left the Department in 1858 to become Professor of Chemistry at Edinburgh and later spent nearly a quarter of a century as a Member of Parliament. For a while he was Vice-President of the Committee of Council on Education.

learned. Beginners, he complained, always set questions which were too difficult, which was like trying to assess the relative physical strength of a group of young men by asking them each to swing a hundredweight about. "You must give them half a hundredweight, and see how they manœuvre that", he insisted, and examination questions must be easy enough to let reason, memory and method have full play. But, although he would have easy questions, Huxley could be hard enough in his marking: "You did quite right in plucking all those fellows", he told an assistant examiner. "I let off a few that you were doubtful about—but the great majority are slain . . . sending up such papers as these is a mere swindle." And, when there were complaints about the numbers who had been ploughed, he told Donnelly that if the 'great heart' of the people and its thick head couldn't be got to appreciate honesty, the sooner they shut up shop the better.

Outside the Department of Science and Art, the great forum of technical education in the third quarter of the century was the Royal Society for the Encouragement of the Arts, Manufactures and Commerce. Huxley was never one of its most active members, but his name keeps cropping up in its records. As a young man he lectured at the Educational Exhibition organised in 1854, and in succeeding years we find him interested in subjects ranging from submarine telegraphy to modes of preserving meat. He played an important part in the Society's conference on technical education in the January of 1868, he helped to organise the Educational Division of the International Exhibition of 1871, and he was one of those who initiated the Society's system of technical examinations. Huxley rarely attended meetings of the sub-committee appointed by the 1868 conference to prepare a scheme for technical education, but this need not mean that a man so expert in string-pulling was without influence on its proceedings. And when, later in the year, the House of Commons appointed its Select Committee on Scientific Instruction, it was to ears well attuned that Huxley and others trumpeted the urgent need for technical education. To breathe the air of those days it is well to repair to the Royal Albert Hall, built originally not for Promenade Concerts but as a meeting-place for men of learning, and read the words of the great frieze inscription: "This Hall was erected for the Advancement of the Arts and Sciences and Works of Industry of all Nations in Fulfilment of the Intention of Albert Prince Consort."

One of the agenda of the January Conference had been to consider how far technical education could be aided by existing endowments, and soon *The City Press*, sensitive to the continual muttering about the vast unused funds of the Liveries, admitted that there was no good reason why they should not be devoted to education. In 1870 a meeting in Common Hall decided to press the Livery Companies to adopt measures for promoting technical education, then Gladstone joined the chorus and suggested that the Companies might use some of their wealth for this purpose, and the time was ripe for Huxley to capitalise those assets of good-will which he had long been accumulating in City circles. Over a period of years he had been a guest at Mansion House banquets, and it would be out of character if in conversation through the courses he did not tie a few strings for later pulling. After 1870 his name figured more prominently in the reports of City feasts, until at the Haberdashers' banquet in 1875, to "upwards of 150 noblemen and gentlemen", only the Lord Mayor, the Vice-President of the Privy Council and the Senior Charity Commissioner had precedence over him. From then on, Huxley was *persona gratissima* to the Livery.

It is not surprising that the City's committee on technical education, set up in 1876, turned to him for advice, and it was with some gratification that he told the Working Men's Club and Institute Union a year later that the livery companies had remembered that they were the heirs and representatives of the medieval trade guilds. The leading part in this movement was taken by the Drapers and Clothworkers and Goldsmiths, and it is presumably more than a coincidence that Huxley's diary for 1878 records engagements with these three very companies. At the Drapers' banquet that year he was publicly thanked for his advice, and five years later the Prime Warden of the Goldsmiths was to recall that his had been the most valuable of the various reports they had received. The outcome of this advice was a recommendation that the Guilds should spend £30,000 in building a new central technical institution ("regard being had primarily—as Professor Huxley suggests—rather to what is wanted in the inside than what will look well from the outside"), and that they should also provide £10,000 per annum for salaries and another £20,000 for exhibitions and technical schools and classes. Huxley was, one of its leading members declared, "really the engineer of the City and Guilds Institute; for without his advice we should not have known what to have done".

Ever urgent, Huxley was not content to sit back and let events take their slow unaided course. In December 1879, presiding at a meeting at the Society of Arts, he took the opportunity to remind the Guilds that they "possessed enormous wealth, which had been left to them for the benefit of the trades they represent . . . that they were morally bound to do this work, and he hoped if they continued to neglect the obligation they would be legally compelled to do it". Continuing his campaign by letters to *The Times*, he complained that the public had not yet been told whether the Guilds had accepted their own committee's report, and rather acidly he pointed out that "The inmost financial secrets of the Church and of the colleges of Oxford and Cambridge have been laid bare by those universal solvents, Royal Commissions; but no Government which has existed in this country for the last century has been strong enough to apply such *aqua regia* to the strong-boxes of the City Guilds". Huxley, having already inspected a potential site in Kensington, knew perfectly well the way things were going, and it seems likely, if we may judge from a letter to the old Chartist George Howell,* that his public admonition to the Livery was a carefully calculated provocation:

> I suppose I have some ten years of activity left in me, and you may depend upon it I shall lose no chance of striking a blow for the cause I have at heart. . . . The animal is moving and by a judicious exhibition of carrots in front and kicks behind, we shall get him into a fine trot presently. . . . The Companies should be constantly reminded that a storm is brewing. There are excellent men among them, who want to do what is right, and need help against the sluggards and reactionaries. It will be best for me to be quiet for a while, but you will understand that I am watching for the turn of events.

This watching was facilitated when, early in 1881, Huxley became Inspector of Salmon Fisheries. Harcourt,† in offering the post, had apologised that "It is not a *grand* place nor as good in its emoluments as I could desire, for it is worth only £700 per ann.", but he pointed out that "Salmon have the good taste to addict themselves to healthy & picturesque localities . . . [and] . . . I do not see why you should not inspect the fish as well as Newton governed the Mint". It is to Huxley's credit that he required hard pressing, but eventually he fell in with this extremely tempting piece of scientific pluralism, and he now found further opportunities to lobby the Liveries. His diaries record many visits to the Fishmongers and Salters Companies; and, since his correspondence at this time refers frequently to technical education, presumably he did not confine his conversation to formal Fisheries business. At any rate, when Huxley was asked to accept the Salters' Freedom in 1883, the Master of the Company wrote "I think you must admit that the City Companies have yielded liberally to the gentle compression you have exercised

---

\* George Howell (1833–1910), the son of a mason, who started work at eight and became a Chartist while still a lad. He eventually became Secretary to the London Trades Council (1861), the Reform League (1864) and the Parliamentary Committee of the TUC (1871).

† Sir William G. G. V. V. Harcourt (1827–1904), Gladstone's Home Secretary. A Liberal MP from 1868, he regularly took a progressive line in Parliament on educational matters, opposing sectarian teaching in the schools and religious tests in the universities.

on them . . . we propose to legitimise your claim for education". Soon the 'City and Guilds of London Institute for the Advancement of Technical Education' had established two technical colleges, the one to be opened in Finsbury in 1883 and the other at South Kensington in 1884. And, when Huxley delivered his Presidential Address to the Royal Society in 1885, he was able to announce that about 250 technical classes in different parts of the kingdom were affiliated to the Institute, and that some of them were already developing into efficient technical schools.

As the fabric of the South Kensington college neared completion, and some in the City began to assume that their work was done, Huxley issued a warning that in fact it had only just started. "That building", he pointed out when distributing the Institute's prizes, "is simply the body, not the flesh and bones, but the bricks and stones . . . and I can assure you making a soul for anything is an amazingly difficult operation." How difficult was to appear very soon. Enrolments at first were few and there were mutterings that the great new venture was already a failure. Soon Donnelly was suggesting that Huxley's "pet institution on the opposite side of the road" should be handed over to the Science and Art Department with a decent income, and by 1887 Huxley himself was beginning to lose heart. He declared in *The Times* that the new college, despite looking so portly outside, was very much starved within; and, taken to task for failure to appreciate the generosity of the Livery, he replied sadly that "munificence without method may arrive at results indistinguishably similar to those of stinginess . . . a man who has only half as much food as he needs is indubitably starved, even though his short rations consist of ortolans and are served up on gold plate". Yet the City and Guilds College was there and was to thrive, joining eventually with the Royal College of Science and Royal School of Mines to form the great Imperial College of Science and Technology.

This year, 1887, was Queen Victoria's Jubilee, and the

Prince of Wales suggested that the occasion might be worthily marked by the foundation of an imperial industrial institution in London. Soon the Press was buzzing with rumours of what the Prince's committee was intending, and before long there arose a rip-roaring controversy. It seems to have been by accident—if any of his controversies were ever entirely accidental—that Huxley became involved. He was unwell at the time of the great inaugural City meeting in January, but at the request of the Prince he agreed to speak. The flirtation of the last thirty years between science and industry, he suggested, had now reached such a stage of intimacy that it was high time the young couple married and set up an establishment for themselves, and he regarded the proposed Imperial Institute as "the public and ceremonial marriage of science and industry". There appears to have been no official intention that he should play more than a minor part in the project, but it was his contribution which caught the public ear. "With the exception of Professor Huxley, whose interesting speech we give in full elsewhere," *The Pall Mall Gazette* informed its readers next day, "everybody was dull, stale, and unprofitable." Striking while the iron was unexpectedly so hot, Huxley wrote to *The Times* emphasising that he had no intention of expressing any enthusiasm for the establishment of a vast permanent bazaar, but hoped for something which would do for the advancement of industrial knowledge what the Royal Society and the universities did for learning in general. For he believed, as he had confided to Herbert Spencer a couple of days before, "the Institute might be made into something very useful and greatly wanted—if only the projectors could be made to believe that they had always intended to do that which your humble servant wants done".

In his *Times* letter Huxley envisaged the Imperial Institute as being placed in the City, convenient for those working there, and he visualised it as "a port of call for all those who are concerned in the advancement of industry . . . a sort of neutral ground on which the capitalist and the artisan would be equally welcome . . . a place in which the fullest stores of industrial knowledge would be made accessible to the public; in which the higher questions of commerce and industry would be systematically studied and elucidated; and where, as in an industrial university, the whole technical education of the country might find its centre and crown". *The Times* declared that his admirable letter should be circulated far and wide and learned by heart by all who would have the organising of the Institute; and, when the Prince's committee came to issue a pamphlet outlining its intentions, Huxley had the gratification of seeing his definition of aims officially adopted. But the cost of a City site proved prohibitive, the Imperial Institute was built in South Kensington where Huxley said it had as much chance of serving the interests of commerce and industry as a fish had of thriving out of water, and history has shown how nearly right he was when he told Michael Foster "The thing is already a failure. I daresay it will go on and be varnished into a simulacrum of success—to become eventually a ghost like the Albert Hall or revive as a tea garden". What he would say of the present plan to move the Institute still further out to Holland Park, instead of seizing the opportunity to bring it in to the South Bank, one almost trembles to think.

With the slow start of the City and Guilds College and the decision against a City site for the Imperial Institute, the spring of 1887 saw the low-water mark of Huxley's hopes for technical education. But by May his resilience was returning and, after urging Lord Hartington to continue the campaign, he wrote in the same sense to Roscoe: * "I may go on crying in the wilderness until I am hoarse, with no result, but if he and you and Mundella will take it up, something may be done." All through the first half of 1887 Huxley's recurrent

* Sir Henry Enfield Roscoe (1833–1915), a Liverpudlian who was Professor of Chemistry at Manchester's Owens College and greatly helped it to achieve university status. He was a member of the 1881–1884 Royal Commission on Technical Instruction, became MP for South Manchester in 1885, and in 1896 became Vice-Chancellor of the University of London.

ill health forced him to alternate between London and the Isle of Wight—although he managed to continue serving on the Council of the Royal Society, examining for the Science and Art Department, presenting one or two papers to scientific societies, attending various committees of the University of London and disputing at large in the *Nineteenth Century*. An attack of pleurisy prevented his speaking at the July meeting which launched the National Association for the Promotion of Technical Education, August and September were spent convalescing in Switzerland, and soon after returning to London he had to leave for Hastings on account of his wife's health. Then, on the 19th November, a terrible blow was dealt him by the death of his darling daughter Marian.

His friends tried to dissuade him from keeping a promise to speak on technical education in Manchester ten days later, but he insisted on fulfilling the engagement. "I am not proud of chalking up 'no popery' and running away . . .", he told Foster, "and, having done a good deal to stir up the Technical Education business and the formation of the Association, I cannot leave them in the lurch when they urgently ask for my services." Braced by his reception at the great meeting in Manchester Town Hall, Huxley was soon writing to Hooker in jubilation:

I was rather used up yesterday, but am picking up. In fact my Manchester journey convinced me that there was more stuff left than I thought for I travelled 400 miles, & made a speech of 50 minutes in a hot crowded room all in about 12 hours & was none the worse. Manchester Liverpool and Newcastle have now gone in for technical education on a grand scale—& the work is practically done—Nunc dimittis!

Now the fruits were ripening fast. In 1889 local authorities received rating powers under the Technical Instruction Act, a year later financial life-blood was provided under the Local Taxation (Customs and Excise) Act, and before Huxley died in 1895 there were half a dozen polytechnics in London and technical colleges all over the provinces.

The Victorians, like us, were divided about the purpose and proper scope of technical education. Magnus * defined its object as being "to train persons in the arts and sciences that underlay the practice of some trade or profession", and Sylvanus Thompson † said that "Education is technical only so far as it is directed to the training of the individual in and for his business in life", but with such narrow views Huxley would have no truck. In the first place, he was not willing to sacrifice the people's education to purely commercial demands; and, in the second, he did not believe that even from a commercial point of view any narrowly technical instruction would be effective.

The dispute about the proper scope of technical education was not an abstract question of definition and terminology: it was the immediately practical question of whether the artisan and his child should be merely instructed to perform their industrial tasks or educated fully to live a rich and fruitful life. When he presided for Thompson at the Society of Arts in 1879, Huxley came out strongly against any attempt to encroach on the limited schooldays of the workers' children for purposes of technical instruction. "Although it was a great thing to make good workmen", he remarked, "yet it was much more important to make intelligent men", and he believed that the elementary schools had quite enough to do without taking on this additional burden. On the other hand, once the earlier stages of education were passed and the worker was faced with the achievement of skill in his particular occupation, Huxley would have him concentrate his attention on that objective as closely as possible. "There are some general principles which apply to all technical training", he told the Easingwold Agricultural Club, "and the first of these . . . is that practice can be learned only by practice. The

* Sir Philip Magnus (1842–1933), Director and Secretary of the City and Guilds of London Institute and later a member of the Technical Education Board of the London County Council.

† Sylvanus Phillips Thompson (1851–1916), who had been a student at the School of Mines before becoming a schoolmaster, Professor of Physics at Bristol and then Professor of Physics at Finsbury and South Kensington.

farmer must be made by and through farm work." Therefore he would not include in a technical scheme for agriculture any courses in the pure sciences as such, but would teach "the history of a bean, of a grain of wheat, of a turnip, of a sheep, of a pig, or of a cow . . . with the introduction of the elements of chemistry, physiology and so on as they came in". He believed that a firm seat could be found on two stools, general preparatory education and specific technical instruction, and he did not propose to fall between them.

Nor was he ready to accept the over-simple view that widespread vocational instruction was all that was needed to ensure for Britain the lead in the economic race of the nations. "Many persons", he pointed out to the London School Board, "thought they had only to have a school for science, and that everything would be done that was needful, that manufactures would flourish henceforth, and that this was the one thing needful; but he believed that to be a profound and mischievous mistake." Perhaps the most succinct statement of his views is to be found in some notes which he drew up in 1887 for the Charity Commissioners:

> Technical education in its strictest sense, is only one of a number of conditions or operations on which the full development of the Industrial productibility of any body of men depends.
> These are
>
> I. Elementary school education as a preparation for life in general.
> II. Technical education proper as a preparation for special callings consisting of
> A. Preparatory Instruction in Science and Art.
> B. Special technological Instruction.
> C. Training and providing teachers in A and B.
> III. Contributory agencies
> A. Capacity catching apparatus.
> B. Physical and moral training.

He told the Commissioners that "the savage of civilisation is a more dangerous animal than any other wild beast; and that sooner or later every social organization in which these ferae accumulate unduly, will be torn to pieces by them", and he therefore urged that in addition to technical education in the narrowest sense the nation should provide "baths, gymnasia, cookery schools, free libraries, Reading rooms & innocent amusements as a contribution to industrial development of prime importance". A comprehensive scheme of technical education, Huxley held, should cover all those means by which the productive capacity of an industrial population may be fully and permanently developed; and it is as true today as when he insisted on it at Manchester that

> Our sole chance of succeeding in a competition, which must constantly become more and more severe, is that our people will not only have the knowledge and the skill which are required, but that they shall have the will and the energy and the honesty, without which neither knowledge nor skill can be of any permanent avail.

Huxley has been criticised for describing medicine, law and theology as "technical specialities", but such statements must be assessed in the light of his general outlook: it was not that he took a low view of professional education. He did not believe that brainwork is, in itself and apart from its quality, a nobler or more respectable thing than handwork, and in his evidence to the 1868 Select Committee he made no distinction of status between the 'profession' of medicine and the 'technology' of engineering. Seven years earlier, indeed, he had suggested the establishment of a professional corporation, to be known as the Royal Mining College, which should stand in relation to mining, metallurgy and geology rather as the Royal College of Surgeons did to medicine. Nearly a century later the suggestion was to be revived and extended, as the recently proposed College of Technologists.

Although he had abandoned the practice of medicine on leaving *Rattlesnake*, Huxley knew a good deal about the usual sort of preparation, and neither his experiences as a student, nor as a lecturer at St Thomas's and Hunterian Professor at the College of Surgeons, had done much to elevate his

thee [*sic*] think?'' The system which I am now adverting to is arraigned and condemned by putting that question to it. When does the unhappy pupil teacher, or over-drilled student of a training college, find any time to think?

Himself a teacher to the finger-tips, Huxley was vividly aware that the profession was one demanding deep thought and high skill. "Teaching in England", he complained to the 1868 Committee, "is pretty much a matter of chance, and the mass of the people are ignorant of the fact that there is such a thing as a scientific method in teaching." It is not surprising, therefore, that he sought to awaken teachers to the implications of their task and to encourage proper training and professional organisation. His diaries record meetings at the College of Preceptors, visits to the training colleges in Battersea and the Borough Road, and a speech for the Teachers' Training and Registration Society in aid of the Bishopsgate Training College for Women (now Maria Grey College). We find him also speaking in connexion with the loan exhibition of scientific apparatus at South Kensington, advising the Society of Arts on syllabuses in domestic science, concerning himself with a scheme to teach teachers the laws of health, and serving as President of the National Association of Science Teachers.

From its inception, one of the stated aims of the School of Mines had been the training of science and technical teachers, but under the influence of the mining engineers and geologists it had contented itself with a few gestures. In 1853 it was resolved to admit members of the College of Preceptors and certificated schoolmasters to courses at half-fee, and a year later it was agreed that the precedent set by admitting two students from Battersea should be extended to training college students in general, but not much more had been done. But Huxley, working with schoolmasters on the British Association's committee on science teaching, had deepened his understanding of the needs of teachers and become increasingly discontented with the inadequacy of their methods.

**THE FATHER**

*This and the sketch overleaf were made by Huxley's daughter Marian*

**THE FAMILY MAN**
'*What I like about the family is the way they all seem to care so much for each other*' (p. 233)

And, when Joseph Payne suggested that if men of science were really in earnest they would condescend to teach in the schools, Huxley accepted the challenge. Early in 1869 he arranged with William Rogers to give a series of demonstration lessons to London schoolchildren, stipulating only "that we shall have a clear understanding on the part of the boys and teachers that the discourses are to be *Lessons* and not talkee-talkee lectures". His great object, he said, was "to set going something which can be worked in every school in the country in a thorough and effectual way, and set an example of the manner in which I think this sort of introduction to science ought to be managed".

One outcome of these lessons was that admirable elementary textbook *Physiography*, in whose preface he emphasised that a general course of science should never become "an *omnium gatherum* of scraps of all sorts of undigested and unconnected information". Yet that, he feared, was precisely what would happen unless teachers had an adequate training. In 1861, lecturing to schoolmasters at South Kensington, he had insisted that "what you teach, unless you wish to be impostors, that you must first know", and in 1869 he pointed out at Liverpool that the teacher without real knowledge would be "afraid to wander beyond the limits of the technical phraseology which he has got up and a dead dogmatism [would result]". In Liverpool again, distributing the prizes at the Institute High School in 1883, he pressed the central point once more:

There are a great many people who imagine that elementary teaching might be properly carried out by teachers provided with only elementary knowledge. Let me assure you that that is the profoundest mistake in the world. There is nothing so difficult to do as to write a good elementary book, and there is nobody so hard to teach properly and well as people who know nothing about a subject.

The passage of Forster's Education Act in 1870 focused attention on the needs of the schools, and it soon became quite clear that teachers competent in science were simply not

L

to be found. So, after extracting from a not usually generous Treasury the considerable sum of £750 to pay lecturers and buy material and apparatus, Huxley set about "a course of instruction in Biology which I am giving to Schoolmasters—with the view of converting them into scientific missionaries to convert the Christian Heathen of these islands to the true faith". A year later, after his accumulating labours on the London School Board had led to a bad breakdown in health, he firmly refused an offer by his friends to relieve him of the course planned for the following summer. "Many thanks for all your kind and good advice about the lectures", he wrote to Tyndall, "but I really think they will not be too much for me and it is of the utmost importance I should carry them on. They are the commencement of a new system of teaching which, if I mistake not, will grow into a big thing and bear great fruit, and just at the present moment (nobody is necessary very long) I am the necessary man to carry it on." By September he was planning the 1873 course, for 1874 he had seventy applications, and year by year there was keen competition for entry. His assistants included people like Sydney Vines, Thiselton-Dyer, Foster and Lankester, and the methods devised for these schoolmaster courses quickly spread to universities and colleges all over the land.

When the South Kensington College became the 'Normal School of Science and Royal School of Mines' in 1881, Huxley felt that at last a long-held ambition had been realised. In proposing the name 'Normal School' he had in mind the Ecole Normale of Paris, and it was often said that he considered the welfare of the teacher students at the expense of those concerned with mining. On the other hand, H. G. Wells, one of those select young pedagogues who, as described in *Love and Mr. Lewisham*, bound themselves to teach science and so received free instruction and a guinea a week, complained that the course was purely and strictly scientific in character with no attention to teaching method. Certainly the schoolmaster students at South Kensington after Huxley's retirement shared Wells's view, and from 1892 to 1894 the College magazine carried a long line of complaints about the lack of any adequate pedagogic instruction. On the other hand, Wells affirms, "That year I spent in Huxley's class was, beyond all question, the most educational year in my life. It left me under that urgency for coherence and consistency, that repugnance from haphazard assumptions and arbitrary statements, which is the essential distinction of the educated from the uneducated mind". The conclusion seems clear: Huxley's own teaching was in itself a pedagogical lesson, he trained schoolmasters well because he was himself a man of high culture and a teacher to the core, but he failed to establish at South Kensington a course systematic enough to ensure that lesser men gave proper training or strong enough to survive his own retirement.

Yet this failure was not due to any lack of thought about the sort of organisation which would be appropriate to professional training. Huxley has left a manuscript note, dated 30 November 1859, which shews that he was already devising a means by which the projected South Kensington college could co-operate with provincial colleges to provide a national system of teacher training. The note suggests that an examining body for the whole group of colleges might be selected from among their lecturers, and 'degrees' granted by the Minister on the recommendation of the examiners. This examining body, it is proposed, should be called not a 'University', but an 'Institute'; and, allowance being made for the fact that there was then no network of local universities to provide nodes of regional organisation, the scheme remarkably anticipates our post-war system of Institutes of Education.

During most of his lifetime Huxley had no confidence that the universities would be able to play any very valuable part in professional education, and he was anxious to keep medical training out of the clerical hands which he considered to be so damaging to teacher training. This is understandable when one recalls how reactionary many of those who then dominated the universities were, and when one considers how hopeless it must have seemed to reconcile the vested interests involved. Yet Huxley was in no doubt that, if the universities were willing to bring themselves into line with the needs of the age, they could become the unifying force of professional education. And towards the end of 1892 he sent the Vice-Chancellor of the University of London a most striking plan. The university, he suggested, should have not only institutions providing for general studies and for research, but also for "Professional education in (a) Law (b) Medicine (c) The Industrial Professions (d) The Scholastic Profession (e) Painting, Sculpture and Architecture (f) Music". Each professional 'College' would be organised on a federal basis ("London Schools & Colleges of medicine organised into one body = *College of Medicine of the University*"), would draw up its own schemes of instruction and examination, and would present its students to the university for the award of professional 'degrees' on an *ad eundem* basis. He feared that it was quite hopeless to expect the various theological institutions in London to combine into a 'College' in the same way as other professional institutions, but he would have welcomed such an arrangement so far as the basic non-sectarian studies were concerned. Cutting across his 'Colleges', Huxley would have had 'Schools' consisting of the lecturers in the various disciplines of scholarship—so that, for example, there would have been regular meetings of philosophers (irrespective of whether they were concerned with professional training in theology or pedagogy or general education in arts or science), and similarly of scientists (whether engaged in pedagogy or the pure sciences or medicine or engineering), and so on. There can be only regret that our present mode of university organisation does not normally provide any such salutary cross-fertilising machinery, but leaves the lecturers in each of the professional departments largely isolated from those in the other professions and those in the basic disciplines. Today, with the example of the University Institutes of Education before us, and with the continuing debate about the proper relationship of the higher technological colleges to the university, we might do worse than return to study Huxley's notes of 1892.

# CHAPTER VIII

# The London School Board

The politicians tell us, "You must educate the masses because they are going to be masters". The clergy join in the cry for education, for they affirm that the people are drifting away from church and chapel into the broadest infidelity. The manufacturers and the capitalists swell the chorus lustily. They declare that ignorance makes bad workmen; that England will soon be unable to turn out cotton goods, or steam engines, cheaper than other people; and then, Ichabod! Ichabod! the glory will be departed from us. And a few voices are lifted up in favour of the doctrine that the masses should be educated because they are men and women with unlimited capacities of being, doing, and suffering, and that it is as true now, as ever it was, that the people perish for lack of knowledge.

*Address to South London Working Men's College, 4 January 1868*

IF ONE HAD to select a single season as Huxley's busiest, it would be that of 1870–1871. During these years he was serving on one Royal Commission on the Contagious Diseases Acts and another on Scientific Instruction and the Advancement of Science, he was President of the Geological Society and the Ethnological Society and the British Association, he became Governor of Owens College in Manchester, and he took on the onerous post of Secretary to the Royal Society. He travelled to give addresses at Leicester and Liverpool and Bradford and Birmingham and Cambridge, he joined with Manning and Knowles to form a relief committee for Paris as soon as its siege was raised, he brought out his *Lay Sermons*,

*Addresses and Reviews* and his *Manual of the Anatomy of Vertebrated Animals*, he produced research papers geological and biological and anthropological, and all the time he was busy arranging to remove the School of Mines from Jermyn Street to South Kensington. There were other miscellaneous commitments connected with the South London Working Men's College and the International College at Isleworth and the University of London, but all this did not prevent his standing for election to the London School Board. No wonder he once remarked to Othniel Marsh * "If I could only break my leg, what a lot of scientific work I could do!" And to George Smalley he explained, "The great secret is to preserve the power of working continuously sixteen hours a day if need be. If you cannot do that you may be caught out any time".

Forster's Education Act of 1870 required for its implementation a comprehensive system of elementary schools and, since there was then no network of local education authorities, the first necessity was the setting up of *ad hoc* School Boards. The Act in general left local option in the matter—John Morley remarked somewhat cynically that "Instead of the School Boards being universal, they should only come into existence where the ecclesiastical party was not strong enough in wealth, influence and liberality, to keep them out"—but in the case of the metropolis the inadequacy of elementary education was so notorious that the immediate election of a London School Board was prescribed. The proceedings of this Board during its first twelve months were taken much as a model for other Boards the country over, and the record of that first year is an impressive one.

All parties recognised the key position which the London Board would hold, and the sects put into the election campaign all the energies which had hitherto been devoted to parliamentary manœuvring. During the November of 1870

* Othniel Charles Marsh (1831–1899), the first Professor of Palæontology in the USA, whose fossil collections at Yale were of major importance in establishing the geological record of evolution.

the newspapers were full of accounts of election meetings, the front pages of *The Times* carried large advertisements of the claims of the competing candidates, and all in all the London School Board election was "the one home subject within the last month which has been able to divert people's attention from the war in France". The Established Church secured the election of powerful people like Canon Cromwell of St Mark's College in Chelsea, Dr Barry of King's College in the Strand, William Rogers of St Botolph's in Bishopsgate, and Lord Lawrence, a distinguished and moderate layman. The Nonconformists had equally eminent representatives—Dr Rigg of Westminster College for the Wesleyans, Dr Angus of Regent's Park College for the Baptists, Benjamin Waugh the founder of the NSPCC for the Congregationalists, and Members of Parliament like Samuel Morley and Charles Reed. The Roman Church, too, had its men; the women's vote was triumphantly organised to return Emily Davies and Elizabeth Garrett (Anderson); and, most significantly for the Board's effectiveness, T. H. Huxley was elected for Marylebone.

Not content with his vulnerability as a non-believer, Huxley took as team-mate a radical carpenter named Cremer,* who had been one of Garibaldi's reception committee on his earlier visit to England and who had signed an *Address of English to French Workmen* calling for united action "against the cajolery and brute force of the so-called rulers". Their joint election broadsheet solicited the Marylebone ratepayers to "Vote for the TWO CANDIDATES . . . who, if elected, will represent two *distinct* and *special* principles: Professor HUXLEY, and Scientific Education, W. R. CREMER, and the Educational Wants of the Working Classes". The polling hours were such that hundreds of working people were unable to vote, and Cremer was not elected, but Huxley (who had remarked at one of his meetings that "no breeder would

* William Randal Cremer (1838–1908), who helped to form the Amalgamated Society of Carpenters and Joiners in 1859 and the London Artisans' Club and Institute in 1868. He became a Member of Parliament for Shoreditch and was eventually knighted.

bring up his pigs under such conditions as those to which the poorer classes of England were now subjected") did not fail to represent both principles.

Arthur Hobhouse * told his wife how "Two most disreputable looking chaps called here yesterday. They were a 'deputation' from Huxley's Committee, or perhaps the Committee itself, to ask me to be the treasurer of the funds collected. They explained that their brethren would feel more confidence in a treasurer above their own rank in life. The treasure, it is supposed, will not amount to more than £100. . . . The only contribution at present is £5 of my own". Very soon, however, the working men on the election committee were reinforced by names like Lubbock, Tyndall, John Stuart Mill and Auberon Herbert, forming as representative a collection of 'workers by hand and brain' as might well be imagined. Huxley had neither the means nor the time for a regular election canvass and, unlike most candidates, he took no newspaper space for advertisement. However, he held four meetings—at St George's Hall in Langham Place, at St Pancras Vestry Hall, at a hall in Paddington, and at St George's Hall in Gray's Inn Road—and explained that he had associated himself with Cremer because, unlike nine out of ten of the other candidates, neither of them had any personal interests to serve.

His election address left the voters under no misapprehension about his attitude to educational expenditure:

It seems to be the fashion for Candidates to assure you that they will do their best to spare the poverty of the Ratepayers. It is proper, therefore, for me to add that I can give you no such assurance on my own behalf.

You may trust me that no waste or extravagance that I can prevent shall be permitted. But every penny levied by an Education Rate and rightly employed, now, means hundreds of pennies taken off the Police

* Arthur Hobhouse, 1st Baron (1819–1904), a highly successful Chancery lawyer who served successively as a Charity Commissioner, a Statutory Commissioner under the Endowed Schools Act, Law Member of the Council of the Governor-General of India, and on the Judicial Committee of the Privy Council. From 1882–1884 he was himself a member of the London School Board.

Rates and the Poor Rates of the future; and thousands of pennies saved and gained by the increase of frugality, the amendment of the habits of life, and the development of the power of production, of the poorer classes of the people.

Of all the illustrators of the "penny wise and pound foolish" proverb, those who object to pay for education are, to my mind, the most outstanding; and my vote will be given for that expenditure which can be shown to be just and necessary, without any reference to the question whether it may raise the rate a halfpenny.

Despite this uncompromising announcement, Huxley came second to Elizabeth Garrett, whose committee had organised the cumulative vote system to great effect in this first important election with female voters.

Huxley was under no illusion that Forster's Act was anything more than a patched-up compromise, but he saw that the situation was one of sufficient flux to allow a determined Board, avoiding both skinflint economy and stultifying sectarianism, to make a decisive contribution to the education of London's teeming children. As recently as 1861 the Newcastle Commission had reported that "none are too old, too poor, too ignorant, too feeble, too sickly, too unqualified in one or every way" to be regarded as suitable for teaching, and the streets of the metropolis were overrun by little arabs who never went to school at all. England had fallen badly behind Germany and France in the provision of elementary education, but at last the conflicting interests of church and chapel had been temporarily reconciled and it was possible to make a start. Huxley's *Contemporary Review* essay, 'The School Boards: What They Can Do and What They May Do', extracts from which were prematurely published before the poll and made a great public impression, indicates that he had thought carefully about the sort of education which the Board Schools should provide.

Naturally he advocated the teaching of science, as of drawing and singing, but first he put physical training, which he regarded as not only necessary for the bodily health of the neglected street urchin but also as an invaluable means of approaching his higher nature. Next—and not exclusively for girls—he put the elements of household work and domestic economy, by ignorance of which the misery of England's poor was intensified, and then came training in the elementary laws of conduct and social responsibility. "But the engagement of the affections in favour of that particular kind of conduct which we call good", he continued, "seems to me to be something quite beyond mere science", and it was necessary not only to teach the science of morality but also to develop a religious sense, to inculcate an ethical idealism.

It had been widely expected that the London School Board would see an immediate head-on clash between Huxley and the orthodox, but he recognised that the law did in fact permit religious teaching of a non-sectarian character and, as he had told one of his election meetings, he "desired simply to administer this Act as an honest man, according to the letter and the spirit of the law, and not to throw difficulties into the way of its operation". In his *Contemporary Review* article he had given clear warning that he would oppose, and if necessary carry an appeal to the Education Department against, any effort to teach theological doctrines in the schools, but Bible-reading was a different matter. The Act permitted it, most parents would desire it, and he did not see how an honest man could oppose it. He must have sympathised with those who, like Lucraft,* wished to restrict religious instruction to Bible-reading without religious note or comment, and with those who, like Chatfield Clarke,† feared that if even this were permitted the teachers would inevitably introduce denominational ideas without knowing it. He must have known how right Rogers was in his remark "A teacher brought up at St. Mark's or Battersea was thoroughly impregnated with the doctrines of his Church, and he was not a

* Benjamin Lucraft (1810–1897), a member for Finsbury, who had been supported by the Labour Representation League and who wished to keep all trace of sectarian teaching out of London's schools.

† Thomas Chatfield Clarke (1829–1895), a member for Finsbury, who held that religious teaching should be left entirely to the Churches.

faithful teacher unless he carried out those doctrines in his teaching". He must have seen the sense in Waugh's * query about who was to ensure that if Bible-reading were permitted no denominational doctrine was taught: "were the children themselves to perform this task, and be made spies for ever on the watch to tell their parents whether the teacher said anything Trinitarian, Unitarian, Ritualistic, or evangelical?" But, above all, he wanted to get the schools working quickly, and to the surprise of some in both camps he supported the famous religious compromise formulated by W. H. Smith: †

That in the schools provided by the Board, the Bible shall be read, and there shall be given such explanation and such instruction therefrom in the principles of morality, and religion, as are suited to the capacities of children, provided always:—

1. That in such explanation and instruction the provisions of the Act, in Sections VII and XIV, be strictly observed, both in letter and spirit, that no attempt be made in any such schools to attach children to any particular denomination.
2. That in regard to any particular school, the Board shall consider and determine upon any application by managers, parents, or ratepayers of the district, who may show special cause for exception of the school from the operation of this Resolution, in whole or in part.

Because of his own agnosticism, Huxley had been forced to give a good deal of thought to the religious education of children. "I go into society", he told Kingsley, "and except among two or three of my scientific colleagues I find myself alone on these subjects—and as hopelessly at variance with the majority of my fellow men as they would be with their neighbours if they were set down among the Ashantees—I don't like this state of things for myself—least of all do I see how it will work out for my children—But as my mind is constituted there is no way out of it and I can only envy you if

* Benjamin Waugh (1839–1908), a member for Greenwich and a Congregational parson, who was mainly responsible for the formation of the National Society for the Prevention of Cruelty to Children.

† William Henry Smith (1825–1891), a member for Westminster and son of the pioneer newsagent. He became Tory leader in the House of Commons, and was once described as 'Smith the Smoother, the quiet, unpretentious reconciler of conflicting opinions'.

you can see things differently." Kate, Lady Amberley, re-cords an interesting conversation with Huxley on bringing up children in a different way from those around them, on the danger of making them pariahs, or of making them think themselves superior to others; and, aware of the dangers of childhood rootlessness, Huxley once said to St George Mivart "Children should be brought up in the mythology of their own time and country, but as they grow up their questions should be answered frankly". His wife took their own children to church, and each time she had one of them baptised it put Huxley in a bad temper, but on the whole he accepted her wishes with good enough grace. "You may judge what my opinions are touching the sacrament of Baptism—", he wrote to Lubbock, "but my wife likes to have the children christened & she has a right to her own way in such matters—I am afraid she is not very orthodox but looks upon the process as a kind of spiritual vaccination without which the youngsters might catch Sin in worse forms as they grow up."

So, he told the London School Board, "If . . . they had to deal with a fresh and untouched population . . . it would not enter into his mind to introduce the religious and ethical idea by the agency of that admirable and venerable book which we called the Bible"; but, he argued with sociological insight, "Any system, to gain the attention of these people to these matters . . . must be a system connected with or not too widely divorced from their own system and beliefs". So far as the England of his time was concerned, he had no doubt that the best medium of ethical instruction was the Bible, and his *Contemporary* essay explained why:

Take the Bible as a whole; make the severest deductions which fair criticism can dictate for shortcomings and positive errors; eliminate, as a sensible lay-teacher would do, if left to himself, all that it is not desirable for children to occupy themselves with; and there still remains in this old literature a vast residuum of moral beauty and grandeur. And then consider the great historical fact that, for three centuries, this book has been woven into the life of all that is best and noblest in English history; that it has become the national epic of Britain, and is as familiar to noble and simple, from John-o'-Groat's House to Land's End, as Dante and Tasso once were to the Italians; that it is written in the noblest and purest English, and abounds in exquisite beauties of mere literary form; and, finally, that it forbids the veriest hind who never left his village to be ignorant of the existence of other countries and other civilisations, and of a great past, stretching back to the furthest limits of the oldest nations in the world. By the study of what other book could children be so much humanised?

Years later he justified his support of Smith in a letter to Edward Clodd:

... though, for the last quarter of a century I have done all that lay in my power to oppose and destroy the idolatrous accretions of Judaism and Christianity, I have never had the slightest sympathy with those who ... would throw the child away along with the bath—and when I was a member of the London School Board I fought for the retention of the Bible to the great scandal of some of my liberal friends who cannot make out to this day whether I was a hypocrite or simply a fool on that occasion.

But my meaning was that the mass of the people should not be deprived of the one great Literature which is open to them—not shut out from the perception of their relation with the whole past history of civilised mankind.

Although it has been claimed that Huxley came to see that his support of Bible-reading was a mistake, eight months before his death he still did not repent of the compromise: "Twenty years of reasonably good primary education is 'worth a mass' ", he told Lord Farrer.

Unfortunately, although Huxley believed that "The persons who agreed to the compromise, did exactly what all sincere men who agree to compromise do ... they accepted what was practically an armistice in respect of certain matters about which the contending parties were absolutely irreconcilable", not all parties had the same high sense of armistice obligations. Within a week the Roman Catholics were seeking authority for children in Board Schools to read the Douai Bible with instructors approved by their parents; and, although Huxley admitted that it might seem hard on Roman

Catholics to have only the authorised version, he insisted that "they could not amend the Act of Parliament; their business was to administer it". The Catholic motion was defeated, whereupon Huxley counter-attacked with a proposal "That in all elementary schools in which the Bible is read, a selection from the Bible, which shall have been submitted to and approved by this Board, shall be used for that purpose". He made it clear that his purpose was not a bowdlerising one —"On the contrary, what we find in the Bible is a plain-spokenness . . . which in many cases I think ought to be imitated at the present day with very considerable advantage to morality"—and he referred with approval to "the good old Biblical word 'harlot' ". But, he remarked, "I don't suppose that any sensible man will maintain that it is desirable to occupy the minds of young children with the laws of Leviticus"; and, more important, "there are, in the Hebrew Scriptures particularly, many statements to which men of science absolutely and entirely demur . . . and what you as honest men must grant, is this, that these tender children shall not be taught that which you do not yourselves believe". However, this the majority would not grant, and his motion was defeated.

After the Board had ruled out both suggestions for revised Bibles, a month did not pass before Canon Cromwell * proposed that it should pay all or part of the fees of poor children attending church schools, and now the fat was in the fire. "Unless [my] ears deceive [me]", Huxley remarked, recalling the Douai episode, "some of those members of the Board who cheered the assertion that the Act was opposed to denominational education were now to be heard supporting the amendment . . . [but] . . . [I do] not wish to go into that now, because men's opinions might naturally change from time to time." He poured scorn on Canon Cromwell's tear-provoking picture of the poor widow who could not afford

* John Gabriel Cromwell (c. 1824–1908), a member for Chelsea and Principal of the Anglican St Mark's College, who in his election campaign had pressed strongly for religious education in the Board Schools.

school fees, and he sincerely hoped that no greater hardship would fall upon the widow whose case had been so pathetically depicted than that of being obliged to send her child to one of the Board Schools. His vigorous attack on this proposal "for the outdoor relief of denominational education" had a marked effect, but Cromwell mustered 23 votes to Huxley's 20.

Quickly laying a stymie by moving 'the previous question', Huxley made it crystal clear that this was the point of no compromise:

> . . . if any motion of that kind became part of the regulations of the Board, he should personally and individually decline to take any share in carrying out conditions which he believed entirely unjust and so utterly opposed to what was expedient and what was right . . . and if such a scheme were carried out, he would undertake to raise a discussion on the case of every child. . . . The time for compromise was over in this matter. . . . He had done his best since he had been at the Board to work harmoniously: very often he had even violated his sense of what was right, for the purpose of enabling this Act to be carried into operation . . . he had . . . given his best support to the carrying of Mr. Smith's resolution—but if he had imagined that the spirit of that resolution would have been so thoroughly and completely violated . . . he would have done his best to vote against it.

Nowhere else in these early records of School Board debates is there a speech so instinct with passion and determination as this; and, although Currie * and Rigg † urged the Board not to submit to Huxley's threat, the sectarians had seen the red light: fifteen abstained, but only a single member voted against 'the previous question'.

Now began a marathon match in which Huxley stonewalled heroically against relays of bowlers. Canon Cromwell's April resolution was still being debated in October— adjourned at 6 p.m. on the 25th, adjourned again at 6 p.m.

---

* Sir Edmund Hay Currie (1834–1913), a member for Tower Hamlets. He was a wealthy nonconformist distiller and later became chairman of the East End's People's Palace.

† James Harrison Rigg (1821–1909), a member for Westminster and Principal of the Wesleyan Westminster Training College.

**THE TEACHER**

*'There is nobody so hard to teach properly
and well as people who know nothing about a subject'* (p. 139)

**THE MAN OF POWER**
*'I always find that I acquire influence, generally more than I want'* (p. xxii)

on the 26th, and at the same hour on the 27th, continued on the 30th, the 31st, and into the early days of November. Huxley declared that, if the proposal were passed, he would oppose any bye-law to make school attendance compulsory, because "he would never be a party to enabling the State to sweep the children of the country into denominational schools". Finally, on 4 November, he delivered a bitter attack on the Roman Church as an engine "carefully calculated for the destruction of all that was highest in the moral nature, in the intellectual freedom, and in the political freedom of mankind", and proceeded with a majestic rebuke to the Church parties in general:

> There were some of them who had made great sacrifices for the sake of peace and for the sake of education. He himself had made a considerable sacrifice, which at the time he fondly hoped would be sufficient. . . . He had hoped that the compromise would be reciprocal, but he could not say there had been any relaxation of those attempts to get back by any means possible, into the hands of the ecclesiastical parties in the country, that denominational education of which it was the whole purpose of the Act of Parliament to deprive them.

Midway through the marathon, Manning wrote to Gladstone "Do not fail to read Huxley's speech. We shall have an Imperial Parliament of little Britain if this goes on", and within a fortnight of this outburst Huxley was being pressed to stand for Parliament. This he refused to consider, but he had halted the wholesale subsidisation of denominational schools in London.

Although it was the debates on religious education whose thunder reverberated across the land in 1871, the great work of the London School Board's first year was the planning of a comprehensive scheme of education. The Scheme of Education Committee (whose appointment was first suggested by Huxley at the Board's second meeting) was faced with an appalling educational position in the metropolis. Even the Home and Colonial School Society's 'model' infant school of 200 pupils consisted mainly of a single room divided by a

M

curtain, the Jews' School at Spitalfields consisted of some 2600 children many of whose parents were described by the master as "the refuse population of the worst parts of Europe", the George Yard Free School in Whitechapel had starving pupils some of whom their teacher had seen fall off the form fainting through hunger, and great numbers of children simply ran about the streets.

Moving the appointment of the committee on 15 February 1871, Huxley defined its task as the consideration of:

> First, the general nature and relations of the schools which may come under the Board. Secondly, the amount of time to be devoted to educational purposes in such schools; and thirdly, the subject-matter of the instruction or education, or teaching, or training, which is to be given in these schools.

It is much to the credit of his colleagues that, recognising his ability despite their dislike of his opinions, they appointed Huxley chairman of this all-important committee. Meeting frequently, and following the principle that it should "obtain some order and system and uniformity in important matters, whilst in comparatively unimportant matters . . . some play should be given for the activities of the bodies of men into whose hands the management of the various schools should be given", the committee progressed rapidly and in four months presented a report comprehensive in scope and liberal in tone.

It was on 14 June that the Board received the committee's report, whose organisational recommendations may be summarised as follows:

i. Day Schools should be Infant Schools (up to 7 years), Junior Schools (7–10 years) and Senior Schools (older).

ii. Infant Schools should be mixed, Junior Schools either mixed or segregated by sex, and Senior Schools segregated.

iii. On grounds of economy, there should be large schools (500+) wherever possible; although Infant Schools might be smaller (250–300).

iv. An Infant School, Junior School(s), Senior Boys School and Senior Girls School should be under one management.

v. For a school of 500 pupils, there should be at least 1 principal teacher, 4 assistant certified teachers and 11 pupil teachers.
vi. Schools should be open for 5 hours daily, 5 days weekly.
vii. There should be women teachers only in Infant Schools, women might take charge of Mixed Junior Schools, only women should teach in Senior Girls Schools, and only men in Senior Boys Schools.
viii. Evening Schools should be formed with the same general character of instruction, but Managers should be left free to adapt the instruction given in the schools to local requirements.
ix. An approach should be made to the Endowed Schools Commissioners to obtain financial help for some Board School children to enter Secondary Schools.

When originally proposing the appointment of the committee, Huxley had strongly urged the establishment of "preparatory, I mean infant schools in which children under the age of six and seven may be collected from the evil education which they are receiving in the streets and gutters, and brought into some state of civilised habit", but there is no reason to suppose that the same suggestion would not have been made without him. The establishment of evening schools was also a particular favourite of his; but it was the proposal to arrange for the diversion of charitable funds to provide scholarships which he made peculiarly his own.

He urged on the Board that "no educational system in this country will be worthy of the name of national, or will fulfil the great object expected of it, unless it be one which establishes a great educational ladder, the bottom of which shall be the gutter, and the top of which shall be [the] Universities", thus providing a figure of speech which caught the public imagination and provided the text for a whole series of articles in the educational Press. Proposing that measures be taken to ascertain which charitable endowments in the London school district ought to be applied, wholly or in part, to the augmentation of the School Fund, Huxley spoke forthrightly about the way in which "that which was originally the birthright of the poor has been converted into a mess of pottage for distribution among the dependents of the rich". He made scathing play of the way in which the "ghost of the pious founder" came in the way of proposals such as his, but "When some great corporate body devotes its funds to the interests of a large and powerful section of society, and that section of society can make itself heard, the voice of the pious founder is completely lost in the din". When he ran into opposition from defenders of the *status quo*, he made the theological concession that "if Alderman Cotton * objected to his saying that the pious founder 'looked down' upon them, he was quite willing to say that the pious founder 'looked up' "; but he insisted that "those children who show ability and capacity in our schools have a legal and moral right to the better education which is afforded at present to the middle classes by the funds". Finally, strongly supported by Lucraft and others, he saw his motion agreed without a division and was even permitted to nominate the members of a committee of inquiry.

The curricular recommendations of the Scheme of Education Committee ran into somewhat heavier weather than those establishing the stages of Infant, Junior, Senior and Evening Schools. In his initial speech suggesting the establishment of the committee, Huxley had taken care to prepare the minds of any members who might be inclined to grudge Board School pupils anything like a liberal education and to warn them that he would not allow his ideas to be written off as unrealistic:

This Board, like all educational bodies, has to steer between Scylla and Charybdis. There is the Scylla of teaching too little, and the Charybdis of teaching too much, and the great practical problem of education, here, as elsewhere, is to avoid both rocks. We have had before us already for some time in this country, a very excellent example of Scylla. I mean the system of trying to teach too little by the Revised Code, which produces instruction in the tools of learning and denies any fragment of real knowledge or information when you have got the tools. It is a sort

* William James Richmond Cotton (1822–1902), a member for the City and later Lord Mayor of London. Although in some ways reactionary, he had an independent mind and a strength of character which made him a valuable member of the Board.

of system which might be described as the teaching a carpenter to go through the motion of the saw and plane, yet never let him have wood to work upon with either (laughter). I am not at all sure that some members of the Board may not think that I am about to furnish them with an example of Charybdis by proposing to teach too much. But I will endeavour . . . [not to exceed] . . . the narrow limits of that which is practicable.

Anticipating objections to the introduction of music and drawing and science, he remarked, "people tell me, 'You might just as well teach them Hebrew'. Why, they are taught Hebrew at present—and taught exceedingly well, too . . . in the East of London"; and, quoting from a German school curriculum, he denied that the young London child was one whit stupider, or less capable of improvement, or one particle less open to these higher studies than the little peasants who ran about Würtemburg.

Later, when he came to present his committee's report, Huxley was unable to defeat an amendment by Canon Cromwell which removed Latin from the list of 'discretionary' subjects that Senior Schools might teach; but when it came to music, which he regarded as "one of the most civilising and enlightening influences which a child can be brought under", he was adamant. One member moved that music teaching should be purely vocal, since "otherwise they might have the piano taught, and he ventured to think that no practical man would propose anything so absurd": Huxley replied, to much laughter, that in fact "they did not intend to teach the piano any more than the harp, the sackbut, or the psaltry", but he succeeded in keeping the door open for the teaching of instrumental music. Urging similarly that as broad an interpretation as possible should be given to the term 'drill' (which he explained, was used because some members had considered his original term 'physical training' too grand), that elementary science should include local geography, that the frequent use of corporal punishment was a mark of incompetency and that there should be regulations restricting its use, at every point Huxley spoke for liberality in the education of the children of the poor. Spalding did not exaggerate when he stated that "This committee, presided over by the late Professor Huxley, rendered signal service to the cause of education in London, and through London, by example, to the country generally. Its report created a revolution in educational ideals".

Reading through these early papers of the London School Board, one is repeatedly impressed by the way in which Huxley seems to have dominated the proceedings; and it is clear that he indulged in no idle boast when telling Michael Foster "I . . . bore the brunt of the battles when the policy of the Board was being settled until the beginning of 1872 when as you know I collapsed". Apart from the two major matters of religious instruction and the scheme of education, he seems to have been involved during the first year in every other issue of importance. He largely prevented the exclusion from London's schools of the inspectors of the Education Department, who, some members feared, might be apt to have fancy notions about cubic space and fresh air and the hygienic standards of the schools generally. He strongly supported Mee * in his (unsuccessful) attempt to establish a pension scheme for teachers, realistically remarking "It was very well to say men ought to make provision for themselves, and so they ought; but very often they did not, especially when they had families and their incomes were of moderate character". He stood for the professional independence of the teacher, opposing a suggestion that Board members be entitled to enter the schools and declaring that they "could not be allowed to come in and set the authority of the teacher at defiance". Further, it was on his proposal that two inquiries were set on foot "in reference to the mode of teaching and the training of teachers"; he was one of the deputation appointed to discuss proposed regulations with the Vice-

* John Mee (1824–1883), a member for Southwark and formerly Secretary of the Church Missionary Society. As Vicar of St Jude's he did excellent work for the poor of London.

President of the Committee of Council; he was one of those charged with the selection of books and apparatus for the schools; he was a member of the Works and General Purposes Committee and the Statistics Committee and the School Management Committee and the Divisional Committee for Marylebone. It comes as no surprise to turn to the memorandum which the London School Board later produced, outlining its work during the first three years of its existence, and there to find that only one member, Professor Huxley, is mentioned by name.

How, one is forced to ask, did this happen? How did a man who had been so anathematised establish leadership of a Board so largely composed of churchmen? And how did such a busy person manage, in the brief fourteen months before his health broke down, to get on to the Minute Book of the London School Board resolutions in favour of practically everything which he had declared should be done?

Largely, no doubt, by his incredible capacity for work. During the election campaign it had been suggested in *The Times* that, while he was qualified in every sense of the word ut that of leisure, he could scarcely be expected to find time for the onerous duties which Board membership would involve; but his working ability had been underestimated. Apart from the holiday period he missed not a single Board meeting until finally he fell ill, he attended altogether some 170 meetings of the Board and its committees during the year, he paid visits to various schools in the metropolis, and he even went to Liverpool's Myrtle Street Gymnasium to see how physical education could be given to children. No wonder that, writing to Anton Dohrn on 3 January 1872, he remarked "I am somewhat 'erkrankt'. . . . Unwillingly, I begin to suspect that I overworked myself last year"—nor that, in the front of his 1872 diary, Mrs Huxley wrote the injunction "First consideration. *Take care of my precious husband & not overwork him*".

Partly the explanation of Huxley's success lies in his genius for lobbying and string-pulling: his diaries for 1870 and 1871 shew that he met privately some of the key witnesses called to the Scheme of Education Committee, and visited Elizabeth Garrett Anderson at her home, and had appointments with Chatfield Clarke and other Board members, and engaged to meet Manning and more than once to visit Westminster Palace—and it would be surprising if he did not use these occasions to smooth the way for his School Board plans. Doubtless he was helped by his eloquence and clarity and his gift of wit and repartee. Yet, in the last resort, it was his statesmanship and charm of character and transparent sincerity which enabled him to do what he did.

But even Huxley could not go on for ever at this pace, and early in the New Year he had to tell Lord Lawrence * that his physician had ordered complete rest:

> I am told, & have every reason to hope, that I shall be quite well again in a short time; but I have now experimentally determined the limits of my powers of work. . . . And, under the circumstances the only course open to me is to place my resignation in your hands. I cannot take this step however without expressing my deep regret, that it is no longer in my power to co-operate with the colleagues whose laborious devotion to their great task has filled me with admiration.

Lawrence was reluctant to accept the resignation and said that he would not place it before the Board without waiting to see what rest and change would do, but Huxley insisted on his letters going forward. On 7 February 1872, when Huxley was already convalescing in Cairo, his resignation from the first London School Board was accepted.

The expressions of regret with which his fellow members received the news ring absolutely true. Dr Rigg referred warmly to "his great fairness and impartiality with regard to all subjects that came under his observation"; Canon Miller,† although "differing *toto caelo* from Professor Huxley in many

---

* Sir John Laird Mair Lawrence, 1st Baron (1811–1879), a member for Chelsea and first Chairman of the London School Board. He is perhaps best remembered as Viceroy and Governor-General of India.

† John Cale Miller (1814–1880), a member for and Vicar of Greenwich.

most important matters", nevertheless could not help saying that he had aroused his admiration by his general deportment at the Board; Charles Reed * thought "the Board might congratulate itself that at any rate for one year they had had the advantages of his services, and that Professor Huxley had left his mark upon the education of the country". Benjamin Waugh was impressed by "his consideration for intellectual inferiors. . . . Towering as was his intellectual strength and keenness above me, indeed above the whole of the rest of the members of the Board, he did not condescend to me. The result was never humiliating. It had no pain of any sort in it. He was too spontaneous and liberal with his consideration to seem conscious that he was showing any. There were many men of religious note upon the Board, of some of whom I could not say the same". And Waugh was not the only one who, despite initial prejudice against Huxley, "was drawn to him most, and was influenced by him most, because of his attitude to a child. He was on the Board to establish schools for children. His motive in every argument, in all the fun and ridicule he indulged in, and in his occasional anger, was the child. He resented the idea that schools were to train either congregations for churches or hands for factories. He was on the Board as a friend of children".

Since his fellow members were men big enough to collaborate with this agnostic tornado of energy which had appeared among them, the London School Board was able in little more than a year to set the shape of English elementary education for three-quarters of a century to come. Much later Huxley was to write "I am glad to think that, after all these years, I can look back upon that period of my life as perhaps the part of it least wasted".

* Sir Charles Reed (1819–1881), the nonconformist philanthropist, whose printing firm became very affluent. A staunch Liberal in politics, and MP for Hackney, he became Chairman of the School Board in 1873.

# CHAPTER IX

# Schools of the Upper Classes

Scientific knowledge is spreading by what the alchemists called a "distillatio per ascensum"; and nothing can now prevent it from continuing to distil upwards and permeate English society, until, in the remote future, there shall be no member of the legislature who does not know as much of science as an elementary schoolboy.

*Address to Working Men's Club and Institute Union,*
*1 December 1877*

IN THE SECOND half of the nineteenth century, when for the first time England was establishing a system of elementary education for the children of the poor, the schools which catered for the upper classes were setting about the reform of their regimen and curriculum. In earlier times, the ancient public schools had included pupils from a wide range of society and had provided an education not unworthy of their origins, but they had been brought nearly to extinction by their harsh discipline and appalling hygiene and lax morality. Dr Arnold and his disciples had transformed the ethos of the public school during the second quarter of the century, but the curriculum was still out of touch with reality. England's expanding economy, moreover, was widening the gap between master and man, and the newly wealthy industrialist was as anxious as the landed aristocrat to see his son taken through a classical curriculum which had become above all a mark of social distinction. In 1850 the public schools were the preserve

of the wealthy and the stronghold of educational traditional-
ism, and even the newer proprietary schools set their faces
against whatever might appear basely mechanical.

Here and there a few traces survived of the eighteenth-
century dissenting academies where eminent scientists like
Priestley had taught, and Mill Hill was teaching astronomy
and chemistry in 1820, but in general the mid-century adult
was quite ignorant of science. Huxley had to be assured that
Tennyson was not joking when he inquired whether the
ascent of sap in plants did not disprove the law of gravitation,
and those responsible for selecting school texts in 1870 could
approve one which declared that "the fly keeps the warm air
pure and wholesome by its swift and zig-zag flight". Not
everyone was content with this state of affairs, and from its
foundation in 1835 the High School of the Liverpool Mechanics Institution employed a full-time 'Philosophical Master'
and gave several hours' science each week to every class; but
in most places a boy like Martin, with a passion for natural
history and experiment, would still have been as much of an
oddity in the 1850s as he was in Tom Brown's schooldays.

Not even the public schools, however, could remain in-
definitely indifferent to new ideas, and a turning-point came
on 23 April 1861 when Grant Duff asked in the House of Commons for a commission of inquiry. Three years later the
Clarendon Commission recommended that natural science
should be taught in the public schools, and in the following
May the House of Lords set up a Select Committee to consider a proposed Public Schools Bill. It was not long before
Lord Wrottesley * was seeking Huxley's advice, and in particular his reply to three questions:

1. In what branches of Physical Science should instruction be given
in our public Schools, & what branches, if any, should be excluded?
2. In what manner should that instruction be imparted? Should

* Sir John Wrottesley, 2nd Baron (1798–1867), an amateur astronomer of
some distinction, who was an active member of the Society for the Diffusion
of Useful Knowledge and chairman of the Parliamentary Committee of the
British Association.

there be periodical Examinations of the Pupils, & prizes for proficiency, & by whom should such examinations be conducted & such prizes awarded?

3. Should instruction in Science be made imperative by positive Enactment, & if not in what mode should it be promoted & encouraged by the Legislature?

Huxley, like the other scientists who were approached, naturally enough answered the first question in the affirmative, but his arguments were more interesting than most. For any study to be regarded as an essential element in education, he suggested, it must be shewn to furnish either indispensable means for the acquirement of knowledge (as with reading and writing), or mental discipline of a kind not to be attained otherwise (the common claim for the classics), or information of paramount practical or speculative importance (as may be gained from history, geography, morality and theology). But, he urged, "The need for scientific education is demonstrable by cogent arguments belonging to all three classes", and especially he advocated the teaching of physics and human physiology. "I am sure", he continued, "that the great aim should be to teach only so much science as can be taught thoroughly; and to ground in principles and methods rather than attempt to cover a large surface of details." As to the manner of instruction, he made his usual plea for practical study and the avoidance of sham verbalism, and to test this he would have the pupils examined by a board constituted from the universities. Finally, he declared, although as a matter of abstract principle he disliked State interference, "in the actual condition of the nation . . . I cannot doubt the wisdom and justice of enforcing the teaching of science upon the public schools by positive enactment".

Pending, and not very much expecting, such positive enactment, the reformers set about securing support for their views. In the autumn of 1865 Huxley discussed with Farrar, then teaching at Harrow, the formation of a small committee of scientists and teachers, to produce a report which would thoroughly arouse public opinion. "This is the main object wh. the Committee wd. accomplish;" wrote Farrar, "& it is almost the only practical way of working on the minds of Head Masters." So, when the British Association met at Nottingham in 1866, Huxley opened up the subject by lamenting excessive specialisation among scientists and tracing it to the lack of adequate general scientific education in the school. Farrar followed with a paper on science teaching, and a committee was appointed to report on the best means of promoting scientific education.

The members—including Tyndall and J. M. Wilson *—met frequently, dining sometimes with Farrar at Harrow and sometimes with Huxley in Marylebone, and they seem to have worked amicably and well. True, Huxley did at one point gravely object that a draft statement, that "reform in education must begin from above", might seem to commit him to theological views which he was not prepared to accept, but badinage of this sort acted only as a stimulant to the committee's deliberations. Its report, adopted at the Association's Dundee meeting in 1867 and presented to the Lord President of the Council, aroused immense interest on its publication and was a milestone in the promotion of science teaching in England. Education in natural science was justified not only on the grounds of utility and mental training, but also because many boys found it interesting and stimulating, because it provided an additional intellectual pleasure for adult life, and because the whole thought of the age had become so impregnated with science that a man was not fully educated without it. Before the year ended there also appeared the celebrated volume of *Essays on a Liberal Education*, and the scientific movement was rapidly gathering momentum. It was at this time that Huxley agreed to give a talk to the Natural History Society of Harrow School, and he wrote to Farrar encouraging

* James Maurice Wilson (1836–1931), at this time a teacher at Rugby and later Headmaster of Clifton. In 1890 he became Archdeacon of Manchester and later Canon of Worcester.

him to continue his efforts at curricular reform. But with the encouragement came a striking warning:

> Do not despair. You are in the thick of the educational fight and must needs feel the struggle more clearly than you can see the inch by inch gain of ground—But you may depend on it victory is on your side —We or our sons shall live to see all the stupidity *in favour* of Science & I am not sure that that will not be harder to bear than the present state of things.

Meanwhile, discontent with the public schools had been sharpened by the 1864 report of the Clarendon Commission, and many groups of forward-looking citizens set about the establishment of educational institutions with fewer cultural and domestic deficiencies. Of these, one of the most intriguing was the International College at Spring Grove. If today it were proposed to found boarding schools in different countries, with similar curricula and methods of teaching so that their pupils might migrate from one to another and thus acquire linguistic fluency and an international outlook without disrupting their studies, what charges of Utopianism might not be made! Yet, nearly a century ago, such a plan was propounded and national committees formed and schools actually started. Those at Chatou near Paris and Godesburg near Bonn presumably came to an end with the Franco-Prussian war, but the London school, of which Huxley was a governor, flourished for more than twenty years.

The scheme originated with a committee, appointed by the commissioners of the Paris Universal Exhibition to award prizes for essays on the advantages of educating together children of different nationalities, and in England the idea was taken up by Cobden and his supporters. When Cobden died in 1865 his place as chairman of the International Education Society was taken by A. W. Paulton, a political journalist who had been educated for the Roman priesthood but instead became a lecturer for the Anti-Corn Law League, and the promoters went ahead undeterred by criticism that the plan would weaken the development of national character. Apart from Paulton and Huxley, the governing body included Tyndall, William Ewart the progressive Liverpool politician, William Smith the translator of Fichte, W. B. Hodgson the former Principal of the Liverpool Mechanics' Institute School, and M. Octave Delapierre the Belgian Consul. Huxley sought to secure the support of John Stuart Mill, but the 'saint of rationalism' did not see how, with his opinions, he could publicly associate himself with a school which would include theology among its subjects of study. The apostle of agnosticism, however, never one to worry about guilt by association, continued to give the scheme his active aid.

The International College opened in temporary premises in Isleworth in 1866, William Ellis * advanced a large part of the money needed to purchase land and erect a permanent building, an eight-acre site in fashionable Spring Grove was approved on sanitary grounds by the Queen's physician, and on 10 July 1867 came the grand ceremonial opening. A large engraving in *The Illustrated London News* portrays great flagpoles bearing the banners of the nations, an enormous marquee presumably for refreshments, and a politely cheering crowd of the well dressed and well fed. At one o'clock the Prince of Wales arrived in a magnificent coach-and-four with police outriders, a gun was fired and the royal standard hoisted, and with a silver spade the Prince planted a *Wellingtonia gigantea*. So, with rich supporters and royal patronage, with the Prince's old tutor Dr Schmitz † as its first Headmaster and eighty pupils in residence in its first term, the International College at Spring Grove got off to a flying start.

"Unfettered by traditional usages," an impressive advertisement in *The Times* announced, "this college, while

---

* William Ellis (1800–1881), who amassed a fortune as a marine underwriter and founded at his own expense five schools which he named after George Birkbeck. He is commemorated by the school of his name in North London.

† Leonhard Schmitz (1807–1890), born at Aix-la-Chapelle and educated partly at Bonn, who was known as a disciple of Niebuhr. He was Rector of the Edinburgh High School before taking up his post at Spring Grove.

preserving what is good in the older institutions, assigns a prominent place in its curriculum to subjects of the utmost importance in our time, viz., modern languages and the natural sciences." The work in languages seems to have been admirable, the pupils discoursing at an open day not only in Latin and Greek but also in French, German and Italian, but the headmaster was apparently reluctant to give science all the school time which Huxley would have wished. However, following several meetings of the College Council during the summer of 1867, Huxley and Tyndall were invited to draw up a scheme for science teaching, and the former produced a most interesting plan.

The first class of eleven-year-olds was to spend three hours per week on "the most elementary truths of Astronomy, Geology, Physical Geography, Meteorology & Natural History", largely in the form of object lessons; in the second year there was to be instruction in elementary physics and botany, "the teaching in the former case to be thoroughly experimental; and in the latter to be based upon the actual observation & working out by each scholar of the parts of common plants"; the third year was to start with elementary chemistry "with as much experimental illustrative practical work as possible", and then continue with elementary human physiology "illustrated by demonstrations upon animal structures"; in the fourth year the pupils were to take more advanced experimental physics and begin the study of social science. "After passing through this preparatory course which should be obligatory upon all scholars," Huxley continued, "option may be given according to the necessities of the administration of the College or to the special gifts & proclivities of the pupil", and he proposed four alternative science courses for the remaining three years. One of the options was to be in mathematical physics, mechanics, astronomy, crystallography and the use of physical instruments; one in advanced chemistry including qualitative analysis; one in zoology, general physiology and "the Natural History of man up to the point at which Ethnology & Archaeology touch History"; and the last in advanced social science including the theory of commerce, law and government. For Tyndall, apparently, Huxley's conception of science teaching was too wide, and he objected to the inclusion of some of the social science. His own proposal, for a logical progression from 'Observational Science' to 'Classificatory Science' and finally to 'Inductive Science', indicates how much more he knew of the theoretical shape of scientific method than of the development of children's interests and the nature of the teaching process.

The extent to which the school managed to achieve its internationalist aim is surprising. The boys must have come from wealthy homes (the school fees were higher than those of Clifton or Lancing or Giggleswick), but they were not restricted by nationality or religion or race. In the early 1870s the pupils included French, Germans, Spaniards, Portuguese, Indians and North and South Americans, and one pupil remembered "raw Brazilians, Chilians, Nicaraguans and what not . . . [and] . . . a negro from Bermuda, a giant of a fellow, who raged over the ground like a goaded bull". This mixed bag of young men, some of them used to settling quarrels by means of a knife, must have been hard to handle, and a local news-sheet records one occasion of open rebellion:

For some reason—doubtless a proper one—the Principal of the International College, Spring Grove, deemed it necessary to stop certain holiday privileges to the pupils. A deputation to the gentleman, headed by the son of a well-known literary man, failed to get a rescind of the terrible denial: and hence a feeling of supposed injustice and ill-advised insubordination. Forming among themselves a Council of Resistance, the boys proceeded to purchase provisions in the shape of hams, preserved meats, bread, biscuits, jams, sweets, tobacco, &c., wherewith to stand the discomfort of a self-imposed siege. A portion of this had been smuggled into the rooms of the College, the remainder being granaried at a "public" somewhere in the neighbourhood, to be delivered by ropes let down at night-time, as the wants of the garrison should demand. On the Saturday evening, a tumbling noise overhead awoke the officials to something unusual. Upon going to ascertain the cause, it was found that the boys had barricaded the doors with chests

N

of drawers and bedding, taking the dormitory-doors from their hinges, and adding them by means of long screws, making admission impossible without the use of great force. In vain they were asked to surrender. The Principal was sent for, but could do nothing. A much-loved under-master's appeal did not alter their determination. As a last resort, on Sunday morning, the aid of the police was sought, and they made short work of the mutineers. Bursting in the doors, they were assailed by brandy-balls from many a catapult! but the Helmet-and-Blue-cloth of law and order quickly brought surrender and subjection. A drum-head school-martial proclaimed the dread sentence of expulsion to ten of the offenders, who were considered principals in the fitful fray—a severe punishment, but a lesson that will stand as a terrible menace to the boys.

The incident, fortunately, does not seem to have interfered unduly with the progress of the College—in 1871 an additional wing and gymnasium brought the expenditure on buildings to £42,000 and soon the boys had the rare luxury of baths with hot and cold water—and as late as 1887 it was apparently flourishing with a staff of fourteen masters. Two years later, however, the premises were sold to Borough Road Training College, and all trace of this fascinating international venture is lost.

Meanwhile, the reform of the older schools of England had been proceeding apace. Already in the 1860s the City of London School was teaching a good deal of chemistry, Wilson at Rugby and Farrar at Harrow had some success in converting their colleagues, and in 1873 the Headmaster's Conference resolved at Winchester "That it is desirable that Natural Science should form part of the curriculum of all first grade schools". Eton had felt sufficiently secure to ignore much of the criticism which came from *The Cornhill* and *The Edinburgh Review* in 1860 and 1861, but the Public Schools Act of 1868 produced a new constitution which gave one seat on its governing body to a nominee of the Royal Society, and this seat Huxley occupied on 13 May 1879.

The Headmaster of Eton at that time was Hornby,* who

* James John Hornby (1826–1909), the first Oppidan and Oxonian to be appointed to that very lucrative post for many generations.

had been appointed in 1868 with the intention that he should initiate reform. The mainly classical masters, however, put up stubborn opposition to all efforts at substantial change, and by the time Huxley arrived at Eton Hornby had largely given up the struggle. A critical Assistant described his Head as 'Hornby the Hermit', and asserted that in his time at the school "taking to drink was a much less serious offence than taking to think", but that is an exaggeration. Outside the regular school work there were many opportunities for boys to follow their own intellectual interests, and some teachers did a great deal to develop the minds of their pupils. The housemasters were still fighting against the attempt to bring them under closer control by the Headmaster, and Huxley told his son that the whole system of paying the Eton masters by the profits of their boarding houses was to his mind detestable. He recognised, however, that the system could not at that time be altered, and concentrated his efforts on the reform of the curriculum.

The reports of the Devonshire Commission during the 1870s had penetrated even to Windsor, and Huxley had been making some moves even before he became a Fellow. Probably a pupil of the time was wrong in his impression that the introduction of science teaching was on Huxley's advice, and a master may be mistaken in believing that it was he who persuaded the school to teach biology, but certainly Oscar Browning * invited him some time before 1875 to give a talk to the boys in his House. Then, in 1878, the Chairman read to the governing body a letter from Huxley on the subject of science teaching and a report was requested on the best means of adapting rooms to that purpose. It is not surprising, therefore, that at his second meeting as governor Huxley was asked to inquire with the Bursar into an application by some of the masters for scientific instruments, and it is clear that he

* Oscar Browning (1837–1923), whose vigorous but not always diplomatic endeavours to reform Eton led to his dismissal in 1875. A fine scholar, he returned to teach at Cambridge, where he became Principal of the University Day Training College.

interpreted the remit widely. The next meeting received a general account of the school's facilities for science teaching:

> Professor Huxley reported that he had been over the Buildings in which science was taught. He considered the accommodation in the Chemical Laboratory Theatre and so forth good and the Museum handy excellent and useful but the Sheds were simply discreditable they could not be looked on with respect and threw a slur on the Teaching they were not well contrived utterly inconvenient and unfit and the Fittings he condemned The Governing Body left it to Professor Huxley to Report on the Requirements to the next meeting.

Within three months Huxley was ready not only with a statement of requirements but also with a rough estimate of cost, which he thought would be about £3000 apart from the site, and the governors agreed to go ahead with the building of a new science block. By the May of 1880 the Bursar had plans and drawings ready, it was resolved "That the Plans be adopted and the work commenced without loss of time", and 'Huxley's Folly' was on its way to erection. It was at this same meeting of the governing body that annual prizes were instituted for biology, and three meetings later the expenditure of £300 on cabinets and specimens and apparatus was approved. Within another three years it was resolved that natural science should be placed on the same footing as classics and mathematics in the examinations for scholarships to the sister foundation at Cambridge, and Huxley could well be pleased with the changes which had taken place at Eton during the first five years of his governorship.

At Eton as on the London School Board, however, he was not concerned solely with science. He was one of a committee appointed by the governing body in 1882 "to obtain information from other Schools as to the Rules or practice which they may have adopted for the instruction of Boys in Music and Drawing", and individually he was asked to obtain further information about drawing from South Kensington and elsewhere. The Headmaster opposed, on the grounds that it would interfere with existing school work, the committee's proposal that all boys should in their first or second year devote up to two hours a week to drawing, but the committee got its way. As to music, however, it was decided "that it would not be expedient at present to make further addition to the regular Studies of the School".

Now a more important issue arose: Hornby was appointed Provost, and it became necessary to elect a new Headmaster. The favourite candidate was Warre,* but a group of progressives campaigned for Welldon,† and Huxley was deeply concerned for the outcome. "I look to the new appointment with great anxiety", he told his son. "It will make or mar Eton. If the new Headmaster has the capacity to grasp the fact that the world has altered a good deal since the Eton system was invented, and if he has the sense to adapt Eton to the new state of things, without letting go that which was good in the old system, Eton may become the finest public school in the country. If on the contrary he is merely a vigorous representative of the old system pure and simple, the school will go to the dogs. I think it not unlikely that there may be a battle in the Governing Body over the business, and that I shall be on the losing side. But I am used to that, and shall do what I think right nevertheless." He travelled up to Windsor for the two meetings which settled the matter and, although the Minutes disclose no details, it would be surprising if he were not one of the two unnamed Fellows who voted against Warre's appointment.

Whether because he had no faith in the new Headmaster, or merely on account of failing health, Huxley's attendance at meetings now became irregular. In 1888 he resigned from Eton's governing body, where, as a fellow-governor put it, he had "stoutly advocated the claims of natural science . . . but

---

* Edmond Warre (1837–1920), a Scholar of Balliol and Fellow of All Souls, who is often ranked as one of the three or four greatest Headmasters of Eton. It was in his time that sport came to reign at Eton.

† James Edward Cowell Welldon (1854–1937), successively Fellow of King's, Headmaster of Dulwich and then Harrow, Bishop of Calcutta, Dean of Manchester and Dean of Durham. He had an infectious personality and made a great impact on Harrow from 1885 to 1898.

earned general respect, as he always did, by the fairness and moderation of his practical views". He had found the public and private schools of England a less favourable field for his peculiar talents than the elementary schools established under democratic control, and perhaps he did not care passionately enough about them to make any major impact. But, if we still have legislators who know less of science than an elementary schoolboy, it is not for want of effort on Huxley's part.

# CHAPTER X

# The Older Universities of England

It is as well for me that I expect nothing from Oxford or Cambridge, having burned my ships as far as they were concerned long ago.

*Letter to John Tyndall, 22 July 1874*

HUXLEY RATHER ENJOYED the feeling of being an outsider (or, rather, he found pleasure in claiming to be one), and certainly it would not have been surprising had Oxford and Cambridge kept him at arm's length. Both universities were governed academically and socially by what Robert Lowe once called "a clerical gerontocracy", and there was a good deal of truth in Huxley's jibe that they were "half clerical seminaries, half racecourses, where men are trained to win a senior wranglership, or a double first, as horses are trained to win a cup". Another side of university life was not unfairly characterised by his ironic reference to "the host of pleasant, moneyed, well-bred young gentlemen, who do a little learning and much boating by Cam and Isis", but things were changing rather rapidly. In Huxley's childhood days there had been a revival of interest in serious learning, and during his early manhood the younger dons who favoured reform were moving slowly into positions of power. By the time Huxley was well established in his first academic post at Jermyn Street, the idea of a university had been given classic shape by Newman in his

Dublin discourses, the Natural Sciences Tripos had been instituted at Cambridge, and the first Royal Commissions on the ancient universities had started their investigations.

An early outcome of the Oxford Commission was the foundation of the Linacre Chair of Physiology, and his friends suggested that Huxley should put in for it. "Such a position," he told Furnivall,* "yielding income enough to render extra work unnecessary and allowing plenty of leisure for the pursuit of original investigation is of all things that which I most covet. . . . Here I am worked to death for a pittance." But already he had theological doubts, and he was never one to give verbal assent whilst making mental reservation. Although brought up in the Church, he explained, he was no churchman; and, despite the wide variation of meaning which attached to the word 'believer', he was not inclined to claim that description for himself. It might be, he admitted, that with the passage of time his doubts would clear up, but he could pledge himself to nothing. Therefore, he asked Furnivall, "Will you ascertain for me whether what I have just said is consistent or inconsistent with the understanding upon which an honest man could become a professor at Oxford?— If it is I will go in for the Chair at once—if not I must give up all thought of it". Debarred from the Linacre Chair by his own integrity, Huxley promoted the candidature of Rolleston,† and his man defeated the nominee of the mighty Sir Richard Owen. "I shall set to work", Rolleston promised Huxley after receiving the good news, "so as never to give you cause to regret the share you have had in my promotion." It was not long before the new professor was consulting Huxley about the conduct of university examinations, and

* Frederick James Furnivall (1825–1915), who took part in the Christian Socialist movement and helped to found the Working Men's College. He later became an outspoken agnostic and offended many by his frankness. He is best remembered as the founder of the Early English Text Society, the Chaucer Society, the Ballad Society, the New Shakspere Society and the Browning Society.

† George Rolleston (1829–1881), a physician of vast knowledge but diffuse thought, who had practised at the Hospital for Sick Children in Great Ormond Street before going to Oxford.

under his influence the 'type system' of zoological study was introduced.

Two years after Rolleston's appointment at Oxford, Huxley visited Cambridge for the 1862 meetings of the British Association. He stayed at Trinity Hall as the guest of Fawcett * and, while there, took the opportunity of founding a "Society for the propagation of honesty in all parts of the world". This 'Thorough Club', so named because its object was the promotion of a thorough and earnest search after scientific truth, seems to have been short-lived, but it served for a while as a useful link between the forward-looking younger men of science. Four years later Cambridge's Professor of Anatomy was writing "Any time you could spare a day we should be delighted to see you & show you the progress we are making—the answer to the question you put at the 'Thorough' dinner here—'What are the universities doing for science?' "

But, despite partial reforms following the first Royal Commissions, there were some at Oxford and Cambridge who wanted more fundamental changes, among them Mark Pattison † and Goldwin Smith.‡ The former complained that the university had renounced her high vocation to take up the easier business of school keeping, and was operating as "a spiritual police to maintain an arbitrary *juste milieu* of Church government and doctrine"; the latter said that the professoriate had fallen into decay and spoke scathingly of "the

* Henry Fawcett (1833–1884), Professor of Political Economy from 1863 to his death. Despite blindness from a shooting accident in 1858, he took an active part in many movements of reform, and as MP for Brighton fought strongly for the abolition of religious tests in the universities.

† Mark Pattison (1813–1884), an erstwhile follower of Newman and Pusey, who had abandoned the High Church party and become heterodox in theology. In 1861 he became Rector of Lincoln College, and over many years wrote vigorously on educational matters.

‡ Goldwin Smith (1823–1910), who became a Fellow of University College in 1846 and Regius Professor of Modern History in 1858. He took a most active part in public affairs, serving as Joint Secretary of the 1850 Royal Commission on Oxford and the subsequently appointed Statutory Commissioners, and as a member of the 1858 Newcastle Commission on elementary education. In 1866 he migrated to the USA to a Chair at Cornell, and thereafter went to Canada.

conjoint operation of celibacy, clericalism and sinecurism". Pattison in particular disliked the dominance of the colleges over the university and the resulting concentration on the tutorial system, and the example of the German universities led some of the reformers to advocate a reversal which would put the professors in power and unseat the tutors. Huxley, however, was not blinded to the essential virtues of the tutorial system by its accidental excesses, and he told the 1868 Select Committee on Scientific Instruction that a major defect in his own School of Mines was its entire dependence on the professorial system. "Both of these systems ought to be combined in any completely organised course of instruction", he believed.

Superficially, it would seem unlikely that there should be much in common between the Darwinian who invented the word Agnostic and the Tractarian who ended as a Cardinal of the Roman Church, but there is a quite marked resemblance between Huxley's views on university education and those of Newman. Certainly Newman's essentially aristocratic outlook was totally alien to Huxley, who would have opened the universities to poor scholars not as a charitable concession but as a social and moral right, and on the fundamental issue of the Church's regency over education they were poles apart. But, while they were both children of England in her heyday, alike proud of their Englishness and even somewhat insular in it, each had a high regard for traditional values going back to the days when Europe was a cultural unity. Both men had a love of exact scholarship which made them suspicious of the tendency to overload curricula to the point of rendering study superficial, and yet each had a universal respect for learning which made him reluctant to admit specialisation to the point of narrowness. Both had a passionate regard for truth and intellectual integrity combined with a contempt for all merely human authority, both were haunted by a feeling that the universe was more complex than nineteenth-century materialism implied. "J.H.N. was simply a sceptic who backed out of it", remarked Leslie Stephen; "Somewhere in Professor Huxley lurks the mystic whose ears are open to the spiritual world", noted *The Quarterly Review*. Perhaps it is not surprising that, although Huxley saw more clearly than Newman how the university could be adapted to the modern world, their educational ideas were more similar than is commonly recognised.

To each the university was, above all, the coping-stone of the nation's system of education, and not simply an academy of manners for the wealthy or a rich store of sinecures for the scholarly. "University education", Huxley declared at Baltimore, "should not be something distinct from elementary education, but should be the natural outgrowth and development of the latter. . . . The primary school and the university are the alpha and omega of education." He would therefore, he told the University of Aberdeen, exclude no subject as in itself unfit for a university, provided that it was studied in depth and with integrity:

> In an ideal University, as I conceive it, a man should be able to obtain instruction in all forms of knowledge, and discipline in the use of all methods by which knowledge is obtained. In such a University, the force of living example should fire the students with a noble ambition to emulate the learning of learned men, and to follow in the footsteps of the explorers of new fields of knowledge. And the very air he breathes should be charged with that enthusiasm for truth, that fanaticism of veracity, which is a greater possession than much learning; a nobler gift than the power of increasing knowledge; by so much greater and nobler than these, as the moral nature of man is greater than the intellectual; for veracity is the heart of morality.

On these grounds, so reminiscent of Newman's discourse 'Knowledge its Own End', Huxley always urged due recognition of the natural sciences, but he also asked "If there are Doctors of Music, why should there be no Masters of Painting, of Sculpture, of Architecture?", and declared "I should like to see Professors of the Fine Arts in every University". Newman, of course, had professors of the sciences at Dublin, and intellectually he accepted science as Huxley accepted letters. But, whereas the man of science had a fine feeling for literary excellence, the man of letters had no real understanding of the scientific mode of thought, and Huxley is the more convincing advocate of a truly catholic university curriculum.

The idea that Newman would have altogether excluded research from the university is quite erroneous—he once spoke of the university as "the high protecting power of all knowledge and science, of fact and principle, of inquiry and discovery, of experiment and speculation"—but he certainly held the prosecution of original investigations to be quite subsidiary to the function of teaching. For Huxley, however, the enlargement of knowledge was of the essence of an up-to-date university, and not a mere accidental:

> The mediaeval university looked backwards: it professed to be a storehouse of old knowledge, and except in the way of dialectical cobweb-spinning, its professors had nothing to do with novelties. . . .
>
> The modern university looks forward, and is a factory of new knowledge: its professors have to be at the top of the wave of progress. Research and criticism must be the breath of their nostrils. . . .

Moreover, whereas Newman considered that specialist academies were more suitable than universities for extending the boundaries of knowledge, and regarded discovery and teaching as distinct gifts commonly found in different persons, Huxley feared the effects of isolating studies in separate institutions and divorcing research from teaching. "I do not think that it is any impediment to an original investigator to have to devote a moderate portion of his time to lecturing, or superintending practical instruction", he said at Aberdeen. "On the contrary, I think it may be, and often is, a benefit to be obliged to take a comprehensive survey of your subject; or to bring your results to a point." And, at Johns Hopkins University, he agreed that the best investigators were usually those who had also the responsibilities of instruction, gaining thus the incitement of colleagues, the encouragement of pupils and the observation of the public.

In the main, therefore, Huxley did not take sides in the

debate about the respective rôles of tutor and professor, but set himself instead to the more immediate task of securing posts at Oxford and Cambridge for men capable of both investigation and instruction. In 1866 he was conferring with Sidgwick * about the best person for a Praelectorship in Natural Science which it was hoped to establish at Trinity, but the proposal was defeated at the December College Meeting. Soon, however, with W. H. Thompson † as Master, Trinity moved to the forefront of Cambridge reform, and in the spring of 1870 Huxley heard from a Fellow that there had been a more positive response to another such proposal:

I read your letter to the Seniority yesterday. Your suggestion as to the Praelectorship of Physiology and the man to fill it, was most favourably received. . . . If Mr. Foster will come and spend a day with me, I can explain everything to him. . . . If he is appointed, we will set to work about establishing the Physiological Laboratory.

His nominee once established in the new post, Huxley had a useful channel through which to influence science teaching at Cambridge, and for the next quarter of a century Michael Foster never ceased to consult him.

In Oxford, the episode of 1860 had not been forgotten and, when it was suggested ten years later that Huxley should be given an honorary degree, there was powerful opposition. "There seems to have been a tremendous shindy in the Hebdomadal Board about certain persons who were proposed;" Huxley wrote to Darwin, "and I am told that Pusey ‡ came to London to ascertain from a trustworthy friend who were the blackest heretics out of the list proposed, and that he was

---

* Henry Sidgwick (1838–1900), Fellow of Trinity and from 1883 Professor of Moral Philosophy. He and his wife were leaders in the movement for the higher education of women.

† William Hepworth Thompson (1810–1886), Regius Professor of Greek from 1853 to 1867, and Master of Trinity from 1866 to his death. He was the author of the famous saying, "We are none of us infallible, not even the youngest among us".

‡ Edward Bouverie Pusey (1800–1882), Regius Professor of Hebrew and Canon of Christ Church. As a Fellow of Oriel he had joined with Newman and Keble in the Tractarian movement, but always opposed the secession of Anglo-Catholics to Rome.

glad to assent to your being doctored, when he got back, in order to keep out seven devils worse than that first!" However, this did not prevent Huxley's being brought in as assessor when Exeter College offered a Fellowship in science in 1872, and his choice fell upon that stormy petrel Ray Lankester. Very soon, however, Lankester was feeling a frustration which comes out clearly in a letter asking his sponsor to look about for another post for him:

> I would not bother you about these personal concerns—if I did not regard you as a father-in-science. . . . No one knows who does not live in the place—the inextricable mess of mediaeval folly and corporation-jealousy and effete restrictions which surround all Oxford institutions.
>
> A commission comes and examines people such as Acland—and of course hears the smoothest, most cheerful account of everything—but many of his statements are untrue and meant to deceive. . . . Other witnesses give necessarily a favourable account of things which they themselves have constructed. . . .
>
> The Colleges are really, without an exaggeration—now nothing more than large proprietary schools. We, fellows, try to get as many fees out of the undergraduates as we can—and to get as many as possible to come to the College and as we can't get many sharp youths we take stupid and lazy ones—and undertake (to their parents) to force them to attend lectures & somehow or other to get them through the degree examination. . . . I am simply kept to my present position—a mere college advertisement "We have a Natural Science lecturer on our staff". . . many men have their lives ruined by taking residential fellowships. They stay up making large incomes (for bachelors) and spending a great deal. . . . Their fellowships are forfeited by marriage so they don't marry. They don't work—for why should they? Their time is sufficiently occupied with routine duties and routine amusements such as riding, dining and whist. To these may be added an occasional visit to London—for unknown purposes. This is the society of Oxford . . .

Lankester, unfortunately, for all his efforts to model himself on his master, never found it easy to take a balanced view of things, and in fact Oxford was rapidly waking up to the importance of science. Already in 1868 there were forty to fifty students attending lectures in physiology, and both Merton and The Queen's College were offering science scholarships. Soon Exeter and New did likewise, and in 1873 Magdalen and Merton held a joint examination for a Fellowship with preference to biology. At Merton and at University College Huxley was brought in to advise on the selection of Fellows, and at Cambridge likewise he did his best to see that new posts were filled by able men. In the autumn of 1873 he sent Michael Foster 'seven teasers' for the written examination for a Trinity Fellowship, and he travelled up to take a personal part in the *viva voce*. The examiners made a new departure by inviting the submission of records of original investigations, and Huxley was so impressed by the research abilities of F. M. Balfour * that he recommended him for the Fellowship. Six years later, when Trinity again asked him to select a biology Fellow, he assured the Master that he would so test the breadth and reality of the candidates' knowledge as to exclude mere "Spider stuffers and Hay botanists", and his promise that the College should have a good man or none was well kept by the appointment of Adam Sedgwick.† Finally, as the diversion of ancient endowments by the 1877 Commissioners strengthened the professoriate, he became an elector to the Cambridge Chairs of Physiology, Anatomy, and Zoology and Comparative Anatomy.

The university world in those days was small and closely knit, and much could be done by a group of friends working well together. In 1872 a party including Huxley, Mark Pattison, Henry Sidgwick and Charles Appleton met at Freemasons' Tavern in London to consider the endowment of research and form the short-lived 'Association for the Organisation of Academical Study', and there were many similar meetings during the 1870s. Some idea of the sort of co-operation which existed between reformers within the

* Francis Maitland Balfour (1851–1882), to whom Huxley had already awarded a natural history prize at Harrow. Later appointed University Lecturer in Animal Morphology, Balfour established the great Cambridge embryology school, and his tragic death in a climbing accident deprived science of the man commonly regarded as Huxley's natural successor in the leadership of British biology.

† Adam Sedgwick (1854–1913), who later became successively Reader in Animal Morphology and Professor of Zoology at Cambridge, and then Professor of Zoology at Imperial College.

walls and those without is given by a few extracts from the letters of Jowett,* the Powerful Master of Balliol:

### To Huxley, 23 April 1877

I am hoping to introduce or rather to persuade others to introduce more physical science in the University. I am inclined to think that some knowledge of it (as of Arithmetic) should be one of the requirements for a degree. Some scientific men appear to be opposed to this on the ground that it will lower the character of such studies. I cannot agree with them: no study can reach a very high standard with the mass of students. Yet it may do them great good & gain something from them in return.

### To Mrs Huxley, 6 May 1877

I want to have the opportunity of talking to Mr. Huxley about a move which I am thinking of trying to make here for requiring a knowledge of Physical Science of all Candidates for a degree.

### To Huxley, 7 May 1878

There are many things about which I should like to have the pleasure of talking to you, specially about the possibility of making Oxford somewhat more of a Medical School than at present.

### To Huxley, 2 December 1885

We are just passing a new medical statute at Oxford which will I hope be successful. . . . I should greatly like to talk with you about Scientific Education at schools & at the University—I would like to make a certain amount of science compulsory as Latin & Greek are: but I do not find that the Professors of Science at Oxford are inclined to support this idea.

One of the schemes which Jowett and Huxley discussed was that of persuading the Royal Society to petition Oxford to allow the sciences to be taken in Responsions, but this reform had to wait until 1920. They and their allies, however, were

* Benjamin Jowett (1817–1893), who had been deprived of the emoluments of his Regius Professorship of Greek for ten years on suspicion of heresy. When he had built up his College's influence, he reputedly remarked "if we had but a little more money, Balliol could absorb the University", and he certainly succeeded in gathering many Oxford strings into his capable hands. Light is cast on certain aspects of his character by the verse devised by students for a Balliol mime:

> I come first, my name is Jowett,
> If it's knowledge then I know it;
> What I don't know isn't knowledge,
> I'm the Master of the College.

more successful in their move to relieve science students of the need to take Latin and Greek in Moderations, and after 1886 the Oxford scientist was free of classical tests beyond Responsions.

A somewhat similar battle, about which more details are available, had been fought at Cambridge some years before. Following an earlier unsuccessful move in 1871, a powerful band of petitioners, including scientists like Huxley and Hooker and Tyndall, men of letters like Arnold and Carlyle, and headmasters like Hornby and Butler * and Abbott,† presented in 1878 a memorial urging that Greek be no longer compulsory in the Previous examination. Impressed by the weight of the signatories, Congregation appointed a Syndicate to consider the memorial and report before the end of the Michaelmas term of 1879. Each petitioner was invited to furnish a fuller statement of his views, and Huxley's was unquestionably the most cogently argued of them all.

He emphasised that in signing the memorial nothing had been further from his mind than any wish to depreciate the value of a study of Greek, either on its own account as literature and history, or as an instrument of education, or as an auxiliary to the pursuit of philosophy, mathematics and science, all of which had Greek origins. But, he argued, he had not noticed any correlation between ordinary Greek scholarship and literary culture, and he did not think that a knowledge of Greek was any more indispensable to a liberal education than a knowledge of Sanskrit or the Differential Calculus or Vertebrate Morphology. Ignorance of any one of these, he admitted, shuts off a large and fertile field of thought, but it was quite possible to become well educated by the aid of other studies. The Greek required for the Previous

---

* Henry Montagu Butler (1833–1918), Headmaster of Harrow from 1859 to 1886 and thereafter Master of Trinity and for a time Vice-Chancellor of Cambridge. He was a brother-in-law of Sir Francis Galton and kept closely in touch with science, which he gave a formal place in the Harrow curriculum.

† Edwin Abbott Abbott (1838–1926), Headmaster of the City of London School from 1865 to 1889 and a prolific author of religious writings and textbooks.

o

examination, moreover, was generally admitted to be but a useless smattering, and he could not doubt that the time spent in learning it might be better employed. But, despite such strong arguments, despite a clear consensus among forty-three headmasters that a change was necessary, despite a recommendation from the Syndicate that students proceeding to a Tripos should be allowed to substitute French or German for Greek in the Previous, the conservatives would not concede. Finally, after long and tortuous discussion, the Grace to confirm the Syndicate's recommendation came to Senate, swollen by the attendance of non-residents from the country, in the November of 1880, and there received only 145 *placets* to 185 *non-placets*. And not until 1919 did Greek cease to be compulsory for entry to Honours courses at Cambridge.

In Oxford, meanwhile, the 1877 Commissioners had considered the desirability of providing for the teaching of English, and in 1885 the university instituted the Merton Chair of English Language and Literature. However, to the indignation of many—and especially of J. C. Collins,* who had himself nourished hopes of being appointed—the electors chose A. S. Napier,† whose interests were almost exclusively in philology. Collins was soon telling Huxley that he proposed trying to block the appointment, and urged "A protest from you in any public paper would I am convinced, have such an effect at Oxford that it would turn the scale when the matter comes before Congregation". No such public protest seems to have been made in time, and the appointment was confirmed. Soon, however, Collins was organising a large-scale attack on the whole Oxford tendency to equate English literature with Middle-English philology, and *The Pall Mall Gazette* printed a series of statements by men of eminence.

---

* John Churton Collins (1848–1909), whose articles in *The Quarterly Review* and *The Pall Mall Gazette* did much to focus attention on the need for a serious study in the universities of their own country's literary wealth. In 1904 he became Professor of English Literature at Birmingham.

† Arthur Sampson Napier (1853–1916), who had thitherto held posts at Berlin and Göttingen.

Matthew Arnold sent Collins a strangely tepid letter, indicating that he would like to see the great works of English literature taken in conjunction with those of Greek and Latin in *Literæ Humaniores*, but not supporting the establishment of a new School for modern literature or modern languages. Huxley, however, came hotly to the defence of his native tongue, and his statement was given pride of place in the *Pall Mall* series. He declared that "the establishment of Professorial chairs of philology, under the name of literature, may be a profit to science, but is really a fraud practised upon letters", and he enlarged on the general question of literary style and culture:

> That a young Englishman may be turned out of one of our universities, "epopt and perfect" so far as their system takes him, and yet ignorant of the noble literature which has grown up in these islands during the last three centuries . . . is a fact in the history of the nineteenth century which the twentieth will find hard to believe; though, perhaps it is not more incredible than our current superstition that whoso wishes to write and speak English well should mould his style after the models furnished by classical antiquity. . . . I mark among distinguished contemporary speakers and writers of English, saturated with antiquity, not a few to whom, it seems to me, the study of Hobbes might have taught dignity; of Swift, concision and clearness; of Goldsmith and Defoe, simplicity. . . . It has been the fashion to decry the eighteenth century, as young fops laugh at their fathers. But we were there in germ; and a "Professor of Eighteenth Century History and Literature" who knew his business might tell young Englishmen more of that which it is profoundly important they should know . . . than any other instructor.

The attack was not without effect: before long Hebdomadal Council appointed a committee to consider the position and, despite procrastination, Statutes were eventually approved instituting a Final Honours School of English and a new Chair of English Literature.

It would be wearisome to detail various other indications of Huxley's influence on the development of the newer studies at Oxford—his letter to the Vice-Chancellor urging the university to support the proposed Plymouth Marine Biological

Station, his backing for a new biological laboratory for Romanes, his securing of the Linacre Chair for Lankester against the desire of the Archbishop of Canterbury that it should go to his cousin, his support for Tylor * in getting Anthropology accepted as a subject for Honours. It is, however, worth while to take a closer look at the two very flattering efforts which were made to get Huxley to go to Oxford himself.

The Commissioners of 1877 had founded a new Chair of Physiology and diverted the Linacre Chair to Human and Comparative Anatomy, and just as these changes were about to come into effect Rolleston died. Now, a couple of decades after he had refused to go in for the original Linacre Chair because of his conscientious scruples, Huxley was pressed to take the modified post. Jowett's anxiety to have his ally within the university is indicated by the almost indecent haste with which he wrote to sound out Mrs Huxley:

> You will have heard with grief of poor Dr. Rolleston's death yesterday. . . . I wonder if Professor Huxley could be induced to stand for his Professorship: We should be delighted to have him here. . . . The Electors are the Presidents of the Colleges of Physicians and Surgeons, the Warden of Merton, the President of the Royal Society, & the Abp. of Canterbury. The three last happen to be friends of mine.

The first four electors happened to be friends of Huxley's, and it is obvious that the hare could have been bagged without the slightest difficulty. The Warden of Merton † waited for Rolleston to be buried before making his approach, but immediately after the funeral he wrote direct to Huxley with a similar inquiry:

> Could you *entertain* the idea of succeeding our friend Rolleston, whom I deeply lament, as Linacre Professor. . . . I do not suppose that

* Sir Edward Burnett Tylor (1832–1917), whose researches into primitive cultures laid many of the foundations of his science. In 1895 he became Oxford's first Professor of Anthropology.

† George Charles Brodrick (1832–1903), who had become an intimate of Huxley's during some twenty-odd years in London as a barrister and journalist. He had become a member of the London School Board and a Governor of Eton in 1877, and later he served as a member of the Selborne Commission on the University of London.

you wd. be willing to become a candidate. The question is whether, if invited to accept the office, you *might* be disposed to do so. . . . If you do entertain the idea at all, it wd. be easy to arrange for talking it over at the Athenaeum.

The post offered £800 to £900 a year, with a Fellowship of £250 or more to accompany it, and Huxley was assured that he would be able to devote most of his time to research. Moreover, Jowett emphasised, Huxley's appointment would not now arouse the theological opposition which it would have done twenty years before, and others agreed with him that it would be the very best thing that could happen to the university. But it was not to be, and Huxley wrote to Brodrick explaining why:

I am getting old, and you should have a man in full vigour. I doubt whether the psychical atmosphere would suit me, and still more, whether I should suit it after a life spent in the absolute freedom of London . . . [but] . . . if I had been ten years younger, I should have been sorely tempted to go to Oxford.

"I am most truly sorry that you are not to come to us", wrote Henry Smith,* "I never supposed, however, that we could hope to catch you."

Later in the year an even greater temptation confronted Huxley, but he put this behind him too. On the death of Dean Stanley,† Dr Bradley ‡ gave up the Mastership of University College to succeed him at Westminster, and Faulkner § tried to get Huxley as the new Master. The prospect was an attractive one, and for a while Huxley wavered:

* Henry John Stephen Smith (1826–1883), the Savilian Professor of Geometry, of whom Jowett said "He was possessed of greater natural abilities than any one else whom I have known at Oxford", and whom Grant Duff described as "the only man in Oxford who was without an enemy".

† Arthur Penrhyn Stanley (1815–1881), who had been Professor of Ecclesiastical History for eight years at Oxford before becoming Dean of Westminster in 1864. He was a consistent supporter of theological liberalism and attracted men of many shades of opinion to Westminster Abbey, whose dignity he did much to restore.

‡ George Granville Bradley (1822–1903), who had been Master of University College since 1870.

§ Charles Joseph Faulkner (1834–1890), Fellow of University College and successively Bursar, Tutor and Dean of Degrees.

I have been thinking very carefully over the proposition which you were so good as to make to me on Friday. I gathered from our conversation that no fixed duties, beyond six months residence, are imposed upon the Master of University College; that a salary of £1300 a year and a house are attached to the office; and, from your coming to me, I take it for granted that there are no theological tests or obligations. . . .

I must confess that after living in London for thirty years the notion of transplanting myself & my family into such totally different conditions as those of Oxford, fills me with some alarm . . . [and this consideration] . . . would still be effective were it not for the prospect of rest & leisure which the the [sic] Mastership offers. . . . .

I have no inclination to be a sinecurist but I want to employ myself to my own liking and it seems to me that if I were elected to the Mastership my thirty years experience of all sorts of work connected with scientific life and education might enable me to be of use to the College to the University [sic]—as a sort of Minister for Science without portfolio—and that at the same time I could secure the opportunity of devoting myself to the best work of which I am capable which I covet.

He feared, however, that the move would involve him in a diminution of income and that the practical working of the Mastership might be very different from what it seemed on the surface, so Faulkner set about removing his doubts. Under the new statutes soon to come into force, he pointed out, the Master's salary would be free of income tax, his house would be free of rent and rates and taxes and kept in repair by the College, and there would be a retiring pension of £500 per annum at the age of seventy-five. As to the duties of the Master, he indicated that these depended almost entirely on the incumbent's own inclinations, and some of his characterisations of other Heads of Houses are illuminating. Plumptre, the Master of University College preceding Bradley, had been left stranded by the reforms of the 1850s because the new ideas were beyond him, and the trivial duties he had performed could have occupied but half an hour a day; Jowett of Balliol stood out in contrast, yet his published work demonstrated that even an active Head could find plenty of time for his own studies; Pattison did absolutely nothing as Rector of Lincoln, and Liddell was able enough but did nothing as Dean of Christ Church; and, to summarise, Huxley's administrative efficiency should enable him to perform the duties of the Mastership without too much expenditure of time. It is difficult to imagine what more Huxley could have wanted; but, despite further correspondence and additional assurances, he decided to stay where he was. The decisive reason, no doubt, was that which he gave to his son Leonard: "I do not think I am cut out for a Don nor your mother for a Donness."

Looking back on the Oxford and Cambridge of a century ago, one is inclined to concentrate on their obscurantism and their slowness to change. But in both places there were vigorous reformers, and it would have been quite impossible for Huxley to exercise the influence he did unless there had been a general movement into line with the needs of the modern world. True, Cambridge lagged behind Breslau and Edinburgh and Dublin in giving him an honorary degree, and Oxford behind Würtzburg also, but both universities managed to get in ahead of Bologna and Erlangen. In the June of 1879 Huxley was able to tell Baynes * "I shall be glorious in a red gown at Cambridge tomorrow, and hereafter look to be treated as a PERSON OF RESPECTABILITY. I have done my best to avoid that misfortune, but it's of no use". Six years later, retiring from South Kensington, he received a similar honour at Oxford, telling Price † that the ceremony would be "a sort of apotheosis coincident with my official death, which is imminent. In fact, I am dead already, only the Treasury Charon has not yet settled the conditions upon which I am to be ferried over to the other side". His early fear, that he had burned his boats so far as the two older universities were concerned, was proved in both cases baseless.

* Thomas Spencer Baynes (1823–1887), the Shakespearean scholar who edited the 9th edition of the *Encyclopædia Britannica*.
† Bartholomew Price (1818–1895), Sedleian Professor of Natural Philosophy from 1853 and Master of Pembroke from 1892.

# CHAPTER XI

# The Universities of Scotland

If your annals take any notice of my incumbency, I shall probably go down to posterity as the Rector who was always
beaten. But if they add, as I think they will, that my defeats
became victories in the hands of my successors, I shall be well
content.

*Rectorial Address to the University of Aberdeen,*
*27 February 1874*

IN SCOTLAND, AS in England, the latter half of the nineteenth century was a period of heated academic debate and
decisive educational reform. The universities north of the
border had never been converted into the *hauts lycées* for the
sons of the wealthy which their southern counterparts had
become, and the survival of the ancient office of Rector still
provided an opportunity for the student body to give periodic
expression to its wishes. Like Oxford and Cambridge, the
universities of Scotland were modelled on Paris, with a little
of Bologna too, but their subsequent development had been
quite different. Three of the four—St Andrews, Glasgow and
Aberdeen—were founded in the fifteenth century by the
bishops of their respective dioceses, and Edinburgh a century
later by the Town Council, and the difficulties of travel in the
northern hills had kept them all fairly local in their appeal.
They also remained quite small—in 1872 St Andrews had but
157 students and Aberdeen only 605—and the comparative
poverty of the country prohibited the development of a rich

194

collegiate structure. The 'colleges' of St Andrews were in effect collateral branches of the university, while those of Aberdeen were independent universities until their jointure in 1858, and in Scotland there was never any danger of the universities' being eaten up by wealthy colleges as had happened in England. But, if the Scots founded no great residential houses like those of Oxford and Cambridge, they endowed in their zeal for education innumerable bursaries, which brought a stream of intelligent lads straight from the soil to the four centres of higher learning. Without affluence or pride of family, the poor students lodged for the most part in the houses of the townsfolk, and were looked on by them as their own. The universities of Scotland maintained into the nineteenth century not only much of their early form, but also their early aims. They were peoples' universities, and their whole functioning and tradition were so different from those of England as to make it almost impossible for most of the leading figures south of the border to play any very effective part in Scottish university reform. Huxley, however, had not been conditioned by an orthodox public school and university education, and he was able to develop wide and influential connexions with the universities of Scotland.

Soon after Forbes left the School of Mines in 1854 to take the Chair of Natural History at Edinburgh, he suggested that Huxley should also go North and deputise for the ailing Professor of Physiology, with the intention of ultimately succeeding him, and the offer was a tempting one made in a flattering manner. But, Huxley felt, "Had I accepted, I should have been at the mercy of the actual Professor—and that is a position I don't like standing in, even with the best of men", so he refused to move. Tragically, however, Forbes died less than two months later, and Huxley was approached to allow his name to be put forward for the vacant Chair of Natural History. "People have been at me about the Edinburgh chair", he told Hooker. "I have written to say that if the Professors can make up their minds they wish me to stand, I will   if not, I will not", and very soon he was able to inform his sister Lizzie that several of the most influential professors had strongly urged him to allow his name to go forward. Huxley was greatly attracted by the prospect of a rise in salary from £200 to £1000 a year, but he was torn two ways. "I dread leaving London & its freedom—its Bedouin sort of life—for Edinburgh & no whistling on Sundays", he confided to Dyster, and he painted an amusing picture of his mixed feelings:

*Apropos* of Edinburgh I feel much like the Irish hod-man who betted his fellow he could not carry him up to the top of a house in his hod. The man did it, but Pat turning round as he was set down on the roof, said "Ye've done it, sure enough, but, bedad, I'd great hopes ye'd let me fall about three rungs from the top." Bedad, I'm nearly at the top of the Scotch ladder, but I've hopes.

One thing to which Huxley particularly objected was the heavy load of lecturing which lay in those days on the professors of Scotland, and in the February of 1855 he withdrew his name from consideration. Edinburgh was still reluctant to lose him, and in April he was within an ace of falling to the financial temptation, but just in time the Government offered him £600 a year at the School of Mines, and in London he stayed.

In 1866, the first British university to do so, Edinburgh conferred on Huxley the honorary degree of Doctor of Laws and he travelled north with Carlyle and Tyndall, who were to be similarly honoured. Evidently not everyone in Edinburgh approved, for the newspapers reported that, unlike his fellow-recipients, he was greeted not simply with "cheers" but with "cheers and slight hisses". The hisses, however, seem to have carried little weight with the university, for in 1869 the Court recognised Huxley's lectures on natural history as a qualifying course for graduation in medicine, and for nearly twenty years candidates for the Edinburgh degree were able to attend his lectures in London in part fulfilment of requirements. A year later the Crown was seeking Huxley's advice about filling the Regius Chair from which he had himself recoiled as a young man:

Private                                                                  Home Office,
                                                                         Oct. 26, 1870.

Dear Mr. Huxley,

You are aware that the Professorship of Natural History in the University of Edinburgh is vacant—

There are four applicants for the post—

Dr. Wyville Thomson
Dr. Macintosh
Dr. Nicholson &
Dr. Anderson (now Director of the Calcutta Museum of Natural History).

I hope you will not refuse to assist me with your advice in choosing the best man.

I have read your testimonial in favor of Dr. W. Thomson. It shows that you think him a fit man. But is he the fittest of the four?—

If you will answer me that question you will greatly oblige me.

                                                    Ever sincerely yours
                                                    H. A. Bruce.

Huxley's reply has not been traced, but perhaps we can guess it from the fact that his friend Thomson * was appointed.

In 1875 Wyville Thomson was to be absent while carrying out a survey in HMS *Challenger*, and Huxley took his place as Professor of Natural History in a concentrated course lasting from May to July. Some 600 students attended the first lecture and the enrolment for the full course was 353, a record for any Edinburgh class. "I . . . positively polished off the Animal Kingdom in 54 lectures", Huxley told Michael Foster on the conclusion of the course. "French without a master in twelve lessons is nothing to this feat." Even he found the feat a trying one, and in mid-course he remarked to Dyster "Talk about brains being important to a man—I believe in bowels". But his efforts were well rewarded, for his agreement with the university had been that he should take the fees and out of them pay his laboratory assistants—a very

* Sir Charles Wyville Thomson (1830–1882), who had studied medicine at Edinburgh and then lectured at Aberdeen, Belfast and Dublin.

satisfactory arrangement for one who could attract so many students. "I cleared about £1000 by the transaction," he told Tyndall, "being one of the few examples known of a southerner coming North and pillaging the Scots."

Meanwhile, Thomson had written from Japan asking Huxley to repeat the course in the summer of 1876, and the university was very anxious for him to do so. In September Sir William Turner * wrote to say "there is no one who would be so acceptable both to the students and to the University generally . . . if you could not come I scarcely feel prepared to recommend that the additional leave should be given to Thomson". Anxious as he was to oblige Thomson, Huxley was reluctant to meet the request lest people said that he was deserting his regular duties for work that paid better, but he was willing to consider the proposal providing the Admiralty urged it and he himself had to take no initiative in the matter. Turner seized on this opening, Christison † also weighed in, and soon the Secretary to the Education Department was writing to tell Huxley that, in consequence of applications received from the Admiralty and the University of Edinburgh, he was granted further leave of absence to deputise again in 1876. He seems to have found some difficulty in getting down to the level of his students, for one of them records that "he had the sense of panting to keep pace with the demands of the lecturer. It was not merely that the texture of scientific reasoning in the lectures was so closely knit . . . but the character of Huxley's terminology . . . presupposed a knowledge of Greek. . . . The strain on the attention of each lecture is so great as to be equal to any ordinary day's work. I feel quite exhausted after them". But, he added, "with all these drawbacks, I would not miss them, even if they were ten times as difficult. They are something glorious, sublime".

---

* Sir William Turner (1832–1916), Professor of Anatomy at Edinburgh, Dean of the Faculty of Medicine, and in 1903 the first Englishman to become Principal.

† Sir Robert Christison (1797–1882), Professor of Medical Jurisprudence and then of Materia Medica and Therapeutics at Edinburgh.

Huxley himself had sufficient energy left after the day's work to get through an enormous quantity of reading, including some tough biological monographs and a few biographies and some novels of George Sand, but he complained that he was harassed with "another confounded commission, on the Scottish universities, which wastes half my time and throws all my plans out of gear". However, membership of this Royal Commission enabled him to learn much more about the University of Edinburgh, he kept contact with the university's many medical men in the metropolis, and ten years later he received evidence of the regard in which he was held by the student body:

The office of Lord Rector of Edinburgh University becomes vacant in the beginning of November of this year, and . . . the Independent Association of the University beg that you will do them the honour of becoming their candidate for the office.

Should you be so good as to give your consent, the success of your candidature would be perfectly certain . . . there is a growing feeling in favour of the object for which our Association exists,—namely, that our Lord Rector should not always be chosen on merely political grounds . . .

. . . there will probably be opportunity for aiding in the progress of University Reform, an object which, it is well known, you have at heart.

The Association most earnestly hope that you will give this request a favourable answer, and allow the Students of this University the opportunity of bestowing the highest honour in their power on one, whom they deem so worthy of it.

Huxley replied that he would have liked to renew his relations with the university, "but my health, though I am glad to say greatly improved is not very solidly rectorial . . . & the attempt to prepare & deliver an address as Lord Rector would probably end in nothing but a forlorn 'Hic Jacet' ".

At St Andrews, also, forward-looking students wanted Huxley as Rector, and Leonard Huxley mentions two occasions when his father's name was mooted—the first in 1872, when he was convalescing abroad after the breakdown which had caused his resignation from the London School Board; the second five years later, when Leonard himself was a St Andrews student and asked his father to stand. What does not seem to be generally known is that, although on the second of these occasions Huxley felt that as a member of the Scottish Universities Commission he could not possibly accede to his son's request, on the earlier occasion his name was actually put to the poll and he was very nearly elected.

The first Huxley heard of the matter was when he was in Naples on the way back to England, and he indicated to Tyndall his annoyance at not being consulted:

> Since my arrival here, on taking up the "Times", I saw a paragraph about the Lord Rectorship of St. Andrews—after enumerating a lot of candidates for that honour, the paragraph concluded "But we understand that, at present, Professor Huxley has the best chance." It is really too bad if any one has been making use of my name without my permission. But I do not know what to do about it. I had half a mind to write to Tulloch * to tell him that I can't and won't take any such office —but I should look rather foolish, if he replied that it was a mere newspaper report and that nobody intended to put me up—

It was, however, more than a mere newspaper report, and the whole story is available in contemporary records. There had already been one contest, but Ruskin's election had been declared invalid on the technical grounds that his Poetry Professorship at Oxford excluded him under a literal interpretation of the Scottish Universities Acts, and the University Court ordered a new election at short notice. It was in these exceptional circumstances, and with Huxley away in Egypt, that a group of students nominated him without consent. At the nomination meeting it was argued that it was time a scientist occupied the high office of Rector, and that Huxley was qualified both by his position in the world of science and by his eminence as an educationist. At another meeting, a few days later, there was a foretaste of the *odium theologicum* which was so fully to flavour the Aberdeen election later in

---

* John Tulloch (1823–1886), Principal of St Mary's College at St Andrews.

the year, one opponent sneering that "Huxley's object in Egypt at present was to visit the Catacombs in search of the primeval jelly from which he asserts all life was evolved". The students, however, were not so easily deterred; and when the result was announced it was seen to have been a near thing:

THE ELECTION OF RECTOR. The election took place on Thursday forenoon. Sir Roundel Palmer and Dean Stanley having been withdrawn the contest lay between Lord Neaves and Professor Huxley. The meeting was very close, Professor Huxley leading for some time but after Neaves got the start he kept his advantage, and at eleven the result was declared in his favour—73 votes being recorded for him and 70 for Huxley.

Where the students of St Andrews just failed to get a Rector who would move with the times, those of Aberdeen just succeeded. In the earliest universities of Europe the Chancellor was appointed by the Church, usually acting through a local prelate; the teachers, organised in their faculties, had corporate voice in the Senate; and the students, grouped according to their nations of origin, chose a Rector to guard their interests. When universities grew up at Oxford and Cambridge, Chancellors continued to represent the Pope (or, later, the King), and Senates still spoke for the teachers, but the students had no voice. Later still, however, when universities were founded in Scotland, the close cultural connexions with France led to the more faithful following of the original model, and the Rector remained in the constitution alongside Chancellor and Senate. At Aberdeen the grouping by nations survived, students from two halves of Aberdeen diocese constituting the 'nations' of Buchan and Mar, those from north of the Grampians making the 'nation' of Moray, and those from the south the 'nation' of Angus. Each nation elected a procurator, the procurators chose the Rector, and in the event of a tie the final decision lay to the Chancellor. The Court of Aberdeen University consisted, after the reorganisation of 1858, of only six men—the Rector, the Principal, and an Assessor each for the Chancellor, the Rector, the Senatus and the General Council—and if the Rector attended in person he had both a vote and a casting vote. Such a situation, where a determined Rector could make effective use of a powerful constitutional position, was one exactly to Huxley's taste.

Some general preliminary discussion about possible candidates had begun before the 1872 summer vacation, and a vigorous newspaper correspondence developed during October and November. The students, infected by the general atmosphere of the times, were dissatisfied with the state of the university, and one of them wrote to *The Aberdeen Free Press* urging that "the office should be a real one, and not an empty title, as was formerly the case, when the Lord Rector was never seen, but when he delivered his inaugural address". Not knowing Huxley, he proceeded to lump him with the other eminent men whose names had been canvassed, asking "What more than an inaugural address can we expect from such men as Darwin, Huxley, Carlyle, Earl Derby, or the Duke of Argyll—men living at a distance and altogether unconnected with Aberdeen?" At a student meeting on 4 November several names, including that of Scotland's Historiographer Royal, J. H. Burton, were proposed; but soon Darwin had declined nomination on health grounds, Gladstone had refused to let his name go forward, and the effective contestants were quickly reduced to two—Huxley and the young Marquis of Huntly.* The Sassenach scientist might have seemed a poor match for the Cock o' the North, whose ancestors for nearly four centuries had exercised powerful influence at Aberdeen, but things did not turn out that way.

When the names of Darwin and Huxley were first mooted, 'A Christian and a Scotchman' informed *The Aberdeen Free Press* of his concern:

* Charles Gordon, 16th Earl and 11th Marquess of Huntly, 7th Earl of Aboyne, 2nd Baron Meldrum of Morven, and Chief of the Clan Gordon (1847–1937), who had high personal distinction as a scholar in addition to the immense prestige accruing from his great estates and position in the clans. In 1890, eighteen years after his defeat by Huxley, he was elected Rector of Aberdeen.

If all men of character and culture are shocked at the coarse profanities of Bradlaugh, and the tribe of obscene lecturers who are engaged in spreading his views through all classes of our people, they have
still greater reason to shudder at the deeper and darker blasphemies (as
we are prepared to prove) of that nest of scientific infidels, of which
Darwin, Huxley and Tyndall form the select committee.

It was asserted that the medical students were not really responsible for Huxley's nomination, but were merely being
used as a 'front' by hidden secularists; and then 'Enquirer'
asked, if the Pope were elected to the Rectorship would not
that be accounted a recognition of Romanism, and would not
the election of Huxley similarly be a recognition of Atheism?
Some of Aberdeen's students, however, were no longer to be
frightened by the comminations of the orthodox, and soon
two letters introduced a type of blackmail by suggesting that,
if Huxley were elected, parents would not wish to send their
sons to a university where there would be so much danger of
contagion by infidelity. A week later, 'P.Q.R.' wrote to protest against "a sort of influence which can only be termed
intimidation" by some professors and parents, one of whom
had threatened to turn his son out of doors if he voted for
Huxley.

By now both gown and town were thoroughly aroused, and
towards the end of November the Editor had to insert a note
that "Our correspondence on this subject is accumulating on
our hands. Our student friends therefore must excuse us if we
are at times unable to attend to their requirements in the
matter of space". Then, as the heat of the debate grew in
letters published day by day, the Editor announced that "This
correspondence is getting a little too personal, and we must
decline to publish any letters in which this element is not kept
in abeyance"—an announcement which, in view of the tone
of the letters which were published, intriguingly implies the
scabrous possibilities of those that were suppressed. Meanwhile, similar correspondence appeared in other local newspapers, a good specimen being the letter of 'T.Q.', who asked

P

"Why has the claimant to the Tichborne title and estates not been brought forward? . . . A man of renown he is—of world-wide renown!", and went on to suggest that the students would surely prefer 'Sir Roger', "to the discomfiture of the Descendant of the Monkey—glorying in that descent". However, discontent with the idea of a simply decorative Rector continued, and the Editor of the *Free Press*, who supported a local man, emphasised the point in an editorial:

> The kind of Rector now wanted is one who, in the first place, has himself had a high educational training; one who, in addition to that, has, by mixing in the world, had opportunity of forming distinct opinions regarding the sort of educational training that will be of greatest service to a young man entering the world; who takes an interest in education; and perhaps most important of all one who will attend the meetings of the University Court, and interest himself in its business.

Huxley sent a letter to a student saying that during most of the year there would be no obstacle to his attending the meetings of the University Court, and there was jubilation among his supporters.

The formal nomination meeting on the 7th December was conducted with the usual clamour, scuffles and throwing of peasemeal projectiles, in which Huxley's supporters had the better of things. After his nominator had been shouldered away in triumph, still waving defiantly the last remnant of his coat, Huntly's backers tried to do likewise, "but it proved abortive from their insufficient numbers, many having gone after the followers of Huxley". A week later the voting took place, with the following result:

| Nation | | | For Huxley | For Huntly |
|--------|---|---|------------|------------|
| Moray  | . | . | 37 | 37 |
| Mar    | . | . | 76 | 52 |
| Angus  | . | . | 79 | 36 |
| Buchan | . | . | 82 | 95 |

Despite Huxley's overall majority of 54, it was a close thing, for, as he explained to Tyndall, "the mode of election is such that one vote . . . would have turned the scale by giving my opponent the majority in that [Moray] nation. We should then have been ties & as the chancellor, who has under such circumstances a casting vote, would have (I believe) given it against me, I should have been beaten". But Huxley's two nations to Huntly's one settled the matter, and the students had the Rector they wanted. No doubt it was in part the rising tide of scientific and medical advance which had swept Huxley into office, but equally important was the desire of the students to have a vigorous Rector who would try to jolt the university out of its traditional grooves. Although initially nominated by medical students, Huxley was also strongly supported by those reading other subjects: and, as he himself commented, "the fact of any one, who stinketh in the nostrils of orthodoxy, beating a Scotch peer at his own gates, in the most orthodox of Scotch cities, is a curious sign of the times".

The central occasion of Huxley's Aberdeen incumbency was his Rectorial address, 'Universities: Actual and Ideal', delivered on 27 February 1874 to an audience of some two thousand. He told his wife that "the students made a terrific row at intervals, though they were quiet enough at times", but he was presumably unaware of just how disorderly these meetings might be. *The Aberdeen Free Press*, more experienced in such matters, reported that "Throughout the whole of the address the greater body of the students listened with marked attention—much more than on any former occasion of which we can remember". As for *The Scotsman*, it described Huxley's speech as courageous, brilliant and wise, and "worth volumes of the emasculate stuff which the Lord Rector of Glasgow University [Disraeli] recently presented to the students who had placed him in his honourable post". That not everyone was pleased is indicated by an anonymous pamphlet, with the unusually intriguing title of *Protoplasm, Powheads, Porwiggles; and the Evolution of the Horse from the Rhinoceros; illustrating Professor Huxley's Scientific Mode of*

*Getting up the Creation and Upsetting Moses. A Guide for Electors In Choosing Lord Rectors*, which followed fourteen pages of abuse in prose with nineteen pages of scoffing in verse, of which the following is a sample:

> The Rector hath a treatise wrote . . .
> The Title of it ought to be—
> *The Book of Huxley's Revelations*;
> And specially should those *savants*
> Most piously peruse the book,
> Who rather would in Huxley trust,
> Than Moses and the Pentateuch.

The students, however, were sufficiently satisfied with their new Rector to institute a new custom by entertaining him to supper in the University Ball-Room, and doubtless some of the orthodox opposition was mollified by his willingness to attend the customary ceremonial Presbyterian service.

In preparing his address Huxley had, he told Michael Foster, "used the Aberdonians for the benefit of Oxford & Cambridge much as Tacitus used the manners of the Germans for the benefit of the Romans", and he congratulated the Scots that they did not make the university "a school of manners for the rich; of sports for the athletic; or a hot-bed of high-fed, hypercritical refinement". But he would not allow the Aberdonians to imagine that their own university was perfect, and he drew attention to the incompleteness of its studies. Candidates for the degree of Master of Arts had to do some natural history as well as classics, but he could not understand why the creative arts were so neglected:

. . . the man who is all morality and intellect, although he may be good and even great, is, after all, only half a man. There is beauty in the moral world and in the intellectual world; but there is also a beauty which is neither moral nor intellectual—the beauty of the world of Art. There are men who are devoid of the power of seeing it, as there are men who are born deaf and blind, and . . . there are others in whom it is an overpowering passion; happy men, born with the . . . genius of the Artist. But, in the mass of mankind, the Aesthetic faculty, like the reasoning power and the moral sense, needs to be roused, directed, and cultivated; and I know not why the development of that side of his nature . . . should be omitted from any comprehensive scheme of University education.

He doubted, in fact, if the curriculum of any modern university shewed so clear and generous a comprehension of culture as did the medieval Trivium and Quadrivium in their time. In the case of medicine, he admitted that all sorts of subsidiary studies might in themselves be valuable; but, since the time available for study was limited, he urged the excision of all that was irrelevant to the purpose of medical training. "Methuselah", he remarked, "might, with much propriety, have taken half a century to get his doctor's degree; and might, very fairly, have been required to pass a practical examination upon the contents of the British Museum, before commencing practice as a promising young fellow of two hundred, or thereabouts. But you have four years to do your work in, and are turned loose, to save or slay, at two or three and twenty." As for natural science, he pointed out that Oxford during the preceding twenty years had spent more than £120,000 on new laboratories, and Cambridge was taking the same course: he did not ask how much Aberdeen was spending, but the question had been set to germinate in his hearers' minds. And, he declared, just as students might go on from the general Arts Faculty for technical or professional training in the specialised Faculties of Theology, Law and Medicine, there should in a modern university be a Faculty of Science to which students might go for further instruction more advanced and specialised than would be proper in the Faculty of Arts.

Within a few days of his election, Huxley had arranged to meet his predecessor in office to discuss the affairs of the university; and he made it clear to his friends that he intended making full use of the ancient Rectorial prerogatives: "Unlike other Lord Rectors", he told Tyndall, "he of Aberdeen is a power and can practically govern the action of the University during his tenure of office." At his first Court meeting it was reported that a student had been deprived of a 'Drum' divinity bursary on the ground that he was not preparing to be a minister of the Established Church, and the Senatus spokesman in the Court objected to the admission of a letter of appeal. Much as he must have disliked doing so at his first meeting, Huxley ruled against the Senatus objection, and he remarked that the time might come when professors of divinity would have to choose between loyalty to their Church and loyalty to their university. However, he received little support, and had to tell Michael Foster "I have been in Aberdeen fighting for the admission of Scotch dissenters to bursaries in my University & getting beaten the parsons being too many for me—but we shall win yet".

At this same meeting Huxley announced receipt of a petition from nearly 200 students—that is, virtually all those reading medicine—requesting changes in the regulations for medical degrees, and he gave notice of his intention to introduce proposals on the matter. Within a few days he was exchanging views with Alexander Harvey (the Professor of Materia Medica) and Alexander Dyce Davidson (his Assistant), who had just been appointed to a Council Committee on the Medical Curriculum, and a letter from Harvey casts an unfavourable light on the condition of medical education in Scotland. When he was a student, he recalled, few Aberdeen medicos had graduated because of the prior requirement of an MA, but had instead taken the London diploma of the College of Surgeons. The minority who went on to Edinburgh to graduate found that their Aberdeen courses were not recognised because they had not included sufficient lectures, and Aberdeen had been forced to follow the Edinburgh example of lectures in each subject five days a week. As a result, students no longer had time to read standard works or spend much time in the laboratory, but sat almost continuously in lectures—another manifestation of the national addiction to long sermons with milestones of heads and sub-heads. And, all in all, the only cheerful feature was that "Your letter leads me fondly to hope, that your influence and exertions as Lord Rector of this University will avail effectually to put matters on a better footing here, and elsewhere".

Encouraged by the knowledge that John Knox's *The Buke of Discipline* was on his side in his wish to free the medical course from choking accretions, Huxley made public through *Nature* the four resolutions which he intended moving in the Court:

I. That, in view of the amount and diversity of the knowledge which must be acquired by the student who aspires to become a properly qualified graduate in medicine; of the need recognised by all earnest teachers and students for the devotion of much time to practical discipline in the sciences of chemistry, anatomy, physiology, therapeutics, and pathology, which constitute the foundation of all rational medical practice; and of the relatively short period over which the medical curriculum extends—it is desirable to relieve that curriculum of everything which does not directly tend to prepare the student for the discharge of those highly responsible duties, his fitness for the performance of which is certified to the public by the diploma granted by the University.

II. That it would be of great service to the student of medicine to have obtained, in the course of his preliminary education, a practical acquaintance with the methods and leading facts of the sciences comprehended by botany and natural history in the medical curriculum; but that, as the medical curriculum is at present arranged, the attendance of lectures upon, and the passing of examinations in, these subjects occupy time and energy which he has no right to withdraw from work which tends more directly to his proficiency in medicine.

III. That it is desirable to revoke or alter ordinance No. 16, in so far as it requires a candidate for a degree in medicine to pass an examination in botany and zoology as part of the professional examination; and to provide, in lieu thereof, that the examination in these subjects shall, as far as possible, take place before the candidate has entered upon his medical curriculum.

IV. That it is desirable to revoke or alter said ordinance No. 16, in so far as it requires candidates for the degree of doctor of medicine to have passed an examination in Greek, and that, in lieu thereof, either German or French be made a compulsory subject of examination for said degree, Greek remaining as one of the optional subjects.

The resolutions came before the Court on 26 February 1874, when Huxley was supported by his Assessor John Webster and the Council's Assessor John Christie, and there was apparently no member of the Court prepared to argue against the principle of the proposals. Campbell,* however, pointed out that such changes might need discussion with the other Scottish Universities and a new Act of Parliament; and an unusually blunt assertion of vested interest came from the Professor of Botany "with reference to his patrimonial rights" —which, under the system of remuneration by means of fees, would be endangered by any relaxing of the ordinance requiring all medical students to attend his lectures. The Court referred the resolutions to the Senatus for its views on the best mode of implementation, the Council accepted unanimously very similar proposals from its Committee on the Medical Curriculum, and Huxley was jubilant. "Did I tell you that I carried all my resolutions about improving the medical curriculum?" he asked his wife in a letter following the Court meeting. "Fact, though greatly to my astonishment. Tomorrow we go in for some reforms in the arts curriculum, and I expect that the job will be tougher."

The reforms in the Arts curriculum came up at the Court on 2 March, on a proposal from the Senatus to institute the new degree of Bachelor of Science. Such a proposal Huxley might have been expected to support strongly, but the pig was in a poke and he was not the man to buy it without full inspection of its pedigree. On examination, it emerged that the proposal of the Senatus was that this so-called 'science degree' should include courses and examinations not only in mathematics and natural science, but also in mental science, Latin, English, and either Greek, French or German: it represented, in fact, a dead-end to which the Council and the Senatus had side-tracked an earlier unwelcome suggestion that science should be put on an equal footing with the tradi-

* Peter Colin Campbell (1810–1876), the first Principal and Vice-Chancellor of the united Aberdeen University.

tional subjects in the Master of Arts degree. By this ingenious device, not only was the MA to be saved from any substantial scientific contamination, but holders of the new inferior degree of BS would not be admitted to the privileges of the magistracy. It transpired, moreover, that the university regulations would allow existing bursaries to be held only by men preparing for the MA—which meant that, in a Scotland of bursary tradition, the proposed new degree would be likely to attract few students. The whole Senatus plan was simply an attempt to avoid giving science a place of real equality in the university. It was too transparent for Huxley's gaze: he accepted the principle of a science degree, but only "providing a sufficient share of the endowments would be devoted to it", and the Court remitted the scheme to the Senatus for reconsideration.

Huxley was familiar enough with the delaying tactics of academic traditionalists, and he can scarcely have been surprised that a stubborn Senatus managed to avoid producing any new scheme for science degrees during his term of office. He warned the Court on 8 May 1875 that "if the University of Aberdeen was not inclined to advance in this matter, it would in all probability stop still and go back . . . the great Universities [of England]—whose example Aberdeen need not be ashamed to follow—were all moving in the direction which was taken by the proposal of the University Court. That was to say, they were allowing candidates for the Arts degree, after passing through a common preliminary examination, to take different lines"; but five months later the Council concluded that a satisfactory solution would have to await a Royal Commission on Scottish university education. Similarly, the proposed changes in the medical curriculum were held up by an opposing petition to the Privy Council from the University of Edinburgh, and by the end of his rectorial term not one of Huxley's desired reforms had been effected.

That, however, was not the end of the story, for a year later a Royal Commission on the Universities of Scotland was appointed, and Huxley was one of its members. He secured from Principal Campbell of Aberdeen an admission that the only science ever included in examinations for bursaries was such as might be crammed from one or two primers, and Principal Grant of Edinburgh had to agree that the lad who learned Latin and Greek at school was also capable of learning science. Principal Caird of Glasgow produced the hoary argument that a prospective scientist needed to know Greek in order to understand technical terminology, but his own scientific knowledge was inadequate to combat Huxley's contention that in such matters etymology is rarely a reliable guide. Huxley's purpose in all this, however, was not to add science to the university entrance examinations, but rather to oppose such examinations altogether as an unnecessary and undiscriminating barrier to higher study. He had in mind not only the boys who came straight from school, but also the older men who saved and scraped to go to a university and then found themselves barred by their ignorance of classical languages. Glasgow's Professor of Divinity suggested that such men might go back to school for a while, but Huxley protested that it was unreasonable to expect adults to sit side by side in class with children and that the university itself should provide tutorial assistance to mature students. Principal Tulloch of St Andrews argued that a fixed entrance examination was necessary to maintain the level of lecturing, but Huxley got several witnesses to admit that some of their best students had been men with no initial knowledge of their subjects, while a professor from Edinburgh agreed that "considering what examinations are at present [it is] sometimes an advantage to have a man coming to you knowing nothing". On the question of science degrees, it was brought out that the proposed Aberdeen BS was a bogus inferior general degree rather than one specially suited to scientists, and it also emerged that the Glasgow BSc required no knowledge whatever of biology. In the matter of medical studies, Huxley pressed witness after witness to agree that much of

the traditional but irrelevant botany, zoology and pharmac-
ology should be excluded; on the general question of examinations he urged the testing of each section of the work so soon
as it was completed instead of allowing it all to accumulate
for a great final examination; and he expressed his dis-
approval of compulsory attendance at lectures. By and large,
he seems to have missed few opportunities of directing attention to the matters in which he advocated change.

When the four substantial volumes of the Royal Commission's report appeared in 1878, Huxley must have been
gratified by its recommendations. A rigid university entrance
examination was looked on with disfavour, and instead it was
suggested that there should be a 'First Examination' to be
taken fairly early in the student's university career. This examination was to include mathematics and English and Latin
for all students, but those intending to study science or
medicine or law were to be allowed to take French or German
instead of Greek, which was to remain compulsory only for
those proposing to read arts. Natural science was to be
added to the examination so soon as conditions in the schools
made it practicable, and the sort of science which it was suggested the schools should teach was simply a summary of
Huxley's recently published *Physiography*. It was proposed
that there should be five alternatives to the traditional course
for the MA degree, the student being allowed to choose between literature and philology, philosophy, law and history,
mathematics, and natural science. For the scientific course
there were to be four alternative subject groupings, so that
each student would study some physics and chemistry and in
addition a selection of physiology, botany, zoology, geology
and applied mathematics. It was also recommended that each
of the four universities should institute a BSc degree for those
wishing to specialise in sciences, and that for this it should be
necessary to take three instead of two of the science subject
groupings. In the case of medical students, the purely scientific studies were to be completed at an early stage so as to

allow subsequent concentration on the professional subjects, and the commissioners suggested that degree examinations in all departments should be arranged in instalments. In view of the narrowness of his own election at Aberdeen, Huxley must have been particularly pleased by the recommendation that rectorial elections should be decided by total votes rather than by numbers of 'nations'; and all in all he could scarcely have written a better report himself. Not everything he wanted was included in the Universities (Scotland) Act of 1889, but that measure included sufficient to justify his forecast that his defeats would become victories in the hands of his successors.

# CHAPTER XII

# The University of London

I had quite given up the hope that anything but some wretched compromise would come of the University Commission, when I found, to my surprise, no less than gratification, that a strong party among the younger men were vigorously taking the matter up in the right (that is, *my*) sense.

In spite of all my good resolves to be a "hermit old in mossy cell", I have enlisted—for ambulance service if nothing better.

The move is too important to spare oneself if one can be of any good.

*Letter to Sir William Flower, 27 June 1892*

DURING THE DECADES when the ancient universities were adjusting themselves to the new demands of the nineteenth century, other institutions of similar rank were emerging at home and fresh universities springing up abroad. There were still many who, like Sir Christopher Mowbray in Disraeli's *Vivian Grey*, "could as easily fancy a county member not being a freeholder, as an University not being at Oxford or Cambridge", but others were less inhibited in their imagination. The second quarter of the century saw the foundation of University and King's Colleges in London and a University at Durham; in the next quarter there came Owens College in Manchester and Yorkshire College in Leeds; in the last quarter there followed Firth College in Sheffield and Mason College in Birmingham and University College in Liverpool.

During these years the first universities were also appearing in England's overseas possessions, and in the rapidly expanding United States of America new foundations followed in quick succession. We keep coming across traces of Huxley's fingers in many of these promising pies, but his most important connexions were with the colleges and university of his native London.

Surprisingly enough, he did not play a very prominent part in the affairs of University College, which had been founded in 1826 by a group of utilitarians and philosophic radicals under the name of 'London University'. To the Christopher Mowbrays of England a non-residential university in Gower Street was incomprehensible; to the supporters of religious tests a secular university was reprehensible; but for Huxley one might have expected it to have had considerable attractions. He was one of its governors and gave evening lectures there from time to time, and his 1870 address on medical education was an event of some importance, but his main activity seems to have been connected with the establishment of the two Jodrell Chairs. Three years after telling the medical faculty that its professors should be so remunerated as to abstain from private practice, he learned that T. J. P. Jodrell, a wealthy *amateur* of science, was prepared to provide an endowment of £7500. Following consultation with Huxley, Jodrell wrote to tell the President of University College that he was advised that the work of the two part-time professors in physiology might be given as efficiently by one full-time professor with the aid of a demonstrator, and he explained that the purpose of the proposed endowment was to induce men of eminent ability to forgo more lucrative sources of emolument and devote themselves to original research. At first the College was reluctant to accept the rather stringent conditions which were attached to the offer, so Jodrell consulted with Huxley again, with an eminently satisfactory outcome: "Since I saw you I have had another interview with the U.C. Deputation at which being fortified by yr. opinion I

assumed a more confident tone & the result was that they ac-
quiesced at once in my view." The intention of the endowment was admirably fulfilled by the first Jodrell Professor of
Physiology, Burdon-Sanderson; * and, when a few years
later the founder's wish to do something more for science
took shape at Huxley's suggestion in the Jodrell Chair of
Zoology and Comparative Anatomy, the first occupant was
that well-loved prodigal protégé, Ray Lankester.

With King's College in the Strand, founded by the Angli-
cans to counter the godless institution in Gower Street,
Huxley seems to have had little to do apart from an unsuccessful application in 1853 for the Chair of Physiology.
Nor, despite his general support for female education, did he
have much connexion with the colleges founded for women,
replying to a request that he should lecture at one of them
with the query "what on earth should I do among all the
virgins, young and old, in Bedford Square? . . . I should be
turned out . . . for some forgetful excursus into the theory
of Parthenogenesis or worse". He gave occasional lectures at
the Birkbeck Literary and Scientific Institution, grown from
the London Mechanics' Institute and later to become Birkbeck College; he helped to establish the Peoples' Palace, the
parent of Queen Mary College in the East End; he did his bit
for the university extension movement. With the medical
schools and colleges of London he was always intimate, and
in South Kensington he was busy building the components
of the future Imperial College. But it was with the original
University of London, founded in 1835 by Lord Melbourne's
government to conduct examinations and award degrees, and
with the movement in the latter part of the century to co-
ordinate the many metropolitan institutions of higher education into a great new teaching University of London, that
some of his most important work was done.

* Sir John Scott Burdon-Sanderson (1828–1905), who had thitherto been
part-time Professor of Practical Physiology and Histology. In 1882 he went
to Oxford as the first Waynflete Professor of Physiology and eventually became Regius Professor of Medicine there.

In 1856 Huxley succeeded Carpenter * as University Examiner in Physiology and Comparative Anatomy, soon he was examining in Zoology also, and during most of the fourteen years until his resignation in 1870 his field ranged from matriculation to eleven different degree examinations in the Faculties of Arts, Medicine and Science. For almost the whole of that period the degrees of the University of London were open to all comers, and those who controlled them were able to determine the curricula of many educational institutions throughout the English-speaking world. In this way, Huxley was able to make his examining a means of spreading the new spirit in biology, and Michael Foster recalls the pleasure with which as a student he looked forward to the *viva voce* test. It was also while Huxley was examiner that the regulations for medical students were altered to require the completion of the preliminary scientific studies before the start of the regular medical course, and he was largely responsible for the introduction of a practical physiology test in 1871.

During the 1850s it was still the dominant view that scientific studies were not sufficiently 'liberal' to form the centre of a university course, but the regulations for the London BA nevertheless allowed candidates to take Honours in a wide range of subjects, including both physical and biological sciences. There was, however, nothing of a standard to suit those who wished to specialise in science, and in 1857 Huxley was one of a group of scientists who urged the Senate to establish a higher scientific degree comparable with that of Master of Arts. A year later, he took the initiative in calling together a group of signatories to a second memorial, raising the question of science degrees in general, and the Senate appointed a committee to consider the matter. The memorial pointed out that the ancient fourfold division of human knowledge into Arts, Theology, Law and Medicine, while

* William Benjamin Carpenter (1813–1885), Registrar of the University of London from 1865 to 1879, when he became a Crown Fellow.

**THE SCHOLAR**

*'Sit down before fact as a little child, be prepared to give up every preconceived notion'* (p. 61)

**THE MAN OF AFFAIRS**
*'Continually taking two irons out of the fire and putting three in'* (p. 109)

possibly adequate to the age in which universities first arose, was quite inadequate since a fifth branch of knowledge, Science, had grown up. It also objected that "Academic bodies . . . continue to ignore Science as a separate Profession; and even the University of London, though specially instituted to meet the wants of modern times, can confer no Degree upon the first Chemist and Physicist of his age, unless he possess at the same time a more than average acquaintance with classical literature". Huxley's evidence to the committee indicates that he was still thinking mainly of a degree at the magistrate rather than the baccalaureate level, but the committee reported in favour of instituting both BSc and DSc degrees. The regulations for the former were based very much on the course which students passed through at the School of Mines, and by 1860 it was possible for the first time in England to graduate in the sciences.

Had Huxley foreseen all the consequences of this success, he might have been less pleased than he was. Once the scientists had their own degree, there were moves to make the course for BA entirely non-scientific, and by 1874 Huxley was having to fight for the retention of physiology. He recognised that it would be impossible for students specialising in the arts to acquire a thorough and practical knowledge of the sciences, but some knowledge they should have:

I apprehend that every degree implies or should imply that the possessor of it has in the first place so much general knowledge as is necessary for the equipment of every fairly instructed person and has undergone a certain discipline which entitles him to the particular degree which he takes. . . .

The possessor of a Scientific degree ought not I think to be ignorant of the existence of Cromwell & of his general significance in English History—though I think it would be most unreasonable to require him to have read Mr. Carlyle's edition of Cromwell's letters & speeches . . . It would be as great a scandal that any person possessing a University degree in Arts should be ignorant of the law of gravitation, or of the chemical fact that air is not an element . . . or of the circulation of

blood in his own body . . . as that a B.Sc. should be ignorant of Cromwell's existence.

And I am quite certain that such knowledge of science though it be
mere information . . . would save our statesmen our public writers our
literary men & our theologians from many of the blunders into which
they are constantly falling & which a properly instructed child would
avoid.

The matriculation examination already required some
knowledge of chemistry, and Huxley urged that physics and
elementary human physiology should be retained in the first
BA examination so as to ensure that no graduate of the university would be devoid of a fair tincture of scientific knowledge. The committee seems to have been convinced, for it
recommended the retention of physiology, but Huxley was
already having second thoughts on the whole question of a
dichotomy between arts and science in degrees at the bachelor
level. In this same year he opposed the institution of a
separate first degree in science at Aberdeen, and a year later
he was advising that university to follow the older universities
of England in the introduction of scientific specialisations for
a common Bachelor of Arts. In the conditions of the 1850s he
could scarcely have done other than fight for the recognition
of the right of science to a degree of its own, but all that we
know of his love of wide culture combined with deep specialisation makes it fairly certain that what he would really have
liked would have been something similar to the flexible
system into which the Triposes of Cambridge have now
grown, with a preliminary general course such as has recently
been devised at the University College of North Stafford-
shire.

In 1883, two years before his retirement from South Kensington, Huxley was invited to become a Crown Fellow and
Senator of the University of London. Ailing badly, he replied
that his many other commitments would permit his attending
meetings only rarely, and that he was unwilling to accept an
office whose duties he could not perform properly, but the
Chancellor's neat retort left him little choice in the matter:

11 Carlton House Terrace.
July 28th, 1883.

My dear Professor Huxley,

Clay, the great whist player, once made a mistake and said to his partner, "My brain is softening", the latter answered, "Never mind, I will give you 10,000£ down for it, just as it is".

On that principle and backed up by Paget * I shall write to Harcourt on Monday.

Yours sincerely,
Granville.

The Home Secretary concurred in this estimate of an only partially functioning Huxley, and in August the appointment was made. As he had warned would be the case, Huxley attended Senate infrequently—only sixteen times in twelve years—but his influence on the university's development was considerable. He was elected to many committees, dealing with matters ranging from the control of the Brown Animal Sanatory Institution to the selection of examiners and the regulation of examinations, but some of these appointments may have been no more than nominal. However, when from 1885 onwards the Senate set about the pressing problem of university reorganisation, his rôle was not merely active but often decisive.

Ever since 1858, when the requirement that candidates for London degrees must have attended recognised colleges was abandoned, there had been discontent that the university could exercise no formal control over the methods of study of those who would be its graduates. Unfortunately, suspicion and recrimination among the many metropolitan quasi-university institutions repeatedly prevented the sorting out of a sorry state of affairs, and by 1880 the situation had become one of great complexity. Some were by then convinced that the only solution was the complete absorption of the London colleges by the university; others would have granted degree-giving powers to the colleges and professional

---

* Sir James Paget (1814–1899), the eminent surgeon and anatomist, whose highly fashionable practice included Queen Victoria. At this time he was Vice-Chancellor of the University of London.

schools; others would have left the existing university as an
imperial examining body and formed a new federal university
for London out of the existing schools and colleges. In addition, and cutting right across these three parties, there was
another tripartite division. Many of the professoriate, influenced by German example and encouraged by the considerable transfer of power in the older universities from
Heads of Houses to the main body of teachers, insisted that
the reorganised university must be effectively ruled by its
professors; the growing body of graduates scattered about
the land wanted more power for Convocation; and a stubborn section of men in authority wanted to retain an essentially autocratic form of university government. It scarcely
seemed that any compromise could be possible.

Then, in 1884, an Association for Promoting a Teaching
University for London was founded, and Huxley was one of
the Special Committee appointed by the Senate in 1886 to
consider its views. The importance he attached to the matter
is indicated by the fact that, despite ill health which repeatedly drove him to Bournemouth and Ilkley and Switzerland, he
managed to attend six committee meetings, and the Vice-
Chancellor kept him well informed of what was afoot in his
absence. Now, however, the position was complicated by the
presentation of petitions to the Privy Council by several of
the existing institutions. The Senate followed the recommendations of its Special Committee in opposing the re-
quests of University College and King's College for a full
university charter, but it was divided about the wish of the
Royal Colleges of Physicians and Surgeons to grant medical
degrees. Huxley thought it unfair that Scottish medical
students might get degrees as a matter of course, while London students obtained only diplomas on the conclusion of
the equally severe conjoint examination, and to those who
argued that a degree should not be given for purely professional studies he replied that "a man who knows no language
but his own, but has had a thorough training in medicine and

its ancillary branches of knowledge, has had a more truly liberal education than the high classic who is devoid of any tincture of scientific culture". He therefore supported a successful motion that the university would not oppose the granting of medical degrees by the conjoint colleges, provided that they were clearly distinguished from the university's own degrees and that their recipients had an adequate preliminary education, and in the June of 1888 the Special Committee asked Lord Justice Fry * to prepare a scheme on these lines. But by this time the air was so thick with schemes and counter-schemes that the Government tried to clear it by appointing a Royal Commission under the chairmanship of Lord Selborne.†

Huxley's Senate attendances had been so few, and his health so poor, that about this time he sought to resign, but Paget persuaded him to continue. "We can always consult you by letter or personally," he wrote, "and be influenced or guided by your opinion." Things were brought to a head by the report of the Selborne Commission, which favoured the establishment of a new federal university substantially similar to that proposed in the earlier petitions of University and King's Colleges; and, when the Senate appointed another Special Committee to consider the report, Huxley was again a member. The proposed new university would have condemned the existing university to a perpetuity of mere examinership, and powerful opposition developed to the Selborne proposals. The House of Commons rejected the Commission's scheme, and it became clear that the only hope of progress lay in some form of federation of the existing colleges and the existing university. At the beginning of 1891, therefore, the Senate produced its own plan, in which the

* Sir Edward Fry (1827–1918), a member of the famous Bristol Quaker family. His early researches held promise of eminence in biology, but he decided to devote his great energies and talents to the law. His connexion with the University of London, in one form or another, lasted for half a century.

† Sir Roundell Palmer, 1st Earl Selborne (1812–1895), the eminent lawyer who was Lord Chancellor from 1872 to 1874 and 1880 to 1885. He entered Parliament in 1847 as a Conservative, but his independent views gradually led him over to the Liberal side.

reorganised university was to be governed by representatives of University and King's Colleges, the Royal Colleges of Surgeons and Physicians, the teachers through the Faculties, and the graduates through Convocation. Huxley attended no Senate meetings during this year, but some pencilled notes on his copy of the Senate's scheme shew the way his mind was working. He proposed to halve the representation of Convocation and of University and King's Colleges, whilst doubling the representation of the university's teachers; he would have added representatives of the Royal Society and the Royal Academy; and he wanted adequate provision for the representation of painting, sculpture, architecture and music. But the Senate's plan was rejected by Convocation, and one more was added to the growing discard of proposals for the reorganisation of higher education in the metropolis.

By the spring of 1892 Huxley seems to have given up hope of any valuable outcome from the complex conflict, and his correspondence was full of despairing phrases. The whole affair, he lamented to Donnelly, was "a perfect muddle of competing crude projects and vested interests"; he told Lankester that "unless people clearly understand that the university of the future is to be a very different thing from the university of the past, they had better put off meddling for another generation"; he warned Weldon * "to take care that no such Philistine compromise as is possible at present, becomes too strong to survive a sharp shake". In the meanwhile, he advised the professors at the Royal College of Science to see that they were not hooked into the hotch-potch, and he saw nothing for it but that the medical, legal and theological corporations should cut adrift and make their own arrangements for professional graduation. A new Royal Commission (the so-called 'Gresham' Commission) was appointed under

* Walter Frank Raphael Weldon (1860–1906), who had recently succeeded Lankester in the Jodrell Chair of Physiology at University College, where he took an active part in the movement for promoting a professorial university in London. In 1899 he moved to the Linacre Chair of Comparative Anatomy at Oxford.

Lord Cowper,* but Huxley saw no reason to expect anything of it. He thought that pretty much what was wanted could be got by "grafting a Collège de France on to the University of London, subsidising University College and King's College (if it will get rid of its tests, not otherwise), and setting up two or three more such bodies in other parts of London", but he had no hope of that's happening. Even when Karl Pearson † and a group of vigorous young teachers in the London colleges set up the Association for Promoting a Professorial University of London, Huxley refused to join it on the Simon Pure ground that it would be improper for a member of Senate to do so—which must have seemed excessively meticulous to those who knew that he had given much help to the earlier APTUL, whilst insisting for tactical reasons that all his contacts should be oral. He was ailing, sadly deaf and deeply dispirited, and he had no confidence that there could be any result worth fighting for.

Then, quite suddenly, opinion began to crystallise, and Huxley's hopes sprang high. The liberal *Speaker* printed on 25 June an editorial praising the new Association and remarking on the extraordinary unanimity evident among those actually engaged in teaching, and within two days Huxley was back in the fray. "I am in great spirits about the new University movement," he wrote to Foster, "and have told the rising generation that this old hulk is ready to be towed out into line of battle, if they think fit, which is more commendable to my public spirit than my prudence." The rising generation decided that the old hulk was seaworthy enough to fly the admiral's flag, and on 7 June *The Times* announced that Huxley had accepted the Presidency of the Association. Karl Pearson, who had signed on most of the

* Francis Thomas De Grey Cowper, 7th Earl (1834–1905), who had served as Lord Lieutenant of Ireland from 1880 to 1882, with W. E. Forster as his Chief Secretary.

† Karl Pearson (1857–1936), the mathematical biologist who virtually founded the science of biometry. He was a brilliant investigator and teacher, but [*DNB*] "was apt to attribute intellectual differences of opinion to stupidity or even moral obliquity".

crew, was delighted that Huxley had come to lead them, but as the fleet set sail he began to have second thoughts. His idea had been to found a university on German lines, with all power to the professors and no compromise with the existing colleges and university, but Huxley had other ideas. Pearson later complained, "Huxley . . . brought his enormous force to work on a small executive committee of which I was secretary to carry out a plan of *his own* . . . with all the force of an old hand [he] completely confused me". The complaint was factually justified, but Pearson should have known that the old warrior would not be content to fly the admiral's flag and let somebody else set the course.

By December the executive committee had been persuaded that the only workable plan was that of a federal university, and Pearson resigned his secretaryship in a bitter open letter in *The Times*. Huxley's reply rebuked Pearson for resigning in the daily Press rather than in committee, and explained why he had opposed the original plan:

> As for a government by professors only, the fact of their being specialists is against them. Most of them are broadminded, practical men; some are good administrators. But, unfortunately, there is among them, as in other professions, a fair sprinkling of one-idea'd fanatics, ignorant of the commonest conventions of official relations, and content with nothing if they cannot get everything their own way. It is these persons who, with the very highest and purest intentions, would ruin any administrative body unless they were counterpoised by non-professorial, common-sense members of recognised weight and authority in the conduct of affairs.

Pearson was a man of genius but tiresome and difficult to work with and, if Huxley managed to get the Association to follow him rather than its founder, that was a cause for legitimate disappointment rather than for accusations of immorality. Huxley's note following an Association meeting, "had to show that I am the kind of head that does not lend itself to wagging by the tail", betokens a certain ruthlessness, but that was the only kind of head which could have brought order out of chaos.

Some of London's more eminent scholars, not unnaturally, wanted a constitution which would ensure that the leaders in each branch of study occupied permanently a position of authority in university affairs, but they found Huxley against them. "That to which I am utterly opposed", he told Weldon, "is the creation of an Established Church Scientific, with a hierarchical organisation and a professorial Episcopate. . . . [Each university teacher], if he is worth his salt, will be a man holding his own views on general questions, and having as good a right as any other to be heard. Why is one to be given a higher rank and vastly greater practical influence than the rest? . . . The besetting sin of able men is impatience of contradiction and of criticism. Even those who do their best to resist the temptation, yield to it almost unconsciously and become the tools of toadies and flatterers." At a meeting of the executive committee of the Association, consisting largely of men who might reasonably have expected to head their respective branches of learning, Huxley found only one supporter against a motion to restrict Senate membership to very senior professors: the following day he suggested (no doubt with his tongue in his cheek) that perhaps he ought to resign his Presidency, and that put 'paid' to all idea of excluding junior teachers from an effective part in university government.

Meanwhile, through the summer of 1892, the Senate's Special Committee had been meeting without making much progress, and at last Huxley put in an appearance. "I am going to a meeting of the University this day week to try my power of persuasion", he told Michael Foster in November. "If the Senate can only be got to see where salvation lies and strike hard without any fooling over details, we shall do a great stroke of business for the future generations of Londoners." The sciences were fairly well represented on the Special Committee, but Huxley was concerned at the possibility that the creative arts and crafts might be overlooked in its plans. "You should see the place I am claiming for Art in the University", he wrote to his painter son-in-law John Collier. "I do believe something will grow out of my plan, which has made all the dry bones rattle. It is coming on for discussion in the Senate, and I shall be coming to you to have my wounds dressed after the fight." If today the metropolitan institutions for painting and sculpture and music are still largely isolated from the University of London, it is not for want of effort on Huxley's part. In the December of 1892 he introduced to the Special Committee a deputation from the Association and, after the Vice-Chancellor had replied for the University, he said that he thought the Senate was moving in the right direction and that details could stand over. Three months later many of the details were filled in, and at its last meeting the Special Committee approved a letter to the Commission which Huxley had drafted. That the University and the Association were substantially at one is not surprising: they were both substantially at one with him.

It must have been with a gratifying sense of accumulated authority that Huxley appeared to give evidence to the Gresham Commissioners. He was President of the Association, Senator of the University of London, Governor of University College; he had long been regarded by the royal medical colleges as an unofficial adviser; many of the other key witnesses were former students or men whose careers he had forwarded—and, to round things off nicely, before the Commission was formed he had been invited to suggest names of suitable members. He urged that a university adapted to modern society must abandon the narrow view of culture introduced in the latter half of the medieval period and revert to the ancient idea of general learning—which, since the modern student has already studied the elements of the Trivium at school, implied that the university must provide an expanded analogue of the Quadrivium, including the natural sciences, historical and literary studies, and the creative arts and crafts. Amidst the existing chaos of conflicting opinions and interests, unusual even in English affairs, he did not venture to ask for the university of his ideal, but he was sanguine enough to hope for some compromise sufficiently flexible to go with the tendencies of the time. The new university should, he declared, unify the existing institutions without fettering them; the professional schools of medicine and law and theology, and where expedient other branches of learning, should be permitted to examine their own students and present them for degrees *ad eundem*; the professors and other teachers should have a large but not preponderant place in the university's government, should have an important voice in the appointment of colleagues, and should be remunerated according to the nature of their work and irrespective of the numbers of their students. There must, he believed, be a central University Chest to receive all fees and State subventions and future endowments, and special provision should be made for instruction in research methods of all kinds. As for the admission of students, he believed that matriculation examinations simply saved the schools the trouble of setting up their own leaving examination, and he did not want any fixed test for entrance to the university. After all, he pointed out, most of the candidates would as a matter of expediency have reached the required standard, and "I say that very possibly the odd tenth may contain persons of defective education, but of a native vigour which makes them more worth having than all the other nine-tenths, and I would not lose them for any consideration".

When the Commissioners reported early in 1894, in the main along the lines for which Huxley had been fighting, he was not unnaturally gratified: "under the circumstances . . . a very considerable achievement", he noted. Ailing badly, he was able to attend only two meetings of the Special Committee on the Report of the Gresham University Commission, appointed by the Senate in February, but in July he went to a full Senate meeting to support a resolution asking the government to appoint Statutory Commissioners to implement the Gresham Commission's proposals. His diary records an

engagement with Lord Rosebery * soon after he became Prime
Minister, but when December arrived, and there was still no
sign of government action, he decided to provoke it. "It is
rumoured that there are lions in the path", he wrote to Rosebery. "But even lions are occasionally induced to retreat by
the sight of a large body of beaters. And some of us think
that such a deputation as would willingly wait on you, might
hasten the desired movement." The Prime Minister immediately agreed to receive a deputation, the various groups involved quickly appointed their deputies, everyone else seems
to have agreed with the University and the Association and
University College that Huxley should speak on all their be-
halves, and in the January of 1895 he fulfilled his last public
engagement. It is one of the most striking things in the career
of this most striking man that, coming out of retirement for
a final fight in the very evening of his days, he was able so to
unify the discordant desires of the capital's many institutions
of higher learning as to allow the Senate of a great new
federal University of London to meet before the end of the
century.

* Archibald Philip Primrose, 5th Earl Rosebery (1847–1929), who had
succeeded Gladstone in March when the latter resigned in opposition to the
Navy Estimate. Although in his later years something of an imperialist, he was
liberal in most home affairs and argued against hereditary political privilege
and denominationalism in education. In 1889 he had been elected first Chairman of the newly constituted London County Council.

# CHAPTER XIII

# To the New World

The question of questions for mankind—the problem which underlies all others, and is more deeply interesting than any other—is the ascertainment of the place which Man occupies in nature and of his relation to the universe of things. Whence our race has come; what are the limits of our power over nature and of nature's power over us; to what goal we are tending; are the problems which present themselves anew and with undiminished interest to every man born into the world . . . thoughtful men, once escaped from the blinding influences of traditional prejudice, will find in the lowly stock whence Man has sprung, the best evidence of the splendour of his capacities; and will discern in his long progress through the Past, a reasonable ground of faith in his attainment of a nobler Future.

*'Man's Place in Nature', 1863*

LOOKED AT FROM the distance of today, the most striking thing about Thomas Henry Huxley is his sheer effectiveness. Whether it was a matter of public controversy or of private lobbying, of reorientating an existing institution or of setting the direction for a new one, of putting the right men into key posts or of selecting the manner in which the nation might be allowed to honour him, he generally seemed to get his way. Of course, this could not have happened had he not wanted what the society of his day needed, but he seems also to have had precisely the character needed to get what he wanted. Compounding a clear view of objectives with immense determination and enormous energy, an unyielding devotion to principle with great flexibility of application, and a capacity for occasional ruthlessness with an habitual captivating charm, he was indeed a formidable figure.

He seems, moreover, to have been formidable from the start. When the young medical apprentice entered a public competition announced by Apothecaries Hall in 1842, his university-taught competitors were apparently unconcerned. At least, no objection was raised to a request that candidates be allowed to complete their answers instead of stopping at four o'clock—but presumably no one imagined that Huxley would still be writing four hours later, and to such effect as to carry off the silver medal. From the start, moreover, Huxley had that immensely valuable quality of being noticed. No doubt he was helped by his innocent audacity towards the hierarchy of scientific society, which allowed him as a lad to buttonhole Michael Faraday by the Royal Institution and receive an exposition of the laws of motion from the first physicist in the land. Perhaps his cavernous eyes of jet and striking lean physique had something to do with it, perhaps the peculiar melancholy which was never quite obscured by the bubbles of his effervescent fun. At any rate, from the time he returned to England the newspapers never left him alone, and in 1858 he was elected to the Athenæum under the 'distinguished persons' Rule at the head of the poll.

It was an adventurous, exciting age, when English society was giving itself a shaking up such as it has rarely known. There was a tumultuous energy about, and a splendid resolution, and the ruling circles had sufficient self-confidence to be unafraid of an upstart young man of evident ability. Huxley had a great gift for seeing that he was in the right, and great skill in using official channels and enlisting the 'best' people in good causes, and as a result he soon acquired a sort of public indispensability. Early in life he had learned that some men of high repute had but commonplace ability, and this gave to his actions a decisiveness and direction which would have been impossible to one who stood in any awe of reputations. He had, moreover, "an organ of 'grin-and-bear-it-iveness' which is large in me by nature & has been developed by all the appliances of art", and he was quite ready to suffer abuse for a few years in the conviction that his cause was righteous and ultimate victory certain.

Huxley's somewhat Quakerish devotion to 'yea, yea' and 'nay, nay' in all his discourse earned him enemies, but not so many as would have been the case in our more mealy-mouthed society of a century later. Occasionally he went too far, and one can sympathise with the badly bruised Duke of Argyll, who complained "He writes as if every believer in Christianity were no better than a blackbeetle beneath his feet", but the Duke was generalising unjustly from his own personal experience. Usually, Huxley's vigour was moderated by an appreciation of opposing sincerity, and in the close-knit society of those days his public intransigeance was largely forgiven for his private charm. "I never came away from your house", Leslie Stephen told Mrs Huxley, "without thinking how good he is; what a tender and affectionate nature the man has! It did me good simply to see him." The Victorians valued goodness, and especially goodness within the family circle, and others besides Lady Monkswell must have remarked after a visit "What I like about the family is the way they all seem to care so much for each other". Huxley's friends were always impressed by his kindliness, and Darwin commented, with reference to the scandalous Belfast address on animal automatism, "I wish to God there were more automata in the world like you". No doubt Alexander Macmillan was foolishly extravagant when he declared "I tell you, there is so much real Christianity in Huxley that if it were parcelled out among the men, women and children in the British Isles, there would be enough to save the soul of every one of them, and plenty to spare", but it is significant that a hard-headed man could make such a statement at all. It is one of the marks of a master that his disciples relate great wonders and fabricate a marvellous mythology, and the Huxley myth acquired in his own lifetime a great and almost autonomous power.

The myth, moreover, was not a narrowly national one. Scientific societies from Dresden to Philadelphia, from Alexandria to Göttingen, from Rome to St Petersburg, all felt it necessary to have Huxley as a foreign member. The Geological Society of Australasia, the Royal Natural History Society of the Netherlands Indies, the Lisbon Royal Academy of Sciences, the Moscow Imperial Natural History Society, the Imperial Geological Society of Vienna—one after another they sent him honorary diplomas. And when, in 1876, he at last found time to cross the Atlantic, the excitement was immense. "The whole nation is electrified by the announcement that Professor Huxley is to visit us next fall", one American correspondent declared. "We will make infinitely more of him than we did of the Prince of Wales and his retinue of lords and dukes." For Huxley the occasion had also a peculiar personal poignancy: he would meet again, after an interval of thirty years, the one member of his father's family for whom his affection had never wavered. "It will be something strange to see any one of my own blood who has any love for me", he wrote to Lizzie before sailing—and immediately corrected himself: "I have written a horrible blasphemy for my children are of my own blood—and they love me well."

Huxley once told Lowell * that he had "a sort of dream of bringing the English speaking men of science together", and his American friends included Asa Gray the botanist, Othniel Marsh the palæontologist, Alexander Agassiz the geologist and Edward Youmans the chemist and educator. Another friend was Gilman,† the university administrator,

---

* James Russell Lowell (1819–1891), the poet, essayist and diplomat. After a tenure of Longfellow's Chair at Harvard, he became US Minister first to Spain and then to the Court of St James.

† Daniel Coit Gilman (1831–1908), who vacated the Chair of Geography at Yale in 1872 to become President of the University of California, and then in 1875 became first President of Johns Hopkins University.

**THE MORALIST**

*'The savage of civilisation is a more dangerous animal than any other wild beast'* (p. 134)

**THE PROPHET**
'*It is the customary fate of new truths to begin as heresies and to end as superstitions*' (p. 90)

who was faced with the exciting challenge of organising the great new foundation of Johns Hopkins. To start off the university's biological studies in a proper manner—that is, his manner—Huxley sent over his former demonstrator Martin * ("young, energetic, very pleasant in manner and a thorough gentleman in all his ways"), and suggested that he should revise the South Kensington scheme of biological teaching "in usum studiosum Yankietatis". But Gilman wanted Huxley in person, and it was arranged that he should pay a visit to Baltimore and deliver the official opening address.

Huxley and his wife set off for America in July in great spirits, leaving their children behind in the care of friends and looking forward to a 'second honeymoon'. As soon as *Germanic* berthed in New York they were whisked away by W. H. Appleton the publisher for a few days' rest at his country house at Riverdale, and then Huxley went to Yale to examine Marsh's collection of fossils. Comfortably housed in a residence placed at his disposal by the millionaire Peabody, and courted by distinguished callers including the Governor of Connecticut, he found time for sufficient palæontological study to become convinced that the horse had originated not in the Old World but the New. Then came a brief visit to Boston, then a short stay at Fiske's summer-house in the White Mountains, and then to Buffalo for the meetings of the American Association for the Advancement of Science. Huxley's lecture on 'Impressions of America' seems to have been enthusiastically received, despite his somewhat ambiguous compliment, "You have among you the virtue which is most notable among savages, that of hospitality", and it was followed by a week's relaxation at Niagara. Then there came the long-awaited meeting with Lizzie at Nashville, Tennessee, where Mrs Huxley was able to pick out on the railway platform the sister-in-law she had never seen, by reason of her

---

* Henry Newell Martin (1848–1896), who had collaborated with Huxley in producing *A Course of Practical Instruction in Elementary Biology*.

R

piercing black eyes. The good townsfolk were not content until Huxley had given them a lecture, 'The Testimony of the Rocks', which with typical thoroughness he based on the local geology of Tennessee; and then, after a visit to Vanderbilt University, he and his wife went north to Baltimore.

The new Johns Hopkins University had from the start set its face against anything in the way of religious compulsion, and Gilman came in for a good deal of criticism for his arrangement of the opening ceremony. "I am very sorry Gilman began with Huxley", wrote one Presbyterian minister to another. "But", he added consolingly, "it is possible yet to redeem the University from the stain of such a beginning." "Huxley was bad enough", it was wryly remarked; "Huxley without a prayer was intolerable." And, perhaps the best comment of all, "*It was bad enough to invite Huxley. It were better to have asked God to be present. It would have been absurd to ask them both*".

Fortunately the Johns Hopkins Trustees were more appreciative, as were others for whom Huxley lectured during his seven weeks in America, and he was able to note in his diary "Say £600 profit on the whole transaction". It must have required some fortitude to turn down the offer of $1000 for a single lecture in St Louis, and Appleton said that if Huxley would stay in America for the winter he could go home with £10,000, but he had to get back to England. Before leaving New York he gave his promised lectures on evolution, filling the Chickering Hall to capacity for three evenings and the front pages of the newspapers on the three following mornings, and on 23 September he set sail to the pleasing tribute of a special commemorative issue of *The New-York Tribune*. It must have been gratifying to hear, shortly after reaching London, that the State University of Minnesota had adopted in its courses "just those elements of the sciences proposed by Professor Huxley", and before long his South Kensington methods were being copied by Princeton and Yale. Harvard, of course, tried to do things in a really grand manner—"Now

is it any use to make any kind of proposition to you. . .?"
Agassiz wanted to know, "we could offer you say $10000 a
year for the benefit of your presence and influence."

Huxley was not to be tempted to settle in the United States
permanently, but this was not due to any lack of appreciation of the cultural potentialities of that still rough and un-
developed land. His only criticism of America was that it was
inferior to England in freedom of thought, and he never made
the mistake of assuming that educational aims and forms
were settled for all time by European experience and tradition. At Baltimore he urged that the school curriculum should
provide "an education fitted for free men; for men to whom
every career is open", and this meant that it must include the
study of written and spoken language, the elements of music
and drawing, some history and social studies, and elementary
mathematics and natural science and psychology. He would
have no rigid test for university entrance, but would admit
any one who could be reasonably expected to profit by the
instruction offered, and he would radically alter the usual
university system of instruction and examination. The necessity to follow many courses concurrently, he argued, led to
the fragmentation of the students' attention, and the need to
remember everything for a final examination led to unin-
telligent cramming. "It is important", he said, "not so much
to know a thing, as to have known it, and known it thoroughly", and he therefore advocated the system practised at South
Kensington, which examined the student at the conclusion of
each course and then allowed him to concentrate his attention on the next course. The widespread adoption of these
principles in American universities might have produced
better results if they had been accompanied by two others:
that "there should not be too many subjects in the curriculum, and . . . the aim should be the attainment of a
thorough and sound knowledge of each", and that the university should eject all students who shewed themselves "deficient in industry or capacity".

One thing which particularly pleased Huxley was that the capital of the Johns Hopkins endowment was not to be spent on magnificent buildings. "A great warrior is said to have made a desert and called it peace", he remarked. "Administrators of educational funds have sometimes made a palace and called it a university." He welcomed the intention to promote research, for "the future of the world lies in the hands of those who are able to carry the interpretation of nature a step further than their predecessors", but he warned that it was very difficult to find a way of encouraging and supporting the original investigator without opening the door to nepotism and jobbery. He had doubts, too, about the wisdom of the constitutional provision for the filling of vacancies among the trustees exclusively by co-option, and he suggested that the governing body should include representatives both of the academic staff and of independent learned societies. Huxley had a peculiar sensitivity to the winds of social change and, although at Baltimore he said relatively little about university organisation, it is remarkable how closely his later plan for reshaping the University of London (with a General Studies College, a series of Professional Colleges, and a Research College) resembles what has since become a popular pattern among the great State universities of America.

To those at the Johns Hopkins ceremony who were charmed by the medieval battlements and ancient towns of England, Huxley pointed out that anticipation has no less charm than retrospect and that there was something almost sublime in the vista of their vigorous young land's future. "Do not suppose that I am pandering to what is commonly understood by national pride", he warned. "I cannot say that I am in the slightest degree impressed by your bigness, or your material resources, as such. Size is not grandeur, and territory does not make a nation." The great issue, he went on, was what they would make of their resources, and "the one condition of success, your sole safeguard, is the moral worth and intellectual clearness of the individual citizen".

The number of these citizens, he suggested in what may turn out to have been a remarkably accurate extrapolation, would reach two hundred millions by the second centenary of American independence, and he forecast some of the problems which would have to be faced—"whether state rights will hold out against centralisation, without separation; whether centralisation will get the better, without actual or disguised monarchy; whether shifting corruption is better than a permanent bureaucracy". Perhaps he was wrong in his further belief, that "as population thickens in your great cities, and the pressure of want is felt . . . communism and socialism will claim to be heard", or perhaps we should wait until 1976 before faulting him on this forecast.

Huxley was deeply convinced of the seriousness of the problems which would be posed by mounting population pressure, and he remarked that it would be just as reasonable to revile Mr Cocker's arithmetic as Mr Malthus's essay on population. Strangely enough, he admitted to Michael Foster that he had never been able to get hold of a copy of *Fruits of Philosophy* (that 'indecent, lewd, filthy, bawdy and obscene book' for republishing which Charles Bradlaugh and Annie Besant were brought to trial), and this may argue, in a man normally so pertinacious, a certain lack of enthusiasm for the popular dissemination of contraceptive knowledge. But when Mrs Besant and Miss Alice Bradlaugh were excluded from classes at University College in 1883, he signed a memorial and attended a meeting in their favour, and he was one of those who met a few years later to discuss the formation of a 'Population Question Association'. He believed that, by concentrating on the greed and ambition of rulers and the turbulence of the ruled, on the decadence of great wealth and the devastation of great wars, historians had missed the real causes of change. "If historical writers could be persuaded that the people at the bottom are of considerably more importance than the people at the top . . .", he noted in 1887, "the importance of the population question as a great factor in history would be more familiar to us—We should know what it had to do with Phoenician colonization with Greek colonization with the everlasting agrarian & proletarian question of ancient Rome; with the barbarian invasions—with the social & political difficulties of every state in modern times. It is the true riddle of the Sphinx of History."

England's apparent immunity from the predicated ills of population density Huxley considered due to a fortunate but temporary concatenation of circumstances, and he had no doubt that her need to import food would increasingly necessitate whatever reduction in the prices of her exports was required to meet mounting competition. Many who shared his fears concluded that the way out was to reduce the wages of the workers, but such a solution was unacceptable to one who commented, in the year before his death, "It is hard to say whether the increase of the unemployed poor, or that of the unemployed rich, is the greater social evil". If, indeed, the only choice for England lay between decent remuneration for the workers, resulting in goods too dear for the export market, and cheap exports produced by means of cut wages, he declared that we should choose the former "and, if need be, starve like men". But he believed that there was a third alternative, to increase scientific and technological efficiency, and that was why in the latter part of his life he made the promotion of technical education into something like a crusade.

His own contributions to science, of course, depended not at all on any social altruism, but were simply the outcome of a lifelong passion for inquiry. He could never afford the luxury of the gentleman-amateur, selecting research problems by personal preference, or he might have done more in physiology. One of the first of the new breed of scientific professionals, he worked in whatever fields were appropriate to whatever job he held. As assistant-surgeon in *Rattlesnake*, with few facilities for preserving specimens and none for experiment, the only possibility was to examine the delicate creatures of the surface seas, dredging and dissecting and drawing as opportunity offered. He was not by temperament a collecting naturalist, but he had skilful hands and sharp eyes and, above all, a mind of philosophic bent capable of seizing the significance of things.

Paid off in England in 1850, Huxley hastened to give an account of his doings to Sir John Richardson, his old official chief at Haslar Naval Hospital. "I paid comparatively little attention to the collection of new species," he explained, "caring rather to come to some clear and definite idea as to the structure of those which had indeed been long known, but very little understood. Unfortunately for science, but fortunately for me, this method appears to have been some-what novel with observers of these animals, and consequently new and remarkable facts were to be had for the picking up." Among the new and remarkable facts which he thus 'picked up' was the common existence of a two-layered cellular plan among the jelly-fish and sea-anemones and corals, thitherto discarded in that old zoological lumber-room, the Radiata, but thereby separated out to form an important new group-ing, the Cœlenterata. Moreover, the homology which he suggested, between the two layers of the cœlenterates and the two germinal layers of higher animals, was to prove basic to later embryology. The same imaginative gift for penetrat-ing superficial differences and discerning fundamental simi-larities informed Huxley's work on the Ascidians (the sea-squirts and their relatives) and on the Cephalous Mollusca (the squids and their near neighbours, the snails and slugs, and the head-bearing shellfish). It was this remarkable achievement, the fundamental reassessment of three widely different groups of animals, which unambiguously established Huxley as a comparative anatomist of the highest distinc-tion while still on the lowest rung of his intended naval career.

More important than the many new facts which Huxley discovered was the method of morphological analysis to which he subjected them. The accepted view of plant and animal types at that time was essentially platonic, each 'type' being taken to correspond with some pre-existent idea in the mind of a creator, and the work of the anatomist was conceived as being simply the description and comparison of the varied representatives of the ideal type. One of the first British biologists to read systematically scientific publications in German (he also read in French, Italian, Norwegian and Danish), and much influenced by the work of von Baer and Johannes Müller, Huxley set about the study of living things in the manner of a physicist investigating inanimate matter, without recourse to the pseudo-explanations of a transcendental philosophy. In his earliest papers the terminology was still at times capable of a platonic interpretation, but fundamentally he regarded a morphological 'type' as simply a summary statement of the structural plan common to a group of organisms. The brilliant success which attended his application of this simple inductive method was largely responsible for freeing taxonomy from idealist preconceptions, and one must take with a grain of salt his later declaration, "I have been oppressed by the humbug of 'Baconian Induction' all my life". What he meant, no doubt, was that the inductive method does not get very far without imaginative insight—but that his own work rarely lacked.

After his appointment in 1854 to Jermyn Street, Huxley concentrated to a considerable extent on the initially uncongenial study of palæontology, and the unpleasant necessity proved to be a blessing. Naturally, he made many new discoveries of fossils of varied kinds, but the really important thing was that he was thus enabled to take a comprehensive view of the whole range of organic nature, both surviving and extinct. Slogging steadily through the structures of vast numbers of organisms, but never becoming submerged by the accumulating data, he regrouped the vertebrates into three great divisions—the Ichthyopsida (fish, amphibia, etc.), the Sauropsida (reptiles, birds, etc.) and the Mammalia. He made the basic tripartite division of the mammals into the egg-laying Prototheria, the marsupial Metatheria and the fully placental Eutheria. He sorted out the birds on a skeletal basis into the reptile-like Saururæ (represented by the fossil Archæopteryx), the Ratites (the ostrich, cassowary, etc.) and the Carinates (the vast majority of living species), and he laid down the foundations of all modern ornithological and mammalian classifications. All this fundamental taxonomy has been so extended and elaborated by later workers as to be almost entirely obscured, but it is given to few men to lay such enduring foundations.

It was in 1865 that Huxley assured Haeckel "It is the organisation of knowledge rather than its increase which is wanted just now", and perhaps he recognised that this was his peculiar power. In his very first lecture, on the subject of animal individuality, he had made a most subtle analysis of the developmental stages and life cycles of colonial organisms; and, despite what the modern zoologist might consider an excessively philosophical endeavour to trace a unity in diversity, this analysis clearly displayed the capacity for illuminating generalisation. A second Royal Institution lecture, in which Huxley emphasised the then still novel view that the important thing about plant cells is not their easily visible walls but their transparent contents, considered the relationship between the properties of an individual cell and those of the organism as a whole. Huxley denied that the cell was the unit of function as it was of structure, that the powers of a living organism were the mere sum of the powers of its component cells. On the contrary, he argued, the cells are not so much the cause of organisation as the result of it, just as the drift line on the sea-shore is the result and not the cause of tidal regularities. At the time there were not many who took his view, later expressed in the apophthegm "the facts concerning form are questions of force, every form is force visible", but now it is commonplace. Precisely because his general attitude to biology was so similar to that of today, most of Huxley's work has become indistinguishably assimilated to the central corpus of fact and theory, and it is only by comparing his research papers with the standard texts of the time that the modern student can form any conception of the originality of his thought. Others have found, as Chalmers Mitchell did, that Huxley's papers read rather like *Hamlet*, "so full of quotations". During his final illness, a group of younger biologists drifted together at a *soirée* of the Royal Society: "Remember", one remarked to the others, "that it was Huxley who made all of us possible."

Huxley's decisive rôle in securing a hearing for, and eventually the general acceptance of, the theory of evolution is well recognised, but his shrewdness towards that theory itself is not so commonly appreciated. Several years before *The Origin of Species*, his own paper on the cephalous mollusca had clearly implied—actually using the word 'evolution'—that the varieties of structure within the group had come about by modification of an original type, but as yet he had no conception of evolution as a widely embracing principle. Darwin's idea of natural selection, however, provided a conceivable mechanism for such evolution, and Huxley accepted it "subject to the production of proof that physiological species may be produced by selective breeding". When Darwin received Huxley's approval he was extremely relieved and wrote "Like a good Catholic, who has received extreme unction, I can now sing 'Nunc dimittis'", but the approval was in fact considerably qualified. Huxley was convinced that Darwin's theory was "as near an approximation to the truth as, for example, the Copernican hypothesis was to the true theory of the planetary motions", but he recognised from the start that selection could stabilise as well as transform, and his were the earliest papers on persistent types. He saw, too, that a weakness in Darwin's work was the absence of any understanding of the laws of heredity such as Mendel was later to provide, and as early as 1861 he was writing "Because no law has yet been made out, Darwin is obliged to speak of variation as if it were spontaneous or a matter of chance. . . . Why does not somebody go to work experimentally, and get at the law of variation for some one species of plant?" As soon as *The Origin* appeared, Huxley told Darwin "you have loaded yourself with an unnecessary difficulty, in adopting *Natura non facit saltum* so unreservedly", and in an even earlier letter to Lyell he had made a remarkably acute anticipation of the idea of unit characters and mutations. "Suppose that external conditions acting on a Species A, give rise to a new species B . . .", he wrote, "I know of no evidence to shew that the interval between the two species must *necessarily* be bridged over by a series of forms, each of which shall occupy, as it were, a fraction of the distance between A & B. . . . In an organic compound having a precise & definite composition—you may effect all sorts of transmutations by substituting an atom of one element for an atom of another element—You may in this way produce a vast series of modifications—but each modification is definite in its composition & there are no transitional or intermediate stages between one definite compound & another. I have a sort of notion that similar laws of definite combination rule over the modifications of organic bodies." As the fossil record accumulated, Huxley's last doubts about the fact of evolution were dissipated, but he never lost sight of the lacunæ in the evidence or underestimated the complexity of the problem, and his speech of acceptance of the Darwin medal was one of striking moderation: "I am sincerely of the opinion that the views which were propounded by Mr. Darwin 34 years ago may be understood hereafter as constituting an epoch in the intellectual history of the human race. They will modify the whole system of our thought and opinion, our most intimate convictions. But I do not know, I do not think anybody knows, whether the particular views which he held will be hereafter fortified by the experience of the ages which come after us."

Huxley's was the last generation in which it was still

possible for an exceptional man to master several sciences, and it would be wrong to think of him as a biologist alone. For several years he was Secretary and for several years President of the Geological Society, and in 1876 he was awarded the Wollaston Medal for his services to geology. He was President of the Ethnological Society and effectively founded the Anthropological Institute, and he produced a plan for collating the anthropometry of all the ethnic groups of the British Empire and actually collected several hundred standard-pose photographs. In these other sciences, as in biology, Huxley was at his best in exploding logical fallacies and expounding methodological principles. His 1862 address to the Geological Society laid down clearly what is now a first principle of stratigraphy, that beds occurring in the same order or bearing the same fossils are not necessarily contemporaneous, and much subsequent confusion might have been avoided if geologists and palæontologists generally had adopted his term 'homotaxis' to indicate correspondence of stratigraphic order. His 1865 paper on the methods and results of ethnology warned against preconceived notions of human races, pointed out the fallacy of basing schemes of biological descent upon philological similarities, and came down in favour of the diffusion of culture as against its independent parallel development in different areas—all principles now recognised to be of prime importance, but all much neglected for many decades after he had propounded them. Sir Arthur Keith has remarked upon the modernity of tone of this ethnological work, which "brushed the cobwebs of racial tradition from the map of Europe". Huxley was aware that the effective populariser of science is liable to be underestimated as a scientist, and this has been his own fate. But the mere titles of his original papers fill a good ten pages of print, and their contents establish him as a research worker of exceptional imagination and ability and as one of the very great methodologists of science.

Huxley had no doubt that with each generation the

methods of science would find ever wider application, so that the time would come when "the frontiers of the new world, within which science is supreme, will receive such a remarkable extension as to leave little but cloudland for its rival". His confidence in the power of science was amusingly expressed after a formal dinner one evening, when he was called on to respond to the toast of 'Science'. He had recently had a dream, he claimed, in which he woke up after death to find himself sitting in a vast and luxurious subterranean hall—attended by waiters whose braided coats did not hide their forked tails. He gave a smart tug to the nearest tail, whereupon the waiter turned round and asked politely, "Yes, sir, what can I do for you?" Huxley ordered a drink—and, since the room seemed somewhat warm, suggested that perhaps the drink might be iced. "Certainly", said the waiter, and shortly returned with the order. Sipping his drink luxuriously, Huxley made a query of the waiter: "I suppose I am not wrong about where I have come to?" "No, Professor, this *is* hell", he was answered. "But surely there has been a good deal of change?" he asked. "This doesn't at all agree with what we used to be told of the place." "Why, no, sir," the waiter replied, "Hell isn't what it used to be. A great many of you scientific gents have been coming here recently, and they have turned the whole place upside down."

This sudden influx of 'scientific gents' into the infernal regions was the consequence of a quite new telluric tendency. It is difficult to realise that the word 'scientist' was only coined in 1840, and the professional scientist became an important social phenomenon only during Huxley's adult years. One aspect of this emerging professionalism was the establishment of many full-time scientific professorships in universities old and new, and Huxley seems to have lost few opportunities to plant his protégés in key positions. Men like Michael Foster and Frank Balfour and Sydney Vines at Cambridge, Ray Lankester and Edward Poulton at Oxford, Morrison Watson and H. M. Ward at Manchester, John

Cleland at Galway and Patrick Geddes at Edinburgh and Wyville Thomson at Dublin and Edinburgh, H. N. Martin at Baltimore and H. F. Osborn at Princeton and Columbia, T. J. Parker at Otago and Enrico Giglioli at Casale and Charles Gould at Singapore—the list of those who owed their jobs to Huxley, or who had been his assistants or students and carried his methods across the world, is indeed a remarkable one. Huxley once boasted, "If I know anything in the world, I know a man when I see him", and it would be difficult to estimate how much the development of university science owed to this talent for selection.

The growth of scientific professionalism was, naturally, accompanied by a change in the nature and number of scientific societies. It was Huxley's generation which restored the initials 'FRS' to their significance of scientific distinction rather than well-connected dilettantism, and it was his high ideal of what the Royal Society might become which made Huxley serve as Secretary for a decade before stepping into the less onerous position of President. As the venerable societies like the Royal and the Linnean climbed back to their former scientific eminence, they found themselves accompanied by newcomers catering for newly developing specialisms. And, cutting right across the formal boundaries of the scientific societies, there were the personal friendships and connexions of individual scientists.

For more than twenty years, "the most powerful and influential scientific coterie in England" was the now almost forgotten 'x Club'. Founded on Huxley's suggestion in 1864, and originally intended to be no more than a means of providing regular social intercourse for a few friends, the eminence of its members made it inevitably into a sort of scientific caucus. The few friends, apart from Huxley himself, were William Spottiswoode the mathematician and royal printer, George Busk the zoologist, Edward Frankland the chemist, T. A. Hirst the mathematical physicist, Lubbock, Hooker, Tyndall and Herbert Spencer—all except the last being Fellows of the Royal Society. Between the nine of them they could muster a Secretary, a Foreign Secretary, a Treasurer and three successive Presidents of that body—to say nothing of six Presidents of the British Association, a Secretary of the Linnean Society, various officers of the Geological and Ethnological and other scientific societies, one Rumford and one Wollaston medallist, three Copley medallists, and five Royal medallists. During the twenty-nine years and 240 meetings of the x Club's existence, no tenth member was ever elected—all suggestions being negatived by an agreement that any new name proposed must contain all the consonants not in the original nine. The x stood in triple symbolism—for the undecided name of the club, for the originally envisaged ten members, and for the undetermined tenth who was never chosen—and the meetings were called by cards bearing the cryptic formula 'x = 21' (or whatever was the appointed date of the month), with the slightly more cryptic 'xs + yvs = 21' for the annual summer outings of members and wives. But lightheartedness of this sort did not disguise the fact that the x Club dined regularly prior to Royal Society meetings, and one can understand the suspicion that the Society was largely run by the Club. Huxley must have chuckled to himself when one day at the Athenæum he overheard a conversation between two other distinguished scientists: "I say, A., do you know anything about the x Club?" "Oh yes, B., I have heard of it. What do they do?" "Well, they govern scientific affairs, and really, on the whole, they don't do it badly."

Despite his conviction that the new world would be one in which scientific method was supreme, Huxley had no naive notion that its attainment would be either simple or without danger. To begin with, he recognised the inadequacy of the mechanical materialism which satisfied many nineteenth-century scientists, and in a letter to Herbert Spencer he had great fun at the expense of their common friend John Tyndall: "In fact, a favourite problem of his is—Given the molecular forces in a mutton chop, deduce Hamlet or Faust therefrom. He is confident that the Physics of the Future will solve this easily." Perhaps he was a little unfair to Tyndall, but his criticism of Spencer on the other flank was fully justified: when the unknowable was given a capital letter, the 'Unknowable' became "merely the Absolute *redivivus*, a sort of ghost of an extinct philosophy, the name of a negation hocus-pocussed into a sham thing. If I am to talk about that of which I have no knowledge at all, I prefer the good old word *God*, about which there is no scientific pretence".

Huxley's appreciation of the power of Berkeleian philosophy made him declare that, if forced to decide between absolute materialism and absolute idealism, he would choose the latter, but it is difficult to take this declaration very seriously. He was never in any real doubt about the primacy of the material universe, and he took sensation to be "the direct effect of the mode of motion of the sensorium". But when Lenin remarked that Huxley's agnosticism was a fig-leaf for materialism, he failed to notice how very dialectical his thinking was. There is no indication that Huxley ever seriously considered, or had even heard of, dialectical materialism, as a coherent philosophy alternative to the simple materialism and simple idealism whose inadequacies he recognised, but it would be an interesting inquiry whether he did not come a good deal nearer to that position than has ever been suggested.

One striking example of Huxley's awareness that novelty may emerge at critical levels of organisation was his suggestion that matter and mind might be "only two out of infinite varieties of existence . . . of kinds which we are not competent so much as to conceive". He would have had no objection in principle to the serious study of what are now called para-normal phenomena, although no doubt he would have required convincing proofs. The latter half of the nineteenth century was a time when many were seeking some way out of the *impasse* of mechanical materialism, and wonderful were some of the ways chosen. There were those who reacted against advancing science by increasing sacerdotalism within established religion, while others sought a compromise in quasi-mystical systems such as the positivist Religion of Humanity and the neo-Hindu Theosophy and the strangely eclectic Christian Science. Others again, like Mr Sludge, combined plain trickery with a confused belief in the reality of spirit-communication, so that in a materialist age even spiritual phenomena became material, and table-rappings tended to replace beatific visions. Huxley himself attended *séances* and detected gross deception, which contributed to his refusal to join the Dialectical Society's committee of investigation into psychic phenomena. Moreover, he explained, "if the folk in the spiritual world do not talk more wisely and sensibly than their friends report them to do . . . the only good that I can see in the demonstration of the truth of 'Spiritualism' is to furnish an additional argument against suicide".

The question of whether there is any necessary conflict between science and religion is largely one of definition, and Huxley's definition of religion was a good deal richer than Arnold's 'morality touched by emotion'. He once said "Teach a child what is wise, that is morality. Teach him what is wise and beautiful, that is religion", but this also oversimplifies his view. Other elements in religion were "the awe and reverence, which have no kinship with base fear, but arise whenever one tries to pierce below the surface of things"; the recognition that "in relation to the human mind Nature is boundless; and, though nowhere inaccessible, she is everywhere unfathomable"; the sensitivity to that strange sadness which comes from an awareness of "the imperfections that cannot be remedied, the aspirations that cannot be realised, of man's own nature . . . this consciousness of the limitation of man, this sense of an open secret which he cannot penetrate". Between science and religion as spiritual aspiration, or religion as humility, or religion as morality, he saw no conflict, and increasingly he found himself attracted to prophetic Judaism. But between science and religion as unhistorical assertion, or religion as hieratic authority, or religion as dæmonology, he could see no possibility of armistice, and his opposition to institutional Christianity never wavered.

It was still possible in Huxley's younger days for a great scholar like Newman to adduce, as an example of the value of revelation, the fact that history unaided would never have been able to discover that man had been preserved in Noah's ark. There was still in Huxley's generation a widespread belief in spirits benign and malign, and he rejoiced that "science, in the course of the last fifty years, has brought to the front an inexhaustible supply of heavy artillery of a new pattern, warranted to drive solid bolts of fact through the thickest skulls". There were some who smiled in a superior manner at Huxley's energetic devotion to the demolition of positions which they thought bound to disappear under a general spread of reason, but perhaps he had a truer appreciation of their stubborn powers of survival. He believed that at the end of the nineteenth century men were at the parting of the ways, and that, unless they accustomed themselves to demand evidence for all assertions, there would be a recrudescence of superstition. The abandonment of the more ludicrous excrescences of belief was not enough: "One does not free a prisoner by merely scraping away the rust from his shackles."

Unlike his friend Matthew Arnold, Huxley was incapable of jettisoning the so-called *Aberglauben* of Christianity and yet continuing to support what unambiguously claims to be an historical religion. "The present and the near future", he remarked scathingly in 1890, "seem given over to those happily, if curiously constituted people who see as little difficulty in throwing aside any amount of post-Abrahamic Scriptural narrative, as the authors of 'Lux Mundi' see in sacrificing the pre-Abrahamic stories; and, having distilled away every inconvenient matter of fact in Christian history, continue to pay divine honours to the residue." Let the process of distillation but continue for another generation, he

sardonically suggested, and a future Bampton lecturer would
be able to declare that, "No longer in contact with fact of any
kind, Faith stands now and for ever proudly inaccessible to
the attacks of the infidel".

Huxley saw no reason why the unavoidable battle between
science and superstition should be fought with gratuitous
injury to personal feelings (Gladstone and Argyll excepted),
and he remarked that "Old Noll knew what he was about
when he said that it was of no use to try to fight the gentlemen
of England with tapsters and serving-men. It is quite as hopeless to fight Christianity with scurrility. We want a regiment
of Ironsides". That was why he was so reluctant to get mixed
up in the Foote case in 1883, when the editor of *The Free-
thinker* was tried for blasphemy, and that explains his annoyance when Charles Watts published a private communication
without permission "among as queer a crew as Jack Fal-
staff's". But although he argued that "rightful freedom is
[not] attacked, when a man is prevented from coarsely and
brutally insulting his neighbours' honest beliefs", he nevertheless signed a petition on Foote's behalf. Huxley stood consistently for the right of the individual to think for himself
and give expression to his thoughts, and we may be sure that
he would be no party to that modern truce between science
and religion which so largely depends on a tacit agreement to
use words with double meanings.

Huxley did not consider that the rejection of religious faith
need imperil ethical conduct, which he believed to be determined by the social formation of the individual conscience.
"Every day and all day long, from childhood upwards . . .,"
he wrote, "associations . . . are formed between certain acts
and the feelings of approbation or disapprobation. . . . We
come to think in the acquired dialect of morals. An artificial
personality . . . is built up beside the natural personality.
He is the watchman of society, charged to restrain the anti-
social tendencies of the natural man within the limits required by social welfare." And, since history shewed that the

great ethical principles had been accepted by societies of many faiths and philosophies, he inquired "if morality has survived the stripping off of several sets of clothes which have been found to fit badly, why should it not be able to get along very well in the light and handy garments which Science is ready to provide?"

In places Mallock's *New Republic* is as wickedly unfair to Huxley as to other members of the apocryphal house-party, but exact justice was done when 'Mr Storks' was made to say that there must be "a universal, intrepid, dogged resolve to find out and face the complete truth of things, and to allow no prejudice, however dear to us, to obscure our vision. This is the only real morality". Huxley had Milton's low regard for a fugitive and cloistered virtue which never sallied out to seek her adversary, and the truth which he found within his laboratory had to be proclaimed without. His great faith in the common man encouraged him (as also, no doubt, did the royalties) to write popular and semi-popular scientific texts which immensely influenced readers in half a dozen tongues, and it was this same faith which set him against all efforts to prejudge the capacities of different social classes. He discovered early "what a heart-breaking business teaching is— how much the can't-learns and won't-learns and don't-learns predominate over the do-learns", but he was sceptical of those who thought it possible to discover in childhood which individuals were capable of much culture and which had best be abandoned as hopeless. "The 'points' of a good citizen are really far harder to discern than those of a puppy or a shorthorn calf", he remarked, and it is not difficult to guess what he would say of an educational policy which virtually determined a child's future by the age of eleven.

Consistently advocating equality of educational opportunity, Huxley wanted Oxford and Cambridge opened not only to the lower middle-classes, but also to "the sons of the masses of the people whose daily labour just suffices to meet their daily wants". The newer provincial university colleges seemed to him essential to the development of any truly national system of education, and he worked closely with Kay-Shuttleworth on the governing body of Owens College after its reorganisation in 1870. Looking to the future, when it would become the nucleus of a great university for Lancashire, he urged the college to take a high view of its functions: "Any corporation of men associated together for the purpose of teaching all forms of precise and accurate knowledge, the object of which was to give the highest intellectual culture that could be given, and to encourage the pursuit of knowledge in perfect freedom and without let or hindrance from any subsidiary consideration, was performing the functions of a university, and was one whatever be its name."

Opening the new medical school of Owens College in 1874, Huxley expressed the hope that the position of the arts faculty in that institution would never by a hairbreadth or shadow be diminished, and he emphasised the importance of placing the different departments close together and thus discouraging any tendency to cultural fragmentation. "Unless we are led to see that we are citizens and men before anything else," he continued, "I say it will go very badly indeed with men of science in future generations, and they will run the risk of becoming scientific pedants when they should be men, philosophers, and good citizens." "We are in the case of Tarpeia," he declared on another occasion, "who opened the gates of the Roman citadel to the Sabines and was crushed by the weight of the reward bestowed upon her. It has become impossible for any man to keep pace with the progress of the whole of any important branch of science. It looks as if the scientific, like other revolutions, meant to devour its own children; as if the growth of science tended to overwhelm its votaries; as if the man of science of the future were condemned to diminish into a narrow specialist as time goes on." And the only way to avoid Tarpeia's fate, he believed, was by a generous sharing of the rewards, by the organisation and extension of scientific education in such a manner as to secure breadth of culture without superficiality, and, on the other hand, depth and precision of knowledge without narrowness. As well as learning some natural science, he always urged, children must master the elements of the social sciences and the theory of morals. It is a remarkable fact that Huxley gave Patrick Geddes the inspiration for his 'regional survey' method; and perhaps even more remarkable that Beveridge's address 'Economics as a Liberal Education', delivered to the London School of Economics in 1920, was avowedly based on a lecture given by Huxley nearly seventy years before. But it was impossible for natural science or social studies or anything else to become an effective instrument of education except through the use of words, and Huxley believed that every child should devote a very large part of its schooling to the careful study of English literature, "and, what is still more important and still more neglected, the habit of using that language with precision, with force, and with art".

This problem of how to avoid an ultimately fatal cultural dichotomy has faced educators for the past century, and perhaps ours is the last generation which will have the chance to solve it. The much older, the perennial, problem is that of steering a path between Plato's *Republic* and Rousseau's *Emile*, of devising an education which will produce neither the man meticulously machined to social conformity nor the man so autonomous as to be socially intolerable. "If individuality has no play, society does not advance", Huxley remarked; "if individuality breaks out of all bounds, society perishes." The great question, therefore, was whether the educational flavour of the new world should be authoritarian, anarchic or agnostic—whether its citizens should grow up believing and behaving uniformly as infallible authority dictates, or believing and behaving indiscriminately as personal preference directs, or recognising that our knowledge is incomplete and that both beliefs and behaviour are best based on the ancient precept, 'Prove all things; hold fast that which is good'.

The great enemy was the closed mind, whether in religion or politics or learning, and Huxley did not delude himself that victory would come automatically with the defeat of either secular or sacerdotal autocracy. After all, he pointed out, "the first-recorded judicial murder of a scientific thinker was composed and effected, not by a despot, not by priests, but was brought about by eloquent demagogues". Socrates he called "The first agnostic, the man who, so far as the records of history go, was the first to see that clear knowledge of what one does not know is just as important as knowing what one does know", and he was "inclined to think that not far from the invention of fire we must rank the invention of doubt. . . . For it is out of doubt of the old that the new springs; and it is doubt of the new that keeps invention within bounds". Not that he wished people to wriggle about for ever in an agony of indecision—on the contrary, he usually set an excellent example of decisive action on the basis of the best available assessment of a situation—but he was repelled by that terrible sclerosis of the human spirit which comes from complete certitude of rightness. At times, it must be admitted, Huxley's rejection of external authority took a form scarcely compatible with a proper agnostic humility about his own opinions, and occasionally his controversial campaigns displayed a certain personal arrogance, but his central thesis was surely valid: "no personal habit more surely degrades the conscience and the intellect than blind and unhesitating obedience to unlimited authority. Undoubtedly, harlotry and intemperance are sore evils, and starvation is hard to bear, or even to know of; but the prostitution of the mind, the soddening of the conscience, the dwarfing of manhood are worse calamities."

It is a strange irony that, as a young man still in his twenties, Huxley told Tyndall that the way to die was in the middle of an unfinished article, "better a thousand times than drivelling off into eternity betwixt awake and asleep in a fatuous old age". The article which he himself left unfinished,

'Mr. Balfour's Attack on Agnosticism', leaves no doubt that he retained to the end his sceptical attitude towards Christian belief. The idea of final extinction was not a comforting one (he once told John Morley "It flashes across me at all sorts of times with a sort of horror that in 1900 I shall probably know no more of what is going on that I did in 1800. I had sooner be in hell a good deal—at any rate in one of the upper circles, where the climate and company are not too trying"), but for him it would have been a dwarfing of manhood to pretend that he believed in an after-life. Stout old Ironside that he was, he could only say "one should be always ready to stand at attention when the order to march comes". For seventy years he had lived his life to the limit, seeking and finding outlets for his many-sided energy, loving and being loved, occasionally hating and being hated, always balanced uneasily between a rational optimism and a temperamental pessimism, making a life of remarkable unity and effectiveness out of a vast range of activities which could so easily have spelled ineffective fragmentation. Had he chosen an epitaph from his favourite Goethe, it might well have been:

> Was Man in der Jugend wünsche,
> Hat Man im Alter die Fülle.*

It is always tempting to indulge in speculations of 'if only' and 'what might have been', and more so with Huxley than most men. If only his childhood love of preaching had led him into the Church, what might have happened to nineteenth-century theology? If his father had been able to afford him an orthodox university education, would he have become a greater Jowett or merely another Romanes? If he had achieved his early ambition of becoming an engineer, and studied physical rather than biological science, what might have been the outcome of his subtle views of the nature of matter? Or if he had remained in the Navy, or gone into

---

\* What in youth a man doth will,
That in age he hath his fill.

medical practice in London, or migrated to Australia, would he still have become one of the leading spirits of the age? Or suppose that he had accepted the offer of an admirer to pay for a legal training, would he have become a great legal theoretician, or the greatest of prosecuting counsel? Or had he submitted to the pressure more than once exerted to enter politics, what heroic parliamentary clashes might there not have been with Gladstone!

Yet, somehow, it is difficult to imagine Huxley in any of these rôles, for they are all too limited. There are some men whose developing qualities express themselves in a sequence of parts played at successive stages of their lives, as the adored young tutor became the powerful Master of Balliol or the silver-tongued preacher at St Mary's became the saintly Cardinal in his Oratory, but the great Professor Huxley was simply young Tom writ large. Almost everything was there from early days—the luminous intelligence, the restless inquiry, the indefatigable industry, the courage and pertinacity, the wide interests, the toughness and the tenderness—and he had to play all his parts at once. He is almost the type-specimen of Plekhanov's 'great man'—he whose personal idiosyncrasies give individual features to historical events, but who above all is great because he possesses qualities which express almost perfectly the social needs of his time and enable him to serve his fellows best by being quintessentially himself. He needed the knowledge that he was both discovering the path to the new world and leading people along it, and it was impossible for him to contract out of the many and varied demands of his age. "Posthumous fame is not particularly attractive to me," he told the old Chartist George Howell, "but, if I am to be remembered at all, I would rather it should be as 'a man who did his best to help the people' than by any other title."

# SELECT LIST OF HUXLEY'S PUBLICATIONS

THIS LIST INCLUDES only items referred to or relied on in the text. The dates and sources given are those of original publication, except that certain lectures whose publication was delayed are listed under their dates of delivery. In the case of items reprinted (sometimes under a slightly different title or expanded or modified) in the *Collected Essays* or the *Scientific Memoirs*, the volume number is given as an additional source.

The following abbreviations are used:

| | |
|---|---|
| *AMNH* | *Annals and Magazine of Natural History.* |
| *BAAR* | *British Association Annual Report.* |
| *CE* | *Collected Essays.* |
| *CR* | *Contemporary Review.* |
| *FR* | *Fortnightly Review.* |
| *JESL* | *Journal of the Ethnological Society of London.* |
| *JLS(B)* | *Journal of the Linnean Society (Botany).* |
| *JLS(Z)* | *Journal of the Linnean Society (Zoology).* |
| *MM* | *Macmillan's Magazine.* |
| *NC* | *Nineteenth Century.* |
| *NHR* | *Natural History Review.* |
| *PRI* | *Proceedings of the Royal Institution.* |
| *PRS* | *Proceedings of the Royal Society.* |
| *PTRS* | *Philosophical Transactions of the Royal Society.* |
| *PZS* | *Proceedings of the Zoological Society.* |
| *QJGS* | *Quarterly Journal of the Geological Society.* |
| *QJMS* | *Quarterly Journal of Microscopical Science.* |
| *SM* | *Scientific Memoirs.* |

Fuller (but in neither case complete) lists of Huxley's publications are given in Leonard Huxley, *Life and Letters of Thomas Henry Huxley* (1900) and in J. R. Ainsworth Davies, *Thomas H. Huxley* (1907).

1845 'On a Hitherto Undescribed Structure in the Human Hair Sheath', *London Medical Gazette*, I, 1340 (*SM*, I).

1849 'On the Anatomy and the Affinities of the family of the Medusae', *PTRS*, CXXXIX, pt. ii, 413 (*SM*, I).

1851  'Zoological Notes and Observations made on Board HMS *Rattlesnake* during the years 1846–1850', *AMNH*, ser. ii, VII, 304, 370 and VIII, 433 (*SM*, I).

'Observations upon the Anatomy and Physiology of *Salpa* and *Pyrosoma*', *PTRS*, CXLI, pt. ii, 567 (*SM*, I).

1852  'Upon Animal Individuality', *PRI*, I, 184 (*SM*, I).

'Researches into the Structure of the Ascidians', *BAAR*, pt. ii, 76 (*SM*, I).

1853  'On the Morphology of the Cephalous Mollusca . . .' *PTRS*, CXLIII, pt. i, 29 (*SM*, I).

'On the Identity of Structure of Plants and Animals', *PRI*, I, 298 (*SM*, I).

1854  *On the Educational Value of the Natural History Sciences* (*CE*, III).

'On the Common Plan of Animal Forms', *PRI*, I, 444 (*SM*, I).

1855  'On certain Zoological Arguments commonly adduced in favour of the Hypothesis of the Progressive Development of Animal Life in Time', *PRI*, II, 82 (*SM*, I).

1856  'On the Method of Palæontology', *AMNH*, ser. ii, XVIII, 43 (*SM*, I).

'On Natural History, as Knowledge, Discipline, and Power', *PRI*, II, 187 (*SM*, I).

1857  'On the Structure and Motion of Glaciers' (with John Tyndall), *PTRS*, CXLVII, pt. ii, 327 (*SM*, II).

'On the Present State of Knowledge as to the Structure and Functions of Nerves', *PRI*, II, 432 (*SM*, I).

1858  'Objects of Interest in the Collection of Fossils', *Builder*, 15 January 1859.

'On the Theory of the Vertebrate Skull', *PRS*, IX, 381 (*SM*, I).

'On Some Points in the Anatomy of Nautilus Pompilius', *JLS* (2), III, 36 (*SM*, II).

1859  'On the Persistent Types of Animal Life', *PRI*, III, 151 (*SM*, II).

'The Darwinian Hypothesis', *Times*, 26 December.

'Time and Life: Mr. Darwin's "Origin of Species",' *MM*, I, 142, December.

1860  'On Species and Races, and their Origin', *PRI*, III, 195 (*SM*, II).

1861  '*A Lobster; or, the Study of Zoology* (*CE*, VIII).

'On the Zoological Relations of Man with the Lower Animals', *NHR*, I, 67 (*SM*, II).

'On the Nature of the Earliest Stages of the Development of Animals', *PRI*, III, 315 (*SM*, II).

1862 'Geological Contemporaneity and Persistent Types of Life', *QJGS*, XVIII, xl (*SM*, II; *CE*, VIII).

'On Fossil Remains of Man', *PRI*, III, 420 (*SM*, II).

'On the New Labyrinthodonts from the Edinburgh Coalfield', *QJGS*, XVIII, 291 (*SM*, II).

1863 *Six Lectures to Working Men on our Knowledge of the Causes of the Phenomena of Organic Nature* (*CE*, II).

*Evidences as to Man's Place in Nature* (*CE*, VII).

1864 *Lectures on the Elements of Comparative Anatomy.*

*Elementary Atlas of Comparative Osteology.*

'Further Remarks upon the Human Remains from the Neanderthal', *NHR*, IV, 429 (*SM*, II).

'Criticisms on "The Origin of Species",' *NHR* (*CE*, II).

1865 'Emancipation—Black and White', *Reader*, 20 May (*CE*, III).

'On the Methods and Results of Ethnology', *PRI*, IV, 461 and *FR*, I, 257, May (*CE*, VII and *SM*, III).

1866 *Lessons in Elementary Physiology.*

'On the Advisableness of Improving Natural Knowledge', *FR*, III, 626, January (*CE*, I).

1867 'On the Classification of Birds . . .', *PZS* (1867), 415 (*SM*. III).

'On some Remains of Large Dinosaurian Reptiles from . . Africa', *QJGS*, XXIII, I (*SM*, III).

1868 'A Liberal Education and Where to Find It', *MM*, XVII, 367, March (*CE*, III).

'On the Form of the Cranium among the Patagonians and Fuegians, with some Remarks upon American Crania in General', *J. Anat. & Physiol.*, II, 253 (*SM*, III).

'On a Piece of Chalk', *MM*, XVIII, 396, September (*CE*, VIII).

'On the Animals which are most nearly intermediate between Birds and Reptiles', *PRI*, V, 278 and *AMNH*, ser. iv, II, 66 (*SM*, III).

1869 *An Introduction to the Classification of Animals.*

'On the Physical Basis of Life', *FR*, V, n.s., 129, February (*CE*, I).

'Scientific Education: Notes of an After-Dinner Speech', *MM*, XX, 177, June (*CE*, III).

'The Scientific Aspects of Positivism', *FR*, V, n.s., 653, June.

'Geological Reform', *QJGS*, XXV, xxxviii (*CE*, VIII and *SM* III).

'On the Ethnology and Archæology of India', *JESL*, I, 89 (*SM*, III).

1869 'On the Ethnology and Archæology of North America', *JESL*,
I, 218 (*SM*, III).

'Principles and Methods of Palæontology', *Smithsonian Inst.
Ann. Rep.* (1869), 363.

1870 *Lay Sermons, Addresses and Reviews.*

'On Descartes' "Discourse touching the Method of using One's
Reason Rightly, and of seeking Scientific Truth",' *MM*,
XXII, 69, May (*CE*, I).

'On Medical Education', *Critiques and Addresses* (*CE*, III).

'The School Boards: What They Can Do, and What They May
Do', *CR*, XVI, I, December (*CE*, III).

'Biogenesis and Abiogenesis', *BAAR*, lxxiii (*CE*, VIII and *SM*,
III).

'On the Ethnology of Britain', *JESL*, II, 382 (*SM*, III).

'On the Geographical Distribution of the Chief Modifications
of Mankind', *JESL*, II, 404 (*SM*, III).

'On Some Fixed Points in British Ethnology', *CR*, XIV, 513,
July (*CE*, VII).

'Extinct Animals Intermediate between Birds and Reptiles',
*Birm. & Mid. Inst. Ann. Rep.*

'Palæontology and the Doctrine of Evolution', *QJGS*, XXVI,
xlii (*CE*, VIII and *SM*, III).

1871 *Manual of the Anatomy of Vertebrated Animals.*
*On Coral and Coral Reefs.*

'Administrative Nihilism', *FR*, X, n.s. 525, November (*CE*, I).

'Mr. Darwin's Critics', *CR*, XVIII, 443, November (*CE*, II).

'Yeast', *CR*, XIX, 23, December (*CE*, VIII and *SM*, III).

'Bishop Berkeley on the Metaphysics of Sensation', *PRI*, VI,
341 and *MM*, XXIV, 147, June (*CE*, VI).

1873 *Critiques and Addresses.*

1874 'On the Hypothesis that Animals are Automata, and its History',
*Nature*, X, 362, 3 September 1874 (*CE*, I).

'On the Classification of the Animal Kingdom', *JLS*(*Z*), XII,
199 and *Nature*, XI, 101, 10 December (*SM*, IV).

'Universities: Actual and Ideal', *CR*, XXIII, 657, March (*CE*,
III).

'Joseph Priestley', *Science and Culture* (*CE*, III).

1875 *A Course of Practical Instruction in Elementary Biology* (with
H. N. Martin).

1876 'The Border Territory between the Animal and the Vegetable
Kingdoms', *PRI*, VIII, 28 and *MM*, XXXIII, 373 (*CE*, VIII
and *SM*, IV).

1876   'Contributions to Morphology. Ichthyopsida . . . Classification of Fishes', *PZS* (1876), 24, (*SM*, IX).

'On the Study of Biology', *Nature*, XV, 219 and *American Addresses* (*CE*, III and *SM*, IV).

'Address on University Education', *American Addresses* (*CE*, III).

'Three Lectures on Evolution', *American Addresses* (*CE*, IV).

1877   *American Addresses.*

*Physiography.*

*Anatomy of Invertebrated Animals.*

'On Elementary Instruction in Physiology', *Science and Culture* (*CE*, III).

'Technical Education', *Science and Culture* (*CE*, III).

'The History of Birds', *PRI*, VIII, 347.

1878   *Hume.*

'William Harvey', *PRI*, VIII, 485, and *FR*, XXIII, n.s., 167, February (*SM*, IV).

'On the Classification and Distribution of the Crayfishes', *PZS* (1878), 752 (*SM*, IV).

1879   *The Crayfish: an Introduction to the Study of Zoology.*

'On the Characters of the Pelvis in the Mammalia . . .', *PRS*, XXVIII, 395 (*SM*, IV).

Preface to English edn. of Haeckel's *Freedom in Science and Teaching.*

'On Sensation and the Unity of Structure of Sensiferous Organs', *PRI*, IX, 115 and *NC*, V, 597, April (*CE*, VI and *SM*, IV).

'On Certain Errors respecting the Structure of the Heart, attributed to Aristotle', *Nature*, XXI, 1 (*SM*, IV).

1880   *Introductory Science Primer.*

'Science and Culture', *Science and Culture* (*CE*, III).

'On the Method of Zadig', *NC*, VII, 929, June (*CE*, IV).

'The Coming of Age of "The Origin of Species",' *Nature*, XXII, 1 and *PRI*, IX, 361 (*CE*, II and *SM*, IV).

'On the Cranial and Dental Characters of the Canidae', *PZS* (1880), 238 (*SM*, IV).

'On the Application of the Laws of Evolution to the Arrangement of the Vertebrata, and more particularly of the Mammalia', *PZS* (1880), 649 (*SM*, IV).

1881   *Science and Culture, and Other Essays.*

'The Connection of the Biological Sciences and Medicine', *Nature*, XXIV, 342 (*CE*, III and *SM*, IV).

'The Herring', *Nature*, XXIII, 607 (*SM*, IV).

1882  'On Saprolegnia in Relation to the Salmon Disease', *QJMS*, XXII, 311 (*SM*, IV).

1883  'On Science and Art in Relation to Education', *CE*, III.
'Oysters and the Oyster Question', *PRI*, X, 336 (*SM*, IV).
'The Pearly Nautilus' (Rede Lecture), *Nature*, XXVIII, 187 (*SM*, V).

1884  'The State and the Medical Profession', *CE*, III.

1885  'The Interpreters of Genesis and the Interpreters of Nature', *NC*, XVIII, 849, December (*CE*, IV).

1886  'Mr. Gladstone and Genesis', *NC*, XIX, 191, February (*CE*, IV).
'The Evolution of Theology: an Anthropological Study', *NC*, XIX, 346 & 485, March & April (*CE*, IV).
'Science and Morals', *FR*, XL, n.s., 788, December (*CE*, IX).

1887  'The Progress of Science: 1837–1887', in T. H. Ward's *Reign of Queen Victoria* (*CE*, I).
'Address on Behalf of the National Association for the Promotion of Technical Education', *CE*, III.
'Scientific and Pseudo-scientific Realism', *NC*, XXI, 191, February (*CE*, V).
'Science and Pseudo-Science', *NC*, XXI, 481, April (*CE*, V).
'Science and the Bishops', *NC*, XXII, 625, November (*CE*, V, as 'An Episcopal Trilogy').
'The Gentians: Notes and Queries', *JLS*(*B*), XXIV, 101 (*SM*, IV).

1888  'The Struggle for Existence: a Programme', *NC*, XXIII, 161, February (*CE*, IX, as 'The Struggle for Existence in Human Society').

1889  'Agnosticism', *NC*, XXV, 169, February (*CE*, V).
'The Value of Witness to the Miraculous', *NC*, XXV, 438, March (*CE*, V).
'Agnosticism: A Rejoinder', *NC*, XXV, 481, April (*CE*, V).
'Agnosticism and Christianity', *NC*, XXV, 937, June (*CE*, V).

1890  'On the Natural Inequality of Men', *NC*, XXVII, 1, January (*CE*, I).
'Natural Rights and Political Rights', *NC*, XXVII, 173, February (*CE*, I).
'Capital—the Mother of Labour', *NC*, XXVII, 513, March (*CE*, IX).
'Government: Anarchy or Regimentation', *NC*, XXVII, 843, May (*CE*, I).
'The Lights of the Church and the Light of Science', *NC*, XXVIII, 5, July (*CE*, IV).

1890  'The Aryan Question and Prehistoric Man', *NC*, XXVIII, 750, November (*CE*, VII, as 'The Aryan Question').

'The Keepers of the Herd of Swine', *NC*, XXVIII, 967, December (*CE*, V).

1891  *Social Diseases and Worse Remedies* (*CE*, IX).

'Illustrations of Mr. Gladstone's Controversial Methods', *NC*, XXIX, 455, March (*CE*, V).

'Hasidadra's Adventure', *NC*, XXIX, 904, June (*CE*, IV).

Preface to English edn. of Rocquain's *The Revolutionary Spirit preceding the French Revolution*.

1892  *Essays on Some Controverted Questions.*

'Possibilities and Impossibilities', *Agnostic Annual* (*CE*, V).

'An Apologetic Irenicon', *FR*, LII, n.s., 557, November.

'Gib Diesen Todten' (verse), *NC*, XXXII, 831, November.

1893  *Evolution and Ethics* (Romanes Lecture), (*CE*, IX).

1893–4  *Collected Essays*, 9 vols. (I. *Method and Results*; II. *Darwiniana*; III. *Science and Education*; IV. *Science and Hebrew Tradition*; V. *Science and Christian Tradition*; VI. *Hume, with Helps to the Study of Berkeley*; VII. *Man's Place in Nature, and Other Anthropological Essays*; VIII. *Discourses, Biological and Geological*; IX. *Evolution and Ethics, and Other Essays*).

1895  'Mr. Balfour's Attack on Agnosticism' (1st part), *NC*, XXXVII, 527, March.


*POSTHUMOUS.*

1898–1903  *Scientific Memoirs*, edited by M. Foster and E. R. Lankester, 5 vols.

1907  *Aphorisms and Reflections from the Works of T. H. Huxley*, selected by Henrietta A. Huxley.

1913  *Poems of Henrietta A. Huxley with Three of Thomas Henry Huxley*.

1932  Draft of 2nd part of 'Mr. Balfour's Attack on Agnosticism', in H. Peterson's *Huxley: Prophet of Science*.

1935  *T. H. Huxley's Diary of the Voyage of HMS Rattlesnake*, edited by Julian Huxley.

# CONSPECTUS OF
# T. H. HUXLEY'S
# LIFE AND TIMES

U

# THE TIMES

| DATE | REIGN | GOVERNMENT | SOCIAL BACKGROUND | CULTURAL BACKGROUND | EDUCATIONAL BACKGROUND |
|---|---|---|---|---|---|
| ANTE PARTUM | REGENCY | | 1810. George III replaced by Regent<br>1812. Ld. Liverpool's government<br>1815. End of Napoleonic Wars. Corn Law<br>1819. Peterloo 'massacre'<br>1820. Regent crowned George IV | *Births.* 1809, Darwin, Gladstone, Tennyson. 1811, Thackeray. 1812, Dickens. 1815, Trollope. 1817, Jowett, Hooker. 1818, Marx. 1819, Kingsley, Ruskin. 1820, H. Spencer, Tyndall, F. Nightingale. 1822, M. Arnold, Pasteur. 1824, Thomson (Kelvin) | 1822. Classical Tripos est. at Camb; Rebellion at Rugby<br>1823. Lond. Mechanics Institute founded |
| 1825 | GEORGE FOURTH | TORY<br>Lord Liverpool | Electorate only ¼ million<br>Combination Laws repealed<br>Australia still largely convict settlement | *b.* Mundella | |
| 6 | | | Police forces being established | *b.* Riemann<br>*Vivian Grey* (Disraeli) | 'Lond. Univ.' (Univ. Coll.) founded. Opened 1828<br>Soc. for Diffusion of Useful Knowledge founded<br>Butler left Shrewsbury |
| 7 | | TORY Canning<br>TORY Goderich | People still transported for poaching | *d.* Canning; *b.* Lister, W. Holman Hunt, Miss F. M. Buss<br>*Evening Standard* started | Arnold appointed to Rugby |
| 8 | | | Emancipation of Nonconformists | *b.* Meredith, Rossetti<br>*Spectator* started | Univ. Coll. School founded. Opened 1830 |
| 9 | | TORY<br>Duke of Wellington | Emancipation of Roman Catholics<br>Peel's Police Reform Act<br>Liverpool–Manchester Railway | *b.* W. Booth, J. E. Millais<br>*Philosophy of Unconditioned* (Hamilton) | King's Coll. Lond. founded. Opened 1831 |
| 1830 | | | Economic crisis, low wages, unemployment<br>Trade unions forming<br>Riots in S & E England | *d.* Hazlitt; *b.* Emily Davies<br>*Principles of Geology* (Lyell), *Lyrical Poems* (Tennyson) | Heavy attack on public schools and universities |
| 1 | WILLIAM FOURTH | | Bristol burned<br>Faraday produced electromagnetic current | *d.* Hegel; *b.* J. C. Maxwell, F. W. Farrar, Miss D. Beale<br>Brit. Assoc. for Advancement of Science founded | Board of Education for Ireland established |
| 2 | | WHIG<br>Lord Grey | First Reform Act, trebled electorate to ¾ million | *d.* Goethe, Bentham; *b.* Tylor, L. Stephen, L. Carroll<br>*Penny Magazine* started | Univ. of Durham founded Charter 1837<br>Rebellion at Eton |
| 3 | | | Keble's Oxford Assize Sermon<br>Factory Act<br>Slavery abolished in British Empire | *d.* W. Wilberforce; *b.* Bradlaugh<br>*Sartor Resartus* (Carlyle)<br>*Tracts for the Times* and *Penny Cyclopaedia* started | £20,000 grant for schools |
| 4 | | WHIG<br>Ld. Melbourne | Tolpuddle Martyrs; riots and arson<br>Poor Law Amendment Act<br>Fox Talbot produced photographs | *d.* Coleridge, Malthus; *b.* Lubbock, W. Morris<br>*Last Days of Pompeii* (Lytton) | Liverpool Mechanics Institute (and High School) founded<br>West Riding Proprietary School founded |

# THE LIFE

| PERSONAL AND GENERAL | SIGNIFICANT PUBLICATIONS | SELECTED LECTURES | SCIENTIFIC ETC. SOCIETIES |
|---|---|---|---|
| George and Rachel (Withers) Huxley married, 1810 | | | |
| Born at Ealing, 4 May | | | |
| | | | |
| | | | |
| | | | |
| | | | |
| | | | |
| | | | |
| To Ealing School | | | |
| | | | |

| DATE | REIGN | GOVERNMENT | SOCIAL BACKGROUND | CULTURAL BACKGROUND | EDUCATIONAL BACKGROUND |
|---|---|---|---|---|---|
| 1835 | WILLIAM FOURTH | CONS. Peel | Prisons Act (Inspectors appointed) Municipal Reform Act (Borough Councils) | *d.* Cobbett, Mrs Hemans; *b.* S. Butler, 'Mark Twain' | Government School of Design est. |
| 6 | | | Railway fever Chartist Movement (→ 1848) Exeter Hall (Evangelical) opened | *d.* Godwin, J. Mill; *b.* Elizabeth Garrett (Anderson) *Pickwick Papers* (Dickens) *Lyra Apostolica* | Examining Univ. of Lond founded |
| 7 | | | Industrial depression developing Pillory still used as punishment | *d.* Constable, William IV; *b.* Swinburne *French Revolution* (Carlyle), *Oliver Twist* (Dickens) | |
| 8 | | WHIG Ld. Melbourne | Charter presented to Parliament Registrar-General's first Report | *b.* H. Sidgwick, J. Chamberlain, J. Morley, Lecky *Elements of Geology* (Lyell), *Proverbial Philosophy* (Tupper) | |
| 9 | | | Anti-Corn Law League founded Roy. Comm. on Police 'Opium War' with China (→ 1841) | *b.* Pater, Henry George *Chartism* (Carlyle), *Researches in Electricity* (Faraday,→1855), *Voyage of 'Beagle'* (Darwin) | £30,000 grant for schools Committee of Council on Education est. (Kay as Secretary). Schools Inspectorate est. |
| 1840 | | | Rowland Hill's 'Penny Post' New Zealand annexed Morse invented telegraph | *b.* Thomas Hardy, Zola *Philosophy of Inductive Sciences* (Whewell) | Battersea Training Coll (St John's) founded Grammar Schools Act |
| 1 | VICTORIA | | Into 'Hungry Forties' Steamship companies developing | *d.* Birkbeck *Tract No. XC* (Newman), *Old Red Sandstone* (Miller), *Heroes* (Carlyle) *Punch* started | St Mark's Training Coll (Chelsea) founded Over 200 Mechanics Institutes |
| 2 | | | Income Tax 7d in £ Chartist riots | *d.* T. Arnold; *b.* W. James *Collected Poems* (Tennyson), *Lays of Ancient Rome* (Macaulay) *Illus. Lond. News* started | Holborn 'National Hall' founded Sheffield 'People's Coll.' founded |
| 3 | | | Trade revival (→ 1846) Smoke Abatement Committee | *d.* Southey; *b.* H. James *Past and Present* (Carlyle), *System of Logic* (J. S. Mill), *Modern Painters* (Ruskin, → 1860) Ethnological Soc. founded | Prince Albert Pres. of Roy Soc. of Arts |
| 4 | | CONS. Peel | 'Rochdale Pioneers' Co-operative Roy. Comm. on Health of Towns Bank Charter Act | *b.* S. A. Barnett, R. Bridges *Eothen* (Kinglake), *Vestiges of Natural History of Creation* (Chambers) *North Brit. Rev.* started | |
| 5 | | | Newman converted to Rome Irish famine (→ 1850) Railways booming | *d.* Sydney Smith *Essay on Development* (Newman), *Sybil, or the Two Nations* (Disraeli), *Cromwell* (Carlyle) | Secular Queen's Coll. in Belfast founded 22 Training Colleges in England and Wales |
| 6 | | WHIG Lord John Russell | Whigs becoming dominant Corn Laws repealed Workhouse scandals | *Leben Jesu* (Strauss, English translation), *Book of Nonsense* (Lear), *British Fossils* (Owen, → 1884) *Daily News* started | Coll. of Preceptors founded Pupil-teacher system est. with training grants and pensions for teachers |

# THE LIFE

| PERSONAL AND GENERAL | SIGNIFICANT PUBLICATIONS | SELECTED LECTURES | SCIENTIFIC ETC. SOCIETIES |
|---|---|---|---|
| Family moved to Coventry End of schooling | | | |
| Reading Hutton's *Geology*, Hamilton's *Logic*, Carlyle's *French Revolution* Learning German | | | |
| Sisters Eliza and Ellen married | | | |
| Began *Thoughts and Doings* (→ 1845) Learning French and Latin, reading science and philosophy | | | |
| Started medical apprenticeship in Rotherhithe Reading for matriculation | | | |
| Free scholarship to Charing Cross Hospital (→ 1845) Silver medal for Botany (Apothecaries Hall) | | | |
| Prizes in Chemistry, Anatomy and Physiology (Charing Cross) Reading Carlyle's *Past and Present* | | | |
| First MB of Lond. Univ., with Gold Medal for Anatomy and Physiology First research paper published | 'Structure in human hair-sheath' | | N.B. *Honorary* includes 'Foreign', 'Corresponding', etc. |
| Entered Roy. Naval Medical Service as Assistant-Surgeon Sailed in *Rattlesnake*, 3 December | | | *Member* Brit. Assoc. |

# THE TIMES

| DATE | REIGN | GOVERNMENT | SOCIAL BACKGROUND | CULTURAL BACKGROUND | EDUCATIONAL BACKGROUND |
|---|---|---|---|---|---|
| 1847 | | | 'Ten Hours' Act / Poor Law Board est. / 5,000 miles of railways in United Kingdom / Chloroform used for anæsthesia | d. Franklin; b. Annie Besant, Edison / *Wuthering Heights* (E. Brönte), *Jane Eyre* (C. Brönte), *Mathematical Logic* (Boole) | £100,000 grant for school / North Lond. Collegiate School (girls) founded |
| 8 | | | End of Chartism (fiasco on Kennington Common) / General Health Act / Bread riots in Britain / Revolutions in Europe | d. E. Brönte, G. Stephenson; b. A. J. Balfour, W. G. Grace / *Communist Manifesto* (Marx and Engels), *Political Economy* (J. S. Mill) | Queen's Coll. (women) founded in Lond. / First Teachers' Certificate examination |
| 9 | V I C T O R I A | WHIG Lord John Russell | Navigation Laws repealed / Christian Socialist Movement developing / Gold in California and Australia | d. A. Brönte, M. Edgeworth, Brunel; b. Pavlov / *Pendennis* (Thackeray), *History of England* (Macaulay, → 1861) | Over 700 Mechanics Institutes |
| 1850 | | | Immense industrial expansion (→ 1860) / Free Libraries Act / 'Papal aggression' / Telegraph cable under Channel | d. Peel and Wordsworth; b. R. L. Stevenson / *In Memoriam* (Tennyson); *Alton Locke* (Kingsley), *Political Economy* (Senior) | Roy. Commissions on Oxford and Camb. appointed (→ 1852) / School of Mines founded / Natural Science Honours School est. at Oxford |
| 1 | | | Great Exhibition and Crystal Palace / Population of United Kingdom, 21 million / Period of prosperity and social stability starting | b. Oliver Lodge / *Yeast* (Kingsley), *Social Statics* (Spencer), *Cranford* (Mrs Gaskell), *Poems* (Meredith), *Moby Dick* (Melville) | Owens Coll. opened in Manchester / Cheltenham Ladies' Coll. founded / Natural Sciences Tripos at Camb. |
| 2 | | CONS. Ld. Derby | New Houses of Parliament opened / 'Eureka Stockade' revolt in Australia | d. D. of Wellington, Pugin / *University Education* (Newman) *Empedocles on Etna* (M. Arnold), *Uncle Tom's Cabin* (Stowe) | Science and Art Dept. est under Board of Trade |
| 3 | | COALITION Ld. Aberdeen | Death duties introduced / Charity Comm. est. / Civil Service Reform proposals | b. C. Rhodes / *Theological Essays* (Maurice), *Hypatia* (Kingsley) | £260,000 grant for schools / Working Men's Coll founded |
| 4 | | | Income Tax 1s 2d in £ / Cholera Report / Crimean War (→ 1856) / Bessemer invented steel converter | b. 'Marie Corelli' / *Hard Times* (Dickens), *Latin Christianity* (Milman), *Light Brigade* (Tennyson), *Laws of Thought* (Boole) | Oxford Univ. Act / Newman Rector of Dublin Catholic Univ. |
| 5 | | | Limited Liability Act / Adulteration of Food Committee | d. C. Brönte / *Principles of Psychology* (Spencer), *The Warden* (Trollope), *Maud* (Tennyson), *Leaves of Grass* (Whitman) / *Daily Telegraph* and *Saturday Review* started | Regius Chair of Technology founded at Edinburgh / Society of Arts examinations started / Civil Service Commissioners apptd. |
| 6 | | WHIG Ld. Palmerston | Life Peerages suggested / Responsible government in Australia / War with China / Perkins synthesised mauve | d. W. Hamilton; b. G. B. Shaw, O. Wilde, F. Harris, J. J. Thomson / *History of England* (J. A. Froude, → 1870) | £451,000 grant for school / Dept. of Science and Art transferred to Privy Council and co-ordinated with Education Dept. / Camb. Univ. Act |

# THE LIFE

| PERSONAL AND GENERAL | SIGNIFICANT PUBLICATIONS | SELECTED LECTURES | SCIENTIFIC ETC. SOCIETIES |
|---|---|---|---|
| Met Henrietta Anne Heathorn in Sydney<br>Working on medusæ and other marine organisms (→ 1859) | 'Blood corpuscles of Amphioxus' | | |
| Nine-month cruise inshore Great Barrier Reef and New Guinea<br>Packeting research papers to England | | | |
| Continuing researches Learning Italian | 'Anatomy and affinities of Medusæ' | | |
| *Rattlesnake* returned to England, 23 October<br>Granted 'special duty' leave for research<br>Living in lodgings (several → 1855) | | | |
| Elected Fellow of Roy. Soc.<br>String-pulling at Brit. Assoc., etc.<br>Joined 'Red Lions' | | | *Fellow*, Roy. Soc. |
| Mother died<br>Gold Medal of Roy. Soc. | 'Animal individuality'<br>'Structure of Ascidians' | Roy. Inst. | |
| Admiralty research leave terminated<br>Working on human, especially nervous, cytology etc. (→ 1857) | 'Morphology of Cephalous Mollusca'<br>'Identity of structure of plants and animals' | Roy. Inst. | |
| Struck off Navy List<br>Appointed at Jermyn Street at £200 per annum<br>Began work on fossil anatomy and classification (→ 1887) | 'Common plan of animal forms'<br>'Educational value of natural history sciences' | Roy. Inst.<br>Soc. of Arts Educational Exhibition<br>School of Mines (general public, 10) | |
| Father died<br>Married Miss Heathorn; moved to Waverley Place, Marylebone<br>Salary raised to £600 per annum; Lectureship at St Thomas's<br>Fullerian Professor to Roy. Inst. (→ 1858, and 1865–68) | 'Progressive development of animal life in time' | Roy. Inst.<br>Dept. of Science and Art<br>Lond. Working Men (6) | |
| Son Noel born<br>Examiner to Univ. of Lond. (→ 1870)<br>To Switzerland with Tyndall | 'Method of palæontology'<br>'Natural history as knowledge, discipline and power' | Roy. Inst. (12)<br>Dept. of Science and Art<br>Lond. Working Men (6)<br>Edinburgh Philosophical Inst. (2) | *Fellow*, Zoological Soc.; Geological Soc. |

| DATE | REIGN | GOVERN-MENT | SOCIAL BACKGROUND | CULTURAL BACKGROUND | EDUCATIONAL BACKGROUND |
|---|---|---|---|---|---|
| 1857 | | WHIG Ld. Palmerston | Bank crisis Matrimonial Causes Act; Divorce Court est. Indian Mutiny (→ 1858) | d. Comte; b. Karl Pearson Missionary Travels (Livingstone), Tom Brown's Schooldays (Hughes), History of Civilisation in England (Buckle) | National School of Design → National Art Training School |
| 8 | | ———— CONS. Ld. Derby | Emancipation of Jews MPs' Property qualification abolished General Medical Council est. | d. Robert Owen; b. B. Webb, E. Pankhurst Darwin and Wallace paper to Linnean Soc. Limits of Religious Thought (Mansel) Englishwoman's Journal started | Oxford and Camb. Local Examinations |
| 9 | | | War with Napoleon | d. Macaulay; b. S. Webb, Havelock Ellis Origin of Species (Darwin), Self-Help (Smiles), On Liberty (J. S. Mill), Richard Feverel (Meredith), Adam Bede (Eliot) Macmillan's Magazine started | £840,000 education grant Newcastle Comm. on Elementary Education (→ 1861) R. Lowe Vice-Pres. of Committee of Council on Education Science and Art Dept. grants for science teaching |
| 1860 | V I C T O R I A | | Income Tax 10d in £ Colonies covered 2¼ million square miles Ironclad warship launched | b. Ben Tillett Essays and Reviews, Glaciers (Tyndall) Cornhill Mag. started | Science degrees at Univ. of Lond. |
| 1 | | | Death of Prince Consort American Civil War (→ 1865) Lagos annexed | d. Mrs Browning Popular Education of France (Arnold), Education (Spencer), Ancient Law (Maine) Natural History Review started | Clarendon Comm. on Public Schools (→ 1864) Lowe's 'Revised Code' First May examination of Science and Art Dept. |
| 2 | | WHIG-LIBERAL Ld. Palmerston | Cotton famine in Lancashire | d. Buckle George Modern Love (Meredith), Pentateuch (Colenso), Four Periods of Public Education (Kay-Shuttleworth), Unto this Last (Ruskin) | 'Payment by Results' introduced Hartley Inst. opened at Southampton Camb. Local Examinations opened to girls |
| 3 | | | Income Tax 7d in £ Taiping rebellion | d. Thackeray, Whateley Water Babies (Kingsley), Antiquity of Man (Lyell) Church Times started | 'New Code' introduced |
| 4 | | | Co-operative Wholesale Soc. founded Rural Housing Report Geneva Convention | d. Landor, George Boole Apologia (Newman), French Eton (M. Arnold) | Taunton Comm. on Endowed Schools (→ 1867) Argyll Comm. on Scottish Schools (→ 1867) Bedford Coll. (women) incorporated Resignation of Lowe, over Inspectors' reports |
| 5 | | WHIG-LIBERAL Ld. Russell | Income Tax 4d in £ Limited Liability Companies formed St Pancras station built Antiseptic surgery | d. Cobden, Palmerston, Mrs Gaskell; b. Kipling Ecce Homo (Seeley), Alice in Wonderland (Carroll), Early History of Mankind (Tylor), Primitive Marriage (McLennan) Fortnightly Review and Pall Mall Gazette started | Education grant down to £636,000 |

# THE LIFE

| PERSONAL AND GENERAL | SIGNIFICANT PUBLICATIONS | SELECTED LECTURES | SCIENTIFIC ETC. SOCIETIES |
|---|---|---|---|
| Bad headaches and tooth-aches; hypochondria becoming frequent | 'Structure and functions of nerves' <br> 'Structure and motion of glaciers' | Roy. Inst. (2) <br> Lond. Working Men (7); Working Men's Coll. | *Honorary*, Breslau Imperial Acad. of Natural History; Dresden Imperial Acad. of Natural History; Giessen Microscopical Soc. |
| Daughter Jessie born <br> Croonian Lecturer <br> Elected to Athenæum | 'Theory of vertebrate skull' | Roy. Inst. | *Fellow*, Linnean Soc. <br> *Honorary*, Imperial Literary and Scientific Acad. of Germany |
| Daughter Marian born <br> Secretary of Geological Soc. <br> 'Darwin's Bulldog' | 'Anatomy of Nautilus' <br> 'Persistent types of animal life' <br> 'Times' review of "Origin of Species" | Roy. Inst.; Lond. Inst. (6) <br> Lond. Working Men (6) <br> Warwickshire Natural History & Archæological Soc. | *Secretary*, Geological Soc. (→ 1862) <br> *Honorary*, Dublin Univ. Zoological and Botanical Soc.; Philadelphia Acad. of Sciences |
| Son Noel died. Son Leonard born <br> Brit. Assoc. 'duel' with Bishop of Oxford | 'Species and races, and their origin' | Roy. Inst. <br> Lond. Working Men (6) <br> Literary Fund Dinner | *Honorary*, Imperial Geological Soc. of Vienna |
| Moved to Abbey Place (Abercorn Place), Marylebone <br> Honorary MA and PhD (Breslau) | 'Early stages of animal development' <br> 'Fishes of Devonian epoch' <br> 'Zoological relations of man with lower animals' <br> 'A Lobster: or the study of zoology' | Roy. Inst. <br> Lond. Working Men (6) <br> Teachers' Course (South Kensington) | *Honorary*, Institute Egyptien of Alexandria |
| Daughter Rachel born <br> Hunterian Professor at Roy. Coll. of Surgeons (→ 1869) <br> Roy. Comm. on Scottish Herring Trawling Acts <br> Formed 'Thorough' Club | 'Geological contemporaneity' <br> 'Labyrinthodonts from Edinburgh coalfield' | Roy. Inst. <br> Lond. Working Men (6) <br> Edinburgh Philosophical Inst. (2); Dublin | *Member*, Roy. Coll. of Surgeons <br> *Honorary*, Odontological Soc.; Imperial Scientific Soc. of Göttingen |
| Brother George died. Daughter Nettie born <br> Working on human fossils (→ 1866) | *Man's Place in Nature* | School of Mines (general public, 10) <br> Hull Roy. Inst. (3) | *Fellow*, Ethnological Soc. <br> *Honorary*, Roy. Literary and Scientific Acad. of Bavaria |
| Income £950 plus royalties <br> Roy. Comm. on Sea Fisheries of United Kingdom (→ 1865) <br> Formed 'x' Club | *Elements of Comparative Anatomy* <br> *Atlas of Comparative Osteology* <br> 'Human remains from Neanderthal' <br> 'Criticisms on "The Origin of Species"' | Lond. Working Men (6) | *Honorary*, Imperial Acad. of Sciences of St Petersburg |
| Son Henry born <br> Governor of International Coll. | 'Methods and results of ethnology' <br> 'Emancipation—black and white' | | *Honorary*, Odontographical Soc. of Philadelphia; Imperial Zoological and Botanical Soc. of Vienna; Roy. Scientific Acad. of Prussia |

| DATE | REIGN | GOVERN-MENT | SOCIAL BACKGROUND | CULTURAL BACKGROUND | EDUCATIONAL BACKGROUND |
|---|---|---|---|---|---|
| 1866 | | WHIG-LIBERAL Ld. Russell | Habeas Corpus suspended in Ireland Report on Jamaica insurrection Telegraph cable under Atlantic ('Great Eastern') | *d.* Keble, Whewell, Riemann; *b.* H. G. Wells *Jewish Church* (Stanley), *Hereward the Wake* (Kingsley) *Contemporary Review* started | Brit. Assoc. Committee on Science Teaching Lond. Mechanics Institute → Birkbeck Literary & Scientific Institute International Coll. founded |
| 7 | | CONS. Ld. Derby | Second Reform Act First Lambeth Conference Paris International Exhibition End of transportation to Australia Canadian Federation | *d.* Faraday; *b.* Galsworthy, A. Bennett *Kapital* (Marx), *Essays on Liberal Education, English Constitution* (Bagehot), *Sound* (Tyndall) | Payment made for extra subjects Halifax Working Men's Coll. est. technical classes |
| 8 | | CONS. Disraeli | End of public executions UK foreign trade four times that of USA | *d.* Brougham, Milman; *b.* Gertrude Bell *Academical Organisation* (M. Pattison), *Ring and Book* (Browning), *Moonstone* (W. Collins), *Scnools on Continent* (M. Arnold) | Public Schools Act Select Committee on Scientific Instruction Degrees in Science and Technology at Edinburgh Univ. South Lond. Working Men's Coll. founded |
| 9 | V I C T O R I A | | New Parliament under 'Household Suffrage' Trades Union Congress founded Irish Church disestablished Suez Canal opened | Mendeléev produced Periodic Table; Mendel's work published *Subjection of Women* (Mill), *Culture and Anarchy* (Arnold), *Hereditary Genius* (Galton) *Nature, Graphic* and *Academy* started | Endowed Schools Acts (→ 1874) National Education League (Secular) and Union (Denominational) founded Girton Coll. (women) founded at Hitchin Headmasters' Conference |
| 1870 | | LIBERAL Gladstone | Patronage in Civil Service abolished Married Women's Property Act Franco-Prussian War Vatican Council | *d.* Dickens; *b.* H. Belloc *Grammar of Assent* (Newman), *St. Paul and Protestantism* (M. Arnold) Anthropological Institute founded | Forster's Education Act est. School Boards Devonshire Comm. or Scientific Instruction (→ 1875) Owens Coll., Manchester reorganised National Union of Teachers founded |
| 1 | | | Local Government Board est. Bank Holidays Act Tichborne Claimant Case (→ 1874) Germany unified | *d.* Grote, Mansell *Descent of Man* (Darwin), *Primitive Culture* (Tylor), *Plato's Dialogues* (Jowett), *Middlemarch* (G. Eliot), *Theory of Heat* (Maxwell), *Nonsense Songs* (Lear) Historical Soc. founded | Religious tests at Oxford and Camb. removed by Univ. Tests Act Newnham Coll. (women) founded International Education Exhibition |
| 2 | | | Secret Ballot introduced Albert Memorial Disraeli becoming imperialist | *d.* F. D. Maurice, Mazzini; *b.* B. Russell, M. Beerbohm *Erewhon* (Butler), *Greenwood Tree* (Hardy), *Voltaire* (Morley) *Daily Chronicle* started | Cleveland Comm. on Oxford and Camb. (→ 1874) Girls' Public Day School Company formed Chair of Education est. a Coll. of Preceptors |

# THE LIFE

| PERSONAL AND GENERAL | SIGNIFICANT PUBLICATIONS | SELECTED LECTURES | SCIENTIFIC ETC. SOCIETY |
|---|---|---|---|
| Daughter Ethel born Member of 'Governor Eyre' Jamaica Committee Comm. on Roy. Coll. of Science for Ireland Honorary LLD (Edinburgh) | *Elementary Physiology* 'Adviseableness of improving natural knowledge' | Roy. Inst. (ethnology course) St Martin's Hall ('Sunday lecture') Nottingham Working Men | *President*, Section D of Brit. Assoc. *Honorary*, Swedish Medical Soc. |
| Learned to smoke cigarettes Working on ethnology and anthropology (→ 1871) To Brittany with Hooker and Lubbock Attending Graphic Soc. | 'Dinosaur remains from South Africa' 'Classification of birds' | Roy. Inst. (ethnology course) Working Men's Coll. Sion Coll. (clergy) Birmingham and Midland Institute (2) | *Honorary*, Imperial Soc. of Natural Sciences of Cherbourg; International Congress of Anthrop. and Prehistoric Archæology |
| Principal of South Lond. Working Men's Coll. (→ 1880) Pres. of Ethnological Soc. (→ 1871) Comm. on Science and Art Instr. in Ireland | 'Crania of Patagonians and other Americans' 'A piece of chalk' 'A liberal education and where to find it' | Roy. Inst. South Lond. Working Men's Coll.; Norwich Working Men Soc. of Arts Conference Univ. Coll. Lond. Birmingham and Midland Institute (2); Newcastle; Edinburgh ('Lay Sermon') | *President*, Ethnological Soc. (→ 1871) *Honorary*, Roy. Medico-Chirurgical Soc.; Jena Medical Natural History Soc. |
| Pres. of Geological Soc. Member of Metaphysical Soc. Coined word 'agnostic' Began frequent attendance at Roy. Acad. dinners, etc. | *Classification of Animals* 'Physical basis of life' 'Principles and methods of palæontology' 'Ethnology of India' and 'of North America' 'Scientific aspects of Positivism' 'Scientific education' | Lond. schoolchildren (12) Lond. women (12) Liverpool Philomathic Soc.; Bradford Philosophical Soc.; Leeds Philosophical and Literary Soc. | *President*, Geological Soc. (→ 1871) *Honorary*, American Philosophical Soc.; Berlin Geological Soc.; Institut de France |
| Elected to Lond. School Board Roy. Comm. on Contagious Diseases Acts (→ 1871); Roy. Comm. on Scientific Instruction (→ 1875) Governor of Owens Coll. (→ 1875), Pres. of Brit. Assoc. Resigned Univ. of Lond. Examinership and Roy. Coll. Surgeons Professorship | *Lay Sermons, Addresses and Reviews* 'Biogenesis and Abiogenesis' 'Ethnology of Britain' 'Distribution of chief modifications of mankind' 'Descartes' *Discourse*' 'On medical education' 'School Boards' | Roy. Inst. Univ. Coll. Lond. Medical School Manchester Working Men Brit. Assoc. (Liverpool) Leicester Literary and Philosophical Soc.; Birmingham and Midland Institute (2); Leeds Literary and Philosophical Soc.; Bradford Philosophical Soc.; Camb. YMCA | *President*, Brit. Assoc. *Fellow*, Anthrop. Institute *Honorary*, Liverpool Literary and Philosophical Soc.; Moscow Imperial Natural History Soc.; German Fisheries Fellowship |
| Income £2,100 Secretary of Roy. Soc. Asked to stand for Parliament | *Anatomy of Vertebrated Animals* 'Mr Darwin's Critics' 'Yeast' 'Bishop Berkeley on the metaphysics of sensation' 'Administrative nihilism' | Roy. Inst. (2); Lond. Inst. (2 courses) Lond. Working Men (6); Manchester Working Men Teachers' Course (South Kensington, 36) Birmingham and Midland Institute; Liverpool (Trades Council) | *Secretary*, Roy. Soc. (→ 1880) *Honorary*, Camb. Philosophical Soc.; Berlin Soc. of Anthrop., Ethnology and Pre-history |
| Health breakdown; resigned from School Board; convalescence in Egypt and Italy Moved to Marlborough Place, Marylebone Elected Rector of Aberdeen Univ. (→ 1874) | | Teachers' Course (South Kensington) | *Honorary*, Manchester Literary and Philosophical Soc.; Italian Soc. of Anthrop. and Ethnology; New Zealand Institute |

| DATE | REIGN | GOVERN-MENT | SOCIAL BACKGROUND | CULTURAL BACKGROUND | EDUCATIONAL BACKGROUND |
|---|---|---|---|---|---|
| 1873 | | LIBERAL Gladstone | Strong republican movement in United Kingdom Population 26 million (France, 36 million) Remington produced typewriter | d. J. S. Mill, S. Wilberforce, Landseer *Autobiography* (Mill), *Rousseau* (Morley) Palæographical Soc. founded | Camb. Univ. Extension Lectures started Oxf. and Camb. Joint Schools Examn. Board est. |
| 4 | | | Trade depression (→ 1879 → 1896) Fear of German trade rivalry Famine in India | d. Livingstone; b. G. K. Chesterton, S. Maugham, G. Stein *Greville Memoirs* (→ 1887), *Life of Christ* (Farrar), *City of Dreadful Night* (Thomson) | Yorkshire Coll. founded at Leeds |
| 5 | | | British economic preponderance ending Disraeli bought Suez Canal shares | d. Kingsley, Lyell, Thirlwall *Renaissance in Italy* (Symonds → 1886) *Encyc. Brit.* (9th edn.) | Lond. Medical School for Women founded |
| 6 | | | Trade Union Amendment Act Queen Victoria Empress of India Atrocities in Bulgaria Bell invented telephone | d. Harriet Martineau; b. G. M. Trevelyan *Principles of Sociology* (Spencer, → 1896), *Daniel Deronda* (G. Eliot), *Roderick Hudson* (H. James) Physiological Soc. founded *Mind* started | Compulsory school attendance, with 'half timers' Roy. Comm. on Univs. of Scotland (→ 1878) Peripatetic science teacher in Liverpool schools |
| 7 | V I C T O R I A | CONS. Disraeli | Politics increasingly dominated by 'Irish Question' Transvaal annexed Russo-Turkish War | d. Kay-Shuttleworth, Bagehot *New Republic* (Mallock), *Life and Habit* (S. Butler), *Physical Basis of Mind* (Lewes) *Nineteenth Century* started | Commissioners appointed under Univs. of Oxford & Camb. Act |
| 8 | | | Berlin Congress Afghan War Microphone invented | d. Cruikshank, G. H. Lewes, Mrs Grote; b. Masefield *History of Eighteenth Century* (Lecky, → 1890), *Dictionary of Music* (Groves, → 1889) | Univ. of Lond. degrees opened to women Maria Grey Training Coll. (women) founded City & Guilds of Lond. Institute founded |
| 9 | | | 'Great Depression' (→ 1896) Popular interest shifting from religion to politics Zulu War | d. Maxwell, W. K. Clifford, Rowland Hill; b. E. M. Forster *Principles of Ethics* (Spencer, → 1893), *Evolution, Old and New* (Butler), *Egoist* (Meredith) *Boys' Own Paper* started | Firth Coll. founded at Sheffield Somerville and Lady Margaret Colls. (women) founded at Oxford Camb. Teachers' Training Syndicate apptd. |
| 1880 | | LIBERAL Gladstone | Mundella (Child Labour) Act Employers' Liability Act Salvation Army founded Bradlaugh seeks to affirm as MP | d. G. Eliot *Progress and Poverty* (H. George), *Spinoza* (Pollock) | Mason Coll. founded at Birmingham Owens Coll. → Victoria Univ. of Manchester |

# THE LIFE

| PERSONAL AND GENERAL | SIGNIFICANT PUBLICATIONS | SELECTED LECTURES | SCIENTIFIC ETC. SOCIETIES |
|---|---|---|---|
| Changed from cigarettes to cigars<br>Order of Pole Star (Sweden) | *Critiques and Addresses* | Teachers' Course (South Kensington) | *Honorary*, Medical Soc.; Buffalo Soc. of Natural Sciences |
| Attended (and exposed) séance | 'Hypothesis that animals are automata'<br>'Classification of animal kingdom'<br>'Joseph Priestley'<br>'Universities: actual and ideal' | Lond. Working Men (6)<br>Brit. Assoc. (Belfast)<br>Aberdeen (Rectorial Address); Manchester (Owens Coll. Medical School); Birmingham (Priestley Commemoration) | *Honorary*, Roy. Irish Acad.; Roy. Swedish Acad. of Sciences; Roy. Acad. of Sciences of Lisbon; Roy. Belgian Acad. of Sciences, Letters and Fine Arts |
| Changed from cigars to pipe<br>Professor *locum tenens* at Edinburgh (and 1876)<br>Vivisection controversy | *Practical Elementary Biology* (with H. N. Martin)<br>Encyclopædia Britannica articles | Roy. Inst. | *Honorary*, Historical Soc. of Lancashire and Cheshire |
| Income £3,000<br>Visited USA, opening Johns Hopkins Univ. and meeting sister Lizzie<br>Roy. Comm. on Vivisection; Roy. Comm. on Universities of Scotland (→ 1878)<br>Vice-Pres. of Working Men's Club and Institute Union<br>Wollaston Medal of Geological Soc. | 'Classification of fishes'<br>'Border territory between plants and animals'<br>'Three lectures on evolution'<br>'On the study of biology'<br>'Address on university education' | Roy. Inst.; Lond. Inst.<br>Lond. Working Men (6)<br>Teachers' Course (South Kensington)<br>Glasgow Science Assoc.<br>USA (Baltimore, Buffalo, New York (3), Tennessee) | *Member*, Physiological Soc.<br>*Honorary*, Literary and Antiquarian Soc. of Perth; Roy. Soc. of Edinburgh; Glasgow Philosophical Soc.; Roy. Soc. of Copenhagen; New York Acad. of Sciences |
| Advised City Companies on technical education | *Anatomy of Invertebrated Animals*<br>*Physiography*<br>*American Addresses*<br>'Elementary instruction in physiology'<br>'Technical education' | Roy. Inst.; Lond. Inst.; Zoological Gardens<br>Working Men's Club and Institute Union<br>Teachers' Course (South Kensington)<br>Birmingham (Domestic Economy Congress) | *Honorary*, Boston Soc. of Natural History; Dutch Acad. of Sciences; Geological Soc. of Belgium |
| Daughter Jessie married<br>Son Leonard to St Andrews Univ.<br>Younger children seriously ill with diphtheria<br>Studying Greek texts<br>Honorary LLD (Dublin) | *Hume*<br>'Classification and distribution of crayfishes'<br>'William Harvey' | Roy. Inst.; Lond. Inst.; Zoological Gardens (Course)<br>South Lond. Working Men's Coll.; Lond. Working Men (6)<br>Roy. Coll. Physicians (Harvey Commemoration)<br>Whitechapel (*re* university extension) | *President*, Queckett Microscopical Club (& 1879)<br>*Honorary*, Academia de' Lincei of Rome; Brussels Roy. Medical and Scientific Soc. |
| Daughter Marian married Leonard to Balliol, Oxford<br>Working on mammalian anatomy (→ 1881)<br>Governor of Eton (→ 1888)<br>Honorary LLD (Camb.) | *Crayfish*<br>Preface to Haeckel's "Freedom in Science and Teaching"<br>'Characters of pelvis in mammalia'<br>'Sensation and sensiferous organs' | Roy. Inst.; Lond. Inst.; Zoological Gardens | *Honorary*, Acad. of Letters of Pernambuco; Roy. Soc. of New South Wales; Natural Science Soc. of Halle; Roy. Belgium Acad. of Medicine; Institut de France |
| Clarke Medal of Roy. Soc. of New South Wales | *Introductory Science Primer*<br>'Cranial and dental characters of Canidae'<br>'Coming of age of "The Origin of Species"'<br>'Science and culture' | Roy. Inst. (3); Zoological Gardens (3)<br>Working Men's Coll.; Lond. Working Men (6)<br>Birmingham (Mason Coll.) | *Honorary*, Roy. Natural History Soc. of Netherlands Indies |

| DATE | REIGN | GOVERN-MENT | SOCIAL BACKGROUND | CULTURAL BACKGROUND | EDUCATIONAL BACKGROUND |
|---|---|---|---|---|---|
| 1881 | | | Bradlaugh-Besant (birth control) trial<br>Traffic in girls exposed by Stead<br>Irish Land Act | *d.* Carlyle, Disraeli, A. P. Stanley; *b.* P. G. Wodehouse<br>*Virginibus Puerisque* (Stevenson), *Anthropology* (Tylor), *Ballads and Sonnets* (Rossetti), *Lectures on Teaching* (Fitch)<br>*Evening News* started | Samuelson Comm. on Technical Education (→ 1884)<br>Univ. Coll. founded at Liverpool<br>Roy. School of Mines → Normal School of Science<br>Camb. Tripos examinations opened to women |
| 2 | | | Second Married Women's Property Act<br>British control est. in Egypt | *d.* Darwin, Pusey, G. C. Rossetti, Trollope, Garibaldi; *b.* James Joyce<br>*All Sorts and Conditions of Men* (W. Besant), *Natural Religion* (Seeley) | Finances of Oxford and Camb. colleges examined<br>Regent Street Polytechnic opened |
| 3 | | LIBERAL<br>Gladstone | Foote (blasphemy) trial<br>Maxim invented automatic gun | *d.* Marx, Colenso<br>*Principles of Logic* (Bradley), *Political Economy* (Sidgwick), *Expansion of England* (Seeley), *Theory and Practice of Teaching* (Thring), *Towards Democracy* (Carpenter), *Story of African Farm* (Schreiner)<br>Soc. for Psychical Research founded<br>*Oxford Magazine* started | Finsbury Technical Coll. opened in City of Lond.<br>Teachers' Guild founded<br>London Univ. Diploma examn. in Education |
| 4 | V I C T O R I A | | Third Reform Act<br>Social Democratic Federation founded<br>Fabian Soc. founded<br>Toynbee Hall opened in South-east London | *d.* M. Pattison, Fawcett; *b.* H. Walpole<br>*Industrial Revolution* (Toynbee), *Huckleberry Finn* ('M. Twain')<br>*Agnostic Annual* started<br>*Oxford English Dictionary* (first part) | City and Guilds Coll. opened in South Kensington |
| 5 | | CONS.<br>Ld. Salisbury | Gordon relieved in Khartoum | *d.* Shaftesbury, V. Hugo, Gordon; *b.* D. H. Lawrence<br>*Arabian Nights* (Burton), *Praeterita* (Ruskin, → 1889), *King Solomon's Mines* (Haggard)<br>*Dictionary of National Biography* (first volume) | Education grants total £3 m. |
| 6 | | LIBERAL<br>Gladstone | First Home Rule Bill rejected<br>Bradlaugh seated in Commons<br>Burma occupied | *d.* W. E. Forster; *b.* S. Sassoon<br>*Bostonians* (H. James), *Victor Hugo* (Swinburne)<br>*Eng. Historical Rev.* started | |
| 7 | | CONS.<br>Ld. Salisbury | Queen Victoria's Golden Jubilee<br>Peoples' Palace opened in East End<br>Eiffel Tower erected in Paris<br>First Colonial Conference | *d.* Thring, Jenny Lind; *b.* Julian Huxley, E. Sitwell<br>*Study in Scarlet* (Conan Doyle)<br>Marine Biological Assoc. founded | Cross Comm. on Elementary Education (→ 1888)<br>Roy. Holloway Coll. (women) founded |
| 8 | | | Local Government Act (County Councils)<br>Select Committee on Sweating<br>Hertz produced radio waves | *d.* M. Arnold, Lear, Maine; *b.* T. S. Eliot, *Dream of John Ball* (Morris), *Robert Elsmere* (Mrs Ward)<br>*Star* started | |

# THE LIFE

| PERSONAL AND GENERAL | SIGNIFICANT PUBLICATIONS | SELECTED LECTURES | SCIENTIFIC ETC. SOCIETIES |
|---|---|---|---|
| Dean of Normal School of Science (→ 1895) Inspector of Salmon Fisheries (→ 1885) Roy. Comm. on Medical Acts (→ 1882) Refused Professorship and Mastership at Oxford | *Science and Culture* 'Herring' 'Biological sciences and medicine' | International Medical Congress Brit. Assoc. (York) Norwich Fisheries Exhibition | *President*, Sanitary Protection Assoc. |
| Offered $10,000 per annum to go to Harvard Working on salmon, oyster, etc. (→ 1884) Honorary MD (Würtzburg) | 'Saprolegnia in relation to salmon disease' | Lond. Women's Medical School | *Honorary*, Physiological Soc.; Clarendon Historical Soc. of Edinburgh |
| Pres. of Roy. Soc. *Ex officio* Trustee of Brit. Museum (→ 1886) Senator of Lond. Univ. (→ 1895) Rede Lecturer at Camb. | 'Science and art in relation to education' 'Oysters' 'Pearly Nautilus' | Roy. Inst. Lond. Working Men (6) Clothworkers Hall (*re* technical education); Mansion House (*re* Peoples' Palace); Lond. Fisheries Exhibition Camb. (Rede) Liverpool (Institute School) | *President*, Roy. Soc. (→ 1886) *Fellow*, Roy. Coll. of Surgeons *Honorary*, Hertfordshire Natural History Soc.; National Acad. of Sciences of USA; American Acad. of Arts and Sciences; Anthrop. Soc. of Washington; Academia Valdarnense of Florence |
| Ill health becoming chronic; to Italy for convalescence Daughter Rachel married Roy. Comm. on Trawl, Net and Beam Trawl Fishing Resigned Presidency of National Assoc. of Science Teachers | 'State and the medical profession' | Lond. Hospital Medical School | *Vice-Pres.* Society of Authors *Honorary*, Brussels Anthrop. Soc. |
| Son Leonard married Resigned Professorship at Normal School of Science Began great controversy with Gladstone Frequent attendance at Literary Soc. Honorary DCL (Oxford) | 'Interpreters of Genesis and interpreters of Nature' | Marine Biological Assoc. | *Honorary*, Geological Soc. of Australasia; Roy. Institute of Higher Study of Medical and Natural Science of Florence |
| To Switzerland for convalescence Strongly opposed to Home Rule | 'Mr Gladstone and Genesis' 'Science and morals' 'Evolution of theology' | Darwin Memorial Statue | *Honorary*, Roy. Coll. of Surgeons of Ireland; Modena Natural History Soc. |
| Renewed ill health; to Switzerland, etc. Daughter Marian died Working on hybridism of gentians Gave up most examining for Science & Art Dept. | 'Gentians' 'Scientific and pseudo-scientific realism' 'Science and pseudo-science' 'Science and the bishops' 'Address on technical education' | Mansion House (*re* Imperial Institute) St Marylebone (*re* free library) Manchester (*re* technical education) | |
| Very had health in spring; to Switzerland, etc. Trustee of Brit. Museum (→ 1895) Copley Medal of Roy. Soc. Honorary MD (Bologna) | 'Struggle for existence in human society' | | *President*, International Geological Congress |

# THE TIMES

| DATE | REIGN | GOVERN-MENT | SOCIAL BACKGROUND | CULTURAL BACKGROUND | EDUCATIONAL BACKGROUND |
|---|---|---|---|---|---|
| 1889 | | | Great Dock Strike Atrocities in Armenia | *d.* Bright, Browning *Lux Mundi, Fabian Essays, Life and Labour in London* (Booth, → 1897) Inst. of Electrical Engineers founded | Universities (Scotland) Act Technical Instruction Act |
| 1890 | | CONS. Ld. Salisbury | Local Taxation (Customs and Excise) Act Parnell-O'Shea divorce case | *d.* Newman, Chadwick, Liddon *Darkest Africa* (Stanley), *Darkest England* (Booth), *Golden Bough* (Frazer), *Principles of Psychology* (W. James), *News from Nowhere* (Morris) *Review of Reviews* started | Univ. Day Training Depts founded in Lond., Manchester, Cardiff, Birmingham, Newcastle, Nottingham Normal School of Science → Roy. Coll. of Science Woolwich Polytechnic opened |
| | VICTORIA 1 | | | *d.* Bradlaugh, Parnell, W. H. Smith *Quintessence of Ibsenism* (Shaw), *Dorian Gray* (O. Wilde), *Sherlock Holmes* (Conan Doyle) | Univ. Day Training Depts founded in Oxford and Camb. Goldsmiths Coll. opened |
| | 2 | | Keir Hardie elected to Commons Independent Labour Party founded | *d.* Tennyson, R. Lowe, Manning, Richard Owen *Widowers' Houses* (Shaw) produced, *Children of the Ghetto* (Zangwill), *Barrack Room Ballads* (Kipling) | Borough Polytechnic opened |
| | 3 | LIBERAL Gladstone | Second Home Rule Bill rejected Third Married Women's Property Act | *d.* Jowett, Tyndall, Fanny Kemble *Agnostic's Apology* (Stephen), *Salomé* (Wilde), *Appearance and Reality* (Bradley) | School-leaving age raised to eleven years Univ. of Wales founded Blind and Deaf Children Education Act |
| | 4 | LIBERAL Ld. Rosebery | Dreyfus trial | *d.* J. A. Froude, R. L. Stevenson, Pater, Helmholtz, Miss Buss; *b.* Aldous Huxley *Man and Woman* (Havelock Ellis), *History of Trade Unionism* (Webbs) *Yellow Book* started | Bryce Comm. on Secondary Education (→ 1895) Chelsea and Battersea Polytechnics opened |
| | 5 | | USA equals UK industrial output Jameson Raid Westminster (Roman Catholic) Cathedral Röntgen produced X-rays | *d.* Pasteur, Seeley *Time Machine* (Wells), *Jude the Obscure* (Hardy), *Red Badge of Courage* (Crane) | |
| POST MORTEM | | CONS. Ld. Salisbury | 1899. Boer War 1900. Labour Party founded (Labour Representation Committee) | 1896. *d.* W. Morris 1897. *d.* Henry George 1898. *d.* Gladstone 1900. *d.* Ruskin 1901. *d.* Queen Victoria | 1898. Univ. of Lond. Act 1899. Board of Education est. |

| PERSONAL AND GENERAL | SIGNIFICANT PUBLICATIONS | SELECTED LECTURES | SCIENTIFIC ETC. SOCIETIES |
|---|---|---|---|
| Health improved slightly Daughters Ethel and Nettie married Began great agnosticism controversy Moved to Eastbourne | 'Value of witness to the miraculous' 'Agnosticism' 'Agnosticism: a rejoinder' 'Agnosticism and Christianity' | | |
| Trip to Canaries Son Harry married Sociological controversy Linnean Medal of Linnean Soc. | 'Lights of the Church and light of science' 'Keepers of the herd of swine' 'Aryan question' 'Government: anarchy or regimentation' 'Natural inequality of men' 'Natural rights and political rights' 'Capital, the mother of Labour' | | *President*, Palæontographical Soc. (→ 1895) |
| | *Social Diseases and Worse Remedies* 'Mr Gladstone's controversial methods' | | |
| Privy Councillor Busy with Lond. Univ. reform (→ 1895) End of 'x' Club | *Essays on Some Controverted Questions* 'Apologetic irenicon' 'Possibilities and impossibilities' | | *Honorary*, Frankfurt Natural History Soc.; Roy. Acad. of Sciences of Amsterdam; Italian Soc. of Sciences in Naples |
| Total assets £14,000 Romanes Lecture at Oxford Honorary MD (Erlangen) Hayden Medal (Philadelphia) | *Collected Essays*, vols I–IV 'Evolution and ethics' | Oxford (Romanes) Camb. (Harvey Celebrations) | *Honorary*, Acad. of Sciences of Bologna |
| Brit. Assoc. Meeting at Oxford Darwin Medal of Roy. Soc. | *Collected Essays*, vols V–IX | Lond. (Salters Company) | N.B. Also member of various literary societies and clubs, *e.g.* Rabelais, Dickens, Literary, Garrick |
| Influenza, bronchitis, renal failure Died at Eastbourne, 29 June Buried, without official ceremony, at Finchley, 4 July | 'Mr Balfour's attack on agnosticism' (unfinished) | | |
| | 1898–1903. *Scientific Memoirs* (5 vols) 1935 *Diary of Voyage of Rattlesnake* | | |

T 283

# REFERENCES

No specific references are given here for general statements or particular incidents which may readily be verified from standard historical or biographical sources, or which are of minor importance. More important or less easily checked points, and nearly all quotations except a few from very well known books, are referred to their sources by means of key words or phrases, printed below in heavy type and preceded by numbers indicating the pages of the text on which they occur. In the case of Huxley's own writings included in the *Collected Essays* or the *Scientific Memoirs*, reference is usually to the volume and page number, the original sources being traceable in the list of his works given above.

Major sources relied on throughout the book are referred to by abbreviations, as follows:

HP    *Huxley Papers*, in the muniments of the Imperial College of Science and Technology.

CE    *Collected Essays*, by T. H. Huxley, 9 vols., 1893–1894.

LL    *Life and Letters of Thomas Henry Huxley*, by Leonard Huxley, 2 vols., 1900.

SM    *Scientific Memoirs of Thomas Henry Huxley*, ed. by M. Foster and E. R. Lankester, 5 vols., 1898–1903.

Otherwise, the titles of books are given in full, or nearly so, with date of edition and with place of publication if outside the United Kingdom. References to journals give the volume and page numbers or the date of issue.

Fuller documentation may be found in the author's typescript, *T. H. Huxley: his Place in Education*, deposited in the library of the University of London

## PRELIMINARIES

P. ii    **'Those who elect'**: H. to Herbert Spencer, 27 December 1880, *HP*, 7.247.

P. xv    **'Any candid observer'**: *CE*, III, 404.
         **humani nihil**: *Nature*, XX, 185, 19 June 1879.

P. xxii    **'Strong natural talent'**: Karl Pearson, *Life and Labours of Francis Galton* (1914–1930), II, 178.

# CHAPTER I

### A MAN SO VARIOUS

*Pages* 1–21

Important sources for this chapter are:

(*a*) EALING LOCAL HISTORY—

> J. A. Brown, *Chronicles of Greenford Parva; or Perivale Past and Present* (1890).
>
> D. F. E. Sykes, *Ealing and its Vicinity* (1891).
>
> Edith Jackson, *Annals of Ealing from the Twelfth Century to the Present Time* (1898).
>
> C. Jones, *Ealing, from Corporate Village to Corporate Town*, (*n.d., c.* 1903).
>
> C. M. Neaves, *A History of Greater Ealing* (1931).
>
> *Kelly's Directory & Cordingley Directory* (various dates).
>
> *Trans. Lond. & Middx. Archæol. Soc.* (*N.S.*, XI, 105).

(*b*) HUXLEY FAMILY AFFAIRS—

> *HP*, 19.79; 31.15–31.65; 31.78–31.85; 31.105; 62.1–62.5.

(*c*) ADMIRALTY—

> *HP*, 30.19–30.27.

*See also:* Cyril Bibby, 'T. H. Huxley and Medical Education', *Charing Cross Hospital Gazette*, LIV, 191, October 1956.

Particular references are as follows:

P. 1 **'If there is anything':** H. to Sir J. Simon, 11 March 1891, *HP*, 26.82.

P. 2 **autobiography:** *CE*, I, 1.
  **'I am a plebeian':** G. W. Smalley, *Anglo-American Memories* (2nd Series, 1912), p. 19.

P. 3 **'I had two years':** H. to Herbert Spencer, 25 November 1886, *LL*, II, 145.

P. 4 **'a bloated mass':** H. to Lizzie (sister, Mrs Scott), 27 March 1858, *HP*, 31.24.
  **'at death's door':** *loc. cit.*
  **'as near mad':** H. to Lizzie, 8 June 1876, *HP*, 31.44.

P. 5 **'of the surprising six people':** *loc. cit.*
  **'nearly lost to':** H. to Lizzie, 17 April 1852, *HP*, 31.17.
  **'sunk in worse':** H. to Lizzie, 22 April 1853, *HP*, 31.21.
  **'Huxley, when not working':** Beatrice Webb, *My Apprenticeship* (1926), p. 25.

P. 6    **'Thoughts and Doings':** The original MS is now (1959) in the possession of Mrs L. Huxley.

       **Carlyle looked up:** *LL*, I, 275.

P. 7    **'used to wonder sometimes':** *LL*, I, 16.

       **First Medical Examination:** H. never, as is commonly stated, graduated as MB. However, he was admitted MRCS in 1862 and elected FRCS in 1883.

P. 8    **'I have taken':** H. to Lizzie, 21 November 1850, *LL*, I, 60.

P. 9    **'I will "roar you"':** *LL*, I, 103–4.

       **'I have been too long':** *loc. cit.*

P. 10   **'To attempt to live':** H. to Henrietta Ann Heathorn (fiancée).

P. 11   **'I will leave my mark':** H. to Lizzie, 21 November 1850, *LL*, I, 60.

       **'Anyone who conceives':** H. to fiancée, 12 July 1851, *LL*, I, 88.

       **'When I last wrote':** H. to W. S. MacLeay, 9 November 1851, *HP*, 30.3.

P. 12   **'My course in life':** H. to fiancée, 6 July 1853, *LL*, I, 84.

       **'I terminate':** H. to Hooker, 6 July 1855, *HP*, 2.14.

       **'bullying was the least':** *CE*, I, 6.

       **'few men have drunk':** H. to Kingsley, 23 September 1860, *LL*, I, 217.

P. 13   **'a complete paradise':** H. to Rachel Huxley (mother), 15 May 1847, *LL*, I, 34.

       **'O thought I':** Mrs H.'s reminiscences, *HP*, 62, 4.

       **'God help me!':** H. to Hooker [May 1855], *LL*, I, 128.

P. 14   **'a fair-haired':** H. to Lizzie, 27 March 1858, *LL*, I, 157.

       **'I like that chap':** *LL*, II, 435.

       **'a Republic':** E. Clodd, 'Evolution and Man', *Nature*, CXV, 725, 9 May 1925.

       **Certainly, his daughters:** Leonard H., 'Home Memories', *ibid.*, p. 700.

P. 15   **'Men, my dear':** H. to Lucy Clifford, 10 February 1895, *LL*, II, 428.

       **'I am prepared to be':** H. to son Harry, 30 January 1890, *LL*, II, 252.

P. 16   **'much more a literary':** G. K. Chesterton, *The Victorian Age in Literature* (1913), p. 39.

       **happy clarity of Stevenson:** E. C. Batho and Bonamy Dobrée, *The Victorians and After* (1938), p. 40.

P. 17   **'perhaps the greatest':** H. L. Mencken, *Unity* (Chicago), 25 May 1925.

       **'I venture to doubt':** H., *Pall Mall Gazette*, 22 October 1886.

P. 17    **'Glassian precept':** presumably refers to the little-known German philosopher, R. Glass, whose 'Kritisches und Experimentelles über den Zeitsinn' appeared in *Philos. Stud.*, IV, 423 (1887).

         **literary analysis:** Aldous Huxley, *T. H. Huxley as a Man of Letters* (1932).

         **'In his case':** E. R. Lankester, *Nature*, XLIX, 311, 1 February 1894.

P. 18    **'the ruling characteristic':** J. Fiske, *Life and Letters of E. L. Youmans* (New York, 1894), II, 215.

         **'Huxley had probably':** J. Skelton, *Table Talk of Shirley* (1895), p. 294.

         **'I have a woman's element':** H. to Lizzie, 21 November 1850, *LL*, I, 60.

         **'If it should be necessary':** *loc. cit.*

         **'Authorities', 'disciples':** H. to W. F. R. Welldon, 9 February 1893, *LL*, II, 315.

P. 19    **'come out in the new':** H. to Darwin [1871], *LL*, I, 364.

         **'O testimonium':** *Quarterly Review*, January 1895.

         **'one of those spotted dogs':** M. E. Grant Duff, *Notes from a Diary, 1892–1895* (1904), II, 112.

         **'As a political operative':** W. Irving, *Apes, Angels and Victorians* (1955), p. 274.

P. 20    **'The truth is':** Lord Avebury, *Nature*, LXIII, 92, 22 November 1890.

         **'Huxley had more talents':** W. Irving, *op. cit.*, p. 71.


# CHAPTER II
## A CULTURE ADEQUATE TO THE AGE

*Pages 22–44*

Important sources for this chapter are:

*Report of the Royal Commission on . . . Certain Schools and Colleges* (Clarendon Commission, 1864).

*Report of the Select Committee of the House of Commons on Education, Science and Art . . .* (1884).

*Reports of the Annual Meetings of the British Association for the Advancement of Science* (various dates).

*See also:* Cyril Bibby, 'The South London Working Men's College: a Forgotten Venture', *Adult Education*, XVIII, 211, Winter 1955; 'Thomas Henry Huxley and University Development', *Victorian Studies*, II, 97, December 1958.

Particular references are as follows:

P. 22    'The modern world': *CE*, VIII, 227.
      'the main, almost sole': Nassau Senior, *Suggestions on Popular Education* (1861), p. 6.

P. 23    'It is in the fermenting': Matthew Arnold, *Culture and Anarchy* (1869), p. 211.

P. 24    'If I were not a man': *LL*, I, 461.
      'Ah, that is interesting': *loc. cit.*
      little Tennessee town: *New-York Tribune*, 23 September 1876.
      'Depend upon it': H. to Hooker, 5 September 1858, *HP*, 2.35.

P. 25    Rio de Janeiro: H. to mother, 25 March 1847, *LL*, I, 32.
      disfigured by such phrases: *CE*, III, 66 *et seq.*
      'English law': *Pall Mall Gazette*, 31 October 1866.
      'the hero-worshippers': H. to Kingsley, 8 November 1866, *LL*, I, 281.

P. 26    no reliable evidence: *Birmingham Daily Post*, 7 and 8 and 12 October 1867.
      'a little Jew': H. to Hooker, 30 January 1858, *HP*, 2.29.
      'If I were a Jew': *LL*, II, 427.
      'the only religion': H. to Romanes, 3 November 1892, *LL*, II, 339.
      Sylvester: Sylvester to H., 20 December 1883, *HP*, 27.152.
      'a pack of': H. to Hooker, 8 October 1868, *HP*, 2.144.
      ingrained liars: H. to Hooker, 2 December 1890, *HP*, 2.373.
      Parnell: *LL*, II, 125.

P. 27    'a pack of disorderly': H. to Jessie (daughter, Mrs F. W. Waller), 7 December 1878, *LL*, I, 488.
      'merely reasoned savagery': *Quarterly Review*, October 1894.
      would be ashamed: *CE*, IX, 231.

P. 28    speak in Liverpool: *Liverpool Mercury*, 15 and 22 September 1870.
      'The State lives': *CE*, I, 259.
      'If continental bureaucracy': *CE*, I, 260.
      he testified: Select Committee on Education, Science and Art, *Report* (1884), *AA*. 1737, 1781, 1748, 1737 (*sic*).

P. 29    'The great mass of mankind': *CE*, III, 421.
      'he did not believe': *Daily Chronicle*, 8 June 1887.
      'One hears this argument': *CE*, I, 252.

P. 30    'We have all known': *CE*, I, 255.
      'I have not forgotten': *LL*, I, 15.
      'a fashionable': *Liverpool Mercury*, 15 September 1870.

P. 31    'He declared': *ibid.*, 19 September 1870.

P. 31    Hope Hall: *ibid*, 27 March 1871.
'What gives force': *CE*, I, 256.
'any social condition': *CE*, III, 448.
'Newton and Cuvier': *CE*, I, 287.

P. 32    'It was known': H. to Lucy Clifford, 22 August 1892, *LL*, II, 325.
Lord Salisbury: *LL*, II, 164.
'The Archbishopric': H. to Hooker, 20 August 1892, *HP*, 2.419.
'Compare your average artisan': *Quarterly Journal of Education*, February 1868.
inborn plebeian blindness: *CE*, I, 257.

P. 33    'I believe in the fustian': H. to Dyster, 6 May 1855, *HP*, 15.62.
Southampton docker: *HP*, 4.337; 24.179–190; 26.174–177.

P. 34    Lady Amberley noted: B. & P. Russell, *The Amberley Papers* (1937), II, 35.

P. 35    'Granting the alleged defects': *CE*, III, 71–72.
'They at any rate': H. to Lyell, 17 March 1860, *HP*, 30.34.
Elizabeth Garrett: L. G. Anderson, *Elizabeth Garrett Anderson, 1836–1917* (1939), p. 89; Barbara Stephen, *Emily Davies and Girton College* (1927), p. 78.
Sophia Jex-Blake: *Times*, 8 July 1874.

P. 36    demonstratrix: Bernard H. Becker, *Scientific London* (1874), p. 192.
Aberdeen University: *Aberdeen Free Press*, 10 May 1875.
'We reply, emancipate girls': *CE*, III, 72.
'no witness is so dishonest': G. G. Coulton, *Four Score Years: an Autobiography* (1943), p. 276.
So we find him supporting: Hester Burton, *Barbara Bodichon, 1827–1891* (1949), p. 168; Barbara Stephen, *op. cit.* p. 159; Maria Grey to H., 1871, *HP*, 17.144–148; Laurie Magnus, *Jubilee Book of the Girls' Public Day School Trust, 1873–1923* (1924); Princess Helena College, *Education Committee Minutes*, 1882–1887; *Cambridge University Reporter*, 11 May 1880.

P. 37    'work to pass': *CE*, III, 228.
'The educational abomination': *CE*, III, 410.
'precocious mental debauchery': *loc. cit.*

P. 38    'In the language of common life': H., *Hume*, (1878), p. 61.
Moberley: Clarendon Commission, *Report* (1864), *A.* 494.
'those who refuse': *CE*, I, 62.
'the conviction': *CE*, I, 16.

P. 39    'Willst du dir': *LL*, I, 151.

P. 39    'Why I was christened': *CE*, I, 3.

'sin of faith': St G. Mivart, 'Some Reminiscences of Thomas Henry Huxley', *Nineteenth Century*, XLII, 985, December 1897.

P. 40    'In the world of letters': *CE*, VII, 218.

'a firm foundation': H.'s preface to English edition of Haeckel's *Freedom in Science and Teaching* (1879), p. xvii.

Liverpool Institute School: *CE*, III, 168–174.

P. 41    a Manchester audience: *Manchester Guardian*, 4 November 1871.

'The value of the cargo': *CE*, III, 154.

'I do not disguise': Select Committee on Education, Science and Art, *Report* (1884), *A*. 1708.

right in believing: *ibid.*, *A*. 1716.

P. 42    'The recent progress': *Pall Mall Gazette*, 1 June 1876.

'I cannot but think': *CE*, III, 62.

P. 43    'The Political Economists': H. to Farrar, 19 December 1894, *LL*, II, 384.

'Settle the question': *loc. cit.*

'That which I mean by "Science"': H. to Kingsley, 4 October 1860, *HP*, 19.198.

P. 44    'That man, I think': *CE*, III, 86.


CHAPTER III

MORALITY AND METAPHYSICS

*Pages* 44–66

Important sources for this chapter are:

(*a*) H.'s FINANCES—
The figures given are computed from various entries in H.'s diaries.

(*b*) METAPHYSICAL SOCIETY—
Alan Willard Brown, *The Metaphysical Society* (New York, 1947).

(*c*) H.'s WRITINGS—
Especially in *Fortnightly Review*, *Macmillan's Magazine*, *Contemporary Review* and *Nineteenth Century*.

Particular references are as follows:

P. 45    'I wish not': H. to Hooker, 6 January 1861, *HP*, 2.85.

'That is the earliest': *CE*, I, 5.

P. 45    'the John Knox': J. Skelton, *Table-Talk of Shirley* (1895), p. 294.

'Pope Huxley': *Spectator*, 29 January 1870.

'right reverend father': H. to Dyster, 9 April 1855, *HP*, 15.60.

'The longer I live': H. to Kingsley, 23 September 1860, *LL*, I, 217.

P. 46    'It was worth': E. Clodd, *Memories* (1916), p. 45.

'Gott hilfe mir!': Julian Huxley (Ed.), *T. H. Huxley's Diary of the Voyage of HMS Rattlesnake* (1935), p. 38.

verses on the death of Tennyson: 'Gib diesen Todten', *Nineteenth Century*, November 1892.

'if some great Power': *CE*, I, 192.

P. 47    'After all': H. to Dyster, 30 January 1859, *HP*, 15.106.

'The proof of his claim': 'On the Zoological Relations of Man with the Lower Animals', *Natural History Review*, I, 67, January 1861.

'that you should have been': J. H. Titcombe to H., 22 November 1867, *HP*, 28.25.

P. 48    'I remember the meeting': Farrar to Leonard H., 25 May 1898, *HP*, 16.27.

delightful conversations: F. W. Farrar, *Men I Have Known* (New York, 1897), p. 151.

'Why, then': J. Fiske, *Life and Letters of Edward Livingston Youmans* (New York, 1894), p. 546.

'Religions rise': notebook of aphorisms, *HP*, 57.

'It is clear to me': H. to Kingsley, 23 September 1860, *LL*, I, 217.

P. 49    'So far from': *CE*, II, 90.

'Great is humbug': H. to Knowles, 13 December 1887, *LL*, II, 187.

P. 50    'the course shaped': *CE*, IX, 195.

'There is no allusion': H. to G. J. Romanes, 22 April 1893, *LL*, II, 353.

'We can only express': *Oxford Magazine*, 24 May 1893.

P. 51    'the fanatical individualism': *CE*, IX, 46.

'Don't you know': H. to Lord Farrer, 5 June 1893, *LL*, II, 358.

'neither a monarchy': *CE*, I, 259.

'men have become': *CE*, I, 268.

P. 52    'Even the blood-corpuscles': *CE*, I, 271.

abolition of private ownership: *CE*, I, 283.

P. 53    **infantile in intellect:** F. Darwin, *Life and Letters of Charles Darwin* (1887), III, 148.

         **awe and inferiority:** A. R. Wallace, *My Life: a Record of Events and Opinions* (1905), II, 39.

         **'Do take the counsel':** Hooker to H., *n.d.*, *LL*, I, 229.

         **'I wake up':** H. to Darwin, 2 July 1863, *LL*, I, 245.

P. 54    **'on—and on':** Hooker to Darwin, 20 March 1871, L. Huxley, *Life and Letters of Sir Joseph Dalton Hooker* (1918), II, 125.

         **'I have been pounding':** H. to Foster, 27 October 1871, *HP*, 4.31.

         **delightful story:** B. Russell, in *Ideas and Beliefs of the Victorians* (BBC, 1949), p. 22.

P. 55    **'the most notorious':** A. W. Brown, *op. cit.*, p. 329.

         **'the arch-miracle':** Morley to H., 9 January 1876, *HP*, 23.24.

         **'Perhaps it is a ruse':** W. P. Ward, *Life of John Henry Cardinal Newman . . .* (1912), II, 333.

P. 56    **'On all sides':** J. T. Knowles to Leonard H., 23 February 1899, *HP*, 20.200.

P. 57    **'man, looking from the heights':** *Proc. Roy. Inst.*, II, 189.

         **'In science, faith':** *Builder*, 15 January 1859.

P. 58    **'regarding the author':** Mrs Lyell, *Life, Letters and Journals of Sir Charles Lyell* (1881), II, 321.

         **'My convictions'** and following passages: H. to Kingsley, 23 September 1860, *LL*, I, 217.

P. 60    **'The world regards':** *CE*, IX, 134.

         **'I know nothing of Necessity':** H. to Kingsley, 22 May 1863, *LL*, I, 242.

         **condemned as a heretic:** H. to Charles Watts, 10 September 1883, *HP*, 28.196.

P. 61    **'My creed may be':** *CE*, IX, 118.

         **'Cinderella':** *CE*, IX, 146.

         **'Have you read':** H. to wife, 2 December 1886, *LL*, II, 146.

         **'Science seems to me':** H. to Kingsley, 5 May 1863, *LL*, I, 240.

P. 62    **'If you are of a different opinion':** H. to Kingsley, 22 May 1863, *LL*, I, 242.

P. 63    **'Huxley's philosophy':** V. I. Lenin, *Materialism and Empiriocriticism* (English edn., 1939), p. 267.

         **'Archbishop Huxley':** Connop Thirlwall, *Letters to a Friend* (1881), p. 317.

         **'What a Paley':** *Quarterly Review*, January 1895.

P. 64    **'When a logical blunder':** *CE*, V, 67.

         **'Nothing has done more harm':** *CE*, V, 93.

P. 64   'one gasp': Knowles to H., 18 March 1887, *HP*, 20.70.

P. 65   'The Ignorance': Holyoake to H., 20 April 1887, *HP*, 18.216.
'effete and idolatrous': *CE*, V, 267.
'incongruous mixture': *CE*, V, 255.
'Catholicism *minus* Christianity': *CE*, I, 156.

P. 66   'I want you to enjoy': H. to Hooker, 30 May 1889, *HP*, 2.344.
'There is a prevalent idea': *CE*, I, 425.

# CHAPTER IV

### SMITING THE AMALEKITES

*Pages 67–88*

Important sources for this chapter are:

(*a*) GENERAL—

F. Darwin, *Life and Letters of Charles Darwin* (1887).

L. Huxley, *Life and Letters of Sir Joseph Dalton Hooker* (1918).

Mrs Lyell, *Life, Letters and Journals of Sir Charles Lyell* (1881).

D. Duncan, *Life and Letters of Herbert Spencer* (1911).

F. E. Kingsley, *Charles Kingsley: His Letters and Memories of His Life* (1877).

J. McCarthy, *Reminiscences* (1899).

A. S. Eve and C. H. Creasey, *Life and Work of John Tyndall* (1945).

(*b*) H.'s WRITINGS—

Especially those in *Select List* above.

*See also:* Cyril Bibby, 'The Prince of Controversialists', *Twentieth Century*, CLXI, 268, March 1957.

Particular references are as follows:

P. 67   'It is assuredly': H. to Hooker, 19 December 1860, *HP*, 2.79.
'in part from force': H. to W. Boyd Carpenter, 16 June 1887, *HP*, 12.118.
'caused such a flow': H. to Skelton, 21 January 1886, J. Skelton, *Table-Talk of Shirley* (1895), p. 298.
'Where there was strife': J. McCarthy, *Reminiscences* (1899), II, 314.
'What an unfortunate man': W. E. H. Lecky to H., 20 January 1891, *HP*, 21.191.

P. 67    'battles, like hypotheses': H. to Lankester, 6 December 1888, *LL*, II, 213.

P. 68    'I am sharpening': H. to Darwin, 23 November 1859, *LL*, I, 175.

P. 69    'Samuel thought it': H. to Dyster, 9 September 1860, *HP*, 15.115.

P. 70    'how durst you': Darwin to H., 5 July 1860, *HP*, 5.123.
         'reversing': F. Darwin, *op. cit.*, II, 196.
         'I by no means': H. to Lyell, 26 June 1859, *American Philosophical Society MSS*.

P. 71    'The only rational course': F. Darwin, *op. cit.*, II, 187.
         'Farewell': Darwin to H., 16 December 1859, *HP*, 5.87.
         '1856–7–8 must still be': *LL*, I, 151.
         'take care of yourself': H. to Hooker, August 1860, *LL*, I, 215.

P. 72    knocking him down: H. to E. Forbes, 27 November 1852, *HP*, 16.172.
         'On my own subjects': H. to fiancée, 5 March 1852, *LL*, I, 97.

P. 73    'Professor Huxley presents': H. to S. Wilberforce, 3 January 1861, draft letter among *Huxley Papers*.
         'The fact is': H. to Hooker, 27 April 1861, *HP*, 2.98.
         The Gorilla's Dilemma: *Punch*, XLIII, 164, 18 October 1862.
         Monkeyana: *ibid.*, XL, 206, 18 May 1861.

P. 74    'Policeman X': *Report of a sad case recently tried before the Lord Mayor, Owen versus Huxley* (1863), no author or publisher given.

P. 77    'We are in the midst': H. to wife, 8 August 1873, *LL*, I, 397.
         'The Four Stages': notebook of aphorisms, *HP*, 57.

P. 78    'I am going to criticise': H. to Hooker, 19 February 1862, *LL*, I, 204.
         'because it was useful': Mrs. Lyell, *op. cit.*, II, 356.
         'If I were in your shoes': Darwin to H., F. Darwin, *op. cit.*, II, 294.
         'I wonder if': H. to Kingsley, 12 April 1866, *LL*, I, 276.

P. 79    'the educated mob': H. to Hooker, 31 December 1859, *HP*, 2.57.
         'You ought to be': H. to Darwin, 1874, *LL*, I, 426.
         'If I do not': Darwin to H., October 1864, F. Darwin, *op. cit.*, III, 28.
         'Hang the two scalps': H. to Darwin, 5 October 1864, *LL*, I, 253.

P. 79   'Sabine': H. to Darwin, 3 December 1864, *LL*, I, 255.

P. 80   'Mr Darwin's work': H.'s notes for speech, *HP*, 41.151.

'There was only': H. to Darwin, 21 November 1877, *LL*, I, 479.

'Controversy': H. to Morley, 7 February 1878, *LL*, I, 488.

one woman was overheard: *LL*, II, 63.

P. 81   'Some of these days': H. to Hooker, 11 September 1871, *HP*, 2.181.

P. 82   'blaspheming': H. to Lord Farrer, 6 December 1885, *LL*, II, 115.

'Do read my polishing off': H. to Spencer, 4 December 1885, *LL*, II, 115.

'the extreme shiftiness': H. to Lord Farrer, 13 January 1886, *LL*, II, 116.

'may I take': Knowles to H., 14 January 1886, *HP*, 20.58.

'He is now castrated': H. to Knowles, 15 January 1886, *LL*, I, 116.

P. 83   arts of advocacy: 'Mr Gladstone and Genesis' is reprinted in *CE*, IV, 164–200.

P. 84   'Benevolent maunderers': notebook of aphorisms, *HP*, 57.

'Yes—Mr. Gladstone': H. to W. Platt Ball, 27 October 1890, *LL*, II, 267.

P. 85   'I had fondly hoped': *CE*, V, 366.

P. 86   'whether the men of the nineteenth century': *CE*, V, 415.

'My object has been': H. to Henri de Varigny, 25 November 1891, *LL*, II, 291.

'Why the fools go on': H. to Hooker, 4 January 1891, *HP*, 2.375.

'As to Gladstone': *LL*, II, 425.

'the contest was like': Grant Duff to Leonard H., 4 November 1898, *HP*, 30.178.

editor on his side: Knowles to and from H., *e.g.* 1885–1889, *HP*, 20.51, 52, 68, 90, 101, 106, 108.

P. 87   'I envy your vigour': H. to Tennyson, 26 December 1889, *LL*, II, 242.

'Since you have forsaken': Knowles to H., 9 February 1895, *HP*, 2.375.

'Mr Balfour has acted': *LL*, II, 395.

P. 88   'I think the cavalry charge': H. to daughter, *LL*, II, 398.

## CHAPTER V

### SCIENCE FOR THE CITIZEN

*Pages* 89–107

Important sources for this chapter are:

(*a*) LECTURES AT ROYAL INSTITUTION—
*Proceedings of Royal Institution*, I, 184; II, 82; II, 189; III, 151; III, 195; IX, 361; *etc.*

(*b*) LECTURES AT LONDON INSTITUTION, ZOOLOGICAL GARDENS, ETC.—
*Times*, 6 December 1876, 2 June 1877, 19 December 1877, 3 December 1878, 2 December 1879, 25 December 1880, *etc.*

(*c*) LECTURES TO PROVINCIAL SOCIETIES—
Birmingham and Midland Institute, *Annual Report*, 1870–1871.
*Birmingham Daily Post*, 7 and 8 and 12 October 1867, 14 and 21 October 1868, 10 October 1871, 3 August 1874; *Hull and Eastern Counties Record*, 9 and 16 April 1863; *Liverpool Mercury*, 8 April 1869; *Yorkshire Post*, 20 October 1869; *Bradford Observer*, 29 December 1869, 30 December 1870; *Leicester Chronicle*, 8 October 1870; *Transactions of Leicester Literary and Philosophical Society*, 1879; *Leeds Mercury*, 31 December 1870.

(*d*) MEETINGS OF BRITISH ASSOCIATION—
*Norwich Argus*, 5 September, 1868; *Liverpool Mercury*, 15 November 1870; *Belfast Newsletter*, 25 and 26 and 27 August 1874; *Ulster Echo*, 25 August 1874; *Banner of Ulster*, 7 September 1874; *Nottingham Review*, 31 August 1866; *Norwich Argus*, 29 August 1868.

(*e*) LECTURES TO ARTISANS AT JERMYN STREET—
*Prospectuses* of School of Mines; H.'s diaries, 27 February 1871, 16 March 1874, 28 February 1876, 29 April 1878, 16 February 1880, 8 January 1883.

Particular references are as follows:

P. 89    'I have said': *Proceedings of Royal Institution*, III, 195, 1860.
P. 90    'History warns us': *CE*, II, 229.
P. 91    'did not care to address': H. to *Leamington Courier*, November 1871, *HP*, 30.172.

298    REFERENCES

P. 91    'Fancy unco guid': H. to wife, 10 April 1861, *LL*, I, 192.
'told them in so many words': H. to Hooker, 16 January 1862, *HP*, 2.112.

P. 92    'blasphemous contradiction': *Witness* (Edinburgh), 11 January 1862.
'I hope you send none': Lyell to H., October 1862, *HP*, 6.70.
'No article': John Morley, *Recollections* (1917), I, 90.

P. 93    'They would perceive' *et seq.*: *Birmingham Daily Post*, 7 and 8 and 12 October 1867.

P. 95    'if it were given to me': *CE*, VIII, 256.
Red Lion Club: Newspaper scrapbook in Belfast Reference Library; *Witness* (Belfast), 28 August 1874.

P. 96    'Notwithstanding the moisture': *Norwich Argus*, 29 August 1868.

P. 97    'Here in my teaching lectures': *LL*, II, 405.
'The English nation': H. to Hooker, 6 October 1864, *HP*, 2.127.
'The respectability': School of Mines, *Council Minutes*, 27 April 1851.
Karl Marx: Dona Torr (Ed.), *Correspondence of Marx and Engels* (1934), p. 141.
'I am sick': H. to Dyster, 27 February 1855, *HP*, 15.54.

P. 98    'are as attentive': H. to Dyster [December 1856], *HP*, 15.80.
'Feeling anxious to hear': B. H. Becker, *Scientific London* (1874), p. 185.
'The intimate alliance': F. Harrison, *Autobiographic Memoirs* (1911), I, 283.
'My working men': H. to wife, 22 March 1861, *LL*, I, 190.

P. 99    'the most perfect': J. Fiske, *Life and Letters of Edward Livingston Youmans* (New York, 1894), p. 149.
'What is the good': F. Darwin and A. C. Seward, *More Letters of Charles Darwin* (1903), I, 230.
'I am, and have been': *CE*, III, 406.

P. 100    'It will be something': *Pall Mall Gazette*, 21 September 1892.

P. 101    'In England': *Illustrated London News*, 30 June 1894.
'one most base': H. to J. Chapman, 23 October 1853, *HP*, 12.169.
'if I chose to join': H. to Hooker, 17 July 1860, *HP*, 2.67.
'The tone of the Review': *loc. cit.*
'It is no use': *LL*, I, 210.

P. 102    'to place before': *Nature*, advertisement to first number, November 1869.

P. 104   **'Anything from you'**: Morley to H., 12 November 1874, *HP*,
         23.20.

         **'I am becoming'**: H. to Morley, 15 November 1874, *LL*, I,
         424.

         **'Knowles and I'**: Morley to H., 27 November 1877, *HP*, 23.33.

         **'The plainest'**: George Gissing, *Autobiographical Notes with
         Comments upon Tennyson and Huxley in Three Letters to
         Edward Clodd* (privately published, 1930).

P. 105   **conspectus of the locality**: *Warwick and Warwickshire Ad-
         vertiser*, 30 April 1859.

         **'the ordinary lumber-room'**: H. to A. Walker, 8 December
         1872, *LL*, I, 136.

P. 106   **'The public exhibition'**: H. to Commissioners of the Manchester
         Natural History Society, 25 January 1868, *LL*, I, 135.

         **'On the present plan'**: H. to M. Foster, 3 May 1886, *LL*, II,
         131.

         **'people stroll through'**: *LL*, I, 134.

         **'stick to the mummies'**: Darwin to H., 23 October 1858, *HP*,
         5.243.

P. 107   **Then in 1870**: H. Cole to H., 11 and 13 June 1870, *HP*, 12.267
         and 12.268.

         **'about the last man'**: H. Spencer, *Autobiography* (1904), I, 404.

## CHAPTER VI

### BUILDING A SCHOOL OF SCIENCE

*Pages* 108–122

Important sources for this chapter are:

*Council Minutes of School of Mines* (under its successive titles).

*Prospectuses of School of Mines* (under its successive titles).

M. Reeks, *Register of Associates . . . and History of the Royal
School of Mines* (1920).

J. S. Flett, *The First Hundred Years of the Geological Survey of
Great Britain* (1937).

*Mining Journal.*

*Royal College of Science Magazine.*

Particular references are as follows:

P. 108   **'To speak nautically'**: H. to Dyster, 18 August 1858, *HP*,
         15.102.

X

P. 108   **of all decades:** G. M. Young, *Victorian England: Portrait of an Age* (1936), p. 77.

P. 109   **'I'll tell you':** H. to Lizzie, 26 November 1854, *LL*, I, 119.

   **taking two irons:** Herbert Spencer, *Autobiography* (1904), I, 404.

P. 110   **'As a class lecturer':** G. B. Howes, *Royal Coll. Sci. Mag.*, VIII, 3, October 1885.

   **'that rich fund':** St G. Mivart, *Nineteenth Century*, XLII, 990, December 1897.

   **'As one listened':** T. J. Parker, *Natural Science*, VIII, 161, March 1896.

   **'sat in face of':** H. E. Armstrong, *Our Need to Honour Huxley's Will* (1933), p. 6.

   **'Dear me!':** T. J. Parker, *loc. cit.*

P. 111   **'namely, as full':** H., *Practical Instruction in Elementary Biology* (1875), Preface.

   **'Capital!':** P. Geddes, 'Huxley as Teacher', *Nature*, CXV, 742, 9 May 1925.

   **'It was a real stroke':** Darwin to H., 12 November 1875, *HP*, 5.324.

   **In Huxley's hands:** T. J. Parker, *loc. cit.*

P. 112   **'How we are to get':** Murchison to H., 18 October 1855, *HP*, 23.147.

   **'a very trying':** H. to Hooker, 15 July 1865, *HP*, 2.134.

   **'he did not find it':** *Council Minutes*, 9 April 1856.

P. 113   **'You want to know':** H. to Lizzie, 27 March 1858, *LL*, I, 158.

P. 114   **Huxley had already sent:** H. to Granville, 13 June 1861, *HP*, 30.56.

   **'I must take leave':** Select Committee on Scientific Instruction, *Report* (1868), *A*. 7958.

P. 115   **a complaint:** *Hansard*, 19 July 1869, CXCVIII, 160.

P. 116   **'Of course, I do not want':** H. to J. N. Lockyer, 20 April 1871, *HP*, 21.270.

   **'A Royal Commission':** *Times*, 6 April 1871.

   **Huxley wrote a letter:** *ibid.*, 11 April 1871.

   **'My Lords direct':** *Council Minutes*, 13 April 1872.

P. 117   **'got up a little':** H., *Nature*, XXVI, 233, 6 July 1882 (*sic*).

P. 118   **'very nice and all that':** Donnelly to H., 14 August 1873, *HP*, 14.12.

   **greatly fortifying to know:** Hooker to and from H., 5 and 14 October 1873, *HP*, 3.16 and 3.212.

P. 118   **an official memorandum** and following passages: *Correspondence between Science and Art Department and Treasury* (1881).

P. 119   **the official invitation:** Lord Spencer to H., 18 August 1881, *HP*, 26.192.

   **'I am astonished':** H. to Donnelly, 18 August 1881, *LL*, II, 36.

P. 120   **it had its advantages:** H. G. Wells, *Experiment in Autobiography* (1934), p. 175.

   **'Surely I may sing':** H. to Donnelly, 3 September 1884, *LL*, II, 73.

   **'Very, very, sorry':** Donnelly to H., 4 September 1884, *HP*, 14.32.

P. 121   **'I am sure':** Mundella to Donnelly, 10 October 1884, *HP*, 23.132.

   **'We decided':** Donnelly to H., 27 December 1884, *HP*, 14.42.

   **Letter about pension:** Mundella to H., 19 June 1885, *HP*, 23.124.

   **An official memorandum:** Donnelly to Lord Carlingford, May 1885, *HP*, 30.138.

P. 122   **'the respective functions':** Donnelly to H., 25 April 1892, *HP*, 14.130.

   **'We are now part':** *Royal Coll. Sci. Mag.*, IV, 104, January 1891.

## CHAPTER VII

### TECHNICAL AND PROFESSIONAL EDUCATION

*Pages* 123–143

Important sources for this chapter are:

*Minutes of Committees of the Royal Society of Arts.*

*Seventh Report of the Commissioners for the Exhibition of 1851.*

*Report of the Select Committee of the House of Commons on Scientific Instruction* (1868).

*Report of the Royal Commission on Technical Instruction* (Samuelson Commission, 1881–4).

*Journal of the Royal Society of Arts.*

*City Press.*

D. Hudson and K. W. Luckhurst, *The Royal Society of Arts, 1754–1954* (1954).

*See also:* Cyril Bibby, 'T. H. Huxley and Technical Education', *J. R. Soc. Arts*, CIV, 810, 14 September 1956; 'T. H. Huxley and Medical Education', *Charing Cross Hospital Gazette*, LIV, 191, October 1956; 'T. H. Huxley and the Training of Teachers', *Educational Review*, VII, 137, February 1956.

Particular references are as follows:

P. 123   'There is a well-worn': *CE*, III, 428.

P. 124   'It is commonly supposed': *CE*, III, 229.

P. 125   'You did quite right': H. to Foster, 17 May 1870, *HP*, 4.22.
        complaints about the numbers: H. to Donnelly, 17 May 1889, *LL*, II, 235.

P. 126   heirs and representatives: *CE*, III, 425.

P. 127   The outcome of this advice: *Guildhall Library*, *Folio Pamphlet* 29.
        'really the engineer': *LL*, I, 474.
        'possessed enormous wealth': *Nature*, XXI, 139, 11 December 1879.
        'The inmost financial secrets': *Times*, 15 December 1879.

P. 128   'I suppose I have': H. to George Howell, 2 January 1880, *LL*, I, 476.
        'It is not a grand place': Harcourt to H., 23 December 1880, *HP*, 18.5.
        'I think you must admit': F. Le Gros Clark to H., 17 August 1883, *HP*, 12.207.

P. 129   his Presidential Address: *Nature*, XXXIII, 115, 3 December 1885.
        'That building is simply': *LL*, I, 475.
        'pet institution': Donnelly to H., 13 February 1885, *HP*, 14.48.
        'munificence without method': *Times*, 21 March 1887.

P. 130   'public and ceremonial marriage': *Pall Mall Gazette*, 13 January 1887.
        'With the exception': *loc. cit.*
        'the Institute might be made': H. to Herbert Spencer, 18 January 1887, *LL*, I, 151.
        'a port of call': *Times*, 20 January 1887.

P. 131   as much chance of serving: *ibid.*, 19 February 1887.
        'The thing is already': H. to Foster, 22 February 1887, *LL*, II, 154.
        'I may go on crying': H. to Roscoe, 1 May 1887, *LL*, II, 155.

P. 132   'I am not proud': H. to Foster, [November 1887], *LL*, II, 180.
        'I was rather used up': H. to Hooker, 4 December 1887, *HP*, 2.301.

P. 133   'to train persons': P. Magnus, *Industrial Education* (1888),
         p. 20.
         'Education is technical': S. Thompson, *Report of Int. Congr.
         Tech. Educ.* (1897).
         'Although it was': *Nature*, XXI, 139, 11 December 1879.
         'There are some general': *Yorkshire Herald*, 11 April 1891.
P. 134   'the history of a bean': *loc. cit.*
         'Many persons thought': *School Board Chronicle*, II, 263, 1871.
         MS notes for Charity Commissioners: *HP*, 42.52.
P. 135   'Our sole chance': *CE*, III, 447.
         Royal Mining College: H. to Lord Granville, 13 June 1861,
         *HP*, 30.56.
P. 136   'I cannot understand': *CE*, III, 320.
         'turned loose upon': *CE*, III, 329.
         'The Public would have': Lord Spencer to H., 30 March 1881,
         *HP*, 26.190.
P. 137   'Ever since I was': H. to Roscoe, 29 June 1887, *LL*, II, 156.
         'I remember somewhere': *CE*, III, 443.
P. 138   'Teaching in England': Select Committee on Scientific In-
         struction, *Report* (1868), *A*. 8000.
P. 139   demonstration lessons: H. to William Rogers, 5 February
         1869, *LL*, I, 309.
         'an omnium gatherum': H., *Physiography* (1877), p. vi.
         'what you teach': *CE*, VIII, 227.
         'afraid to wander': *CE*, III, 129.
         'There are a great many': *CE*, III, 170.
P. 140   'a course of instruction': H. to Dohrn, 7 July 1871, *HP*, 13.202.
         'Many thanks': H. to Tyndall, 3 June 1872, *HP*, 8.120.
P. 141   'That year I spent': H. to Wells, *Experiment in Autobiography*
         (1934), p. 201.
         MS plan for Institute of Education: *HP*, 42.194.
P. 142   MS plan for University of London: *HP*, 42.110.

## CHAPTER VIII

### THE LONDON SCHOOL BOARD

*Pages* 144–163

Important sources for this chapter are:

*Report of the Royal Commission . . . [on] . . . Elementary Instruc-
tion* (Newcastle Commission, 1861).

F. Smith, *A History of English Elementary Education, 1760–1902*
(1931).

*London School Board Minutes.*

*First Report of the Scheme of Education Committee* (1871).

*The Work of the First Three Years of the London School Board*
(*c.* 1874).

*Final Report of the School Board for London, 1870–1904* (*c.* 1905).

*School Board Chronicle.*

*See also:* Cyril Bibby, 'The First Year of the London School
Board: The Dominant Rôle of T. H. Huxley', *Durham Research
Review*, II, 151, September 1957.

Particular references are as follows:

P. 144  'the politicians tell us': *CE*, III, 77.

P. 145  'If I could only': *LL*, II, 9.

'The great secret': *Natural Science*, VII, 297, October 1895.

'Instead of the School Boards': J. Morley, *Life of William Ewart
Gladstone* (1903), II, 303.

P. 146  'the one home subject': *Times*, 16 December 1870.

'Address of English': *Beehive*, 5 December 1863.

joint election broadsheet: in archives of Imperial College.

'no breeder': *Times*, 22 November 1870.

P. 147  'Two most disreputable': L. T. Hobhouse and J. L. Hammond,
*Lord Hobhouse, a Memoir* (1905), p. 54. The committee is
not specified as that for the School Board Election, but
probably was so.

unlike nine out of ten: *Times*, 22 November 1870.

P. 148  'none are too old': Newcastle Commission, *First Report*, p. 90.

Article on 'The School Boards': *Contemporary Review*, December 1870 and *CE*, III, 374.

P. 149  'He desired simply': *Times*, 22 November 1870.

'A teacher brought up': *SB Chronicle*, I, 40.

P. 150  'were the children': *ibid.*, I, 71.

'That in the schools': *LSB Minutes*, 8 March 1871.

'I go into society': H. to Kingsley, 30 April 1863, *HP*,
19.212.

P. 151  Kate, Lady Amberley: B. and P. Russell, *The Amberley Papers*
(1937), II, 27.

'Children should be': St G. Mivart, *Nineteenth Century*, XLII,
993, December 1897.

'You may judge': H. to Lubbock (Lord Avebury), 4 May 1864,
*Lubbock MSS*.

'If . . . they had to': *SB Chronicle*, I, 44.

'Take the Bible': *CE*, III, 397.

P. 152   'though, for the last': E. Clodd, *Thomas Henry Huxley* (1905), p. 41.

'was a mistake': J. A. Picton, *The Bible in School* (1901), p. 12.

'Twenty years': H. to Lord Farrer, 6 November 1894, *LL*, II, 283.

'The persons who agreed': H. to Peter Bayne, 18 October 1894, *HP*, 10.251.

P. 153   'they could not amend': *SB Chronicle*, I, 135.

'That in all elementary': *LSB Minutes*, 29 March 1871.

'On the contrary': *SB Chronicle*, I, 200.

'Unless [my] ears': *ibid.*, I, 237.

P. 154   'if any motion': *loc. cit.*

P. 155   'he would never be': *ibid.*, II, 326.

'carefully calculated': *ibid.*, II, 360.

'There were some': *loc. cit.*

'Do not fail': Shane Leslie, *Henry Edward Manning, his Life and Labour* (1921), p. 175.

P. 156   'First, the general nature': *LL*, I, 341.

'obtain some order': *LL*, I, 347.

P. 157   'preparatory, I mean infant': *SB Chronicle*, I, 7.

'no educational system': *loc. cit.*

'that which was originally': *ibid.*, I, 393–395.

P. 158   'When some great': *loc. cit.*

'if Alderman Cotton': *ibid.*, II, 38.

'those children who show': *ibid.*, I, 395.

'This Board, like all': *ibid.*, I, 8.

P. 159   'one of the most civilising': *loc. cit.*

'otherwise they might': *ibid.*, II, 165–168.

'they did not intend': *loc. cit.*

P. 160   'This committee': T. A. Spalding, *The Work of the London School Board* (1900), p. 92.

'I . . . bore the brunt': H. to Foster, 11 January 1874, *HP*, 4.66.

'It was very well to say': *SB Chronicle*, II, 231.

P. 161   Myrtle Street Gymnasium: *Liverpool Mercury*, 20 November 1870.

'I am somewhat "erkrankt"': H. to Dohrn, 3 January 1872, *HP*, 13.213.

P. 162   'I am told': H. to Lord Lawrence, 6 January 1872, *HP*, 21.176.

The expressions of regret: *SB Chronicle*, IV, 387 *et seq.* and *LL*, I, 350–352.

P. 163   'I am glad to think': *CE*, III, 431.

## CHAPTER IX

### SCHOOLS OF THE UPPER CLASSES

*Pages* 164–176

Important sources for this chapter are:

*Report of the Royal Commission . . . [on] . . . Endowed Schools* (Schools Inquiry, Taunton Commission, 1867).

*Report of the Royal Commission . . . [on] . . . Certain Colleges and Schools* (Clarendon Commission, 1864).

*Report of the Select Committee of the House of Lords on the Public Schools Bill* (1865).

*British Association Report* (1867).

*Reports of the Royal Commission on Scientific Instruction and the Advancement of Science* (Devonshire Commission, 1871–75).

*Minutes of Provost and Fellows of Eton College.*

L. S. R. Byrne and E. L. Churchill, *Changing Eton: a Survey . . . since the Royal Commission of 1862–64* (1937).

L. Wiese, *German Letters on English Education, Written During an Educational Tour in 1876* (tr. L. Schmitz, 1877).

*See also:* Cyril Bibby, 'A Victorian Experiment in International Education: the College at Spring Grove', *B. J. Educational Studies*, V, 25, November 1956.

Particular references are as follows:

P. 164   **'Scientific knowledge is spreading':** *CE*, III, 421.

P. 165   **Tennyson was not joking:** F. Harrison, *Autobiographic Memoirs* (1911), II, 86.

      **'the fly keeps':** *School Board Chronicle*, II, 57, 1871.

      **Liverpool Mechanics Institution:** C. Foster, *The Influence of Science Teaching on the Development of Secondary Education* (PhD thesis, University of London, 1940).

      **Grant Duff:** *Hansard*, 3rd series, CLXII, 983, 23 April 1861.

      **three questions:** Wrottesley to H., 23 May 1865, *HP*, 29.250 and 29.251.

P. 166   **H.'s evidence to Select Committee on Public Schools Bill:** *House of Lords Parliamentary Papers*, XXI, 308, 1865.

P. 167   **'This is the main object':** Farrar to H., 1 October 1865, *HP*, 16.21.

      **Huxley did at one point:** *Pall Mall Gazette*, 24 December 1886.

P. 168   'Do not despair': H. to Farrar, 6 October 1867, F. W. Farrar, *Men I Have Known* (New York, 1897), p. 152.

P. 169   the governing body: *Illustrated London News*, 7 September 1867.

John Stuart Mill: Mill to H., 8 and 18 April 1865, *HP*, 22.223 and 22.235.

William Ellis: F. W. Robinson, *William Ellis and His Work for Education* (MA thesis, University of London, 1919).

a large engraving: *Illustrated London News*, 20 July 1867.

'Unfettered': *Times*, 10 June 1871.

P. 170   The work in languages: *Middlesex Mercury and County Advertiser*, 20 July 1872.

was apparently reluctant: W. B. Hodgson to H., 25 June 1868, *HP*, 18.204.

Huxley and Tyndall: J. F. Tremayne to H., 10 December 1868, *HP*, 42.35.

a most interesting plan: *HP*, 42.38.

P. 171   For Tyndall: *HP*, 1.57 and 42.50.

'raw Brazilians': M. Hewlett, 'The Gods in the Schoolhouse', *English Review*, XII, 43, December 1912.

'For some reason': *Our Neighbourhood* (Ealing), December 1870.

P. 172   progress of the College: *Thomason's Local Directory for Hounslow, etc.*, 1871 and 1887.

Two years later: *Middlesex Independent*, 31 July 1889.

P. 173   'taking to drink': H. S. Salt, *Memories of Bygone Eton* (1928), p. 210.

the whole system: H. to Leonard H., 6 July 1884, *LL*, II, 134.

a pupil of the time: Gilbert Bourne to Henry Roscoe, 26 April 1912, *Eton Muniments*.

a master: M. D. Hill, private communication to author, 20 March 1953.

Oscar Browning: *Times Educational Supplement*, 21 November 1958.

a letter from Huxley: *Eton College Minutes*, 14 May 1878.

at his second meeting: *ibid.*, 28 July 1879.

P. 174   'Professor Huxley reported': *ibid.*, 11 November 1879.

Within three months, etc.: *ibid.*, 11 February and 11 May 1880, 8 February 1881, 12 February 1884.

not solely concerned with science: *ibid.*, 9 May and 14 November and 12 December 1882.

P. 175 'I look to the new appointment': H. to Leonard H., 6 July 1884, *LL*, II, 134.

who voted against: *Eton College Minutes*, 29 July 1884.

'stoutly advocated': G. C. Brodrick, *Memories and Impressions, 1831–1900* (1900), p. 258.


CHAPTER X

THE OLDER UNIVERSITIES OF ENGLAND

*Pages 177–193*

Important sources for this chapter are:

*Report of the Royal Commission . . . [on] . . . Cambridge* (1852).

*Report of the Royal Commission . . . [on] . . . Oxford* (1852).

*Report of the Select Committee of the House of Commons on Scientific Instruction* (1868).

*Third Report of the Royal Commission on Scientific Instruction* (Devonshire Commission, 1873).

*Report of the Royal Commission . . . [on] . . . Oxford and Cambridge* (1874).

*Oxford University Gazette.*

*Cambridge University Reporter.*

C. Mallet, *A History of the University of Oxford* (1924).

A. I. Tillyard, *A History of University Reform from 1800 . . . the University of Cambridge* (1913).

D. A. Winstanley, *Later Victorian Cambridge* (1947).

*See also:* Cyril Bibby, 'T. H. Huxley's Idea of a University', *Universities Quarterly*, X, 377, August, 1956.

Particular references are as follows:

P. 177 'It is as well': H. to Tyndall, 22 July 1874, *HP*, 9.84.

'a clerical gerontocracy': A. P. Martin, *Life and Letters of the Rt. Hon. Robert Lowe . . .* (1893), I, 27.

'half clerical seminaries'; *CE*, III, 79.

'the host': *CE*, III, 203.

P. 178 'Such a position': H. to F. J. Furnivall, 24 November 1856, *Huntington MSS.*

'Will you ascertain': *loc. cit.*

'I shall set to work': Rolleston to H., May 1860, *HP*, 25.148.

P. 179 Thorough Club: *LL*, I, 198 and *HP*, 31.120.

'Any time': G. M. Humphrey to H., 22 March 1866, *HP* 18.332.

P. 179  'a spiritual police': M. Pattison, *Suggestions on Academical Organisation with Especial Reference to Oxford* (1868), pp. 127–129.

P. 180  'the conjoint operation': G. Smith, *The Reorganisation of the University of Oxford* (1868), p. 6.

   'Both of these systems': Select Committee on Scientific Instruction, *Report* (1868), *A*. 7957.

   'J.H.N.': Leslie Stephen to H., 8 April 1889, *HP*, 27.57.

P. 181  'Somewhere in Professor Huxley': *Quarterly Review*, January 1895.

   'University education should not be': *CE*, III, 237–241.

   'In an ideal University': *CE*, III, 204.

   'If there are Doctors': *CE*, III, 206.

P. 182  'the high protecting power': J. H. Newman, *Christianity and Scientific Investigation* (1859).

   'the mediaeval university': H. to Lankester, 11 April 1892, *HP*, 30.448.

   'I do not think': *CE*, III, 226.

   the best investigators: *CE*, III, 255.

P. 183  'I read your letter': W. G. Clark to H., 2 April [1870], *HP*, 4.172.

   'There seems to have been': H. to Darwin, 22 June 1870, *LL*, I, 331.

P. 184  Exeter College: H. to A. Dohrn, 5 June 1872, *HP*, 13.218.

   'I would not bother you': Lankester to H., 18 December [1872], *HP*, 21.39.

   Already in 1868: Select Committee on Scientific Instruction, *Report* (1868), *AA*. 2699 and 484.

   Soon: *Oxford University Gazette*, 23 January and 24 December 1872, 5 April and 10 June 1873.

P. 185  Huxley was brought in: Rollaston to H., [?1880], *HP*, 30.117; and G. C. Brodrick, *Memories and Impressions, 1831–1900* (1900).

   'seven teasers': H. to M. Foster, 29 September 1874, *HP*, 4.92.

   F. M. Balfour: J. W. Clark, *Old Friends at Cambridge and Elsewhere* (1900), p. 285.

   'Spider stuffers': H. to W. H. Thompson, 19 December 1880, *HP*, 30.119.

   he became an elector: *Nature*, XXVII, 167, 214 and 450, 14 and 28 December 1882 and 8 March 1883.

   Freemasons' Tavern: *Times*, 23 November 1872.

P. 186  **Letters written by Jowett:** to H., 23 April 1877, *HP*, 7.9; to Mrs H., 6 May 1877, *HP*, 7.11; to H., 7 May [1878], *HP*, 7.15; to H., 2 December 1885, *HP*, 7.58.

P. 187  **were more successful:** *Oxford University Gazette*, 23 November 1886.

        **similar battle . . . at Cambridge:** *Cambridge University Reporter*, 25 March 1879, 9 April, 4 May, 15 June, 2 and 6 November 1880.

P. 188  **'A protest from you':** J. C. Collins to H., 24 March 1885, *HP*, 12.289.

P. 189  **a strangely tepid letter:** M. Arnold to J. C. Collins, 24 October 1886, *Three Letters of John Churton Collins* (privately published, 1910).

        **'That a young Englishman':** *Pall Mall Gazette*, 22 October 1886.

        **various other indications:** *Oxford Times*, 20 June 1885; *HP*, 25.230; *HP*, 21.123, 131, 133; *HP*, 28.61.

P. 190  **'You will have heard':** Jowett to Mrs H., 17 June 1881, *HP*, 7.35.

        **'Could you entertain':** Brodrick to H., 21 June 1881, *HP*, 11.85.

P. 191  **Moreover, Jowett emphasised:** Jowett to H., 4 July 1881, *HP*, 7.37.

        **'I am getting old':** H. to Brodrick, 22 June 1881, *LL*, II, 30.

        **'I am most truly sorry':** H. J. S. Smith to H., 12 July 1881, *HP*, 26.119.

P. 192  **'I have been thinking':** H. to C. J. Faulkner, 9 October 1881, *HP*, 16.34.

        **removing his doubts:** Faulkner to H., 10 October 1881, *HP*, 16.38.

P. 193  **'I do not think':** H. to Leonard H., 4 November 1881, *LL*, II, 32.

        **'I shall be glorious':** H. to T. S. Baynes, 9 June 1879, *LL*, II, 4.

        **'a sort of apotheosis':** H. to Bartholomew Price, 20 May 1885, *LL*, II, 110.

## CHAPTER XI

### THE UNIVERSITIES OF SCOTLAND

*Pages* 194–214

Important sources for this chapter are:

*Calendars* of the four Scottish universities (various dates).

*Report of the Royal Commission on the Universities of Scotland* (1878).

*Court Minutes of University of Edinburgh.*

*Council Minutes of Aberdeen University.*

*Edinburgh Evening Courant.*

*St Andrews Gazette and Fifeshire News.*

*Scotsman.*

*Aberdeen Free Press.*

*Aberdeen Daily Express.*

*Aberdeen Herald.*

*See also:* Cyril Bibby, 'T. H. Huxley and the Universities of Scotland', *Aberdeen University Review*, XXXVII, 134, Autumn 1957.

Particular references are as follows:

P. 194  **'if your annals':** *CE*, III, 191.

P. 195  **'Had I accepted':** H. to fiancée, 14 October 1853, *LL*, I, 113.

**'People have been at me':** H. to Hooker, 24 November 1854, *HP*, 2.4.

P. 196  **strongly urged him:** H. to Lizzie, 26 November 1854, *LL*, I, 119.

**'I dread leaving London':** H. to Dyster, 5 January 1855, *HP*, 15.46.

**'Apropos of Edinburgh':** *loc. cit.*

**the newspapers reported:** *Scotsman* and *Edinburgh Evening Courant*, 3 April 1866.

**for nearly twenty years:** *University of Edinburgh Court Minutes*, 8 November 1869 and 18 July 1887.

**the Crown was seeking:** Bruce to H., 26 October 1870, *HP*, 11.131.

P. 197  **'I . . . positively polished off':** H. to Foster, 11 August 1875, *LL*, I, 446.

**'Talk about brains':** H. to Dyster, 9 June 1875, *HP*, 15.135.

P. 198  **'I cleared about £1000':** H. to Tyndall, 13 August 1875, *HP*, 9.91.

**'there is no one':** W. Turner to H., 30 September 1875, *HP*, 28.44.

**'he had the sense':** *LL*, I, 442.

P. 199  **'another confounded commission':** H. to E. L. Youmans, 27 June 1876; John Fiske, *Life and Letters of Edward Livingston Youmans* (New York, 1894), p. 334.

**'The office of Lord Rector':** J. T. Morrison to H., 24 January 1886, *HP*, 23.92.

P. 199 'but my health': H. to J. T. Morrison, 1 February 1886 (draft), *HP*, 23.94.

P. 200 'Since my arrival': H. to Tyndall, 31 March 1872, *HP*, 9.50.

P. 201 'Huxley's object in Egypt': *St Andrews Gazette and Fifeshire News*, 30 March 1872.
'THE ELECTION OF RECTOR': *loc. cit.*

P. 202 'the office should be a real one': *Aberdeen Free Press*, 30 October 1872.

P. 203 'If all men of character': *ibid.*, 29 October 1872.
if the Pope: *ibid.*, 8 November 1872.
'a sort of influence': *ibid.*, 22 November 1872.
'Our correspondence': *ibid.*, 21 November 1872.
'This correspondence': *ibid.*, 27 November 1872.

P. 204 'Why has the claimant': *Aberdeen Herald*, 23 November 1872.
'The kind of Rector': *Aberdeen Free Press*, 14 November 1872.
'but it proved abortive': *Aberdeen Herald*, 14 December 1872.
results of voting: *ibid.*, 21 December 1872.
'the mode of election': H. to Tyndall, 1 January 1873, *HP*, 9.63.

P. 205 'the fact of any one': *loc. cit.*
'the students made': H. to wife, 1 March 1874, *LL*, I, 407.
'Throughout the whole': *Aberdeen Free Press*, 28 February 1874.
'worth volumes': *Scotsman*, 28 February 1874.
anonymous pamphlet: *Protoplasm, Powheads, etc.* (1875), in Aberdeen University Library.

P. 206 'used the Aberdonians': H. to Foster, 23 February 1874, *HP*, 4.73.
'a school of manners': *CE*, III, 203.
'the man who is all morality': *CE*, III, 205.

P. 207 'Methuselah': *CE*, III, 221.
just as students might go on: *CE*, III, 215 and 223.
meet his predecessor: H. to M. E. Grant Duff, 17 December 1872, *Grant Duff MSS*.
'Unlike other Lord Rectors': H. to Tyndall, 1 January 1873, *HP*, 9.63.

P. 208 professors of divinity: *Aberdeen Daily Free Press*, 17 April 1873.
'I have been in Aberdeen': H. to Foster, 22 April 1873, *HP*, 4.50.
a Council Committee: *Aberdeen University Council Minutes*, 9 April 1873.

P. 208   'Your letter leads me': A. Harvey to H., 15 April 1873, *HP*, 18.68.

P. 209   Huxley made public: *Nature*, IX, 21, 13 November 1873.

P. 210   'patrimonial rights'; *Scotsman*, 27 February 1874.

      the Council accepted: *Aberdeen University Council Minutes*, 15 April 1874.

      'Did I tell you': H. to wife, 1 March 1874, *LL*, I, 408.

P. 211   'providing a sufficient share': *Scotsman*, 3 March 1874.

      'if the University': *Aberdeen Daily Free Press*, 10 May 1875.

      an opposing petition: *Aberdeen University Council Minutes*, 13 October 1875; *Scotsman*, 25 September 1875.

P. 212   Huxley's questions to witnesses: Royal Commission on Universities of Scotland, *Report* (1878), *QQ*. and *AA*. 115–136, 165–172, 571–572, 617, 726, 729, 740, 927, 1197–98, 1390, 1587, 1731–1732, 1834–39, 1958–63, 3392.

P. 213   Royal Commission's report: *ibid.*, I, 26, 28, 29, 30, 152–156, 159.

# CHAPTER XII

## THE UNIVERSITY OF LONDON

*Pages 215–230*

Important sources for this chapter are:

*Minutes of Senate.*

*Minutes of Committees. Printed for the confidential use of the Senate* (1867–1880).

*Minutes of Committees and Official Memoranda. Printed for the confidential use of the Senate* (1881–1890).

*Report of the Committee appointed to Consider the Propriety of Establishing a Degree or Degrees in Science* . . . (1858).

*Calendars.*

*Report of the Royal Commission* . . . [on] . . . *new University or power* . . . *in London* (Selborne Commission, 1889).

*Report of the Royal Commission* . . . [on] . . . *the Draft Charter for the proposed Gresham University* . . . ('Cowper', 'Gresham' Commission, 1894).

W. H. Allchin, *An Account of the Reconstruction of the University of London* (1905–1912).

T. L. Humberstone, *University Reform in London* (1926).

Particular references are as follows:

P. 215  'I had quite given up': H. to W. Flower, 27 June 1892, *LL*, II, 313.

P. 216  telling the medical faculty: *CE*, III, 315.

Jodrell Chairs: H. Hale Bellot, *University College, London, 1826–1926* (1929), p. 315 and *HP*, 19.70–19.74.

'Since I saw you': Jodrell to H. [1873], *HP*, 19.72.

P. 217  at Huxley's suggestion: Sir G. Young to H., 17 January 1879, *HP*, 29.266.

'what on earth': H. to F. J. Furnivall, 14 December [1856], *Huntington MSS*.

P. 218  recalls the pleasure: *LL*, I, 238.

in 1857 Huxley: *Minutes of Senate*, 8 July 1857.

he took the initiative: H.'s draft memorial, *HP*, 42.143.

P. 219  'Academic bodies': *Minutes of Senate*, 12 May 1858.

Huxley's evidence: Committee [on] Degrees in Science, *Report* (1858), pp. 65–70.

based very much: Select Committee on Scientific Instruction, *Report* (1868), *A.* 2028.

for the first time: The Natural Sciences Tripos had already been instituted at Cambridge, but it was open only to those who had already otherwise qualified for a degree.

'I apprehend': H.'s draft evidence, *HP*, 42.34.

P. 220  retention of physiology: *Minutes of Committees* (1867–1880), p. 106.

P. 221  'Clay the great whist player': Granville to H., 28 July 1883, *HP*, 21.213.

P. 222  kept him well informed: Paget to H., 2 February 1887, *HP*, 24.10.

'a man who knows': H.'s memorandum to University of London, *HP*, 42.179.

P. 223  Lord Justice Fry: *Minutes of Committees and Official Memoranda* (1881–1890), p. 86.

'We can always': Paget to H., 28 April 1888, *HP*, 24.12.

Senate produced its own plan: *Minutes of Senate*, 28 January 1891.

P. 224  some pencilled notes: *HP*, 42.81.

'a perfect muddle': H. to Donnelly, 30 March 1892, *LL*, II, 311.

'unless people clearly understand': H. to Lankester, 11 April 1892, *HP*, 30.148.

'to take care that': H. to Weldon, 27 March 1892, *LL*, II, 308.

P. 225    'grafting a Collège de France': H. to Lankester, 11 April 1892, *HP*, 30.148.

'I am in great spirits': H. to Foster, 27 June 1892, *LL*, II, 333.

P. 226    Pearson later complained: Pearson to F. Galton, 14 July 1906, K. Pearson, *Life and Labours of Francis Galton* (1914–1930), III, 289.

bitter open letter: *Times*, 3 December 1892.

'As for a government': *ibid.*, 6 December 1892.

'had to show that': *LL*, II, 314.

P. 227    'That to which I am utterly opposed': H. to Weldon, 9 February 1893, *LL*, II, 315.

resign his Presidency: H. to Weldon, 25 January 1893, *HP*, 28.232.

'I am going to a meeting': H. to Foster, 9 November 1892, *LL*, II, 314.

'You should see the place': H. to Collier, 8 November 1892, *LL*, II, 307.

P. 228    which Huxley had drafted: *Minutes of Committees and Official Memoranda* (1881–1890), p. 229.

invited to suggest names: Donnelly to H., 29 March 1892, *HP*, 14.118.

evidence to Gresham Commissioners: *HP*, 42.104 and Cowper Commission, *Report* (1894), p. 554 *et seq.*

P. 229    'I say that very possibly': *ibid.*, p. 563.

'under the circumstances': *HP*, 42.141.

P. 230    engagement with Lord Rosebery, H.'s diary, 26 May 1894.

'It is rumoured': H. to Rosebery, 4 December 1894, *LL*, II, 317.

## CHAPTER XIII

### TO THE NEW WORLD

*Pages* 231–259

Important sources for this chapter are:

(*a*) AMERICAN VISIT—

Special commemorative issue of *New-York Tribune*, 23 September 1876.

'Address on University Education', *CE*, III, 235–261.

Johns Hopkins University, *MS* material *re* official opening.

Y

(b) Huxley's Contributions to Science—

This general assessment is based partly on an examination of H.'s *Scientific Memoirs*, partly on M. Foster's obituary notice in *Proc. Roy. Soc.*, LIV, 55, partly on P. C. Mitchell's *Thomas Henry Huxley: a Sketch of his Life and Work* (1901), and partly on assessments by many leading scientists in the special supplement published on the centenary of Huxley's birth by *Nature* (CXV, 697–752, 9 May 1925).

(c) The *x* Club—

This general account is based on many incidental references in the biographies, memoirs and correspondence of its members and some of its occasional guests, including the John Tyndall MSS at the Royal Institution.

(d) Owens College—

*Minutes of the Court of Governors.*
*Minutes of the Council.*
*Minutes of the Senate.*
*Reports from the Council to the Court of Governors.*

Particular references are as follows:

P. 231   'The question of questions': *CE*, VII, 77 and 154.

P. 233   'an organ of grin-and-bear-it-iveness': H. to Foster, 28 April 1809, *HP*, 4.16.

'He writes as if': Argyll to Tyndall, 29 January 1891, G. D. Argyll, *Autobiography and Memoirs* (1906), II, 526.

'I never came away': *LL*, II, 433.

'What I like': E. C. F. Collier, *A Victorian Diarist . . . 1873–1895* (1944), p. 35.

'I wish to God': Darwin to Huxley, 27 March 1882, *LL*, II, 38.

'I tell you': H. A. Harper, *The Personal Letters of John Fiske* (private circulation, Torch Press, Cedar Rapids, Iowa, 1939), p. 217.

P. 234   'The whole nation': *LL*, I, 460.

'It will be something strange': H. to Lizzie, 8 June 1876, *HP*, 31.44.

'a sort of dream': H. to Lowell, 14 November 1883, *Harvard MSS.*

P. 235   'young, energetic': H. to Gilman, 20 February 1876, *Johns Hopkins MSS.*

P. 235 'in usum studiosum': H. to Martin, 2 April [187?], *ibid.*

'You have among you': *New-York Daily Tribune*, 26 August 1876.

P. 236 based on the local geology: *ibid.*, 11 September 1876.

absence of religious compulsion: the tone was set by a notice displayed on the campus: "A brief religious service will be held every morning at 8.45 in Hopkins Hall. No notice will be taken of the presence or absence of anybody."

'I am very sorry': *Johns Hopkins MSS.*

'Huxley was bad enough': F. Franklin, *Life of D. C. Gilman* (New York, 1910), p. 221.

'It was bad enough': *Johns Hopkins MSS.*

$1000 and £10,000: W. H. Appleton to Mrs H., 22 August 1876, *HP*, 10.108.

Minnesota: W. W. Forbes to Gilman, 30 September 1876, *HP*, 17.54.

Princeton: H. F. Osborn, *Impressions of Great Naturalists* (New York, 1924), p. 6.

Yale: L. Huxley, *Life and Letters of Sir Joseph Dalton Hooker*, (1918), p. 208.

Harvard: A. Agassiz to H., 8 November 1882, *HP*, 6.146.

P. 237 freedom of thought: *HP*, 31.105.

'An education fitted for free men': *CE*, III, 238.

'It is important': *CE*, III, 251.

'there should be not too many': *CE*, III, 243.

'deficient in industry': *CE*, III, 242.

P. 238 'a great warrior': *CE*, III, 256.

'the future of the world': *CE*, III, 254.

'Do not suppose': *CE*, III, 260.

'the one condition of success': *CE*, III, 261.

P. 239 'whether state rights': *CE*, III, 260.

'as population thickens': *loc. cit.*

Mr Cocker's arithmetic: H.'s unpublished MS, 1887, *HP*, 42.58.

Fruits of Philosophy: H. to Foster, 18 July 1883, *LL*, II, 56.

Mrs Besant and Miss Bradlaugh: *LL*, II, 56.

Population Question Association: Minutes of a private conference, 9 March 1888, *HP*, 49.66.

'If historical writers': *HP*, 42.58.

P. 240 'It is hard to say': *CE*, IX, 212, *f.n.*

'and, if need be': *CE*, IX, 219.

P. 241 'I paid comparatively little attention': *LL*, I, 58.

P. 242 'I have been oppressed': *LL*, I, 485.

P. 243 'It is the organisation': H. to Haeckel, 7 June 1865, *LL*, I, 267.

'the facts concerning': British Association, *Report*, 1866.

P. 244 'so full of quotations': *Nature*, CXV, 707, 9 May 1925.

'Remember that it was Huxley': P. C. Mitchell, *New Review*, August 1895.

'subject to the production': *CE*, VII, 150.

'Like a good Catholic': Francis Darwin, *Life and Letters of Charles Darwin* (1887), II, 232.

'as near an approximation': *CE*, VII, 149.

'Because no law': H. to Hooker, 4 September 1861, *LL*, I, 227.

P. 245 'you have loaded yourself': H. to Darwin, 23 November 1859, *LL*, I, 175.

'Suppose that external conditions': H. to Lyell, 25 June 1859, *American Philosophical Society MSS*.

'I am sincerely': *Times*, 1 December 1894.

P. 246 'brushed the cobwebs': A. Keith, 'Huxley as Anthropologist', *Nature*, CXV, 722, 9 May 1925.

P. 247 'the frontiers of the new world': *Nature*, LI, 1, 1 November 1894.

He had recently had a dream: P. C. Mitchell, *Thomas Henry Huxley* . . . (1901), p. 204 (1913 edn.).

P. 248 'If I know anything': *HP*, 31.105.

'the most powerful': Fiske to wife, 8 December 1873, E. F. Fiske, *Letters of John Fiske* (1940), p. 144.

P. 249 'I say, A.': *LL*, I, 259.

'In fact, a favourite problem': H. to Herbert Spencer, 3 August 1861, *LL*, I, 230.

P. 250 'merely the Absoluter edivivus': H. to F. J. Gould, 1889, *Literary Guide*, January 1902.

'the direct effect': *CE*, VI, 307.

'only two out of': *CE*, VI, 286.

P. 251 'if the folk in the spiritual world': *LL*, I, 420.

'Teach a child what is wise': Edwin Hodder, *Life and Work of the Seventh Earl of Shaftesbury* (1886), III, p. 282.

'the awe and reverence': *CE*, III, 393.

'in relation to the human mind': H., *Crayfish* (1879), p. 3.

'the imperfections': *CE*, I, 33.

P. 252 Newman: M. Pattison, *Memoirs* (1885), p. 105.

'science, in the course of': H., *Hume* (1878), p. 59.

'One does not free': *CE*, V, 13.

P. 252   'The present and the near future': *CE*, IV, 237–238.
P. 253   'No longer in contact': *loc. cit.*
    'Old Noll': *LL*, II, 322.
    'among as queer a crew': H. to Tyndall, 25 November 1883, *HP*, 9.144.
    'rightful freedom': *LL*, II, 407.
    he nevertheless signed: James Sully to Leonard H. [1900], *HP*, 27.131. [The contrary impression is widespread, owing to an error in *LL*, II, 406.]
    'Every day': *CE*, IX, 30.
P. 254   'if morality has survived': *CE*, IX, 145.
    'a universal, intrepid': W. H. Mallock, *The New Republic . . .* (1877), p. 56 (Rosemary edn.).
    'what a heart-breaking business': *CE*, VII, vii.
    'The "points" of a good citizen': *CE*, IX, 23.
    'the sons of the masses': *CE*, III, 203.
P. 255   closely with Kay-Shuttleworth: *Owens College, Manchester, Court Minutes*, 1870 *passim*.
    'Any corporation of men': *Manchester Guardian*, 3 October 1874.
    'Unless we are led': unidentified newspaper cutting in Manchester University Library.
    'We are in the case of Tarpeia': H. F. Osborn, *Impressions of Great Naturalists* (New York, 1924), p. 93.
P. 256   gave Patrick Geddes: P. Mairet, *Pioneer of Sociology: the Life and Letters of Patrick Geddes* (1957), p. 72.
    Beveridge's address: W. Beveridge, *Power and Influence* (1953), p. 247.
    'and, what is still more important': *CE*, III, 185.
    'If individuality has no play': *CE*, I, 277.
P. 257   'the first-recorded judicial murder': *CE*, VI, viii.
    'The first agnostic': *loc. cit.*
    'inclined to think': unpublished fragment, *HP*, 45.104.
    'no personal habit': *CE*, IX, 243.
    'better a thousand times': H. to Tyndall, 22 October 1854, *LL*, I, 121.
P. 258   'It flashes across me': J. Morley, *Recollections* (1917), I, p. 114.
    'one should be always ready': H. to Romanes, 28 September 1893, *LL*, II, 368.
P. 259   almost the type-specimen: G. V. Plekhanov, *The Rôle of the Individual in History* (English tr., 1940).
    'Posthumous fame': H. to Howell, 2 January 1880, *LL*, I, 476.

# INDEX

*Names of persons and periodicals are in general indexed only where the entry is of some significance apart from the mere receipt of a communication. All such communications are documented in the* **References** *beginning on p. 285.*